Bird Without Wings

Faebles

Cally Pepper

LODESTONE BOOKS

Winchester, UK
Washington, USA

First published by Lodestone Books, 2013
Lodestone Books is an imprint of John Hunt Publishing Ltd., Laurel House, Station Approach,
Alresford, Hants, SO24 9JH, UK
office1@jhpbooks.net
www.johnhuntpublishing.com

For distributor details and how to order please visit the 'Ordering' section on our website.

Text copyright: Cally Pepper 2012

ISBN: 978 1 78099 902 9

A CIP catalogue record for this book is available from the British Library.

Design: Lee Nash

Printed and bound by CPI Group (UK) Ltd, Croydon, CR0 4YY

We operate a distinctive and ethical publishing philosophy in all
areas of our business, from our global network of authors to
production and worldwide distribution.

For my mum

Chapter One

I'm sixteen today. It's my last exam this morning. Last day in Year 11. Last day of school.

I spot Sasha waiting for me outside the school gates. She's leaning against the wall, her jet black hair glinting in the morning sun. She's laughing. She looks amazing. She always looks amazing. Sasha and I have been best friends since the beginning of high school. She's more like a sister than a friend.

My insides feel as though they're turning to liquid as I approach her, somewhere between that warm feeling of familiarity and the harsh dread of the unknown. I take a deep breath and brace myself as she turns to face me.

'What's the matter with you, you mad cow?' Sasha screams into my face, and I catch my breath. 'You attacked my brother, you put him in hospital. What are you, a freak?'

My stomach tightens and I stare at the floor, hoping my eyes won't show how much her words hurt, pretending I haven't noticed the small crowd of interested onlookers beginning to gather.

Let me explain. Jasper is Sasha's brother; he's 18 and dropped out of school last year. And just about every girl fancies him. He's good looking, tall, muscular. No…good looking just doesn't describe him. He's damn near perfect. He's an Adonis. He has dark brown eyes, tanned skin, almost-black hair, which grows in tight curls, and he wears cut very short. He's slim and muscular, and you really have to hear his voice – deep and smooth, like melted chocolate. But even forgetting all that, he has a kind of confidence, I suppose arrogance, something you can't put your finger on that just seems to pull the girls like a magnet. Something that other lads in our school don't have, they don't even come close. And the girls in my Year treat Jasper like a god, they giggle when he's within earshot and flirt like mad if he so much as looks at them. It's embarrassing to watch them.

So when Sasha said Jasper liked me, I admit I was flattered. Boys just don't seem to fancy me, and I couldn't believe Jasper would be interested in someone like me. It's not that I'm ugly or anything, but I wouldn't say I was that pretty either. I can't be, because I've never had a real boyfriend. Most of the other girls in my class are going out with boys, bragging about sex and stuff, especially Sasha. Sasha always has plenty of boyfriends, and boasts that she lost her virginity at 13, although I know for a fact that isn't true.

'I was defending myself,' I hiss back at Sasha, feeling my face turn pink. 'He was the one who attacked *me*. Sasha, can we leave this 'til after? It's our last exam today.' Some of the spectators are sniggering and whispering.

'Why?' Sasha sneers, her voice getting loud and raucous. 'You don't want anyone to know you're frigid?' She laughs nastily and her face screws into something quite mean and ugly. I hear muttering from the expanding crowd. I can tell Sasha's enjoying the attention.

'You broke his arm, punched him on the jaw and kicked him in the nuts!' Her eyes widen with mock-surprise as she looks round at her audience. Most of the kids in our Year have crowded round, enjoying the show. 'You should be locked away!'

'That's not how it happened,' I splutter, feeling out of my depth. I've never been good at arguments and Sasha knows it.

'He only wanted a kiss!' Sasha says, rolling her eyes at her audience. There's a roar of laughter.

I decide to say nothing more, push my way through the crowd and towards school. I roughly wipe away the tears that are welling in my eyes.

'There's something wrong with you,' she yells. 'You're a FREAK!'

That's not fair, it's just not right. She's supposed to be my best friend. My pace slows as her words filter into my mind. I start to see red, Sasha is just so wrong. She wants to make a scene; well two can play at that game. I spin round and march back, straight at her. Sasha looks a little startled, she visibly shrinks. Some of the girls start to back away.

'Listen, Sasha,' I say loudly, looking her straight in the eye. 'Are you seriously suggesting that I beat up your six-foot brother with my bare hands, in his own home…' I make an overly-grand gesture towards my own skinny frame. 'For absolutely no reason at all?'

Sasha's mouth drops open and her tongue tries to wag, but there's absolutely nothing she can say. I spin on my heel and march back up the path towards school. At least I've shut her up for now. But I know this isn't the last of it.

And the worst part is, what Sasha has accused me of, is actually true. I *did* beat up her six-foot brother with my bare hands.

I make it as far as the school doors before I hear Sasha scream, 'You're a FREAK, Scarlett Moon!'

I pause momentarily to hear her say loudly, 'As if Jasper would want to bang her anyway, she's pig-ugly.'

I cringe and feel a pricking behind my eyes, but carry on walking with my head held high, hoping that by some miracle the whole school hadn't just heard that.

I finish my exam paper in plenty of time and check it over carefully for stupid mistakes. I turn the answer sheet over and place my pen by the side, lining it up with the edge of the paper. Most of the kids are still scribbling away or sitting with their head resting on their hands, scratching around in their minds for inspiration.

All the desks are carefully lined up so that every student is sitting at a single desk and no two desks are touching. The space between every desk is exactly the same as the width of each desk. The teachers measure the gap with almost exact precision. They have to. I like this; it satisfies my need for things to be exactly right. It's not that I'm a perfectionist, I'm not. It's a sort of control thing. If I can control my environment and make it right, then perhaps all the rest of the stuff will start to fall back into place. Start to mend. Maybe even go into reverse and undo all the bad that has happened. It's something to do with all the shitty things that have happened this year; I can get a bit controlly about things, objects mainly.

I sometimes find myself making up little rules, like 'if I don't put the pen exactly in the middle of the desk then I won't pass the exam'. I carefully place my pen exactly in the middle of the desk. You know, just in case.

But I'm not superstitious or anything, I know that's just silly. I wouldn't, for example, kid myself that if I 'touch wood' then my dad will come home, because I know, deep down, that it's not going to happen, he's never going to come home. I feel a slight panic rising in my throat as I glance around the room looking for some wood to touch. Well I've said it now, haven't I? I lean over and lightly touch the wooden floor with my finger. You know, just in case.

The trouble is, this need for things to be right, it's going the wrong way, because now I've lost my best friend too. But I don't care. I pick up my pen and start doodling on the top of my question paper. Boxes inside boxes, inside boxes. Boxes with no opening, no way in and no way out.

I glance over at the desk where Sasha's sitting, towards the front of the hall. She's still writing. I can see the back of her head, her long, poker-straight black hair cascading down her back with no apparent effort. And yet she will have spent an hour getting her hair that straight before school.

I feel lonely, discarded. Another loss. I seem to have lost so much this year, first my dad, then my cat died. And now Sasha's friendship. It's like I'm losing parts of my body. An arm perhaps. I glance down at my arm. Maybe not an arm, it's not like losing an arm. No, every time I lose something, it's like I'm losing a chunk of my heart. I wonder how many more things I will lose before I run out of heart altogether.

I inhale deeply, breathing in the smell of the school, the polish on the wooden floor, pencils and paper. Strange, surely paper and pencils are odourless? And a sort of bare-feet smell – the exam hall is normally the school gym, converted for exams once a year.

I can't see through the windows from where I'm sitting, they're too high. But I can see the sky, and it looks bright and pure and blue. A seagull soars above the rooftops, so high it looks tiny to me sitting below in this huge synthetic room. The gull seems motionless in the sky, gliding on an air current, then suddenly changes direction and swoops away, beyond my line of vision. I blink in the brightness. I feel like a caged bird, waiting to fly out into the world. A bird without wings.

I feel a tightness in my throat. It's my birthday, but it doesn't feel like it. I'm sixteen. I thought I might feel more grown up. Sixteen is adult really, isn't it? I wish I could turn into a real adult right now. Adults don't seem to have to put up with complicated people. I wonder what happens to evil kids when they become adults. Do they grow into nice people or just find more sophisti-cated ways of being vile? I try to picture what I might look like when I'm 30. I can't imagine. Old. I bet Sasha will still be beautiful even when she's 30. Sasha looks lovely even when she's not trying. She looked amazing last night.

Last night...

Chapter Two

Last night. Sasha had arranged for us to go out, as a pre-birthday treat for me. I didn't want to celebrate my birthday this year. Not without Dad. So I agreed to go out the evening before..

I was excited and scared, and it took me hours to get ready. I finally decided to wear my new pink blouse and a short skirt. It'd been a warm day so I went barelegged and put on my new pink wedge sandals. I knew I looked nice, but wasn't sure if it was nice enough. I'm skinny and would like to be more curvy. It makes me self-conscious. Boyish. And there was nothing I could do about my red hair. And face. There's nothing actually wrong with my face, and thankfully I haven't got too many freckles yet this summer. But next to Sasha I always feel ordinary. I did wonder if the skirt was a little too short. No makeup, just some lip-gloss.

I'd arranged to meet Sasha and her 'boyfriend-of-the-moment', Ben, and of course Jasper, at the Multiplex. I arrived too early so I collected my ticket and bought myself a large Coke. We were going to see *Superteen*, a spoof film about some teenage superhero. Not my choice. The others were late. As soon as Jasper entered the foyer a group of girls started to giggle flirtatiously and call out, 'Jasper, Jasper.' He ignored them and sauntered towards me, ahead of Sasha and Ben. He looked fantastic in black Versace jeans and an Armani top, and a trendy pair of leather ankle trainers. He had a way of walking that somehow told you he knew he was being watched. Not exactly a swagger, but close.

The girls who had been drooling over him must have wondered what he was doing with such an ordinary girl. He grabbed my hand and led me into the cinema, straight up towards the back, without saying a word. I felt in awe, he was so confident, sure of himself. I was excited, Jasper was out with me. *He chose me.*

My bubble wobbled when he took my Coke out of the armrest

and drank it down in one go. Which I thought was a bit cheeky. I frowned at him and he winked back at me and did a sort of clicking noise with his tongue that wound me up a bit. I started to feel a little bit irritable. He'd hardly said a word to me.

During the film Jasper laughed out loud at all the appropriate bits, and made the occasional comment towards the screen. I stole a glance at him once or twice. He really is good looking, there's no doubt about it. His dark liquid eyes with thick black eyelashes curling up over his tanned skin. Even the tiny chicken-pox scar near his eye. And yet the pock-mark doesn't detract from his looks, if anything it makes him more appealing. A sort of vulnerability.

After the film ended I stood up to leave but Jasper pulled me back down into my seat. 'Not so fast, Babe,' he said and kissed me on the mouth. I hadn't been expecting it and he somehow managed to get me off-centre and bang teeth. I pulled away, a bit embarrassed. What a disappointment. He winked and did that clicking noise again. I hurried to catch up with Sasha and Ben.

Once outside we all walked back towards Sasha and Jasper's house. Jasper walked slightly ahead of me and I had to keep doing little half-runs to keep up with him. And then he started talking on the way home, boasting mainly, about himself, and how he'd taught his dog to hunt rabbits. He didn't shut up. He said the 'F' word a lot. I think he thought he was impressing me. But he could've seen from my face that I wasn't interested. I've seen his dog when I slept over at Sasha's and it looks vicious. Sasha makes it sleep in the shed when Jasper's away because she hates it.

And he went on about how he'd got a car and a motorbike and how he'd been driving his dad's car since he was ten, I half-wondered how a ten-year-old boy could see over the bonnet of a car but frankly I couldn't be bothered asking. I just wanted to go home.

When we got back to their house, Sasha invited me in for a

cold drink and I agreed; I'd been feeling thirsty ever since Jasper drank my Coke in the cinema.

The house was empty; their dad must have been out. Sasha's mum died when she was a baby so she lives with her dad and Jasper. And they're away a lot on business, so Sasha often asks me to sleepover. She's not allowed to have friends over when her dad's home. I don't think he's very nice. Sasha always seems glad when they're away, we order pizza and lie in her double bed watching adult films until really late, replaying the naughty bits.

Jasper and Ben grabbed some beer from the fridge and Sasha poured out something fizzy and lime green and handed it to me. It tasted okay, sweet and fruity, and I drank it fast, the sugar rush making me feel light-headed. I decided to make my excuses and leave after I'd finished it.

I was feeling fuzzyheaded and sleepy but the next thing Sasha and Ben seemed to have disappeared. I remember thinking I'd better get home to bed; perhaps I was starting with a cold. I felt so strange. I stood to leave, but felt Jasper place his hand on my arm. 'Where you going, Babe? The night is young.' Then he did that annoying clicking with his tongue again.

I've never had a real boyfriend, sometimes I feel unattractive, childish. And I'm not sure about sex. I know all the facts, who does what and stuff. But don't really understand why. And I was pretty sure I didn't want to find out last night with Jasper.

'Another?' Jasper had said. His lips curled into a smile as he had handed me some more bright-green liquid.

My thoughts are brought back into the exam hall with a jolt as I hear the exam moderator woman shouting out 'FIFTEEN MINUTES.' I glance sideways at the boy sitting at the desk next to me. Luke. He smiles. I feel a flush coming to my cheeks and I quickly look down at my answer paper.

Luke sits next to me in Maths; it's the only subject where Sasha and I are in different sets. He's always been nice to me, if a little quiet. I feel myself relax, the tension of the morning starting to unwind with his small gesture of friendship. I glance back at him but he's busy reading through his answer paper. One or two kids have started to fidget; most of the class have finished now and are looking around the room, trying to have conversations with their eyes only.

I drift back into my own thoughts and Sasha's cruel words from this morning are suddenly being replayed over and over in my head. She called me 'frigid'. Half my school Year would have heard that. Some of the kids in the exam room seem to be staring at me. I can feel their eyes on me. I feel prickles at the back of my nose and hope that I'm not going to cry. I blink quickly and then close my eyes tight, rub my face with my hands. Maybe I really *am* frigid. Perhaps there *is* something wrong with me. After all I'm sixteen now. I'm even older than Sasha; she's not sixteen 'til next week. And she's had *loads* more experience than me. Well Sasha's had more experience than most of the girls in our class actually.

I keep my eyes tight shut, wishing I was somewhere else. Anywhere. It's dark inside my head and I want to disappear into the gloomy shadows of my mind. What's the matter with me? I clench my stomach as I see a flashback from last night, like an action-replay. With Jasper, on the settee, I can remember everything so very clearly.

'No, Jasper,' I had said as he leaned over me on the sofa. I pushed my forearm firmly against his chest, but he was too strong for me. I felt I was suffocating. The sweet green drink had made me feel woozy, everything sounded muffled.

'Playing hard to get?' he breathed into my face, laughing, sneering. He had started to undo the buttons on my blouse. I pulled away, but he tugged harder at the fabric and I heard a slight rip.

'Stop it, Jasper, I mean it, this isn't funny.' I pleaded with him. His face was so close to mine that he looked distorted. His mouth pressed together in a fine line.

'Nobody says *no* to me,' he said, his lip curling nastily. And I realised it was probably true.

I leaned forward to get off the settee but his hand clamped onto my arm like a vice. He yanked me back down. I lost balance and fell awkwardly.

'Ow!' I yelled as my head bounced off the back of the sofa, and tried to prise his fingers from my arm, he was hurting me.

His eyes were jet black and angry; he ran his tongue over his lips. 'Don't play games with me, Babe,' he said. I started to feel scared.

His face came towards me and his mouth clamped over mine. I gagged as he stuck his tongue in my mouth. I could smell beer and stale cigarette smoke on his breath. I tried to push him away, feeling sick, but he was holding me down and I couldn't move. He was surprisingly strong. As he came up for air I could feel his hand sneaking under the fabric of my blouse. He was laughing now and it sounded nasty. Creepy. It chilled me to the bone.

I pushed at him, managed to release my arm and move away, tried to stand up, but my legs didn't feel quite real. Jasper grabbed my arm again and it hurt. 'Please stop, Jasper.' I tried to keep my voice from shaking but the fact is I have never been so frightened in my life. My eyes searched for the door, his hold tightened even more, and his face flashed with something sinister.

It was as if he was crazy, he was breathing heavily and his face was flushed. One hand was holding me down whilst the other was groping awkwardly beneath my skirt. Then his eyes locked onto mine, his face was no longer pretending to smile – all that was left was a malignant leer.

What happened next is a bit of a blur, I remember bouncing off the cushion as I was shoved backwards. I was gripped by panic and I screamed even though I knew there was nobody to hear. He leaned over me, pinning me down with his weight. My flesh crawled as I felt his fingers touch me and I held my breath with revulsion. I pushed at him with my wrists but his free arm grabbed me so hard I cried out.

I tried to disconnect my thoughts from what was happening. 'Stop,' I whispered, more to myself as I knew it was futile. 'I don't want this, let me go.' I let the tears flow down my face; my breaths were coming in sobs. I knew that if I tried to move again, his grip would tighten, I knew it would be so easy for him to really hurt me. I felt I was choking, my body clamped down by his legs, he was heavy, I tried to scream again but there was no sound, my voice had gone. I realised that I was defenceless to stop him. I heard him unzip his flies and I closed my eyes.

But it was as though something suddenly snapped in my head. Like a rage, a fury. How dare he think he can just take what he wanted. Something seemed to happen, I felt a prickling in my fingertips and then an acute pain in my shoulders, and then an exploding sensation shot up through my spine and into my arms, driving a surge of hot angry fuel into my veins. The rage surged through my body like a hot ripple of pure power, gathering in intensity, and as the heat locked into tissues, I could feel my muscles firm and strengthen.

As Jasper fumbled I felt an enormous strength. I took a deep breath, formed my hand into a solid fist and whipped my arm upwards, slamming my knuckles hard into his belly. I surprised myself how much force I had been able to muster. 'Umph-wheeze,' the noise came from him as the air was knocked out of him. The surprise caused him to relax his grip on me, and as he gasped, struggling to put oxygen back into his lungs, I flung my arm back across his face, slapping him hard with the back of my fist. His face whipped round, throwing him backwards. Blood appeared on his cheek where my Claddagh ring had ripped his skin. I was up on my feet immediately and made a dash for the door.

As I felt for the door handle I turned to look at him, still on his knees, his pants hanging half way down his legs. He looked dazed, like he didn't know what had happened. He struggled to his feet, staggering towards me.

'You little bitch, you'll pay for that.'

He lunged at me but I caught his wrist in my hand and twisted it round hard. There was a sickening crunch and he screamed in pain, dropping to his knees and cradling his arm. It was just so easy. I stepped towards him. He looked afraid, his eyes wide and scared.

'Please don't hurt me,' he whimpered.

It was so pathetic, I almost wanted to laugh. He had shrunk down to almost nothing, a shrivelled, defenceless little worm. I wanted to leave, but I couldn't erase the feeling I'd had just moments earlier, when he'd controlled me. Terrified. Powerless. Violated. What he would have done; how he would have just taken what he wanted. Before I could think twice, I stepped forward, jerked my leg upwards hard and there was a satisfying *thuck* as my foot struck him hard in the groin. He crumpled in pain, dropped to the floor, curling into a ball, his eyes bulging as he struggled to breathe, gasping and retching.

I leaned over him, he probably couldn't hear but I was going to say it anyway. Loudly.

'*NO* means *NO!*' I shrieked. And I spun on the heel of my new wedge sandals, opened the door and strode out of the house without looking back.

Chapter Three

'TIME'S UP, PLEASE STOP WRITING, MAKE SURE THAT YOUR NAME AND EXAM NUMBER IS WRITTEN ON THE TOP OF EVERY SHEET. PLEASE REMAIN IN YOUR SEATS UNTIL ALL THE PAPERS HAVE BEEN COLLECTED. WHEN YOU HEAR THE BELL, YOU CAN LEAVE THE EXAM ROOM.'

I gulp loudly as my thoughts are brought back into the classroom.

Five more minutes and school will be over. Four minutes. But I feel no real joy in that fact because I know they'll be waiting for me at the school gates. They, of course, being Sasha and her entourage. Word will be out, there's a vacancy for Sasha's best friend. Every girl in our Year will be hovering around her, hoping to be picked out. I sigh, pick up my pen and unzip my pencil case. I check my answer papers are in the correct order.

The papers are being collected from the front of the hall towards the back, and after their papers are gone people are starting to whisper. Relief, nerves, excitement. I can see the back of Sasha's head, bent low whispering to Becca. Becca's shoulders shake as she giggles. She looks over her shoulder, catching my eye. They're talking about me. I know they'll all be out there, waiting to humiliate me again after school. Perhaps Jasper will be there too. I shudder. Sasha's going to turn the whole school against me. I don't care. I open my pencil case quickly and jab a pencil hard into the palm of my hand. I look down in shock as a small purple circle appears and a drop of blood oozes at the entrance of the tiny hole. *What am I doing?* I put my pen away quickly and rub my hand with my thumb. I've got to get out of here, I'm going mad.

I glance over at Luke again. A friendly face. He smiles, and I smile back this time. I feel soothed. You'd never think he was a year younger than the rest of us. He's good at science and maths so he's doing his exams a year early. Most of the fast-track kids are quite nerdy looking. Not Luke. He's arty, different to the other boys. It's like he doesn't need to make an effort, doesn't care whether people like him or not. He's skinny, longish blond hair with an unruly fringe. It looks like it's been hacked by a kitchen knife, all spiky and choppy. He has vivid blue eyes, which are usually hidden by his blond messy mop. But a nice smile. He often comes to school with paint smudged all over his hands, and sometimes his face. He draws pictures on his arms in black and red ink – elaborate images of dragons and winged creatures, they looked like tattoos – but the next day they'll be gone, only to be replaced by another fantasy scene. I've noticed him sketching doodles in his jotter during Maths lessons, usually fantasy figures and monsters, dragons, unicorns, elves. It's funny; I've sat next to him in Maths for a year and yet have hardly spoken to him at all. I like sitting next to him, I never feel under pressure to speak if I don't want to.

I jump as the bell rings out marking the end of the exam, end of day, end of term, end of Year Eleven, end of high school. The whole class rises together, the sound of chairs being scraped back fills the hall and the smell of relief intoxicates the air. The moderator is shouting but the sound is lost beneath the noise of sixty teenagers trampling for the door. I grab my pencil case and peer to see if I can spot Sasha out in the corridor, perhaps I could make a run for it. But Sasha's already out there.

I feel a hand gently tugging on my arm from behind, it's Luke. He thrusts a scrap of paper into my hand with a telephone number on it. I turn around but he's already gone. I shove the note in my pocket and make my way down the corridor. A feeling of doom creeps over me like cold sick.

I welcome the feel of the fresh free air as it slaps me in the face, and I draw a deep breath as I turn towards the school gates. As I approach the school boundary I see a swirl of smoke above the wall and somehow know that it marks the spot Sasha will be waiting. I clench my fists and walk a little faster. I've done nothing wrong. How dare she treat me like this, she doesn't even know what really happened. I'm tired and I want to go home.

'Here she is,' sings Sasha as I turn the corner. 'It's freaky frigid Scarlett!'

She's leaning against the six-foot wall that encircles the school. Some of Sasha's fans are scattered about, standing, talking, smoking, laughing. Demob happy.

Sasha holds a cigarette to her lips and takes a drag. She's not even a smoker really. She only does it because she thinks it makes her look older. I know because we used to do pretend smoking in her bedroom, take photos on our phones, then we'd judge which was the best look, smoking or not smoking.

I quicken my pace in a vain attempt to pass her. I don't want another confrontation. I stare at the ground and try to push through the crowd but someone grabs me by my arm and I spin round to see Jasper's face just inches from mine. I freeze.

He blows smoke into my face. 'Stuck up little Bitch,' he spits as he leers down at me, blatantly peering down the front of my blouse. There's a red scratch on his face where I hit him last night and his arm is immobilised in a splint. The smoke catches in my throat, I cough and start to move away.

'Look at me I'm Sandra Dee,' Sasha sings out in a stupid voice. I turn and glare at her, my face burns and my fists clench. How *dare* she. Jasper grabs my arm again and I yank it away. Okay, I tell myself, walk away now. *Just turn and walk.* But a group of kids close in around me, wanting to get a better look, creating a circle. I look at their faces, every one familiar, many of them in my class and some of them supposed to be friends. I start to feel hot, trapped.

'Back off!' I shout, seeing their hostile expressions, struggling to control myself. My body is beginning to tremble. Sasha steps towards me, her lip curling into a sneer. 'What you gonna do Sandra Dee? Beat us all up like you did my brother?' She bends towards me and I can feel her breath on my face. She smells of stale smoke and expensive perfume.

'Stop it, Sasha,' I say quietly and calmly, my eyes narrowing. 'Let me go.' But the feel of her hand tightening on my arm triggers the feelings of panic from last night.

She tilts her head towards me, says something quietly into my ear but I can't hear, don't want to hear. Too many voices, too much noise. My eyes lock onto hers. I can't read her expression. I yank my arm away from her. She glances at her brother. He nods, the gesture loaded with meaning. I don't understand.

Sasha suddenly screams out, 'What happened to your dad then Scarlett, did you beat *him* up too? Is he buried under your patio?' I feel the blood drain from my face as laughter rings out around my ears.

'You...BITCH!' I gasp, struggling to control myself. I feel my body start to vibrate with rage, my muscles are changing and strengthening just like last night, a hot flow of energy radiating from my spine and through my tissues, my muscles tightening with anger. And she's just looking at me. I can't read the expression on her face as she glances towards her brother.

Jasper suddenly lurches forward. 'Nobody calls my sister a bitch,' he hisses through clenched teeth. 'You and me...we have unfinished business.' He grabs a handful of my hair and yanks my head back so he's looking directly into my face. I hold my breath; his face is inches from mine. The crowd goes deathly silent. Just a couple of seconds but it feels like a lifetime, waiting. I know, and he knows, that he only has to make a move now, to hurt me. But then he winks, and he does that disgusting clicking noise with his tongue. I shudder. The crowd cheer.

'This is not over,' he mutters into my ear. He releases his grip on my hair with such force that I'm propelled backwards. I feel myself twist and overbalance, I try to grab out at something to steady myself but I feel weightless as I watch myself crash to the floor. Time seems to slow right down as I float through the air, my senses heighten, I can hear every sound, every laugh, every sneering comment, and in the distance I think I even hear the sound of birdsong. But that is away from here, in another lifetime, in the gardens, the woods, where things are easy, uncomplicated – free. As the concrete floor comes up to meet me I know I'm going to land badly. *This is going to hurt.* My arm goes out to break the fall but my head crashes down onto the flagstones, my face cracking against the edge of the pavement.

A bolt of pain shoots through my head, I cry out, my hands go to my face and I feel something warm and sticky. I've struck my face just below my right eye, and it's throbbing with pain. I feel sick, things are fuzzy, I hear a roaring sound and then everything goes silent and black.

As I start to come round I struggle to focus. I try to get up off the ground. Sasha and the other kids have backed away, looking alarmed. I can hear murmurs, whispers. 'She just fell,' and 'Unbelievable, she's so clumsy.' I can just see the back of Jasper disappearing into the crowd. My shoulder feels stiff and painful, my head spins and the side of my face feels like it has exploded. My vision's blurred and my head's swimming.

I sway as I struggle to my feet and wipe at my face with the sleeve of my blouse. It turns blood red. I feel nausea rise to my throat and wobble as I straighten my skirt, turn on my heel and stagger away. Nobody says anything, not one person comes to help me, not a kind word. My face throbs and the path seems to be swaying from side to side. I feel blood running down my cheek, or perhaps it's tears. How can everybody be so against me? Is Sasha so popular that she's turned the whole school against me? Did nobody actually see what happened here? Is there no ounce of kindness in this whole bloody school? Or is everybody so afraid of Sasha and Jasper that they don't dare defy her. They saw what happened to me and they didn't want that to happen to them. These people, they're like a flock of mindless sheep. All gutless. Gutless and lacking in imagination.

As I stand at the bus stop, leaning against the bus shelter, I think I hear a muffled voice coming through the zooming sound in my ears, it sounds like Sasha.

'Scarlett!' I don't bother to look round, it hurts too much. 'Scarlett,' she says again.

I turn my head and wince; it feels like I have a sack of potatoes resting on my head.

But I suddenly feel hopeful. There at the bus stop, leaning against the bus shelter, in that tiny miniscule of a moment I see a ray of hope. *She's realised she's gone too far, she's going to apologise.* After all, surely five years of friendship is worth something. *Everything's going to be all right.*

Her face comes into my vision, she looks concerned. She looks like the old Sasha, my friend. *My best friend.* Her hand touches my arm gently, and I feel my expression soften as I look into her eyes. She leans towards my swollen cheek, and I think for a brief moment she's going to kiss my cheek.

'Scarlett,' she says gently. There are tears in her eyes.

There's a sound from behind her and she glances over her shoulder, Jasper is walking towards us. Sasha suddenly straightens up, and screams into my face,

'You're a FREAK Scarlett and I never want to see you again.'

I peer at her in disbelief. She glares at me but a tear escapes and runs down her cheek. She doesn't brush it away. *I don't understand.* Then she turns and moves towards Jasper. He spits on the ground, points his finger at me and then runs his finger across his throat in a threatening way and then turns and walks away. Sasha doesn't look back as she rushes to catch up with him. I feel faint; the air feels thick and foggy. I think I'm going to throw up. Surely our friendship means something to her. *Why is she being like this?*

Chapter Four

The bus driver stares at me openly but I don't care, I just want to get home and lock the door. I know my face is streaked with blood, the small cut beneath my eye has stopped bleeding but I have a splitting headache, the bruise on my cheek is throbbing, swollen and tender. My school blouse has blood-red smears down the front and on the sleeve. Luckily I won't ever need to wear my school blouse again.

I make my way shakily up the stairs and am relieved to see that I have the whole of the top floor to myself. I choose a seat towards the front of the bus and stare out of the window, trying to blank my mind. As the bus moves away, the school disappears from sight and we trundle on past the row of cottages that line the edge of the village, I start to relax. I sniff hard to try and stop the tears from flowing. The hypnotic, familiar rhythm of the bus relaxes me and I start to unwind, I think I'll make myself a mug of hot chocolate when I get home. And have a warm soapy bath. Maggie won't be home until late tonight.

I peer through the thick murky glass. We've quickly left the little village behind and the landscape is dominated by the tall trees that edge Gossamer Woods, with the odd cottage scattered here and there. My eyes relax and blur as I settle back into my seat.

'Excuse me,' comes a small voice from over my shoulder and I jump, I hadn't noticed anybody else getting on the bus. 'Do you mind if I sit here?'

I wonder why the old lady wants to sit next to me when the rest of the bus is empty.

'Okay,' I shrug, and wince in pain.

The old woman and I sit in silence. I try to remember what happened outside the school, what Sasha said, it's all a bit fuzzy. We've been friends for such a long time. And why was *she* crying? She was the one being vindictive. I was the one who cracked my face on the pavement. I feel so alone. I miss my dad so much, but no, I'm not going to think about him now. I won't get upset. I sniff and get a tissue out of my bag, blow my nose noisily.

'Are you all right, dear?'

It's strange that rage thing, last night with Jasper – how could I have mustered enough strength to thump him like that? Am I turning into some kind of freaky muscle woman? I'm not under any illusion that I could beat up a grown man, under normal circumstances. It was as though my anger released something inside. It felt as though some kind of fuel was being poured through my veins, feeding my tissues and muscles. Like a sort of strength. *Oh my God I'm turning into the Incredible Hulk.* I laugh inwardly but glance at my hands to make sure there are no tinges of green. But seriously, it was when I got angry, something powerful, but not just an ordinary temper thing. This was different. It seemed to be physical, like it came from my body. It started around my back, my spine, my shoulders. It seemed to radiate outwards, energising and giving me the strength. I mean, how else could I have beaten up Jasper like that. It's quite scary. *Freaky.* Sasha's right, I *am* a freak. Dad had always said that redheads have a temper, but this is something else altogether.

'I hope you don't mind me asking?'

I glance towards the old lady sitting next to me.

'Sorry, were you talking to *me*?'

'Well there's nobody else on the bus, dear.' She laughs, but it's a kind laugh.

I smile in spite of myself, and then wince as my face hurts.

'Sorry,' I say. 'I was miles away.'

'Are you all right?' she says. 'It's just that you seem very sad. You look like you've been in an accident?'

A bubble of self-pity wells up inside, and I fight the tears back. But I appreciate her concern and I'm glad of the distraction. I swallow hard.

'I'm fine, thank you. I just had a run-in with some school bullies who were entertaining themselves at my expense. But the bump on my head was accidental, I slipped and fell over.'

'Oh that's awful,' says the old lady. 'But you know, dear, they're probably mean to you because they're jealous, you are a very beautiful young lady.' I laugh out loud, she must be blind: swollen eye, blood splattered face, matted ginger hair...*beautiful*? But I secretly hug myself; nobody has ever called me beautiful.

I glance round at her. Actually she's not that old, maybe sixty. But she looks as though she's suffered a lot in her life. She has a nice face, kindly. And the most vivid deep blue eyes. Wise eyes. More like a younger person's eyes. And a sweet smile.

'What school do you go to?' she says.

'Aspen High School. But it was my last exam today, so theoretically I actually don't go there anymore.' My heart gives a little skip. No more school worries for almost three months.

'Oh, yes I know,' the old lady replies, 'my grandson goes to that school.'

I nod and turn back to the window. I drift back into my own thoughts and watch the scenery flash by in a blur. I'm relieved that my headache's starting to diminish.

'My grandson will be about the same age as you. Luke Woods. Do you know him?'

I stare at her in surprise. *Of course I know him. Luke from Maths. I have his telephone number scrunched up in my bag somewhere.*

'Yes, I think so,' I say, suddenly feeling a little shy. I turn back to the window. Luke from Maths is her grandson. He has the same vivid blue eyes.

'I *do* understand,' the old lady suddenly says softly, and gently touches my hand. I shiver at her touch but I don't mind, it feels nice, her bony hand is surprisingly comforting, cool and gentle. I realise that not many people touch me these days. She reminds me of Miss Marple, although she appears to be a bumbling old lady, I'll bet her mind is as sharp as...well, something sharp.

We sit in companionable silence for the rest of the journey, the old lady and me. I feel comfortable sitting with my new friend. The old lady's compassion is almost palpable, and it reminds me of a time when all was well in the world. When my dad was still here, and I felt loved and happy. Even though I've never had a mum, I've never missed out on anything in my life. I suppose what you've never had, you don't miss. I always had Auntie Maggie close by. And there was my secret visitor too. But I don't talk about her to anybody.

Well okay, I'll tell you. When I was little I used to have an imaginary friend. I used to call her my Angel Lady, and sometimes I imagined her sitting on the chair in my bedroom. But she wasn't really there of course; she was like an air painting. She was awesome, like a kind of angel. She had a kind of shimmery rainbow around her. I imagined they were angel's wings. She was tall and slim with lovely long legs. And silver toes. Lovely long red hair, like mine. And I used to pretend that she was real and that she was my mother, come to visit me. I would lie in my bed and peep over the covers at her. Sometimes she would talk to me, tell me stories about a world of fantasy, fairies and wonderful winged creatures. I loved it when the Angel Lady came to visit me.

'This is my stop,' the old lady says and I jump. She squeezes my hand and gets up carefully as the bus slows down. 'It's been lovely to meet you, Scarlett. I hope you enjoy the rest of your birthday.'

I turn and smile at the old lady, she raises her hand to my cheek and strokes away an old tear with a pure white soft cotton embroidered handkerchief, a calm floods over me like a warm blanket. She presses the cool hankie into my hand.

'Keep the hankie, dear. My name is Pandora, you can trust me,' she says.

I frown questioningly, but I lift the cotton hankie to my hurt cheek again, it feels cool and tingly, as though a glass of fizzy water is being poured over my bruise. I feel comforted, it reminds me of when I was little and my dad would wrap me in a big warm towel after my bath. I felt so safe then, when I was little. I wish I was little again. *I wish my dad was still here.*

I watch through the window as the old lady steps down from the bus, and I smile as she turns and waves to me through the window.

I pull my mirror out of my bag and study my face. It's smeared with blood and tears, but I'm surprised to see that the cut is starting to heal over already, and the swelling has gone down. There's a small pink mark where, I assume, the bruising is going to come, but it's not half as swollen as I thought it would be. I snap my mirror shut and frown out of the window, feeling a bit of a fraud for feeling so sorry for myself.

That's strange, I suddenly think with a start. How did the old lady know my name? And then I sit bolt upright in my seat. How did she know it's my birthday?

Chapter Five

An hour later I'm perched on the edge of the bath with a bottle of pink bath foam. 'A fragrant bath soak to de-stress and relax'. I unscrew the cap and turn the bottle upside down, pouring a generous glob into the steaming water. I try to blank my mind as I watch the bath fill with mountains of bubbles and the room clouds with herb-scented steam. I clutch my towelling robe tightly around me until the bath is filled to the brim; dip my toe into the pink fragrant water. Just the right temperature. I shiver as I slip out of my robe and drape it over the towel rail, then step into the mountain of aromatic bubbles.

I sigh heavily as I sink into the reassuringly warm water, letting go of the tension and allowing the warmth to envelop me, the stress of the day seeping out through my pores. I duck my head below the surface and listen to the muffled sounds of bubbles rising through the soapy water. I can feel the strain of the last few days slipping away. I start to wash myself, bit by bit, so that I don't miss even an inch. The stale dried blood disappears from my face and leaves my pale pink flesh as though it's been untouched. I relax in the bath for a long time, topping up with hot water every time it starts to cool down.

When I do finally emerge from the water, the cool air hits my skin like a slap. As the steam rises from my flesh, my skin reacts, tightening, raising goose bumps down my arms and legs. Exposing my body to the air is like exposing my mind to its real thoughts and feelings, I gasp and shiver, grab at my towelling robe, which has fallen to the floor.

As I slip my arms into my robe, my body starts to tremble. I fight for breath as my emotions catch up with me. I feel as though somebody is sitting on my chest and I can't get any air in. The strength has disappeared from my legs, they buckle under me and I slide down onto the cold bathroom floor, clutching at the fluffy towelling fabric of my robe. The icy tiled floor bites into me and I gasp for air, trying to control my thoughts. It's as though I'm reliving the events of the last 24 hours, over and over again. My body shakes and my teeth chatter. *I'm going to die.* It keeps coming back, in flashbacks. I can feel his hands on my skin, his breath, his clammy hot hands and those lustful eyes. I shudder with disgust. I want to erase it all, everything that's happened these last few days. Weeks. Months. But it's like a bubble, no matter how much I push it down it still bobs up to the surface, larger than life. It's my fault, it must be. I must have done something to bring all this on. *Perhaps if I had done something different.* I take several deep breaths to control my breathing. I hate myself for this weakness, I'm sixteen, for God's sake, get a grip.

I fight to control my breathing, my face crumples and I start to sob violently. I want my dad. I need to be a little girl again, just once more. I need to be held and to feel safe. I'm shaking so hard the bath is vibrating. Something is exploding inside my head, a pain so bad I almost wish it were real. I want to hurt, to hurt badly, to hurt myself. That would be a pain I can control. I make a fist with my hand and with all my force I ram my knuckles into the ceramic tiles on the wall. The pain is excruciating, I scream out into the silent empty house and double up on the floor for a while, seconds, minutes, maybe more. I'm sobbing so much I can't breathe, my arm clutches my stomach as I try to suck air, as though I'm paralysed between breaths, holding, I feel the blood rush to my head and my ears begin to roar, on the edge of consciousness, it's my choice, breathe or slip away. Live or die. I suddenly gasp, short sharp breaths, and then coughing. Coughing and retching. I drag myself along the floor to the toilet and vomit, my body judders violently as I heave and sob.

Moments later my breathing has calmed and the pain from my bruised fingers returns. I wrap my throbbing hand in a damp towel and lie curled on the floor, cradling my hand; it somehow helps to have physical pain to focus on. Real pain, pain that I can understand. *Control.* It's easier to deal with that real pain than the confusing pain that comes from inside. And whilst my hand throbs and aches it masks the emotional pain. And I cry. I cry for myself, for how powerless I felt last evening. I cry for my dad who's been missing for two months now and I miss him so much that sometimes when I think about him it actually physically hurts. And I cry for Maggie, my aunt, who I hear weeping softly into her pillow at night. Not only did she lose her beloved elder brother, she gained custody of a troubled teenage girl.

But most of all I cry because it's been such a hideous, crappy, shitty, year so far.

When the sobbing starts to ease I reach for the toilet roll. I sniff hard and blow my nose noisily into the tissue and flush the chain. I don't know exactly what time Maggie will be home, but I don't want her to know about last night, or today. She's had enough to worry about. I take a deep breath and try hard to swallow all my sadness, hurt and humiliation. The grief, the loneliness and confusion. *Grow up, Scarlett, stop feeling sorry for yourself.*

I splash cold water onto my face and wipe away the steam from the mirror. And gasp in surprise. My face is unblemished. There's no sign of the cut, the bruise or the swollen cheek. Amazing. Unbelievable. In fact I feel a bit silly. *What a drama queen.*

But at least now I won't have to mention all this to Maggie. If she thinks I've got problems she might try and cancel her trip to Spain with her friends next week. And I know how much she's looking forward to it.

I examine my hand, my wrist, where I'd punched the ceramic tile. *Stupid, stupid.* It's red and swollen; I move my fingers around and wince in pain. No broken bones, that's good, very difficult to explain. I suddenly want to laugh out loud.

Then I remember the little white cotton hanky that the old lady on the bus gave me, the one that felt so cool and healing on my face. I run through to my bedroom and empty my bag onto the bed. There it is. It's soft white cotton with a tiny embroidered flower in one corner, it's really very pretty. I wrap the hanky around my sore hand. Lovely comforting feeling, so cool, so calming. I can feel the flesh of my hand throbbing and tingling, as though it's starting to heal. I sniff at the hanky, can't smell anything like a balm but there must be some kind of ointment on the hanky, something to help things heal.

I lay the hanky over the top of my hand, over the knuckles, can feel it resting there lightly. I hold my hand out, still, very still. I can feel my skin creeping beneath the hanky, ever so slightly. I lift the edge of the cotton hanky, and stop breathing. The cut over my knuckle is moving, tightening, the skin knitting together, before my eyes. I pull the hanky back over my hand quickly. Oh my God.

Something very strange is going on, but not in a bad way. Not something I will be rushing to tell my school friends about. A magic hanky? I don't think so.

Chapter Six

I slip into my pyjamas and go downstairs, the white cotton hanky still wrapped around my hand. I check all doors are locked and then make my way around the house, closing all the curtains and switching on the heating. It hasn't been so warm today and I need the comfort of the warm central heating, the reassuring gurgling of water through the pipes. By the time I'm relaxing in front of the television I'm feeling brighter and more positive, pushing away all remnants of the day. I have the whole summer ahead without having to deal with Sasha or Jasper, or the rest of those spineless kids in my year. I have to stay positive, stay strong.

I hear the front door click and then slam, and the familiar sound of Maggie's heels clicking through the hallway. She looks tired. She kicks off her shoes then goes straight to the fridge and pulls out a bottle of white wine. She glances at me and grins, and I smile back. I understand. This is her crutch, her way of coping with losing her brother. I know it's as bad for her as it is for me. Maggie and her brother Sam, my dad, have always been close.

'Happy Birthday!' Maggie sings. 'I know you said you didn't want to celebrate without your dad, but I got you a few bits anyway.' She smiles apologetically and hands me some wrapped presents.

I'm pleased she did, I love opening presents. She's bought me perfume and a couple of tops I liked when we were shopping last week. And some scented candles.

'Thank you, Maggie.' I lean over and kiss her on the cheek. She snuggles down into the couch and cradles the glass of wine in her hand. She looks so lovely when she smiles, her eyes light up and she looks much younger. She reaches round and fumbles with her hair clip, shaking her head to liberate her hair as it bounces out of the ponytail and cascades down her back. She has the same brown wavy hair and big hazel-brown eyes as my dad. Dad always used to say his hair was the same colour as a field mouse. But I like field mice. It's better than having hair the colour of...I don't know what kind of animal has red hair. A ginger kitten. But Maggie's hair is darker now; she tints it to mask the grey hairs that have begun to appear in the last year or two. She's kept the length; it's almost down to her waist. She ties it up for work, but as soon as she gets home her hair is the first thing to unwind. In fact Maggie's hair is even longer than mine. I smile fondly as she tucks her legs beneath her and sips at her wine glass.

I don't know what I'd have done these last few months without Auntie Maggie. I'd probably be in some kind of foster care. I know how much Maggie gave up when she came to live with me. She's never been married but she has a busy social life, and that all went to pot when she adopted her teenage niece. She has to work longer hours now to support both of us, and she doesn't get to see her friends as often as she used to. But she's never once complained. If I had a mum, I'd want her to be just like Maggie.

'Scarlett,' she says hesitantly, breaking into my thoughts. 'I found something today, something I had forgotten all about. It's a present your dad wanted to give you on your sixteenth birthday. I have no idea what it is, I found it all wrapped up, he mentioned it to me months before he...went.' Her voice falters, and I touch her arm. 'I thought I should give it to you now anyway. In case it's important.'

Maggie puts her wine glass down on the bookcase and goes over to the chest of drawers. My heart feels like it's going to pound right into my throat. She pulls out a package, wrapped in cream tissue and tied with large green satin ribbon. I swallow and stare at the present. Maggie stares too, she perches on the edge of her chair so that she can watch me open it.

The shape of the parcel doesn't give anything away; it's about a foot square, about an inch deep, and quite heavy for its size. Maggie grins as I shake it gently, hold it to my ear, and then sniff at it.

'Well it doesn't smell, and it doesn't rattle,' I conclude.

'I hope not, if it rattles you've probably broken it!' She laughs, it's a real 'Maggie laugh'.

I don't hear the sound of Maggie's laughter very often these days and it warms me right through. It reminds me of summer days when I was little, playing in the garden. Dad and Auntie Maggie would be laughing at some joke that I was too young to understand. But I'd laugh along with them anyway. Maggie's the only mother figure I've ever known and she's been a part of my life for as long as I can remember.

It's been over two months now. Since Dad disappeared. It was the 1st of April. April Fool's Day. He went out to work that morning, and that was it. He never came home. He never even turned up at the university where he works. He just disappeared into thin air. Even now, I still half-expect him to burst through the door, his glasses sliding down his nose, his hands running through his hair in frustration with the traffic. He always insists on cycling to work even though he hates the way the car drivers treat cyclists. But when he didn't come home I was convinced it was some kind of April Fool's joke. It would have been just like him. But it wasn't a joke, because he never did come home. The police listed him as a 'missing person' and told us that people sometimes do this; they just walk out of their lives. Well perhaps some people do, but my dad doesn't. He just wouldn't do that, he couldn't, he would never leave me.

Maggie and I walked the streets looking for him, looking for a clue. We telephoned everybody we knew, went everywhere, all the places he could possibly have gone, where he had perhaps had an accident and couldn't get help. The university where he works swears Dad never turned up, his security card wasn't used that morning. His bike was gone too, he had taken it out of the shed, locked the shed carefully behind him, and then disappeared into thin air. It's a horrible feeling, not knowing. Both

Maggie and I went over and over in our heads where he could be, and both came to the same conclusion. He must be ill, lying in a gutter somewhere. Or lost his memory. You hear stories of people who get amnesia.

We rang all the hospitals, every couple of hours, for weeks, not quite knowing what we wanted to hear. Perhaps no news was good news. Or better news. But after a couple of weeks Maggie started to assume the worst. He must be dead. But I have never allowed myself to believe that. I feel deep inside, somehow I'd know. And if he's dead how come nobody found him? If he'd been beaten up and left in a gutter, even if his wallet had been stolen, somebody would find him. And his bike would be somewhere wouldn't it? If they'd stolen his cards then the police would be alerted when they were used. We begged the police to keep looking, but they lost interest. Apparently lots of people go missing every year. 'If he wants to come home, he'll come home,' the police sergeant had said with a sympathetic smile, 'don't you worry.' It was so frustrating. Patronising. I wanted to yell at him, *he's my dad, he hasn't run away!* So we were left on our own.

Maggie moved into my house and has stayed ever since. Social Services said that she could be my guardian especially as I was almost sixteen. We didn't have to bother with formal fostering arrangements. And we had to accept that we may never see him again. We do try. Maggie spends her waking hours working at the hospital and hiding her pain in a bottle of wine in the evenings, and I throw myself into preparing for my exams. I stopped talking about him, even to Sasha. But it never goes away, not just because you say it must. It never stops hurting.

For me, the hunt has turned inward. Searching my mind for an explanation, it's taken over my life, my thoughts, and my actions. If perhaps I'd been home that day, if I'd done my school work, if I hadn't stayed out so late, if I'd worn different clothes. Maggie says I have 'a spot of OCD', obsessive compulsive disorder. But in my head it's like the butterfly theory. I read somewhere that when a butterfly flaps its wings in one part of the world it can cause a hurricane in another part of the world. That makes perfect sense to me.

So I've tried to work out what I could have done differently to have made him stay. What I can do now to bring him back. And that's why I have to be very careful. Very careful that I don't do anything else wrong. Whatever I did to make this happen, I mustn't do it again. I can't lose anything else, anybody else. So everything is kept in order, I have to control everything, I like to see things straight, tidy, doors have to be closed and locked, and I have to do the right thing. Always. Every puzzle has an answer. I have to make it right. Because deep down, somewhere deep in my heart, I secretly hope, expect, *know* that he will walk back through the door.

'Oh for crying out loud, Scarlett, OPEN IT!' Maggie's voice shocks me out of my indecision; she looks like she's going to burst with anticipation. 'I've known about this present for months now and I can't wait another minute, if you don't open it, *I will.*'

I don't delay any longer and rip the tissue paper off the parcel, revealing a brown cardboard box. I turn the box over looking for a way in, I find the opening and run my finger under it and the flap to the box springs open.

Inside is some pale yellow tissue, and beneath that, a large picture frame with a colour photograph inside it.

I hear myself gasp and my hand covers my mouth, the picture frame falls from my hand and plops onto the couch.

'What?' says Maggie, looking anxious. 'What is it?'

I open my mouth but no words will come. Maggie is craning to see what was in the package.

Eventually I pick up the picture and look at it again. The woman in the photograph is slim and elegant, she has dark red hair. A beautiful face, stunning. She wears a lemon and cream dress that looks like it is part of her, she wears a band of bright yellow and cornflower blue flowers in her hair, and her bare toes are painted with silver polish.

It's Angel Lady. It's the lady who used to visit me in my bedroom, in my dreams. I feel a little nauseous. *Who is she?*

I stare at the photograph. I swear that I can see something weird. Okay it's slightly out of focus, but they are there. Just like the Angel Lady. Behind her shoulders. If you really use your imagination. *Wings.* If you had a good imagination.

I pick up the frame quickly, it's ridiculous. *Get a grip.* It's just the picture that comes with the frame. It's just my rubbish mind playing tricks on me. I take a few deep breaths. It's okay, it's just me. I'm being stupid.

I turn it over in my hands; stare at the back of the frame. It's lined with a silky-soft material and the whole of the frame is backed in lemon-coloured leather.

It's actually awesome. Dad probably bought it so that I could put my own photograph into it. I'll put a picture of Dad in the frame. And get rid of that photo. Of the woman.

Angel Lady.

Maggie looks like she's going to explode with anticipation.

'It's a photo frame,' I say. 'Not of anybody we know, just, you know, just a frame. It's lovely. Dad probably thought I'd put a photo of him in it. And I will. A photo of Dad. You know, take that photo out. Cos it's just the photo that comes with the frame.'

Maggie is looking at me very oddly. *It's just a photo frame.*

I pass the frame across to Maggie. She looks at the photo and frowns, and then glances back at me. She places the picture on the coffee table, wipes her hands on her jeans and reaches for her glass of wine. She takes a sip, replaces the glass and then scrambles around in her handbag for her cigarettes.

Maggie has gone awfully pale.

I stare at the photo frame sitting on the coffee table. The leather is a lovely pale lemon colour, looks like it's been hand-made. Imprinted in the leather on the front cover, in gold lettering, is one word, 'Fae'.

'What does that mean?' I say out loud. Maggie frowns. As I pick up the tissue paper to clear it away, a piece of paper falls out. I recognise Dad's handwriting. Written on creamy yellow thin parchment paper.

To my Fairy Princess,
Now you're Sixteen I can tell you who you are, how you got here, and what is your destiny. I will be able to answer some of the questions that you will be starting to ask now that you are sixteen, and you will soon be in Transition.
Happy Birthday darling, I'm proud of you,
All my love, Dad.

The tears are rolling down my cheeks as I pass the letter over to Maggie. I used to like him calling me his Fairy Princess when I was a kid, but as I got older he just used to do it to embarrass me in front of my friends. That feels like a lifetime ago.

I hear Maggie reach for her hanky and blow her nose. But what on earth does he mean when he says I need to know who I am? And how I got here? All I know is that my mother abandoned me when I was a very young baby. Dad never spoke about her, so I never asked. I suppose I always felt we would talk about it one day.

'What does he mean by *Transition*?' I say out loud.

Maggie shrugs and shakes her head. She places her wine glass on the mantelpiece and comes to sit next to me.

We sit in silence for a while, I feel puzzled and tearful. What did Dad mean when he said he could tell me who I am and where I came from? I know some odd things have happened lately but that's nothing to do with my birthday, more to do with Jasper and Sasha and my sudden ability to beat up grown men with my bare hands. And that odd woman on the bus. And the strange hanky. But Dad couldn't have known about all that. I feel frustrated and, well, angry. Angry at Dad. Why isn't he here to explain all this?

'What did Dad actually *say* about the present?' I half-snap at Maggie.

'He just said he wanted to put it away for your birthday. I wish I'd paid more attention now.'

Silence again. Maggie looks like she's going to cry.

The photo frame is sitting on the coffee table in front of us. I'm avoiding looking at it. And I get the feeling Maggie is avoiding looking at it too.

'Do you know who that is, Maggie? In the photo frame?' I ask accusingly.

'No,' says Maggie, perhaps a bit quickly. 'As you say, it's probably just the picture that came with the frame.'

'Well maybe it will all become obvious soon,' I say, suddenly feeling the need to reassure Maggie. She's tapping her fingers on the arm of the sofa, she looks unnerved. 'Perhaps it's one of those things you have to not think about to be able to work out. Like when you're trying to remember someone's name and then it pops into your head when you're doing something else.'

'Yes, yes.' Maggie nods profusely. She finishes her wine and gets up to pour herself another glass.

Maggie comes back into the room holding her re-filled glass and a cigarette. She takes a drag and glances over at me like a naughty child. She never used to smoke in the house, Dad didn't like it. I know she smokes in the lounge after I've gone to bed, I can smell it in the morning. She takes another puff on the cigarette, looks like she's trying to suck the life out of it. Her eyes glisten with emotion.

She attempts a watery smile and places her wine glass on the side. She hesitates, takes another drag on her cigarette and stubs it out on a saucer. She bites her lip, wipes her tears on the back of her hand and sniffs loudly, and then says, 'There's something I think I need to tell you, Scarlett.'

Chapter Seven

Maggie taps the cushion beside her. I jump onto the settee and pull my legs up, sinking back into the soft cushions. My heart is hammering in my chest.

'As Sam's not here, I think I should tell you. It's about your mother, and how you got here.'

I'm a little surprised to hear that Maggie knows about my mother. I've always imagined I was the product of a one-night stand, and that my mother turned up on his doorstep one day to dump the baby on him. Like in *Three Men and a Baby*.

'The story's a little unbelievable, like a fairytale, but you'll have to bear with me.' Maggie cradles her wine glass.

'Okay,' I say. Maggie's silent for a moment.

'When Sam and I were young, I was about seven and he'd be nine. We used to play in the woods here behind the cottage, Gossamer Woods.'

I nod.

'Everything was much safer in those days. At least it seemed that way. Kids would play out all day and as long as they were back in time for tea nobody worried where they were.'

I nod and smile. Actually, Maggie doesn't know this, but my dad *did* allow me go and play in the woods when I was young, he used to say that there were a lot of bad people in the world and dangerous things, but the woods were relatively safe because the woodland folk would look after children. He made me promise I wouldn't go deep into the forest, never further than the old oak tree. And during the long summer holidays I would go off for the afternoon, with my little bag full of sweets and a book to read. Sometimes Dad would come and join me, and occasionally I'd go with a school friend. But mostly I liked to go on my own.

I blink myself back and wait for Maggie to begin.

'We had a friend, a little girl who we'd play with in the woods.

She was a little older than me, nearer Sam's age. Her name was Tate and she was a lot of fun. She used to know all these daring games, and she would teach us all about the trees and the woodland creatures. And the used to make up the most amazing stories.' Maggie laughs a little, and takes a sip from her wine glass.

'Where did she live, this friend?'

'Tate?' Maggie muses for a moment. 'As a child I always kind of assumed she lived in the woods. She was different. Tate was different from us.'

'What do you mean, *different*?'

Maggie sighs, and glances towards me and then away quickly. She settles back into the cushions, takes a sip from her glass. And then she lights another cigarette and takes a huge drag on it. She glances at me, and then looks away. Then she looks me straight in the eye.

'Tate was a fairy.'

I laugh, but it comes out sounding strange.

'A...*fairy*?'

'Well obviously *not* a fairy,' Maggie says quickly, coughing gently into her hand. She takes another gulp from her wine glass. Her eyes move around the room and then back to mine.

'A fairy?' I say again, more impatiently.

'Yes,' Maggie says decisively. 'Tate was a fairy.'

'Right,' I say.

'Right,' Maggie says.

We're both silent, staring at each other. Maggie has that look she used to get when she was arguing with Dad and she knew she was right. Dad used to say she was like a stroppy teenager. He also said I get that look too when I'm arguing. I feel a sudden need to break the silence. I don't want Dad to be right, not when he's not here anymore.

'So where is she now, this fairy?'

'Well that's just it,' Maggie says. She slaps the wine glass down on the shelf and shuffles her legs under her, still looking a tad grumpy.

'Look, Scarlett,' she says, 'I can only tell you the story like this, through the eyes of a child. I was six or seven years old, we're talking about an age when we believe in Father Christmas, the tooth fairy brings gifts in exchange for baby teeth, and the woods are inhabited by fairies. As far as I was concerned, our little friend Tate was, well, special. She was different, she wasn't like us. I always believed she was a fairy.'

'Okay,' I say, touching her arm gently in truce. 'So when did you stop seeing your little friend Tate in the woods?'

'We used to go and play with her for quite a number of years. She seemed to be there all the time, playing by the oak tree. But as we got older it was harder to find her – like we knew she was there but we just couldn't see her. By the time I was thirteen or fourteen, I guess, I started getting interested in other things, clothes and boys. So I stopped going into the woods with Sam.'

'But Dad still went to see Tate?'

'Yes, Sam still used to go and meet Tate. He would have been fifteen or sixteen when I used to tease him that he was in love with her. You know what it's like with brothers and sisters. Of course he hated that and would get really grumpy and moody, so he stopped telling me about his rendezvous with Tate. He became secretive. He wouldn't talk about her, refused to tell me things they had done, things they had talked about. Dreamed about.'

'I'm not surprised if you teased him about it.'

'I know. But because he wouldn't tell me about her, I got curious. He became different. I suppose he was just growing up. But he used to sneak out of the house at every opportunity to see her. So one day I followed him.'

'What!'

'I know. He used to slip out in the evenings when our dad, your granddad, was in bed. Granddad was quite poorly by then and he'd go to bed straight after tea. So I waited 'til Sam had slipped out of the back door and I went after him. It was about six in the evening, the summer was nearly at an end but it was still warm and bright in the evenings. I followed him into the woods, making sure he didn't see me.' Maggie smiles and takes a sip from her glass.

'I hid behind a tree and watched, laughing to myself thinking about how I'd tease him the next day. But then Sam seemed to disappear. One minute he was there, and the next minute he was gone. It was really weird.'

'You mean you lost sight of him?'

'No, I mean he disappeared. I was watching him, he stood there in the clearing close to the old oak tree, and then he was gone. He couldn't have moved, or hidden, I was staring straight at him and then he was gone.'

'O-kay.' I feel a little shiver down my back.

'So what did you do?' I say politely, not wishing to annoy her again.

'I sat down under that old oak tree, the huge one near the clearing?'

I nod. I know the tree, everybody does, it's meant to be hundreds of years old. Maggie's staring into the distance, concentrating hard as though trying to remember every detail of that evening.

'I waited, I thought sooner or later he would reappear, he couldn't be gone forever. But I'd been getting a lot of hay fever that summer and my eyes were itchy and hazy. I was finding it more and more difficult to focus. And then I saw Sam again. But he seemed to keep disappearing and then reappearing – it was as though I couldn't focus properly in the light. It suddenly all changed, it was more colourful and bright, and it would hurt my eyes. Like in the old days when TVs were first in colour, and everything was super-bright and unreal.'

She looks at me and I blink. I have no idea what she's talking about. She puffs her cheeks out in annoyance and closes her eyes to continue.

'Everything was more vibrant and clear, sounds were twice as loud, scents more potent. The sky was filled with butterflies and winged insects, the foliage was lush and the wild animals were tame. And the woods were filled with Gossamer Orchids, those gorgeous yellow flowers that used to inhabit our woods. They had already been extinct for years and years. We hadn't seen them since we were very young.' Maggie is lost in her thoughts.

'And then I saw Tate. Sitting on a fallen tree. She was lovely as a child, but as a teenager she was the most beautiful girl I had ever set eyes on. She was sixteen now, a young woman really. Her little baby fairy wings had grown into huge shimmering iridescent wings spreading behind her. She was beautiful, with pale skin and long red wavy hair, which seemed to catch the sunlight. She had the most stunning deep sea-green eyes I have ever seen.'

I gulp; I also used to know a person who looked just like that. *The Angel Lady.* I glance over at the picture in the photo frame.

'In fact, from what I remember, Tate looked a bit like the woman in that picture. Obviously she was younger when I saw her.' Maggie nods her head towards the photo frame and I shiver. The sooner I replace that picture with a photo of Dad, the better.

'In fact Tate looked a lot like *you*.'

I snap out of my thoughts and realise Maggie is looking straight at me. I blush. Okay so I have red hair and green eyes, but I'm not beautiful. And I don't have wings, Ha!

'Go on, Maggie, what happened then?'

'Blimey, the acorn doesn't fall far from the tree does it, Miss Impatience!'

I pull a face and Maggie pulls one back and takes a large gulp from her wine glass before she continues.

'Well we all sat together and talked, Sam, Tate and me. It was like we were kids again. Tate was just as I had remembered her, gentle and sweet natured, but of course she seemed so grown up now. It's no wonder your dad fell for her.'

Maggie gently touches my arm. 'Scarlett, your dad didn't come home that night. They told me that they were in love. Your dad and Tate. And the following day Sam told me that they had made love for the first time that night. They slept together under the great oak tree, and he said he never wanted to wake up, couldn't bear to be parted from Tate. They slept in each other's arms, right there under the stars.'

'Wow,' I breathe.

'Sam never saw Tate again after that night. He went back the following evening, but Tate was nowhere to be seen. He looked everywhere for her, he went back into the woods every day, but he never saw her again. He hunted for hours, asked everybody he met if they'd seen her, tried to find out where she had come from, where she lived. But nobody knew her name. He thought he was going mad. Sam went back into the woods every day, camped out there, slept there several nights, but he never found her. I was the only person who knew about Tate, and I tried to make him forget about her. I even tried to convince him that she was just in our imagination, like an imaginary friend. That he should forget about her and move on. That she had never existed. It was eating away at him and I was worried…I was worried that he would send himself mad. Especially with your granddad being a little dotty anyway, I wondered if perhaps it could run in families.'

'He never found her?'

'No, but he never stopped looking.'

'Wow.' I feel a little choked.

I pull myself to my feet and go into the kitchen, fighting back tears with no idea why. I crack open a can of Coke from the fridge. Wow, Dad was in love with some girl from the woods. I wonder if she was a vagrant or a gypsy. Maggie said she was a fairy. I smile to myself. Maggie was always obsessed with fairies when she was young, I know that because she let me read all her old school books – nearly every story she wrote was about fairies in the woods.

I slide down onto the floor, pull my legs up and lean back against the soft couch. I close my eyes and think about Maggie's story. I feel warm and woozy. Wouldn't it be nice if Dad was with Tate now, if he was living with her in an 'imaginary friend' world in the woods. I feel the warm skin from Maggie's legs against my arm, and I wrap my arms around her legs, like cuddling a soft toy. Maggie's fingers play with my hair and I love the feeling. I feel safe and warm.

Then Maggie leans forward a little and I feel her hair brush my cheek gently, can smell the faint odour of wine and light perfume, as she murmurs into my ear.

'Tate is your mother.'

Chapter Eight

'What?' My mouth has dropped open. 'Tate's my mother? Did Dad find her then?'

'No, he never saw Tate again but he never stopped hunting for her. He would camp out in the woods sometimes, and as soon as he got home from college he'd be out there looking. It was several months later…nine months later to be exact, he was back in the woods, still hoping to see her, to find her, to discover proof that she existed, that their love had been real. It was a lovely evening, warm and still, and he decided to rest for a moment. He sat down under the oak tree, and he fell asleep.' Maggie is lost in her thoughts again, and then catches her breath.

'It was summertime by now. The trees had started to get their leaves, and when your dad woke up he noticed a clearing where the sunlight shone through the trees.'

Maggie reaches for her wine glass and takes a sip, places it back on the shelf. Leans her head back on the sofa and closes her eyes.

'It struck him as strange because it had been such a dull day, but the sun was shining so brightly through the trees. And he had a feeling that someone was watching him. Although he couldn't see anybody, there was nobody there. But he felt that somehow he wasn't alone.'

Maggie's voice has diminished to a whisper and I squeeze her hand in encouragement.

'Sam noticed that the sunlight streaming down through the gap between the trees seemed to be beaming onto one spot in the grass, like a spotlight on a stage, pointing at one spot in the grass. It lit up all the gorgeous butterflies that were caught within this shaft of light, like a slice of light bursting through the trees…' Maggie pauses, lost in her thoughts.

'Go on, Maggie,' I say, 'what happened next?'

'Well...' Maggie laughs.

'Well?' I say, urging her to go on.

'Well that was when Sam noticed the bundle under the tree, caught beneath the beam of sunlight. A sort of package made up of leaves and petals. It struck him as odd because the leaves were a greeny-red, more like autumn leaves and yet it was only June.

'Something made him go over to the bundle. He told me it was as though somebody had left a parcel for him, and was pointing him towards it with the beam of sunlight.'

I've a feeling I know what's coming next. 'What was in the bundle?'

Maggie smiles, she won't be rushed. 'Well, when he leaned over the pile of leaves he realised that they were sheltering a parcel of something wrapped in the middle. The leaves were all tangled together, like a vine. The leaves were wrapped around and intertwined with flowers and soft dried green moss. Like a warm blanket.

'So what was inside?' I ask again, wanting desperately to know, but also a little afraid of what Maggie is going to say.

'As Sam peered over the bundle, he thought he could hear something like a whispering around him, but there was nobody there. And then he saw something move, inside the parcel, he pulled the parcel wrappings back carefully, and there was the most captivating little baby he had ever seen. You were pink and warm and beautiful.'

'Me?' I say, breathlessly. 'I was the baby?'

'Yes, Scarlett, it was you. He could tell you were just sleeping, and he picked you up carefully and held you very close, so close he could feel your hot little breath on his cheek and your moist little mouth left a damp patch on his skin. Sam always said it was like a fairytale. He sat down in the leaves and cradled you. He said your little face was like the face of a little angel. Like a gift from heaven. He fell in love with you, and has loved you ever since. He knew straight away that you were his and Tate's baby daughter. It was exactly nine months since that night he had spent with Tate, the very last time he saw her.'

My throat feels like it's closing up.

'So what did he do?' I croak. 'Was there any sign of the person who had left me? Somebody must have left me there while he was sleeping. Was anybody there?'

'I don't know,' Maggie replies, after a moment's hesitation. 'Your dad couldn't see anybody, but you were warm and well fed, you couldn't have been there very long. But he *felt* like there was somebody there, watching over you. He knew you had been left for him to find, you hadn't just been abandoned.'

I feel a shiver up my back and my heart beats a little faster. We are silent together for a moment. Maggie is smiling.

'Then you opened your eyes and looked straight at him. It was as if you had opened your eyes for the very first time. You had the most amazing, dazzling vivid green eyes. Tate's eyes. The colour of the sea on a clear sunny day. Stunning. You can't have been more than a few hours old, but when your dad looked into your eyes it felt as though he could see your soul. He knew that you belonged to him and that for some reason you had been left for him to look after. So he wrapped you up in his jumper, and carried you home.'

'And he never saw anybody, nobody at all?'

'We-ell,' Maggie glances at me a little hesitantly. 'As he was walking back through the woods there was someone. A woman from the village. She was taking a walk through the woods.'

'Could she have been my mother?' My heart is pounding now.

'Oh no,' Maggie laughs. 'She would have been old enough to be your grandmother. In fact her grandson goes to the same school as you.'

'So what did Dad do with me after that?'

'When he got you home he showed me the baby. I was only fifteen at the time and he was seventeen. Your gran had died a few years earlier and of course your granddad was quite poorly by that time. So Sam and I decided we'd better call the police. But before the police arrived, we examined the bundle of leaves and cloths, and there were some papers in between the layers of fabric that you were wrapped in – we found a document, your birth certificate.'

Maggie wriggles her toes into her slippers and walks over to the bureau, takes out a large brown envelope. She comes back to the sofa and sits down, emptying the contents of the envelope onto the cushions. My heart is pounding in my chest. I pick up the sheet of paper, it's a birth certificate.

'Your birth had somehow been registered, and your mother had named you Scarlett. Your mother was listed as simply Tatham Sage, and your father was listed as Samuel Moon.'

I stare down at the name on the Certificate. Tatham Sage. *Wow.* My mum.

'Oh my God, so Dad really *is* my dad. And Tate really is my mother?' I can hardly read the writing on the paper through my blurry eyes.

'Yes, we didn't know where Tate was, or how she managed to get the birth registered, but she clearly had it all worked out. And she had intended for Sam to find you in the woods that day. Wherever she had been, and wherever she is now...there must have been a good reason why she left you for Sam to look after.'

'What did the police say?'

Maggie laughs and flicks her hair, as though she's back there sixteen years ago.

'The police thought we were two crazy teenagers who'd had a baby together. They somehow assumed that I was Tatham Sage, the mother, and that Sam was the father. And we didn't put them right.' Maggie giggles like a schoolgirl. 'And as all the paperwork was in order, and there was clearly another adult living in the household, your granddad, they left us to it. They referred us to social services but the social worker never took a lot of interest. They could see that you were healthy and happy so they left us alone after a couple of visits. I promised Sam that I'd always be there to help him bring you up, especially after Granddad died. You were always so much more to me than just a niece. I couldn't have loved you any more if you'd been my own daughter.'

'I know that, Maggie,' I say, tears welling in my eyes once again. 'So what happened that night? After the police left?'

'Well we bathed you together that first night, and that was when we noticed your little wing-shaped birth mark in the middle of your back, it was as though you were meant to have little fairy wings on your back.'

'Huh, well if Tate is a fairy as you say, then maybe my birthmark really is fairy wings, maybe I'll have a go at flying...' I giggle as Maggie punches my arm.

My two symmetrical wing marks haven't faded as I've grown older; they've deepened in colour and grown with me. I like them; they make a pattern like a pretty tattoo in the middle of my back, near my shoulder blades.

I pick up the birth certificate and hold it in my hand, run my fingers over the writing. Tatham Sage. Wow, that's my mother. Tatham Sage. I'm not sure what I feel, perhaps a little numb inside. It's such a lot to take in.

I pick up the photo frame. With the picture of the person who might look like her. A bit. Perhaps. Just a coincidence. *Obviously.*

I place the picture frame back on the coffee table and sniff loudly and wipe away a tear with the cotton hanky that is still wrapped around my hand. I feel exhausted.

Maggie leans towards me, peering at the scabs on my knuckles. 'Have you hurt your hand, honey?'

'I slipped and banged it in the bathroom after my bath.' Well it's the truth. Kind of.

'That's a pretty hanky, where did you get it?'

'An old lady gave it to me, I was sneezing on the bus and she said I could keep it.' I can hear how lame that sounds.

'The little flower in the corner of the hanky,' says Maggie, 'looks just like those Gossamer Orchids that used to be in the woods. The ones that are extinct now.'

I look down at the hanky. But something is niggling me, at the back of my mind, tapping at my head.

'Maggie,' I say, thoughtfully, 'that woman in the woods, the one who was there the day Dad found me when I was a baby.'

'Oh yes, she lives the other side of Gossamer Woods. Her grandson goes to your school.'

'What's her name, the old lady, what's her first name?'

'Her name's Pandora.'

Chapter Nine

Oh my God, today is turning into such a weird day. Dad was so right when he said there were questions to be answered.

Upstairs in my bedroom I carefully lock the door from the inside and lean against the wall for a few moments, clutching the photo frame to my chest with my eyes tightly shut.

Then I walk over to the window and close the curtains. I straighten my duvet and tuck it back in behind the wall. I slowly unbutton my pyjama top and slip it over my shoulders, untie the waist string on my pyjama trousers and step out of them. I like these pyjamas; they're warm and soft, white with pink hearts all over them. I hug the fabric to my skin for a moment. What's going on? And what was it that Dad was going to tell me now I'm sixteen? What does *Transition* mean? Who is Tate and where is she now?

I place the photo frame on my bedside table and stare at it. It's a stunning picture frame. So unusual. I wonder what 'Fae' means. Isn't that an old word for fairies? Perhaps it's the name of the shop it comes from. Yes, it'll be a shop selling all stuff to do with fairies and things.

The woman in the photo looks *so* like the Angel Lady. Is Tate the Angel Lady? *Is this a photograph of my mother?* I shake my head as though to rid my head of the thought. I'll change the photo for a nice picture of Dad. I will. Tomorrow. Soon, anyway.

I fold my pyjama trousers and place them carefully on the bed, fold the pyjama top and place that over the trousers, lining it up exactly with the edge of the bed. Then I stare at the pyjamas as though seeing them for the first time. *What am I doing?* I'm going to bed, why have I just taken my pyjamas off? I roll my eyes at myself. But it's warm in my bedroom and it feels nice to be naked.

I wander around my bedroom, pick up a book off my bedside

table and put it back down again, straighten the edge of the book so that it lines up with the edge of the cabinet. It's not that I'm obsessional about things being straight or anything. Obviously. It's just, well it looks better that way. The pin board over my bed is covered with photos and mementoes – tickets and receipts and bits of paper to remind me about good stuff. But I like the photos to be straight on the board, not crooked or anything. It would be nice if the colours all matched, or maybe if I arrange them so that the colours go from one side to the other. Like my jewellery. I like to organize my necklaces in order of length, and sometimes I colour-coordinate them. And my clothes. I start with blue on the left and go through the colour wheel – green, yellow, red, and ending with purple on the right. Just so that I know where to find things. And they look so pretty like that.

I perch on my bed and lay my hand lightly on my picture frame, cast my eyes around the room. The walls are a lovely pale sage green, which I chose myself, and the furniture is painted white eggshell. Dad got some old wooden bedroom furniture at the Salvation Army shop but none of the wood matched, so we painted it all. I must have only been ten or eleven at the time. I smile to myself when I think back, the image of my dad with splodges of paint all over his clothes, his face, his glasses, even his hair.

But the furniture still looks amazing. And Maggie bought some green velvet fabric for curtains (which I made myself) and I made cushions to go with it. I love my room. The dark blue carpet doesn't really match the colours but we found a big fluffy white rug to put by the bed and Mags bought me a fabulous huge white fluffy cushion last Christmas. It's nothing like Sasha's made-to-measure designer bedroom with matching furniture that gets changed every couple of years, but I like it.

I walk over to the wardrobe and open one of the doors. There's a full-length mirror stuck to the inside of the door with yellow flowers all around the outside from when I was going through my stencilling phase.

I study my reflection. Skinny. I hate my body, I would prefer more curves. I touch my breast. Too small. Tiny hips, tiny bum. It's not so much that I don't go in at the waist; it's more that I don't come back out because my hips are so thin. Sometimes I think I still have the body of a child. I push a hand either side of my waist and press my hands inwards, forcing an hourglass figure.

I sigh, turn so that my back is facing the mirror and pull my hair over my shoulder so that I can see my wing-shaped birthmark. Slightly darker than my skin colour, quite large now. The mark seems to increase in size as I grow older. I open out another wardrobe door and angle the second mirror so that I can see my back in the front mirror without straining my neck. The birthmark is mid-brown, like a henna tattoo. It seems to rise from the middle of my spine, upwards and outwards towards my shoulder blades, and then round and downwards. It looks like a pair of tightly folded wings. Just beneath the skin. I stretch my arm round my back and touch the skin. Doesn't feel any different, not like a scar or a burn or anything. As I prod the area my skin prickles, as though there are sensitive nerve endings beneath the skin. *Well, of course there are, it's the spine.*

As my fingers prod through the skin, my flesh tingles, like a deep itch. *It's nice.* No, not an itch. More a need, a craving to scratch. I kneel down on the floor and push my back against the chest of drawers. Yes that's the spot, just between my shoulder blades, and a little lower. The middle of my back. I push harder, the more I do it, the more I feel it. The more I like it. Crave it. I want to get my hands round on my back and really press, massage the skin, dig my fingers deep into my muscles. I flop back onto the floor and push my back against the carpet, pressing hard, pushing against the wardrobe with my feet. I groan to myself and then giggle. I once saw a cow scratching itself on a fence like this.

The whole of my body is starting to tingle and I get back up onto my knees again. My skin feels as though it's catching fire, my senses seem heightened, I can feel the cool air move against my body, can smell the scent of my skin, can hear the faint beat of my heart. Bu-bum, bu-bum. I move slowly, twisting and turning, feel every movement of my muscles, my sinews, every cell in my body feels alive. I hold my breath and run my hand across my belly, I crave something but I don't know what.

I glance at the mirror, what a sight, my hair is a mess from rubbing on the floor, my eyes dark and wild, I'm bright red in the face. But my skin feels hot and silky smooth.

I lie back heavily on the soft bedroom rug and cry out softly as my spine sends little bolts of crackling energy upwards through my back and shoulders and downwards into my pelvis, burning out as it reaches my arms, legs, feet. The fizzling, the heightened feeling radiates outwards in ripples and surges, slowing and decreasing in intensity as it travels, like molten liquid pulsing through my veins.

And yet despite the turbulence from my spine I feel a strange calm. I run my hands across my skin, following the rippling movement as it radiates out from the small of my back, up into my shoulders and flooding out into my arms.

And then I notice. *Oh my God.*

I hold my arms in the air and stare at them, my heart pounds in my chest. Bu-bum, bu-bum. Goosebumps rise on my flesh as I watch my muscles rippling, rising and falling like very shallow bubbles bursting just beneath the surface. I shudder and clasp my forearm with my hand, stilling the movement. As I release my arm the rippling slowly begins again, subtle and yet quite visible now I'm aware of it. My arm muscles are working by themselves. Developing and strengthening. My body is changing.

My flesh tingles, like I'm catching fire and yet the touch of my hand intensifies the sensation. I run my hands over my skin trying to satisfy this craving, this burning need. My back, my belly, I seem to come alive as I explore. I close my eyes and groan, my heart pounding in my throat, trying to focus on the feeling. It's as though I'm losing control. I *want* to lose control.

A slight panic rises in my throat. I try to resist, keep in control, but as my hand skims my breast I feel my skin tighten, I cup my breast in my fingers and feel the softness, wonder how it would feel for a boy, a real boy to touch me. *Luke.* I draw in my breath sharply as another ripple of pleasure shoots down my spine. Something changes deep inside and I begin to lose myself in the moment.

I close my eyes again and bring my finger up to my lips and feel an imaginary kiss, as the kiss leaves my lips it travels down my spine and into the depths of my belly somewhere. *Luke.* I don't know what I'm doing, or whether I'm doing it right, but I don't want it to stop. I feel a fluttering in my back, strong, deep, red hot as I press my back hard against the floor. I want something, I don't know what.

I screw my eyes tightly and gasp, muffle a cry, my back muscles go rigid and my spine arches off the floor. I hold my breath; I want to hold on to this feeling as long as I can. *Don't lose control.* And yet the intensity is unbearable, pleasure and yet searing pain. Inside my abdomen I feel my muscles tighten but almost as quickly an intense crippling pain grips my shoulder-blades as though somebody has grabbed my shoulders and is tearing them away from my body, my muscles ripping away from my back. Hot searing agony and yet deep intense ecstasy at the same time, I don't know whether to laugh or cry. And then it's all over.

My whole body shudders to a halt and I gasp in relief. All the strength has melted out of me and I feel limp and helpless. I can feel the muscles in my arms, legs, back, abdomen, deep down, still gently contracting rhythmically as though they're winding down from some immense feat of strength, weakening, relaxing and then fluttering, the nerves in my back pulsating in time with it. I'm breathing quickly, almost panting.

And I start to laugh. *What on earth?* I'm lying on my back, my arms wrapped around myself in an embrace, red and swollen and exhausted.

After a moment I struggle to my feet, shaky and weak. It feels wrong, like I've indulged in some guilty pleasure. I look in the mirror again. I somehow look, well, different. More toned. Curvy. Not by Sasha's standards, but there is a definite curve. I know it's crazy, but my breasts actually look bigger. I cup my breasts in my hands and push them up, like Sasha does with her push-up bras. I'm almost a woman. What on earth have I just done to myself? Must be the mirror, or the lighting. It's got to be.

I turn to study my back in the mirror again, stare at the two wing-shaped birthmarks. And the strangest thing. *Oh my God.* They've changed colour. Too weird. I shut my eyes; it's been a long and emotional day. I open my eyes slowly and turn so I can see my back clearly in the double mirror. The wing marks, the ones that had always been a little darker than my skin tone. They're pure white. And slightly, slightly *fluorescent*. I shudder and recoil from the mirror.

But what if…what if I really am special, what if I actually do have some strange power? What if Tate, what if she really did have wings too. Maggie said she thought Tate was a fairy. Of course there's no such thing as fairies. *Obviously.* But what if, what if I am actually growing wings? Perhaps Sasha was right; I really am some kind of freak. I laugh out loud to myself. Must be the lighting in the bedroom or something, playing tricks.

I march over to the wall and flick off the light switch, the room fills with darkness. There, that's sorted that, no more imagining things.

I feel my way across the room towards my bedside lamp, but something catches my eye in the mirror, a kind of light. Something glowing. I look closer and recoil backwards from the mirror, startled. The wing marks on my back…they are…they're very faintly...*glowing*, and...and shimmering, like something is under my skin. Something alive. I quickly pull my arm round and prod my back. My fingers chase my muscles around beneath the skin, as though they're not attached. It feels like something's there. Just beneath the surface, *like tightly folded wings.* And looking into the mirror, it's like it's, well, *fluttering.* Just beneath the skin.

Oh My God. No, no, no, no, NO! That's just too weird. I pull my pyjamas back on quickly and jump into bed, lie down quickly. This is just my imagination. So much has happened today, I'm letting my mind play games with me. I close my eyes tightly. My heart's pounding in my chest.

I won't think about it.

Chapter Ten

I don't know how long I've been asleep when I awake suddenly with a sharp stabbing pain in my forehead, like an ice-cream headache gone wrong. I close my eyes tight and moan gently, holding my head in my hands. It has to pass in a minute.

Bright white light flashes before my eyes like strobe lights, intermingled with swirls of colour going fuzzy around the edges. I open my eyes; the room is spinning, like a kaleidoscope of colours going round and round. *Here we go – a migraine.*

But it feels different to usual, I feel quite giddy, try to focus through the darkness, seeking something in my bedroom, any object, an anchor to stop the world from spinning out of control. I sit up in bed and peer into the room as it sways before me. The pain in my head is diminishing but my vision is blurry. Coloured lights are blinking at the edge of my eyesight. I can smell something metallic and damp. I can just about make out some objects, but it doesn't feel like my room. I chase around in the darkness to find something familiar. *Bloody migraine.*

Lights are still flashing in my eyes but yes, I can make things out. My eyes are starting to adjust. Beginning to focus. There's something in the corner, but it's not my familiar wardrobe and chest of drawers. It's a desk. Or something. I peer through the darkness and the swirls of light. Oh my God my eyes hurt.

It's a person. Somebody's in my room, I jolt in shock, my bare feet landing on the bare floor. I'm rooted to the spot, try to open my eyes wide but it hurts too much, I groan again, but I can see the room now. It's not my room. It's somewhere else. I feel cold, shiver. I hug my arms around me, I want to shout out to the person but I'm afraid, my voice doesn't work. Where am I? I can hardly breathe. The swirls of colour are beginning to fade, moving to the edge of my vision. *Where am I?* It's dark and dirty, like I'm inside a shed or barn. I feel gritty rough wooden boards beneath my bare feet. I smell dirt. Oil. Animals, like in a cowshed or a stable. My vision is clearing.

I'm standing inside a barn. It's empty, except for a person in the corner. A man, he's sitting at a desk, and his head is resting on his arms. Is he asleep? Is he ill? *Is he dead?* The bright white lights suddenly flash like sheet lightning grabbing my thoughts and senses in a vice grip. I drop my head into my hands, groan and close my eyes tightly as another bolt of pain shoots through my head like a nail being driven into my skull. I try make out what's happening. A pure white light illuminates the room, for just a split second, I can see brown curls on the top of the man's head, he looks up from the desk. *Dad?* It looks like Dad. The white flashes are making it difficult to see. The image is fading, no, Dad where are you? There's somebody else, in the corner. But the image is fading, he's disappearing. I hear his voice. I can't make out what he's saying. *Dad?*

But it's pitch darkness again. My toes feel my fluffy bedroom rug beneath my feet. It's warm and I smell hand cream, fresh bed linen, scented candles. I can't make out if I'm awake or still dreaming. I reach out my hand towards my bedside lamp and switch it on. Brightness floods my bedroom. I'm alone.

My eyes spin around the room, examining everything carefully as though I somehow expect to see a bale of hay and a cow grazing in the corner. My heart is thumping in my chest and I can't get my breath. I start to shiver. The air's warm but I feel exposed. I walk to the window and pull the curtain back to peer outside. The moon is almost full and the garden looks magical in this light. I shiver again and reach up to close the window, lock it. I close the curtains carefully and glance around the room again. Just checking.

I get back into bed, snuggle the bedclothes close to my face, wrapping myself tightly in the duvet. What the hell was that. A migraine? A dream? It was Dad, I only got a look at him for a fraction of a second, but I know it was him. It didn't feel like a dream. What's happening to me? *Where are you, Dad?* Is this somehow a sort of message sent from Dad? *Don't be ridiculous.*

I eventually slip into a restless sleep.

Chapter Eleven

I'm up and dressed early the next morning, I pull my padded gilet around me and zip it up, step out into the early morning air. The ground mist brings with it a chilly nip as it rolls across the fields and hovers inches above the grass. The sun, sitting very low in the sky, is just starting to smoulder through the damp fuzzy morning haze. By midday the sun will be bursting through the sky, warming the air, burning away the mist and drying off the damp grass. It's going to be a beautiful June day.

I set off down the footpath, away from our cottage. I'm wearing my favourite linen cropped pants and a plain white t-shirt. The pants are bright apricot and the colour matches my mood. As I open the front gate I glance back towards the cottage. Maggie is standing at her bedroom window waving and I raise my hand in a quick finger wave. She's beaming; I can't remember the last time I saw her looking so happy. She's looking forward to her week away with her friends. But I think she's also relieved that she's finally told me about my mysterious mother, and how I was abandoned in the woods.

My spirits are high, and I have to resist the temptation to skip down the lane like a child. I've got over my 'episode' last night when I imagined I was growing wings, and the dream about Dad. This morning I checked in the mirror and although my birthmark looks a little paler, there's no sign of any wings. For goodness sake, wings!

School's over, it's going to be a lovely day, and not a Sasha or a Jasper in sight. Or a bloody wing.

My muscles feel achy and stiff today, as though I've spent three days dancing non-stop or something. But moving around is helping; the more I flex my arms and legs, the more my muscles are easing. Must be all that squirming around last night on the bedroom floor. I cringe as I recall my embarrassing secret and glance back at Maggie. I feel like everybody who looks at me today will know.

Maggie moves away from the window and I close the gate. Our cottage is the last one in the lane, nestling within a gathering of trees, the neck section of Gossamer Woods; they stretch for about two miles and cut the village in two. As I turn towards the woods, I heave my backpack onto my shoulder and it bounces on my back as I stride along in the chilly morning air. The gravel footpath quickly narrows, and then diminishes, becoming a ribbon of dry dusty dirt weaving its way between the trees, this way and that.

As I enter the woods I listen to the sound of a single wood pigeon singing his monotone mantra with a chorus of different tunes from the other birds that inhabit the woodlands. I hitch my backpack higher onto my shoulder and head deeper into the woods, my pace slowing as I pick my way between the centuries-old trees. On a day like this I could forget about all my worries, and I intend to do just that.

As I'm enveloped by the trees I'm hit by an explosion of scents and sounds, the atmosphere is cool and aromatic. The woods seem alive with music, an orchestra of birds tweeting and twittering, harmonising with the soothing rustle of leaves as the light breeze whips through the trees. I spent most of my childhood playing in these woods and know the position, size and nature of nearly every tree. I've climbed most of them and fallen out of many. I could probably find my way through the woods blindfolded. I inhale the familiar smell of dry wood and gentle herbal fragrance, an aromatic fusion of the foliage inhabiting the woods alongside the mature deciduous trees. Deeper into the wooded area the landscape becomes more dense, a dark forest where few people venture as the sunlight rarely breaks through to light up the pathway.

I know exactly where I want to go, and make my way towards the large oak tree. Although the pathway leading between the trees is dry and dusty, the tufts of grass lining the pathway are damp with dew, my fabric pumps are soon sodden and my feet feel the biting cold. I walk through the muddle of trees and out into the clearing where the hazy sun is already pouring down onto the lush green grass, starting to evaporate the ground mist that has gathered in the clearing. As I emerge into the sunshine I look up at the sky and smile at the fresh breeze as it licks my face with an almost minty freshness. I always feel happy when I come here. I turn slowly to face the oldest tree in the woods, the large old oak tree, and take a deep, respectful breath.

Some of the trees in this woodland are over 400 years old, but it's rumoured that this great old oak tree has stood for over a thousand years. The trunk is easily seven feet in diameter, and when you stand under it and look upwards towards the sky, you can't even see to the top. The tree's span is as wide as it is tall and it stands alone, like a huge mushroom with a green frilly cap. All the other trees in the wood leave a respectful distance around the great oak so it stands in its own patch of sunlight.

When I was little, Dad used to say that this tree was special, it had magical qualities. He used to tell me of legends about fairy folk, dragons and elves living in the tree and although I don't remember actually believing the tales, I can see now where he got the stories. If Maggie was right and Tate really was a fairy. *Not that I believe that for one minute.*

I've always been in awe of the old oak tree, I still am, impressed by its grandeur, fascinated by its symmetry. I like to think that for every single leaf there's an identical one on an opposite branch. It's like the great-grandfather of the woods and as I stand looking up at the great master tree in wonder I speculate what amazing stories it could tell, if only it could speak.

I think about what Maggie said about theatrical lighting effects coming from the sky, lighting the base of the trunk. No matter what time of day, the rays of light burst through the tree's boughs, splitting into colours like a prism, the colours dancing upon the roots at the base of the tree giving it a magical quality. Like the end of a rainbow. Or the beginning.

I can almost believe that the whole world begins at the base of this tree and the sun, moon and stars revolve around this deciduous masterpiece. In fact many hundreds of years ago, people could very easily have mistaken this great tree for some kind of god, something awesome to worship. Perhaps Heaven itself is sitting on the highest bough, perhaps if I just climbed up and up and up...

I drop my backpack onto the damp ground and sink down into the mossy earth beneath the tree, leaning against its great trunk, and look upwards. If I were to climb up to the top, I could see everything. I might even see my dad. I wonder for a moment if Dad came back here on the day he disappeared. I'd really like to believe that. Maybe he's with Tate now.

I kick off my shoes and wiggle my cold damp toes. Even though the bark on the trunk is hard and rough, much of it is coated in a thick cushion of soft velvety moss. I nestle in a hollow between the roots, like a padded cradle. This is where I was found as a newborn baby.

Although the ground is damp and I know my pants will be wet before long, the sun's rays are warming me from the outside in. I lay my head back against the trunk of the tree and close my eyes. I feel at home here, did I begin my journey from this very spot? I wonder who Tate really is? Why couldn't Dad find her? Maybe Dad found her, and wherever he is now, he's with her. I hope so.

Just for a moment I allow myself to speculate what might have happened to me if Dad hadn't come along, hadn't found me. Did the person who left me, whether Tate or somebody else, know what happened to me? What's she like, this Tate, my supposed mother? Why did she leave me? Is she still alive? Did she hang around to make sure somebody found me? I open my eyes, sigh.

What sort of person would abandon me, a newborn baby, in the woods and leave me to die? I close my eyes again and delete that thought from my mind. I prefer to think that whoever left me, did it for the right reasons. I drift off to sleep.

I awake with a start and flick at my ear with the back of my hand; something nipped my ear, an insect or something. *Damn midgey.* I've lost track of time and am not wearing a watch so I can't be sure how long I've slept. I look around; the sun has moved in the sky and is now beating down directly overhead. I reach out my hand, the ground is bone dry. I'm not sure if my trousers are still damp but I'm feeling stiff, I stretch my arms out in front of me.

I stare at my arms. I might be imagining it, but they seem more toned. More muscley. Not in a gross body-builder sort of way. But I have such skinny arms and legs and somehow they look more shapely. I look down at my legs, and run my hands down my thighs, am I imagining it or do they feel more meaty? Just a teeny bit, not so anybody else would be able to tell. Except me. Blimey, that exercise last night, if I could call it exercise, has really done some good. I smile guiltily.

I hear a rustling nearby and see a squirrel scurrying in the grass, hunting for food and probably daring itself to come and investigate my bag. 'There's nothing here for you,' I whisper, but as I feel my stomach gurgle with hunger I remember there are some sandwiches in my bag. I take out my lunch, break off a piece and throw it towards the squirrel, wondering if they like cheese sandwiches. This one does.

After I've eaten the rest of my sandwich I relax back against the tree again, listening to the birds and watching the squirrel busying himself with his food hunting. I feel relaxed and lazy. As my eyes glaze over my thoughts go to my dad once again. Nothing has been the same since he went missing. I still wake in the middle of the night, trying to puzzle it out. He's such a gentle man. Kind. Funny. Strong. He's a worrier. I used to go mad trying to find out what was worrying him, but he would never tell me. He would make a joke and pull his face as though I was still six years old. But I loved him when he did that. *Dad.* I feel a prickling behind my nose when I think of the daft faces he used to pull, his silver-rimmed glasses sliding down his nose and his fringe sticking up at the front because he's been running his fingers through his hair trying to work out some formula or other. His eyes would twinkle and he'd tell me that everything was fine.

He'd never have just walked out, walked away from his life, left me. That was what the police had implied. With all those questions about whether he had done this before, whether he might have had another life. It was crazy, why won't they listen? He'd never have done anything like this. *And yet he did.* But where is he? *Where are you, Dad?* People don't just disappear. Do they? Last night's strange dream about him in a barn has spooked me a little.

Suddenly I'm startled by something flashing past my line of vision, like a spiral of dust, whipping past my eyes so fast I can't see what it is. I spring to my feet and blink, my heart pounding, looking all around but there's nothing there. Everything is peaceful and the squirrel is frozen to the spot staring at me, alarmed by my sudden movement.

I tut to myself and flop back down.

Now I really can feel the dampness on the underside of my linen pants and I fidget awkwardly on the mossy cushion. The ground is dry but my pants are still wet where the air wasn't able to circulate. I move my shoulder to see if it still hurts from my fall yesterday. It doesn't. I gently prod the area under my eye, and wonder how my cut has healed so quickly. There was no sign of a bruise, or even a mark, when I looked in the mirror this morning. In fact I feel more pain from my stiff muscles after my antics last night, than I do from my injuries. Maybe I should dig out the old lady's hanky for my stiffness; it seems to be the cure-all.

'Do you believe in magic?' I say out loud to the squirrel. 'I think that old lady Pandora is a witch. I think that hanky she gave me was magic.' The squirrel ignores me and nibbles at some crumbs he missed earlier. 'You know what, squirrel, you're better company than *any* of the kids at school.'

All the events of the last 48 hours flit through my mind. The attack from Jasper and fighting him off like that, the strange strength I seemed to get. Then the run-in with Sasha, and falling onto the pavement hurting my face and shoulder. Then meeting Pandora on the bus. And Pandora's hanky. She was in the woods that day. And she turns out to be Luke's gran. Weird that. Luke's face bursts into my mind, complete with floppy blond fringe. Perhaps I should ring him, where did I put that bit of paper he gave me with his number on? The way things are at the moment, I need all the friends I can get.

I smile to myself. *Luke.* He reminds me of my dad in some ways. Eccentric. I always think of Dad as a sort of mad scientist, Luke is sort of genius too but in a more arty way. He never wears standard school uniform, there's usually something missing or he has cut-off pants or a heavy knit waistcoat, or his tie hangs around his neck like a bandana. And his clothes hang off him, like getting dressed was an afterthought. And yet…and yet he looks good. *Amazing.* But chaotic. Dad's kind of chaotic too but there's a kind of method in his madness. But Luke's not like that, he's just messy. I'm not sure I have room in my life for Luke's kind of chaos, not whilst things are, well, like they are.

I jump as another insect nips at me, this time on the end of my nose. I waft my hand to try to brush it away, but it's on my ear now. It didn't feel like a bite, more like somebody flicking my ear.

I shrug and lie back down. I feel very relaxed and calm after my sleep, I gaze into the distance and enjoy the warmth of the sun on my skin, and the feel of the soft earth between my fingers. My eyes relax and gradually go out of focus, staring into the distance, at nothing. I see something move. But there is nothing there, my imagination playing games with me again.

Then I definitely see something.

If I let my eyes relax, blur, I see something in the corner of my eye, it flits past but when I look it disappears. I focus on the distance again, and there it is, on the outer edge of my vision, like a sort of dragon-fly. But it isn't a dragon-fly, I know that. It isn't a dragonfly, but it has wings.

Oh my God. It's…it's a person. A person with wings.

Noooooooooo!

Chapter Twelve

I sit bolt upright. This is just my imagination. Or a dream. There's nothing here in the woods with me. I'm not stupid. The thing I think I saw, the thing with wings. It didn't look threatening, it didn't frighten me. *It was a fairy.* The flicking on my ear starts again. *Keep calm.*

'Stop it!' I shout angrily and brush my hand across my ear. The flicking stops, but I think I hear a muffled giggle.

Ok I've finally lost it. Not only am I imagining that I'm growing wings, now I'm imagining fairy folk too. And talking to myself. Time to go home. I start to pack my things back into my bag, my eyes dancing around anxiously.

But everything looks different. The sunlight in the woods seems too bright, the colours too vibrant. The sky is too blue. As the sunlight filters through the trees, it splits into a thousand colours, so vivid I have to shield my eyes. And the dazzling blue sky is alive with movement, butterflies – with huge exquisite wings so fragile, like a swarm swaying in the breeze, a huge colourful Mexican wave. Why have I never noticed this before?

And then the hairs on my arm stand on end. The flowers – they look just like Gossamer Orchids, I've seen them in photographs. But they're all over the place, waving in the breeze, large as life. Maggie said they're extinct. She said these woods used to be famous for Gossamer Orchids; this was the last place in the UK where they still survived. But Maggie said they were there, that night, when she met Tate again. The night I was conceived.

A shiver runs through me and I remember Pandora's hanky. I drag it out of my pocket, study the little embroidered flower in the corner. It's a Gossamer Orchid. And Pandora was there in the woods the day I was found. What does she know about this strange place? And the Orchids? But they're here, hundreds of them, thousands. Bright yellow Orchids with lime green leaves. They must be attracting the butterflies. I'm mesmerised. The colours. The sound of fluttering wings wafts by my ears, like a wave of colour all moving together, in and out of the yellow flowers. I stare in disbelief and my throat bunches up painfully. I've never seen anything like this.

Something else moves, something bigger. *I'm not alone.* It looks like... *Ignore it, I'm imagining things.* I'm spooking myself now. I refuse to look at it. I pick up the wrapper from my sandwiches and empty the crumbs out onto the grass for the squirrel to snack on later. A couple of baby rabbits hop over to me and I gasp. *So sweet.* They come right up to my hand. The baby rabbit tilts his head to one side, and then turns his back on me, searching in the grass for food. *I'm not alone.*

It's a girl.

She's sitting on a low branch of the tree. I blink. Still there. She seems almost dream-like. Quite perfect. I blink again. Still there. She doesn't seem real, almost like a photograph, but she's moving, she's swinging her legs. Perhaps she's a kind of hologram. She's watching me. She holds out her hand to the butterflies and they swarm towards her as though she's vacuuming them in. I catch my breath.

Ignore it. Ignore her, you're imagining this, she's not real, ignore her. I have to shield my eyes to see, the light so clear, pure. Like a person who has bad eyesight suddenly putting on their glasses...or like you have been looking through a murky window and then you clean it...or the colours of the TV are all wrong and suddenly you brighten them up, and—

'Hello.'

My head shoots up and I stare at the girl.

'Hello,' she repeats. I'm so astonished I don't know what to do.

'I think you'll find,' says the girl, 'that the polite thing is to say hello back.'

I swallow hard.

'Hello,' I squeak, my throat so dry I can hardly make a sound.

'There,' she says, 'that wasn't so bad was it?'

I look around, nervously. She must be about my age, perhaps a little younger. She has black hair, cropped close to her head and cut around her ears. Like a boy. Her ears are an unusual shape, long and thin, and a bit pointy at the top, a little button nose, and strikingly beautiful amber-coloured eyes with long dark lashes and pale pink lips. Exquisite. Her cropped black hair frames her face, illuminating her smooth white porcelain-like complexion.

She's wearing a thin floaty top. *It's see-through.* The sheer fabric is greeny-ochre with strands of silver all the way through. I stare, I can see right through the fabric. *She's virtually naked underneath.* She's quite lovely. Beneath the tunic top she has very short creamy-coloured semi-translucent leggings, they start well below her navel and end half way down her thighs. Her legs are long and slim. And silky. She has nothing on her feet, and her toenails are painted pale green with a little silver crystal embellishing each one.

The girl coughs. 'It's rude to stare.'

'Sorry.' I look away quickly. And then look back again, I can't help myself.

The girl hops off the tree bough; she seems so light you'd think she was no weight at all. She dances over to me and holds out a long slim hand.

'I'm Ainsel,' she says, 'very pleased to meet you.'

'I'm Scarlett, er, pleased to meet you too.'

Ainsel laughs, a silvery laugh. I'm enchanted. I can't take my eyes off her.

'That's the formalities over then,' she says and dances around in a circle like an excitable puppy. She finally sits on the ground, crossing her legs in front of her and I decide to do the same. It reminds me of when I was back in junior school and I laugh but I'm not sure why.

'Do you live near here?' I say.

The girl laughs too, and I feel myself blush, wondering if she's laughing at me or with me.

'I live *here*.'

'Here?' I glance around me, half-expecting a house to suddenly manifest itself between two trees.

'Here,' she says and sticks her lower lip out like an impudent child.

'I don't think so!' I say and laugh rudely. I'm confused. Nobody lives in the woods. But a voice is nagging at me. Maggie said that Tate lived in these woods.

There is a sound from behind the girl, a rustling, and the girl twists away from me to look behind her, and I gasp in horror. I'm staring at her back, it's like her back is unfolding, and I can't believe what I'm seeing. The girl has, well...she has... Okay, she has wings. *Wings.* The most beautiful wings. Not that I have anything to compare them with, or course. They're semi-transparent like dragonfly wings, and they're almost as long as her body. As they shimmer, silvery, green, yellow, pink...as they catch the sunlight the colours appear to change colour, giving off a kind of silvery dusty haze. *Fairy dust.* Her body gracefully lifts into the air and onto a low bough of the oak tree. I look away, flustered. *It's just a dream, enjoy it.*

Again the nagging voice in my head is trying to remind me. Maggie said that Tate had wings. Is this the place Tate lives? Is she here now?

I hear another noise and jump to my feet, I spin around but I can't see anybody else. Ainsel's sitting just a couple of feet away at eye-level and she locks eyes with me, she's pouting like a child. She breaks off a twig, never breaking eye contact, and fiddles with it between her long dainty fingers, peeling back the bark and splitting it. I'm fascinated. She suddenly leans forward so that her nose is nearly touching mine.

'Are you real?' she asks, almost petulantly.

'What?' I splutter.

'Well how did you get here?' she says, frowning. She reaches out a dainty slim finger and pokes at my arm rudely.

I'm astonished, am I dreaming about the girl, or is the girl dreaming about me? This is too complicated. But I can't take my eyes off her wings. They have stilled now and are folding inwards, tucking in behind her. Like one of those expensive convertible cars when the roof folds down and disappears inside a compartment within the body of the car.

'I love your wings,' I finally gasp, 'they're awesome!'

'Thanks! I'm rather proud of them.' Ainsel's face breaks into a beam and she leaps up, her wings bursting, shimmering so fast that all I can see is sparkly dust. She gracefully lifts herself onto a higher branch of the tree. *Show off.*

'Are you…' I pause, once I say this I can't take it back. 'Are you a…a…*fairy?*'

The girl Ainsel explodes with laughter. It sounds like a thousand tiny bells all tinkling in harmony, and as she laughs the butterflies hover over her, seeming to dance in tune with her laughter.

'A fairy, of course not!' Ainsel splutters. 'Fairies don't exist!!'

I feel stupid. *Of course bloody fairies don't exist. I'm going to kill Maggie.*

'Sorry,' I say, and stare at my hands.

Ainsel pushes off the bough with her feet and floats gracefully to the ground, landing so softly she must be as light as a feather. I look away. I feel so stupid. *Why did I say that?* She reaches out and takes hold of my hand, her other hand gently turns my face to look at her. Her fingers feel like soft suede against my cheek. She looks into my eyes and I feel I'm entering her soul, her large honey-coloured eyes are so deep and soft I feel I'm going to melt. She strokes my palm. Her hand feels silky like a rose petal and her touch makes my skin tingle. She smells of spring flowers and sparkling mineral water. She leans towards me, her face only inches from mine.

'Fairies are made-up by people who don't understand what we are.'

She says it very seriously and I'm not sure what to say. I don't know if she's offended or making fun of me.

'What *are* you then?' I say hesitantly.

'I'm a Fae!'

My eyes widen, and I feel a rush of blood to my face. That word again. Fae. I shiver.

'A what?' I say nervously.

'I'm a Fae. F-A-E. This is the Fae world, we are the Fae people.'

'Is Fae the same as fairy?'

The Fae girl shrugs and sighs. 'Well you can call us fairies if you want, but the word fairy originally came from Fae anyway – Fae-rie. Don't you know anything? You're a Fae too!'

'Oh, no!' I say quickly. 'I'm not a Fae, I'm just normal.'

Ainsel laughs. 'Well that sounds very unlikely to me!'

She studies me carefully. 'No, you *are* a Fae.' She nods to herself as if to confirm the fact. 'You're a Hybrid.'

I frown at her. 'I'm *not* a Hybrid,' I spit before I can think about it. 'What's a Hybrid anyway? Isn't it some sort of greenfly or something. An insect?'

'No, that's an aphid.' This time she really is laughing at me. I scowl. 'You're a Hybrid. You are half Fae, half everyday people.'

'Everyday people?'

'You know, I suppose you'd call yourself human.'

'Well aren't *you* human?'

'Duh, what have I just said. I'm Fae!'

Just then something else flits across my vision, too fast for me to catch what it is.

'Eldridge!' Ainsel calls out. 'I told you to keep out of sight.'

The Fae girl turns to me. 'Eldridge is my brother, take no notice of him. He can be a pain.'

Ainsel sighs and leans towards me again, whispering, 'Don't ever let a Fae boy hear you call *him* a fairy!'

I giggle. A boy fairy? Now I *know* I'm dreaming.

A face peeps from behind the trunk of the tree. I can't make out the face properly because the sun's in my eyes, but I can tell it's a boy.

'Do Fae boys have wings too?' I say. Ainsel rolls her eyes.

'Yes, of course. Boys' wings are smaller than ours, and stronger. Have you gone through Transition yet?' She leans over to peer at my back and beckons me to come closer.

I gasp. What's *Transition*? My mind flits back to Dad's letter. And why does she think I'm a Fae Hybrid? I lean towards her eagerly but a low branch of the tree is in the way and a twig snags in my eye.

'Ow!' I cry, and shut my eyes tight as they water up, holding my fist to my eye until it stops stinging, and then blink quickly. Ow, ow. I close my eyes again, and blink quickly. That's better. I peer through the watery mist covering my eyes but can't focus properly. I close them again and rub them with my finger. When I open my eyes, my sight has cleared but I'm alone.

Ainsel's disappeared, and so has the boy. I blink again, and then again, but they've both gone. The whole world seems to be suddenly very dull, as though the sun has gone behind a cloud and a grey blanket of fog has come down over the forest. There are no swarms of colourful butterflies, only swarms of midgeys. And the gorgeous yellow Orchids have disappeared. I shake my head in bewilderment. Where did it all go? And the lovely half-naked girl, Ainsel? With the amazing wings? Maybe they're still here, but I can't see them for some reason. Perhaps it's something to do with this fog. I wonder if they can see me. Or hear me.

'Bye,' I say to nobody. I wonder if I'm going mad. Everything logical tells me that this is not happening. And yet it feels so real.

I sling my bag onto my shoulder and start to make my way home, trying to work out if it was another crazy dream, like last night seeing Dad. Am I going mad? But if this is madness then it's better than reality. Sitting there by the oak tree, talking to that fairy thing, is the first time I've felt free, really free, since Dad disappeared. Today, for the first time in weeks, months, perhaps longer, I haven't felt the need to control my environment.

My step is light and my head is clear. This is the happiest I've been for a long time, it was a very strange dream, or fantasy, or whatever it was. But one thing I'm sure about, dream or no dream, this is the place where my dad and Maggie used to play with Tate. And Maggie's right, Tate really was a fairy. Tate must have been a Fae, like Ainsel. Maybe I'll come back again and see if I can meet with those Fae people again. Maybe Tate is here too. Maybe Dad came back here; perhaps he's in the Fae world right now, stuck and somehow unable to come home. And I'll be able to find him, and bring him home. Maybe Tate is here, and I'll find her too, and…

Ok, I know. One thing at a time. But I'll come back again soon, that's for sure.

Chapter Thirteen

I switch on the computer and pick up my can of Coke. There's no point sitting waiting for it to boot, it always seems to take forever, longer if I sit and watch it.

I walk over to the kettle, glance at the wall clock. Maggie will be home soon, I'll boil some water ready for her coffee. She'll be busy tonight packing for her trip; they leave early in the morning and typical Maggie she hasn't even started to pack yet.

It took me weeks to convince her to go ahead with her trip – her very oldest and best friend is getting married next month, and they arranged this 'hen' trip months ago, a week in Barcelona with six other 'girls', most of them were at school together and have kept in touch ever since. She was going to cancel but I convinced her to go ahead. I'm actually looking forward to the time alone, and I know that she's really excited about it now she's made the decision to go. She's given up so much of her old life since she moved in with me and I love to see her happy like this.

I've decided not to tell Maggie about my encounter in the woods today. With the fairy person. Not until I've looked into it a bit more. I'm not even sure why. I know Maggie was convinced Tate was a fairy of some kind so it wouldn't come as too much of a shock. I smile at the absurdity of what I'm thinking; perhaps there really is a streak of madness running through our family. If I'm honest, the main reason I don't want to share this with Maggie is that I'm not yet ready to say out loud 'I think I'm growing wings'. *Not sure I ever will be.*

I open the kitchen door and breathe the fresh summer air. I can smell the herby scent from the woods. A small bird flies overhead, up towards the trees, flitting its little wings furiously and then soaring, gliding, enjoying the freedom of the sky. I envy the little birds and the animals in the woods. They don't have exams or school bullies.

The computer occupies a small corner of the kitchen on a solid oak desk. The keyboard is perched precariously on top of a pile of Dad's books, magazines and a folder crammed full of his papers which neither Maggie nor I want to move. Somehow if the papers are still there, waiting for him, there is always a chance he might come home. The police have gone through all his stuff, searching for a clue as to where he went, but when they returned Dad's folder Maggie dropped it back onto the desk. I understand. We both work around Dad's folder, things get moved, the desk is cleaned, books come and go, coffee is spilt and toast crumbs are scattered. But Dad's folder stays exactly where he left it.

I pick up an old coffee mug from the desk, and walk over to the sink. I'm not sure how long that cup's been sitting on the desk, but something is floating on the top and not in a good way. I pour the remnants of it down the sink, wash and dry the mug ready for Maggie's fresh drink, and then return to the desk, deep in thought.

Our kitchen is small, but squeezed into it are several solid oak kitchen units, a small pine dining table and mismatching chairs, the oak desk in the corner, and a large range oven, which overpowers everything else in the room, but keeps the kitchen warm and toasty even on the coldest of days. It's my favourite room in the cottage.

As I perch on the edge of the chair with my can of Coke, I stare at the monitor, waiting for my desktop to appear, willing it to go faster. I click to make the computer dial-up to the internet. We can't afford broadband so we still use dial-up and it's so slow and frustrating that I often go down to the library to do my homework. But that's a bus ride into town, and I want the information quickly. Like now.

As soon as the internet browser appears I go into my search engine, and carefully type in the word f-a-i-r-y. I hit Enter and wait. After what seems like days, a page of websites are listed, and I scroll through them. An abundance of information comes back at me, all giving opinions as to what a fairy is. Human in appearance. Magical powers. Young. Winged. Small. Tiny. There is an assortment of variations on the name, feirie, fairie, faie, faery, faerie, faery, faierie. I stare at the screen. I go back to the search engine and type in 'Transition'. The computer seems to take forever before the screen clears and the results are displayed. It doesn't say anything about fairies, or magic, or wings. As far as I can tell it just means changing, converting, altering from one state to another.

Oh my God, am I going to change into a fairy?

I go back into one of the fairy sites and sigh. I'm just about to switch the computer off when I hear a sound behind me. I spin round, knocking over my can of Coke.

'It's only me!' Maggie sings out, banging down her shopping on the kitchen table loudly and then rushing to help me mop up the Coke before it seeps into the keyboard. I grab my dad's folder and dab at it with the sleeve of my jumper, but it's soaked and sticky. We carefully empty the documents out of the folder and lay them out on the kitchen table to dry. Luckily only the top corner of each sheet of paper is damp.

'You're jumpy!' Maggie says, laughing at me as I try to mop up the remaining Coke from the floor. I give her a sharp look.

'If you didn't creep around with your fairy footsteps I would have heard you.'

I clamp my mouth shut. *Bloody fairies on my mind.* I shoot a glance at Maggie but she's humming to herself and dabbing at the papers with a paper towel. I switch off my computer and go to flip on the kettle to make Maggie's coffee.

'Coffee, Mags?'

Maggie is still humming to herself happily.

'Maggie?'

'Yes, dear?' She turns and smiles, still in a little world of her own.

'Mags, I know how much you gave up for me, when you moved in here. You never get the chance to go out with your friends now, and I really hope you have a great time next week in Spain.'

Maggie gives me a huge silent bear hug, then says, 'I really didn't give anything up at all, I've always loved you like you were my own daughter.' Her voice cracks with emotion.

'I know that. But still, I just wanted you, you know, to know that I know.'

'I do know that you know you know,' she grins and I frown at her in mock-confusion.

'Oh, Mags!' I blurt, suddenly wanting to jump up and down in the spot like a three-year-old. 'The Gossamer Orchids, I saw them today, hundreds of them, they were beautiful!'

As soon as I have said it my mouth clamps shut and I bite my lip. I definitely saw the Orchids, but...when the Fae girl Ainsel had disappeared, and all the butterflies...they had disappeared. They must have been part of the other world, the Fae stuff. *Oops.*

'What do you mean you saw the Orchids?' Maggie says, frowning. 'Have they grown back?'

'Oh, no,' I say, feeling my face redden, 'I mean that I was looking on the internet and there was an article about them, and pictures.'

'Oh yes,' Maggie says with enthusiasm, stirring her coffee quickly, 'they were so lovely. It's such a shame they've all gone, the ground used to be like a bright yellow carpet from June to September. But then they died out gradually. Something to do with the atmosphere and the hole in the ozone layer. Or something.'

Maggie's silent for a moment. 'But the Orchids were definitely back that day when I followed your dad into the woods.' Maggie's face creases into a frown again. 'Did you say you saw the Orchids in the woods today?'

'No, no,' I say quickly, 'I just found them on the internet. An article.'

Maggie's eyes lock onto mine. As a kid she always knew when I was lying. I could get away with anything with Dad, but Maggie always knew. After a few seconds she sighs and smiles.

'Your grandfather used to say that the Orchids had healing properties, if he fell over and cut his knee, he just had to rub his skin with the Gossamer Orchid petal and it would heal over.' She chuckles. 'The things they used to believe in those days, eh!'

I laugh too, but I can hear in my own ears how false it sounds.

Maggie shuffles through the papers from Dad's folder, and puts some of the dry sheets back inside. A few of the sheets are still damp and sticky, and I cover the table with newspaper to help soak up the liquid. One sheet catches my eye; it has something written on the top, in Dad's handwriting. 'I'll leave these here until the morning,' Maggie says, placing them carefully on the newspaper. 'We'll put them back in the folder tomorrow.'

'Yeah,' I say, but I can't take my eyes off the sheet with Dad's handwriting.

Maggie goes upstairs to start her packing and I sit down at the kitchen table and pick up at the sheet of paper. It's a local map of the area, an OS style map with contours and paths, much of it taken up with Gossamer Woods. There's a circle drawn around a section of the woods, like a kind of boundary. At the top, in Dad's handwriting, it says:

Shadow Fae, Gossamer Paddock. April 1st

My heart is pumping so hard I can hardly breathe. *Fae.* That word again. And the date – April 1st. That was the day Dad disappeared. Did Dad know about the Fae people? *Dad where are you?* Why is it dated April 1st? It must have been one of the last things he wrote before he disappeared.

I touch the paper lightly, tracing my father's handwriting with my finger. 'I need you, Dad,' I whisper, as though perhaps he can hear me. The sheets of paper are mainly printouts from the computer, screen dumps and internet research. The topics range from local history and weather charts, to information about what chemicals to use to clean bird poo from your car.

My hand trembles as I slide the piece of paper towards me, carefully fold it into four and slip it into my bag. I listen to Maggie moving around upstairs and wonder if she can hear my heart thumping on the walls of my chest.

I check the back door's locked and close the curtains, start to walk upstairs.

'I'm off to bed,' I sing as I peer round Maggie's bedroom door. 'Early night.'

Maggie smiles and nods. 'Night sweetheart.' I glance around her room and smile at the mess. An abundance of clothes, shoes and makeup spilling all around the room, on the bed, on the floor, not an inch of any surface is showing. *She's happy.*

Once I'm inside my room I perch on the edge of my bed, my stomach feels quivery. I plug my phone into my speakers and punch some buttons to set it to play random music, on low. I puff up my pillow and lay my dad's piece of paper on the bed beside me. I feel a little empty knowing Maggie will be gone tomorrow for six whole days and nights and somehow seeing my dad's handwriting beside me helps.

I flop back down onto the pillow and close my eyes. I really have to start making new friends, getting out more. It's clearly not good for me to be spending so much time on my own, making up these imaginary friends. *Luke.* I sit up bolt upright. After all he has given me his phone number.

I try to bring his face into my conscious mind. I can picture his blond hair flopped over his eyes, I can see his hands doodling in his maths book. But I can't picture much more, except that he sometimes makes me feel uncomfortable when he looks at me. His piercing blue eyes, they seem to look into your soul. I reach into my bag again and my fingers search the bottom of the lining for the bit of paper he gave me. It isn't there. I press my palm into my forehead, where did I put it? I was at school...after exam…piece of paper…turned around, Luke gone and…ah, I put it in my pocket.

I yank my headphones out of my ears and leap across the room, hoping Maggie hasn't stuck my clothes in the wash. That would be typical, just when I really need… I'm relieved to see my skirt still folded neatly on my chair, where I left it. I shove my hand into the pocket, feel the crumpled paper in my fingers and drag it out. It's all creased and torn. I straighten it out on the bed next to my dad's sheet of paper. I feel like a million manic butterflies are dancing inside my stomach. *Just ring him.* I suddenly feel panicky. What if he laughs at me. *Do it now before you chicken out.*

I dial his number, and then I lie back on my bed whilst I listen to the line connect and then ring. My mouth's dry. What if I can't speak? Shall I put the phone down? It's not too late. What shall I say? *Hey, Luke, guess what? I see fairies.* I'm just about to press the red button when I hear a click…

'Hello?'

I sit bolt upright.

'Hello, Luke, it's Scarlett. From school. Scarlett Moon,' I blurt.

'Hey, Scarlett.'

'Hi.'

There is an awkward silence as my mind goes blank. I should've planned what to say. Finally I say, 'I found your note, I'd forgotten about it.'

'Yeah.'

Silence. I screw up my face in frustration. Say something, I urge myself, say something that's not stupid.

Finally Luke fills the silence. 'Erm, d'ya wanna to come round for a coffee sometime?'

'Yes,' I blurt, glad to have the silence broken, 'that would be good, how about tomorrow?'

Coffee would be okay, wouldn't it? And judging by this short stunted conversation, coffee won't take very long at all.

'Yeah great.'

Silence.

'D'ya wanna come to mine?' I hear Luke say. 'I could show you my paintings?'

'Isn't that just a cheesy line?' I laugh nervously. Luke goes silent and I kick myself. How lame. 'I mean, you know, show you my etchings. Didn't they used to…' I cringe. *Okay stop talking now.*

'No, I just thought…' Luke's voice peters out.

'Yeah that would be great,' I say quickly, wishing I could press 'undo' like you can on the computer. 'Would about eleven be okay? My aunt's going away for a few days and I'd like to see her off.'

'Yeah that's great, I'll do some painting 'til you come.'

Another silence.

'So where do you live?' I say, and laugh nervously.

'Oh, thought you knew. It's the first cottage on the other side of the woods to you. Number Ten. Red door.'

'Oh! We're Number Twelve!' So close. Well, about two miles away actually.

'So I guess that kinda makes me the boy next door.' I hear him laugh and it makes me feel warm and tingly.

'Okay, I'll see you tomorrow then.' The line goes dead.

As I press the 'end' button, my heart is thumping in my throat. I feel my face break into a wide smile. I chuck my mobile onto the bed, flop back and hug my pillow. Coffee. Good, it's not like I have to try or anything. He's just the boy next door. More or less. If you don't count the acres of woodland separating our two houses.

What am I thinking? I don't even like coffee.

Chapter Fourteen

When I reach Luke's house I glance around warily. It's an old cottage, like a dormer bungalow, and the whole of the front is covered in an old ivy-type creeper, the windows peep out like poky eyes. You'd never believe that it's the exact same cottage as the one Maggie and I occupy, obviously constructed by the same builder at about the same time. But whereas our cottage has been modernised over the years, new windows, rendering, front door, Luke's cottage is like a real country cottage straight off a calendar.

A stream runs through the garden from the direction of the woods. The sound of babbling water rushing through the garden makes me think I might need to pee. A small rustic bridge spans the stream, connecting with the path leading into the woods.

The garden is a mass of colour, like somebody has scattered seeds randomly. The flowers, shrubs, plants, trees are a wall of colour, a living breathing world exploding with fragrance, alive with the sound and movement of birds, bees, butterflies, insects.

I hesitantly approach the bright red front door. I reach out my hand for the doorbell but the door swings wide open.

'Oh!' I take a step backwards.

'Hi,' Luke says, 'sorry if I gave you a fright.'

I'm not sure I have ever heard Luke laugh before, and for some reason I feel myself blush. I glance down self-consciously and shuffle my feet. I tug at my cropped top, trying to cover the half inch of tummy it exposes. My mouth feels dry.

He seems taller than I remembered; he's wearing a white, baggy, brushed cotton shirt with no sleeves. And by the look of the frayed seams, they've been ripped off rather than cut. The front of his shirt is smeared with paint, as though he's dragged his painty fingers across his chest. His arms are thin and tanned with inky doodles stretching all the way up. Apart from the oil-paint stains, the white shirt is squeaky-clean, as though he's just taken it out of the laundry and ironed it. His jeans are clean, well-worn pale denim. At some point they've been converted into shorts – ripped off (or cut roughly with blunt scissors) just above the knees. My eyes linger on his long tanned legs. He catches me looking and I glance away quickly.

Luke leads the way into the kitchen and fills a shiny hob-kettle with water. I feel tongue-tied so I pretend to look interested in the furniture. The kitchen is similar to ours in its layout but the cupboards are outdated and some of the appliances look like they've stood in the kitchen since it was built. My eyes come to rest on a large appliance in the corner; it looks like a fridge or a dishwasher, or perhaps a twin-tub.

'Is your gran here?' I say nervously.

'No, she's out shopping.'

I nod, thinking about the day I met her on the bus. I wonder if she's mentioned it to Luke.

I follow Luke as he wanders back into the hall. He pauses beside a large solid oak door and turns to face me.

'I'd like to show you my studio.' His chest puffs out with pride.

My mouth drops open as I walk into the room. The contrast between this room and the rest of the house is startling. It's obvious that this is Luke's private space; he's stamped his personality on the room. Vivid colours with huge expression. Walls coated with pictures, sketches, paintings. Even the wooden floorboards are daubed with paint, splashes of colour, doodles, blobs, like his ideas have taken a life of their own, climbing onto the walls and manifesting themselves in the shape of any particular canvas. Every picture sucks me in, as though I'm climbing inside it, and each image relates to another. The corners of the room are piled high with books, canvasses, bottles, tubes, pots with brushes, palette knives. The room smells of oil and distilled turps, chalk, carbon, wood. There are rags, paints, pens and chalks scattered. A burst of light streams in through large patio doors, adding to the crazy colour storm. The disorder in the room confuses my need for order, for symmetry and control. It's utter chaos.

He laughs self-consciously. 'I like to play around with colours and tones. There's something I'm trying to get, to achieve, a colour or something, it's just outside my reach but I know I'll find it someday.'

'Mmmm,' I say, 'your parents must be very tolerant.' My dad wouldn't have allowed me to make such a mess in the house.

'My mum and dad died when I was seven,' Luke answers. 'I've lived here with Gran ever since.'

'Oh. I'm sorry…'

'No it's okay,' Luke assures me. 'I don't mind talking about it.' He nods as though to convince himself.

There's a rickety chair in the corner of the room, a pale yellowy wood with a woven seat. I walk over and touch it. There's something familiar about it.

'You can sit in it if you like,' Luke says. 'It's almost exactly the same as the chair Van Gogh painted in Paris. It's my inspiration. He created a whole new way of representing colours just by the way he applied paint to the canvas, he broke the mould. That's what I need to do, create something new, I can see it in my head but I can't reproduce it on canvas. It drives me half crazy sometimes.'

I sit on the wooden chair and view the room. Such disarray, confusion, mess. Such madness. It muddles my mind, confuses my basic need for order, my need to control my surroundings. It is utterly fantastic. It makes me feel free.

A shrieking whistling noise comes from the kitchen and I jump.

'Coffee?' Luke says.

'Actually'—I lick my dry lips—'do you have anything cold?'

He rolls his eyes. 'You could have said before I put the kettle on.'

'Sorry.' I swallow. 'Luke?'

'Yeah.'

'I love your studio, it's amazing.'

The corner of his mouth curls upwards but he quickly turns and leaves the room. He returns a moment later holding two cans of Coke and hands one to me.

It's icy cold in my hand, dripping with condensation. I snap the can open and drink from the edge of the can thirstily, the first fizz biting into my thirst and rushing down my throat in greedy gulps. I wipe my lips on the back of my hand, rest my head back in the chair and close my eyes. When I open them Luke is watching me, his eyes vibrant and stormy beneath the confusion of lights and colours inside his crazy studio. He glances away. I raise my Coke can to my lips to hide my smile. I like it here, I like it a lot.

A huge painting propped on a large easel demands my attention. It's semi-abstract, an apparent mess of colours and shapes. I think it's only half finished. But in the centre of the image I can see clearly the great old oak tree in the woods. When I screw my eyes I can see perfectly the grain of the bark, the wispy grasses, the sunlight trickling through the foliage above, I can almost smell the light scent of the herby forest, feel the sun on my skin. And if I half close my eyes, it's almost as if there should be a figure there, nestled in the hollow beneath the trees.

'That painting...'

Luke nods. 'The old oak in the woods, it's not finished. There's something missing, to bring the painting alive. A person, or an animal or summat. I can't move on with it until I can work out what's missing.'

He slides down onto the floor, leaning against the wall, pulls his legs up so he's resting his chin on his knees and stares at the big unfinished painting. We slurp our drinks in silence. I feel myself relax, at peace. The visual chaos is comforting, and for the first time in many, many months, I no longer feel the need to straighten anything, change anything, or control my environment. I don't need to do anything. I can just be me.

'I could sit in this room forever,' I murmur, more to myself than to Luke.

My eyes are drawn to a painting in the corner, leaning against the wall. It's a picture of the countryside, quite different to the style any of the others, realistic, more like a photograph. I stare at the canvas; can almost feel I'm there inside the picture.

As my eyes relax and my mind wanders, I imagine I'm walking down the winding lane in the painting. The scene comes alive in my mind. As I wander down the lane in my imagination, I can see the wild flowers swaying in the slight breeze, purple foxgloves, blood-red poppies and yellow buttercups. A little rabbit scampers across the road in front of me. So *sweet*. A red car appears in the distance. Quick, hop out of the way little rabbit. The rabbit lollops across the road and disappears into the hedgerow as the car approaches. I smile to myself. I see two people in the car. A couple. They look happy. The man at the wheel glances at the woman and she smiles. The man looks a bit like Luke, he has the same colouring. The woman is laughing, her eyes twinkle. There's another car close behind them. A black SUV. It is being driven erratically, there is a young boy at the wheel, and he's beeping his horn and flashing his lights. Maybe nine or ten years old, he can only just see over the bonnet of the car. He's trying to overtake the red car, but it's a narrow road. He's waving to the couple in the estate car, as though he knows them. My heart's pounding in my chest as I try to blink myself back into the real world, back inside Luke's studio. But I'm locked into this picture. It's like I'm stuck in a dream. And there's a video running, I can't get out of it, and I can't stop the film.

The black SUV is alongside the red car, too close, there's a screeching of brakes, a crunch, the cars bounce off one another. I rub my eyes; I can't seem to wake myself out of this daydream. I have no control. There's a sharp turn in the road, there's another scrunch of metal as the SUV steers into the red estate car, the red car skids. I see their faces, panic, horror, the car spins and then careers off the road. The edge of the road, there's a drop. A sheer drop. I try to scream, but I can't do anything. The crash, deafening, the smell of hot metal, hissing, the car is upside down at the bottom of the valley, steam from the bonnet, fuel pouring from the engine. Wake up, WAKE UP. The horrible image is starting to fade. I'm coming back into the room. But not before I hear an enormous explosion, then the boy's face fills my vision, he's only young. He's smiling. He has black curly hair and almost-black eyes, and a faint pockmark over his eye where he has scratched a chickenpox spot. *Jasper.* I try to scream.

I return real life with a jolt and stare around at Luke's paintings, his easel, his mess. I stare at Luke with wide eyes, my heart pounding and my hands sweating. Luke's staring back at me and I suspect I might have made a sound. I cough. And then cough again.

I stand, cautiously hanging on to the back of the chair. I don't dare look back at the painting in the corner. In case it sucks me back in. I know it was just my mind wandering but why would I fabricate of such a horrible scene? Most normal girls daydream about boy bands, puppies, new clothes. Normal things. Not car accidents.

'Shall we go for a walk?' I say a little shakily, feeling flustered and embarrassed. Did I actually scream? My legs feel wobbly like a jelly.

Chapter Fifteen

As we walk out into the sunshine, my worries melt away. Luke's garden is long and thin, and seems to diminish towards the bottom as it dissolves into the woods. We continue walking, saying very little. Luke's hand is inches from mine. The sun beats down on my neck and arms. I take a deep breath of fresh air and sigh loudly.

'I'm not very good at this,' Luke says gruffly, misreading my sigh for boredom.

'Good at what?'

'Talking and stuff. People. I'm not very good at conversation.'

It doesn't matter. I feel content in his company.

'Why don't you tell me about yourself?' I say, brushing my fingers over a large peach-coloured poppy flower. The petals are crinkled and creased as though they've been folded tightly by hand and stuffed into the flower bud. It must have only just burst its way out; the petals are all creased as though they've been set free after having been scrunched up. I feel happy for the flower. It must feel very relieved to be free after being tightly bound for so long. To feel the moisture of the morning dew. The sun baking onto its vivid orangey-peach perfect petals…

'I hate it when people say that.' Luke breaks into my thoughts. 'Never know what to say. Ask me a question.'

'Okay.' I pause for a split second. 'Oh, okay, what's your favourite colour?' My eyes are still exploring the peach poppy flowers.

'That's easy,' he says, 'green.'

'Why green?'

'Because that's the colour of the trees, leaves, grass. The colour of nature.' He stares at the ground. 'And your eyes.'

'Okay,' I say, turning away so he can't see me blush. 'Now you ask me a question.'

'Any question?' he grins cheekily. 'Okay, erm, what's your earliest memory?'

'Oh,' I say, relieved. My eyes look upwards towards the blue sky, trying to recall. 'I was probably about three, my dad found a tiny stray kitten on a country road. He brought it home, and he told me that I could keep it. I can remember now as if it was yesterday. It was as light as a feather, just tiny ball of ginger fluff. She had claws like tiny needles. She crawled up my chest, her little claws digging into me as she climbed, until I could feel her fluffy face against my cheek. Then she meowed, like she was really cross with me, and head-butted me. She had such a loud purr. I loved my kitten. I called her Jelly Tot because she was so tiny. And of course they were my favourite sweets.'

'Seriously though, Jelly Tots were your favourite sweets?' Luke laughs. He bends down to remove his trainers and continues barefoot, carrying his shoes.

'Well if I got a kitten now it would have to be called Toblerone or Galaxy.'

A sudden gust of wind whips around my midriff, sending a wave of cool pleasure through me. I shiver as goosebumps rise on my forearm.

'Do you still have her? Jelly Tot?'

'No,' I say, looking at the floor, 'she died a few weeks ago, not long after Dad went missing. Some kind of animal killed her, probably a fox or a dog or something.'

'I'm sorry, that's tough.'

'I really miss her, sometimes I forget and find myself looking for her, expecting her to appear, purring and rubbing against me.' I try to make my voice sound extra bright and cheery to hide my sadness.

'Okay my turn to ask again,' I say quickly, anxious to change the subject. 'What's your greatest aspiration?'

'Oh that's a bit deep'—Luke grins easily—'but it's easy. My greatest aspiration is to paint the perfect picture.'

'What would that be of?' I say, turning towards him. He looks away quickly and I think I see his cheeks turn pink.

'That's two questions. It's my turn again now.'

'Okay,' I laugh. 'Go on then.'

'Describe your first kiss,' he says quickly.

It's my turn to go pink and he grins cheekily.

'Okay,' I say, very aware that he may have heard Sasha's outburst at school the other day. *Frigid Scarlett.*

'I was seven years old, and it was with Christopher Littler behind the bike shed at Aspen Green Juniors. He was a year older than me and I was two-timing him with Thomas Chapel from my class. I'd promised Thomas I'd marry him the day before.'

Luke laughs out loud. 'You're shameless.'

'Yeah, I went through a bit of a dry spell after that, serves me right I suppose.'

I laugh nervously. The truth is I haven't actually had my first kiss yet. Well not a proper kiss. I've a dated a few boys. Well, two. Daniel McNeil and Kyle Murray. But I was never particularly interested in either of them. Daniel took me to McDonalds, he brought his Nintendo DS with him on the date. I saw it poking out of his pocket. And he picked his teeth all the way home. The other one, Kyle Murray, took me to the park and talked about football for three hours. I texted Sasha 'RING ME WITH EMERGENCY' and she rescued me. We spent the rest of the afternoon shopping. I smile as I remember how Sasha and I laughed about it afterwards.

Okay,' I say quickly, 'my turn again, next question...have you ever been in love?'

'That's easy, yes,' answers Luke immediately. 'About four years back I had an almighty crush on the girl presenter from Blue Peter. Can't remember her name now.'

Luke's walking a step behind me as we pass through a narrowing in the thick bushes. I hold a thin branch away from my face as I pass by and let go of it quickly. 'Ow!' I hear from behind as it slaps him across his cheek.

'Sorry,' I say without looking around. He leans forward and smacks me lightly across my bum. 'Oy!' I complain, but I'm smiling.

'My turn again,' he says quickly. 'What's the worst thing that ever happened to you?'

The path widens and Luke skips to catch up alongside me. I sigh.

'That's got to be when my dad disappeared in April. I know you've lost your parents too.' I pause, I don't want to dig up any bad memories for him. I see him nod encouragingly so I continue. 'He just didn't come home one day and we still don't know what happened to him. It's horrible because we can't get on with our lives. It's as though time has stood still.' I stop walking suddenly and stare at my feet. 'I miss him.'

I'm mortified to realise that I'm crying.

Luke takes hold of my hand and gently holds it between his fingers, his hands are bigger than mine and smeared with dried paint, but they feel soft and warm. My shoulders shudder as I try to gain control.

'I'm sorry,' I say, 'please don't be nice to me.' I laugh, and then snort as I muffle a sob. I laugh some more, alternating between hiccups and sobs and giggles. Luke cups my face in my hands and gently wipes the tears from my cheeks with his thumb.

He pulls me close to his chest and I feel his arms around me. My face is buried in his chest. His soft cotton shirt smells of fabric softener. I can feel the heat from his body, his arms are tight around me and his fingers are playing with my hair. His shirt is soon damp from my tears, I relax against his body and I feel a heartbeat but can't tell if it's his or mine. The warmth of his hold makes me feel strange inside. I wrap my arms around his waist, his hand smoothes down my back and I feel his fingers brush my skin beneath my top. I like the feel of his touch against my skin.

I look up into his blue eyes and realise that for the first time in my life I want a boy to kiss me.

'I can't imagine how it feels for you, not knowing where your dad is,' Luke says softly. He turns to continue our walk, but keeps hold of my hand. 'If that had happened to me, I'm not sure I could have coped. When I lost my parents, it was nine years ago and yet I can remember it as though it were yesterday, when they came to tell us. That feeling, the words that make the bottom drop out of your world. Nobody would actually tell me they were dead. I heard lots of those stock phrases being muttered...sorry for your loss...deepest sympathy...but I just wanted someone to tell me what had happened. They kept saying stuff like "Mummy and Daddy were taken by the angels" and "they're in heaven now." It was the policeman in the end who sat down with me at the kitchen table and told me what had happened. I will never forget him. He treated me like a real person, not just a seven-year-old kid. "Your mum and dad were in a car accident and they were both hurt very badly and they died." I wanted to hear those words but once they have been said, nothing's ever the same again. It stung like mad at first but we were able to bury my parents, to say goodbye, and up to a point I knew what had happened and why. But I can't imagine how hard it is for you. I'm really sorry.'

I smile a watery smile. Luke is still holding my hand and I like it.

'What do you mean *up to a point* you know what happened?' I say, my heart racing a little in my chest.

'Well they never found out what caused the accident. It seems that my parents' car was run off the road, but the other car didn't stop and there were no witnesses. A couple from the village said they saw a car being driven crazily down the street afterwards, by a young kid, ten or eleven years old, but they didn't get any details and there was nothing to connect this kid to the accident, and nobody knew who he was anyway. But the only important thing is that they died, and they aren't here now. But I was the lucky one, I was able to come and live with Gran. She's really something, I can't wait for you to meet her.'

We walk in silence for a while, listening to the sounds of the forest, each lost in our own personal, confused thoughts. I fight with my conscience, trying not to think about that weird daydream I had when I was in Luke's studio.

It's just my mind playing games.

We walk for most of the afternoon, stopping once to perch on a fallen trunk of tree. I've not felt this relaxed for a long time. The day speeds by in a blur, we laugh a little, talk a lot and hold hands for the whole of the afternoon.

It's six o'clock when we arrive back at Luke's house. As I walk into his studio my eyes are drawn towards the painting in the corner on the floor. The one that seemed to trigger that horrible daydream about the car accident.

I'm so shocked that I cry out slightly.

'What?' says Luke, coming in behind me. 'What's up?'

'That canvas on the floor…' I say. 'I was looking at it earlier, it had a painting of the country road, and now it's blank.'

I stare at the pure white canvas leaning against the wall.

'No, *that's* the one you were looking at earlier, of the woods,' says Luke kindly, pointing to the large painting on the easel.

'Yes, but then I was looking at this painting, on the floor. It was a picture of…'

My voice trails off as I realise that I don't really know what the picture was.

'Doing anything tomorrow?' says Luke, a slight hitch in his voice as though he's nervous.

'Not really.'

'Wanna come round again?'

I fight to hide the smile that wants to creep across my lips.

'Yeah sure.'

Chapter Sixteen

I spend most of the morning pondering what to wear but decide on my stonewashed jeans, silver canvas pumps, and pink top. Maggie always tells me not to wear pink because it clashes with my red hair but honestly how can you possibly match clothes to your body parts? Well, hair. Anyway it's a nice top. And sexy.

I spot her as soon as I step out into my front garden. Sasha. Walking down the lane towards our cottage. I glance back towards my front door and hesitate, if I nip back inside now maybe she won't see me. *Coward.* No, I'm going to walk down my front path with my head held high. My legs feel a little wobbly.

Sasha looks stunning, as always. She's wearing her lilac print maxi dress with a flouncy scarf; she always looks fantastic in that dress, so tall and curvy. She has some new glittery white wedge flip-flops, her toenails are a work of art with stars and tiny crystals. I can't help but admit she looks amazing, as always. As she approaches my front gate she lifts her D&G sunglasses to the top of her head, her hair flops around her ears like a halo. The sun catches her earrings. You'd never think she's still only fifteen, a week younger than I am. Yet she could easily pass for twenty. To my surprise she stops and places a hand on the gate.

'Scarlett!' she exclaims, as though I'm the last person she expects to see walking down my own front path. I glare at her.

'I'm really sorry,' she says quickly. 'Please can we be friends again?'

I feel my chin jerk up defensively. How *dare* she. After all she said, after all she called me. She made such a show of me.

'Really, Scarlett, I don't expect you to forgive me right now, but I just want you to know that I'm sorry. I was upset. I didn't know the whole story. I realise now that Jasper was in the wrong, you had every right to deck him.'

She turns to leave. As she drops her sunglasses back down I

realise her eyes are red-rimmed. *She's been crying.*

'Wait,' I say, hesitantly, 'wait.' She turns and takes off her sunglasses again. She smiles. I have seen that smile so many times. I've slept over at Sasha's house so often, when her dad and Jasper are away. It's a big house. Well, more like a mansion. Gossamer House. It nestles right on the edge of Gossamer Woods, only a five-minute walk from our cottage but it could be a million miles away. I guess it isn't that easy being the daughter of a wealthy property developer. A field full of ponies isn't going to make up for not having your dad around very often. I should know that, and I don't even have any ponies. I don't even have a cat now.

'Look, Sasha,' I say, 'you said stuff that was really hurtful. And unforgivable. It'll take time for me to forgive you.'

Sasha gives me her best Victoria Beckham pout. She used to practise that look in front of the mirror for hours whilst I sat on her bed, awarding her marks out of ten and trying out her various hair products. Sometimes I wonder what part of Sasha is real, or whether it's all just an act. But I feel a tugging, deep inside my heart, a longing for things to be right, the friendship, the feeling of belonging, everything that went along with being best friends with Sasha. I know she's self-centred and pretentious, but deep down she's okay. After all it's not her fault her brother is some kind of sociopath. And something inside me wants to giggle at her ridiculous pout. She really needs to work on that.

I glance back towards my house. Part of me craves for things to be how they used to be, if only we could turn the clock back. Just a couple of months. When Dad was still here and Sasha and I would laugh until we cried over some silly thing.

'Time for a quick coffee?' I say.

Sasha grins, more like the old Sasha. As she dances over the threshold to my house, a waft of her expensive perfume catches on my breath. The last time I smelt that perfume was on the last day of school, just a few days ago. I wonder if I'm doing the right thing. But even if you can't mend something, perhaps you can build a bridge over it.

I snap the kettle on and grin stupidly at her. Sasha is a real coffee lover and hates fizzy drinks. I always used to think she was so sophisticated. She doesn't own an item of clothing that isn't a designer label. She takes a tissue out of her bag and gives the kitchen chair a wipe round and then sits down on it, and smiles back at me. Well if I'd paid £250 for a dress I'd be careful where I sat too.

But strangely enough, Sasha looks a bit fake to me today, sitting in my kitchen, her eyelashes long and thick. *Fake.* The big smile. *Fake.* The Victoria Beckham pout. *Fake.* The unexpected feelings of remorse. *Fake.* I suddenly feel cool towards her.

'So, what have you been doing with yourself?' she asks, glancing around the kitchen with a poorly disguised look of disdain. I feel very conscious that Maggie and I don't keep the kitchen as tidy as we might.

'Not a lot really,' I mutter, a little lost for words. I feel I want to impress her with some interesting tale.

She laughs quietly. 'Yeah, you can't survive without me.'

I narrow my eyes as I pour the hot water into her favourite Green Day mug. I feel annoyed. No, angry. She thinks I can't have fun without her. She thinks I need her. *Well I don't.*

'Actually I've been seeing Luke Woods, you know from our year at school. I've been seeing quite a lot of him,' I lie. *Childish, I know.*

'Ah, Luke,' Sasha says, her eyes burning with something I can't quite read. 'Ah yes, been there, done that, bought the condoms...'

My face must be pure unadulterated shock. Sasha and Luke? Sasha? And Luke? *No.*

Sasha watches my face as she cradles her mug and gently blows across the surface of her steaming coffee. With her big pouty lips and her manicured nails, and her boobs almost falling out of her top. I feel something nearing disgust in the pit of my stomach.

What chance do I have with Luke if she's been there. Been there, done it. Luke has been with Sasha. They've had sex. *No.* Actually, no, I'm not sure I can believe that. *Believe it.* She's so beautiful that's no mistake. But he doesn't seem the type. I catch her eye, she's enjoying this. *No.* She's just being manipulative. Mean. It's not true.

'He's a bit dull but he's got a cute bum,' she says and then she laughs, her perfectly shaped eyebrows rising with expression. 'Oh yes, of course I forgot, you don't *do it*, do you?'

She leans towards me, conspiratorially. 'He definitely does, in fact he's obsessed with me, won't leave me alone, keeps texting me.'

She smiles, but her smile doesn't reach her eyes. I turn my back on her and open the fridge door. *Think, think.* I take my time finding a can of Coke, messing with the contents of the fridge while I wrestle with the emotions that are threatening to rise to the surface.

I slam the fridge door decisively and hold the icy damp can in my hand. *Throw it at her.* I can feel the anger manifesting itself in my shoulders. *Throw it at her.*

'Get out,' I say.

Silence. Her mouth drops open. I speak again, low and controlled.

'Please leave, now.'

Sasha gapes and then rolls her eyes, stands up, picks up her mauve Gucci handbag. She opens her mouth to speak but I push past her and march to the front door ahead of her, open the door wide.

'Get out.'

She follows me through the hall and stands facing me. 'You're just upset because of your dad.'

I see red, I really want to hurt her, how dare she mention my dad. She's not good enough to even say his name. I grab hold of her hair at the back and yank her head close to me. She's making a yelping sound, like she's really frightened.

'What are you doing?' she squeals.

I quickly release my grip and she steps away from me, as she smooths her hair, her scarf slips from her neck and I notice a darkened purpley area, like a bruise, just above her collarbone. On her neck. Like finger marks. I stare. *Oh my God did I just do that?*

Sasha is bright red, livid. 'Freak!' she splutters, pulling her scarf up over her neck. 'As if Luke would be interested in you anyway, he's obsessed with me, OBSESSED. Once you've tasted tenderloin you're not going to settle for a burger.'

She pushes past me and steps out into the sunshine with a supercilious smirk on her face. *Stupid toffee-nosed stuck up cow.* She starts to turn back to say something, but I give the door a shove and it slams shut in her face. *Cow, cow. Slut. Bitch.*

I flop down on the kitchen chair, gasping to gain control of my breathing. I really have to do something about this rage thing. It's so not me. Did I really cause that bruising on Sasha's neck? *Oh my God.* I'm turning into a thug. But no, I don't think I touched her neck. I might have tugged her scarf when I grabbed her hair, but bruising doesn't come out that quickly, surely. But I wonder how she got the marks? It looked like someone had grasped her around the neck. I didn't do that. *Did I do that?*

An image flits through my mind, of Sasha that day outside the school, with Jasper. She looked a bit in awe of him. A bit scared actually. *Did Jasper hurt her?*

No, it was probably just a love bite. Yep, it could have been a love bite. Then I go cold, perhaps Luke gave her the love bite. When they had sex. When they, when they...

Just then my phone bleeps. It's Luke.

WHERE RU?

I go hot and cold. What if Sasha is telling the truth about

Luke, why would she lie? She said he texts her all the time. I pick up my mobile and throw it across the room, it falls apart as it smacks against the wall. I take Sasha's mug over to the sink and pour the still-hot liquid into the bowl.

I put the mug on the drainer and let out the plug, watching the hot coffee encircle the plughole with a gurgle. Tears well up in my eyes as I rinse the sink out and chase the last bit of soap around with a cloth. Then I squeeze out the cloth and wipe the sink around again. My tears are splashing down into the sink as I clean, scrubbing, trying to make the stainless steel shine like a mirror. Why did she have to have Luke, couldn't she have left one boy for me. Just one. There are still some coffee splashes in the sink, like stains, what can I use to get them off? I look in the cupboard and find a pan scourer. My tears flow as I scrub at the sink, scrub and rub and cry. I have to get it clean. Scrub. My hands are sore and I want to scream, I get the scourer and scratch it over the back of my hand, it hurts like mad but it feels clean. I scrub harder; the skin on my hand is red raw and starts to bleed. *Stop it, just stop it. Get a grip.*

I gasp as I force myself to take a deep breath and run my hand under the cold tap. It's bleeding and it stings like mad but the pain feels good. I turn off the tap and lay a kitchen towel over my hand to dry it, a watery pink imprint seeps through the paper towel. What's the matter with me, why do I keep hurting myself like this? I really *am* a freak, whoever heard of anybody deliberately hurting themselves.

I walk upstairs slowly, my breath hitches as I take Pandora's cotton hanky out of the drawer and wrap it around my hand. The same hand I stabbed in the classroom and then hit against the tiles in the bathroom. I'm going to have to stop abusing my hand.

But the hanky feels different today, it doesn't feel as cool, soothing. Perhaps the power of the hanky has diminished. Whatever balm was impregnated in the hanky, it's lost its effect. I've worn it out.

I go back downstairs, I feel weak and shaky. My hand is stinging but I feel somehow released. More relaxed. I peel away the hanky and peer at the skin beneath. The bleeding has stopped but in places it's oozing a kind of clear fluid. Yuk.

I pick up my mobile phone from the floor. It's dead – there's no light on. The back has come off and is lying on the floor, along with the battery. I put it all back together and it bleeps at me as soon as I switch it back on.

THERES AN ICE COLD COKE HERE WITH YOUR NAME ON IT…RU COMING TO CLAIM IT?

I swallow, and text back.

SORRY CANT MAKE IT TODAY. SOMETHINGS COME UP.

A text comes straight back as my eyes sting with disappointment.

OK ☹ SEE YOU SOON X.

My fingers hover over the buttons, wanting to text back, to say yes, yes, I'll be there in a bit. I stare at the screen. A voice in my head is saying don't be so childish. Just go to Luke's house. Go and have a good time. You know you want to.

But another stupid, stubborn, self-pitying voice is stopping me.

Chapter Seventeen

I've spent the last three days lurking at home feeling sad and confused. I've picked up Dad's letter dozens of times, and put it down again. I've tidied the house, cleaned my bedroom, done my laundry, emptied the bins and watched daytime TV until I was nearly insane.

I woke up this morning remembering that it's Sasha's birthday today. And I half wonder what she's doing. I have a card and a present for her in my bedroom drawer but I'm too stubborn to take it round.

Luke has texted me a couple of times and I'm going to ring him. I am. Quite soon.

Anyway I've turned a corner; I won't be a victim any more. Maggie will be home in a few days and I don't want to spend any more time in an empty house wallowing in self -pity.

I walk down my front path and turn towards Gossamer Woods. The air's warm and dry and the sun's starting to burn through the light misty cloud cover. As I enter the woodland I kick off my canvas pumps and stuff them into my bag, relax as I feel the warmth of the long dry grass beneath my feet. I stretch and yawn, and wriggle my toes. I start down a sandy path through the trees, the soft sand warming the soles of my feet, the air feels balmy and I inhale deeply. I begin to smile inside, I always feel good here in the woods, I can't ever imagine feeling depressed for very long here, embraced by the trees and surrounded by natural sights and sounds.

I feel an anticipatory warmth as I approach the small sunny clearing near the old oak tree. I slump down in my special spot at the foot of the tree and sigh deeply, letting go of all my negative thoughts and feelings, fears and worries. I close my eyes, try to clear my head.

I hear a slight sound, and when I open my eyes, Ainsel is

standing a little way away. I smile. I'm neither surprised nor alarmed. Ainsel is stepping up and down onto a tree stump, whispering to herself. I can't make out what she's saying. I focus my eyes on the curve of the nape of her neck, her cropped hair makes her neck appear long and slender. She's wearing a pale lemon translucent dress with tiny spaghetti straps; it falls and clings to the shape of her body, ending just below her hips where it holds itself in soft frills and flounces. I marvel at the lovely shape of her body beneath the silky fabric. She has little tiny yellow cropped shorts beneath her dress, cut so low that they're little more than a ribbon of fabric barely covering anything at all. She seems unaware that I'm here and I feel I should look away, but somehow my eyes are drawn to her. A dozen or so colourful butterflies flitter downwards and rest on her little moving body, clinging to her arms and back as though they form part of the outfit.

I notice the same strange light again; everything is crystal clear and tainted in slightly different colours. The light bounces off colours and explodes into prisms, as though I'm looking through the facets of a crystal. The air is humming with winged creatures, butterflies, bees and huge dragonflies, cosseting the carpet of extraordinary woodland blossom, kissing each flower and moving on. Ainsel's wings suddenly unfurl, they seem to appear from the folds of her outfit, emitting a breathtaking shimmering aura. The wings are almost fluid, like liquid silk, they move and change form almost as though they have a life of their own, they contain every colour of every butterfly, including colours my brain can't even register. I gasp and shiver, feeling suddenly quite emotional.

I could stare at this amazing creature with the breathtaking wings for the rest of my life. The tint and shade of her wings constantly move and change, now aqua, and then suddenly the light explodes like a sparkler on a dark night and flush deep pink and, what's that colour? Like a red, not purple, sort of like...I screw up my eyes and peer. I can't make it out; I don't seem to be able to focus on it. In fact my eyes hurt when I look at it.

'Hello again,' Ainsel's silvery voice breaks into my thoughts. I jump and feel my face redden.

'Hi, Ainsel.'

She's turned to face me and I find it difficult to look directly at her. Her dress, like her top the other day, is transparent. I find myself breathless and hot. Unnerved. Her face splits with a wide grin showing a row of little pearly white teeth. I watch her run her dainty fingers through her closely-cropped black hair and I shiver, wondering what it feels like, perhaps a velvety-peach.

'You remembered my name,' she says. 'I'm glad you came back. I wasn't sure if I'd see you again. Some people can't seem to find their way.'

'It's really not that difficult,' I laugh, focusing my attention on my dusty bare feet. 'There's a path leading right here, it splits off a few times but nearly all the paths in the wood lead to this clearing, this tree.'

'Noooooo,' Ainsel snorts and I start to giggle in a kind of hysterical way. She frowns darkly at me, which makes me worse. Then she just giggles with me and continues. 'I mean I didn't know if you would be able to find your way back *here*, to the Fae world. Some people, they come once and then can't work out how they got here. And then they try and pass through the membrane and it's so funny watching them. Making big eyes and batting their eyelids. We sometimes just sit and watch them for fun, sometimes we *ping* them. It's to do with the eyes, you see, Eldridge says it's like a magic eye picture. If you can learn how to look at a magic eye picture and see what is there, that's how you get into the Fae world.'

'What do you mean 'ping', and what's a magic eye?'

'Haven't you ever looked at a magic eye picture? They just look like jumbled up colours. And you have to focus on the centre really close to your nose and then move it away from your face and then you suddenly see the picture inside. And then it's obvious and you wonder how you couldn't see it in the first place. Well apparently for everyday people, the Fae world's a bit like that. It takes some practising to get here – mostly it's just a fluke when people find themselves here for the first time.'

I haven't a clue what she's talking about, membrane, magic eyes. But apparently I must have the knack. For the first time in my life there's something I'm actually good at. I suddenly feel alarmed. 'How do I find my way back to my world then?' I imagine myself stuck in this place for the rest of my life.

'Well you just have to do the same thing as you did to get here, but in reverse.'

I'm not sure that helps. I shrug, but frankly going home's the last thing I want to think about right now. A rabbit scampers out from behind a tree; it goes right up to Ainsel. She lifts her foot and tickles it with her toes. The rabbit stretches out on the warm sand whilst Ainsel teases it.

'Wow,' I breathe, 'he's so tame, is he yours?' I glance around wondering where Ainsel keeps his hutch. Ainsel explodes with laughter again, and I feel stupid, although not sure why.

'You really don't know much about Fae do you?'

'No, I don't know *anything* about Fae. I don't understand – this is Gossamer Woods, I come here loads but I've never heard anything about the Fae world. And I've never seen a Fae person before.' My eyes are drawn back to Ainsel's wings. They shimmer constantly, changing colour with the light, generating an aura of fine glittery dust. 'Do the fairies live on the other side of, did you say a *membrane*?'

'Yes, there's a membrane between the Fae world and the everyday world, that's how we keep the air clean and pure.'

'What's an everyday world?'

'That's what *we* call *your* world, the other side of the membrane. A lot of non-Fae call it the 'real world' but that's just rubbish. Fae are real people too.'

'So what's the membrane called?'

'Membrane.' Ainsel grins cheekily.

I hold out my hand to see if I can feel anything. Ainsel laughs again. It is a lovely sound, almost musical.

'You can't feel the membrane. You can sometimes see things on the other side of the membrane, they're a bit blurry, but the people on the other side can't see us. Well, not very often. Years ago, before the membrane thickened, they didn't see things exactly as they are – the membrane would act as a concave lens so they would see things much smaller than they are...that's why everyday people think fairies are small.' Ainsel leaps up onto a high branch of a tree and leans down, still talking. 'But very few everyday people are actually able to enter this world these days. Mostly it's Fae Hybrids.'

'You've mentioned Fae Hybrids before, what *are* Hybrids?'

'They're half-Fae and half-everyday people. Like you.'

'I'm not half-Fae.' I laugh nervously.

'Okay then,' she says, and leaps out of the tree and flutters gracefully down to the ground, landing lightly on her toes. She pulls at her ear.

'Why do you call us 'everyday' people?' I say.

'Because you live in the everyday world.' She rolls her eyes.

Fair enough.

'But if the Fae world and the everyday world are separated by the membrane, how come Fae Hybrids can happen, how can Fae people meet non-Fae people and have babies?'

'Well it doesn't happen much these days, but everyday children sometimes used to pass through the membrane.'

'Like I'm doing now!' I say.

'Duh no, not like you're doing now. Because you're a Fae Hybrid. Don't you listen?'

Ainsel pulls at her ear and flashes her eyes in annoyance. She pauses, almost waiting for me to argue with her, but when she realises I'm going to say nothing she pouts like a child.

'The lighting's so powerful here,' I say, deciding to ignore her childishness. 'It's so clear and the colours are amazing.'

'That's because it's more pure here,' Ainsel replies. 'People can't see the damage they're doing to the atmosphere in the everyday world, every time you spray an aerosol or pour bleach down the toilet it releases pollutants into the air which after years and years cause the air to fog over. Of course you can't see it, your eyes have adjusted to get used to it, but from our side we can clearly see the damage that's been done. You're used to seeing things through the haze so when you come over to this side of the membrane, where the air is pure, you see things as they really are.'

'So how is it that I'm sitting in the exact same position that I was in the everyday world, just under the oak tree, and yet now I'm on the other side of the membrane? Which side of the membrane is the oak tree now? If it's here, has it disappeared from the other side?'

'You ask so many questions,' she says, and tugs at her ear again. 'The Fae and the everyday world share the same space, the same land. The easiest way to explain it is that the membrane is flexible and it allows us both to occupy the same space at the same time, sort of parallel living. It's just that our air is purer. You have polluted your world so we've separated our atmosphere from yours. So we live here on the clean side, and you live on the mucky side.'

'But what about things, objects. I'm on the Fae side, am I also on the other side?'

'No of course not, either you're in the Fae world or in everyday world. A lot of animals choose to come and live in the Fae world, which is why there are so many animals here. Particularly winged creatures, your smog is really bad for their wings.'

I look around at the little furry creatures running in and out of the bushes. Rabbits, squirrels, I think I see a fox, and deeper into the woods I can see two deer grazing. But there are also butterflies, dragonflies, bees, all flitting around in swarms, like a huge magic carpet flying across the sky.

'You'd better close your mouth or you'll swallow a butterfly!' Ainsel says.

'So what about the grass, the trees, where are they, the everyday world or the Fae world?'

'They're part of the surroundings, they're in both worlds. It's just the atmosphere, the air, that's different, and the creatures that live here. We even have some animals that everyday people believe to be extinct. They've chosen to come over to the Fae world because the everyday world has clogged up with gunk over the years.'

'It's not *that* bad!' I scowl. 'How would *you* know, you've never been there!'

'Well look for yourself.'

I follow Ainsel's pointing finger, and just beyond the mid-distance there is a murky foggy hazy area. 'That's your air, beyond the membrane. The membrane's clear, but from this side you can see how mucky your air is, the sun can't get through, you're living and breathing the poisonous yuck.'

I peer into the gloomy area that's moving. I stand and walk towards it. 'How come I can see the membrane here but not in other parts?'

'It just depends where the membrane happens to end at that moment. It moves all the time, but it never goes beyond the edge of the woods. It forms a sort of backdrop to our world, like a false wall, which moves as we move towards it. It's like we're living in a huge bubble, we can go wherever we want and the bubble moves with us. But here at the oak tree, the membrane is thinner. It's a kind of entrance to the Fae world for anybody coming through. Like you. Which is why Eldridge and I are often here. It's our job to check out anybody coming through the membrane and alert the Fae villagers of any danger.'

I laugh rudely and stare at her. 'What possible danger could there be, what do you think we 'everyday people' are going to do, catch a butterfly or something?' *They must all be paranoid.*

I'm staring at the murky membrane, which is moving away. It looks like a rolling mist moving slowly backwards and forwards. When I turn back towards Ainsel I recoil in shock.

'ARGH!' I gasp.

Ainsel is crouched on all fours like a wild cat about to pounce, her wings held stiffly above her like a weapon. There's a kind of sound, rather like a snake, escaping her lips.

'Black-Wingssssss,' she hisses mysteriously, the rigidity of her body making her voice sound shrill.

'Wh-what?' I snort. Black-Wings, for goodness sake, what possible danger could there be in these woods? What are Black-Wings? Bats, maybe? Perhaps they have some sinister significance in the Fae world or something. She certainly seems scared of them.

Ainsel sees my startled reaction and her body relaxes, she rises out of the crouch and her rigid wings soften and gently fold towards her back. She touches me reassuringly on the arm; the softness of her touch sends tingles up my arm leaving goose-bumps on my skin.

'Black-Wings, they are the most dangerous creature in the land,' she says in her normal silvery voice.

'Ah!' I say. 'Okay.' I'm still breathing heavily from the shock of her reaction. I daren't ask what Black-Wings are. Some kind of bird? Perhaps a hawk, maybe she's afraid for her little rabbits. She obviously takes it very seriously anyway.

I stare at the ground and wiggle my toe in the dry sandy earth, wondering if this girl is just making fun of me. *Black-Wings indeed.*

'Okay, look at it this way.' Ainsel breaks into my thoughts, she's completely normal again now. *If you consider wings and virtual nudity to be normal.* 'Think about the radio. There are sounds in the air waves that you can't hear. Loads and loads of different radio channels, all using the atmosphere around us. We would never know they were there. They're totally silent to our ears. But switch on a radio, it can tune into one channel, or another, and you can hear the sound as clear as day. It's *magic.*'

'No it's *not* magic,' I protest. 'It's science!'

'Duh,' she says, and I feel like slapping her. 'Yes, of course it's science, and so is *this*. It's just a type of science that *everyday* people haven't yet discovered. But that doesn't mean it isn't real. When you tune into our Fae world, it's like you are picking up a different channel on your personal radio.'

She tugs at her wings and narrows her eyes at me. And then laughs quickly, her wings unfold gently like the petals of a flower and her body is gracefully lifted onto the branch of the tree. I 'tut' loudly because I'm still unsure what to make of her, and I'm still not totally convinced she isn't teasing me.

I reach down and pluck a flower from the ground. It's really quite extraordinary, the brightest yellow you can imagine, rather like a highlighter-pen yellow, with almost luminous glittery orange stamens. A Gossamer Orchid. And they're all over, covering patches of the woodland floor like a resplendent yellow carpet. I'd love Maggie to see this. As I tear the flower away from its deep green stalk, a pale yellow liquid oozes from the torn stem and I gaze at it in wonder. It looks like a light golden runny honey. Maggie said these flowers had healing qualities, I wonder whether this oozing liquid has medicinal qualities. I take some of the honey-like liquid and spread it onto the top of my hand where I scrubbed my skin raw a few days ago. As I spread this golden liquid over my hand, the skin smooths over, the scabs dissolve and the redness diminishes, leaving a slight pinkness marks. Wow, that's pretty impressive. Like a kind of exfoliator for damaged skin.

Something flits past like a streak of light, a figure dives behind Ainsel. I squint my eyes in the bright light and can just make out a boy. He's wearing nothing on top, only a pair of shorts. Ainsel glares at him.

'I thought I said to stay out of sight,' she hisses at him. I try to make out his face, he has short black hair like Ainsel, but the colours are so bright I can't focus on him.

'Who's that?'

'Eldridge, he's my younger brother, he's only fifteen.'

I'm wondering how old Ainsel is, surely she can't be much older than me.

'How old are you?' I say.

'Nearly sixteen,' she says. She pulls at her ear and glares at me belligerently. I laugh, she's so sweet. But how can she be the same age as her younger brother. Maybe he's only just turned fifteen and she's nearly sixteen, or...I'm suddenly distracted by something murky moving in the middle distance.

'Hey, did you see that? Is that the everyday world I can see there?'

'Yes, somebody's there in the woods. Let's ping him,' Ainsel says excitedly.

'*What* him?'

'We can ping people in the everyday world. We're not supposed to. It's sort of against our law. But we do it anyway. If we can get close enough to the membrane we can twang it, sort of like elastic, and it flicks the person – like on their ear or their nose. They think they've been bitten by an insect. It's quite funny.'

Ainsel leads me by the hand. When we reach the membrane I can make out the outline of the figure, it's murky and unclear but I can tell it's a man, probably a young man. Ainsel reaches out her hand and grasps at the fog, it's almost like we are standing inside a bubble, and lets it go – *twang*. The man slaps his hand against the side of his head. It's weird to be standing so close to this murky figure and yet know that he can't see us and has no idea we're here. Ainsel giggles loudly and I wonder if he can hear us. This is obviously what happened to me in the woods when I thought I'd been bitten by a fly. 'Ping'-ing, indeed! It's nothing but mischievous fairies having a joke at our expense.

Something moves behind me and I spin round, it's Eldridge, he darts behind a tree.

'Eldridge, either come and sit down or go away. Stop eavesdropping,' Ainsel shouts.

He sits down in the grass a little way away. I still can't see him properly; the light is so bright here. But he doesn't look like any fairy I've ever seen in drawings. For a start he's taller than me. I can't see his face properly but he's wearing bright red shorts. His skin's not as pale as Ainsel's, his hair is black like hers and thick like a mop. He has large almond-shaped amber eyes framed by thick black lashes, just like Ainsel. He glares at me so I turn away.

The membrane has moved away, and the figure in the woods has disappeared. No wonder, he probably thinks he's being eaten alive by insects.

'If the Fae world is sharing the same space as the everyday world,' I say, 'how come we don't bump into each other?'

'Well there's always the membrane between us. If a person in the everyday world walks towards us, then the membrane comes towards us, forcing us backwards and keeping us separate. If we don't move backwards then the membrane will engulf the person in the everyday world. This is why Fae people live in woods. And we tend to avoid people anyway. Unless we're pinging them, of course.'

The Eldridge boy whistles softly to himself. I lean closer to Ainsel and cup my hand around her ear, whispering, 'Your brother, Eldridge, is he a fairy? He doesn't look like one, he looks too tall. And he has strange ears.'

As I say it, I remember that Ainsel's ears are pointy also. She glares at me, and leans over and pokes my ear rudely with her finger.

'So have you,' she says.

'Oh!' My hand goes to my ears and my fingers follow the shape self-consciously. I suppose they are a little pointy at the top, I've never noticed before. My ears are nearly always covered by my hair. And it's not like you can actually see your own ears.

'Like I said, you're Fae,' Ainsel says and I make a 'pah' noise. 'You can call us what you like, fairy, elf. I suppose in your folklore, the boy fairies would have been called elves. After all, it's not very flattering to call a boy a fairy'.

I giggle and look at Eldridge. I'd love to call him a fairy. I can see him clearly enough to realise that he's scowling. I lie back in the grass and look upwards towards the sky. Just for a moment I want to believe that I am one of them. It'd be nice to belong.

Perhaps I really do belong. If Tate was a Fae. That would mean…in that case…Ainsel could be right. I could be half Fae. A Fae Hybrid.

Which explains the wings. Growing inside my back.

Oh my God. I'm a fairy.

Chapter Eighteen

I don't actually know how I managed to get back through the membrane into the real world. Okay then, *everyday* world. I decided I should maybe think about going home, and soon after everything went very grey and Ainsel and Eldridge were gone, along with the Orchids and the butterflies. Almost like my body knew how to do it without thinking.

I feel quite sad to be away from that beautiful place, but I'm ravenous so I decide to make my way back home. I'm amazed how dull and muted everything seems now I'm back in the real world. Okay, everyday world. It's like I've put sunglasses on.

As I turn reluctantly towards home, my eyes are still searching for the flowers, the butterflies. It feels empty. Like there's been an Armageddon or something and all living creatures have been wiped out. I stand very still. Of course it's no different to usual, it's just after the Fae world it all seems kind of barren.

I smell something, it doesn't belong, feels wrong. It smells vaguely pungent and nasty. I inhale the incongruous scent but my mind struggles to place it. Then I feel a shadow, behind me, a movement, a sound, a feeling. I spin round.

Sasha.

An icy feeling drips down my spine.

'What do you want?'

Sasha's eyes dart around anxiously as though she's expecting somebody else. The scent of her expensive perfume is even more pungent now, and smells so out of place here in the woods. *She* looks out of place, actually, as I look at her. She looks ridiculous. I've never seen her like this, she looks a mess. Her peach-coloured wedge sandals are dusty and dirty, her Armani skirt is streaked with dirt as though she's been sitting on the floor for hours. She paid a small fortune for that skirt. And her three-quarter sleeved top is caked in sweat. She looks like a fish out of water dressed like that, here in the woods. It's all wrong.

'What do you want?' I say again, my tone openly hostile.

'Scarlett,' she says. 'Scarlett, I'm really sorry. They make me do it. Please Scarlett stay away, stay away from me and my brother, please don't trust anybody.'

'What do you mean?' I say, suspiciously. 'What are you talking about? You stalk me and then you tell me to stay away from you?'

To my astonishment Sasha sinks to the floor and begins to cry. Loud juddery sobs that shake her entire body. A feeling of compassion sweeps over me, and yet something prevents me from going to her, rescuing her. I feel a sudden thickness in my throat.

Sasha looks up at me through streaming eyes, and as she reaches for a tissue from her Prada satchel, her cardigan slips off the shoulder revealing a massive bruise, deep dark purple on the outside and redder in the middle. Her shaking hand lifts the tissue to her nose and she blows loudly.

'Oh my God, Sasha, what happened?' I gesture to her bruised shoulder. There's a wobble in my voice, I remember the bruise on her neck the other day. 'Did you fall off your horse?'

Sasha quickly pulls her cardigan up over her shoulder and winces in pain.

'Please, please, Scarlett, don't trust anything I say. Please.'

She's spooked by something and her head jerks up, she spins round but there's nothing there, her eyes are darting around.

'I love you, Scarlett, please don't hate me.'

I feel uneasy, my heart lurches for my old friend but a voice inside is telling me not to trust her. I've no idea what she's talking about. How did she get those awful bruises? What's she doing here in the woods?

I get the feeling we're being watched. Sasha's jumpy, she looks haunted, the hairs on the back of my neck start to move and I spin round. Nobody's there. Sasha's looking at me pleadingly, as though she's trying to tell me something but I can't hear what she's saying. I'm confused. She looks genuinely frightened and those bruises look real. I feel like I'm missing something.

'Sasha.' I want to go to her, but there's something in her eyes, like a warning. I take a faltering step towards her, reach out my hand.

'I'm sorry, Scarlett,' she says, flinching, her eyes dart around nervously. And then she quickly turns and runs, leaving her sandals on the floor by my feet.

'Sasha!' I shout, but she's gone. I listen, and there's no sound at all. The silence is almost palpable. Unnatural. I shiver.

What does she mean? I can't work out which is the real Sasha: the fake designer Sasha who draws a crowd and shouts hurtful things to me; the giggly fun Sasha who used to lie in bed with me and eat chocolate muffins in Disney pyjamas and make me promise I wouldn't tell anyone; or the bruised terrified Sasha who has just sped through the woods without her shoes?

She told me to stay away from her. Well okay, I can do that. With pleasure. She's such a drama queen. She probably fell off her horse or something. I think back to a couple of years ago, she got her foot stuck getting out of her dad's car. Went headfirst, ended up with a black eye and a twisted ankle. She milked that for weeks.

I start to move slowly through the woods, walking blindly, deep in thought and not paying a lot of attention to anything. The late afternoon air tastes fragrant and musky but Sasha's spicy perfume has left a nasty smell.

It must be getting towards teatime judging by the position of the sun, and I'm feeling hungry. I tune into the music of the birdsong and marvel at the different sounds each one makes. I turn my head upwards, the sky's pale blue with wispy clouds. A shaft of sunlight is bursting through the tree branches and I pause beneath it, soaking up the warmth. I close my eyes. I can feel the fluttering of the wild birds flying from branch to branch.

I listen closely and I try to recognise which bird is making which song. Like so many times recently I wish I was a bird up in the sky, ready to fly away, feel the freedom of flight, the warm air beneath my wings and the wind in my face.

I open my eyes, a song thrush is perched on a branch high up and I can see its beak opening and closing in time with its song. The tall trees rise and merge as though I'm standing at the bottom of a bright funnel, diverging as it reaches the top. The sun's rays split and focus down on me as though I'm on a stage with the spotlight directed on the star dancer.

I start to sway to nature's music, the rustling of the trees, the chirping of the birds, the clicking of a grasshopper on the ground near my feet. I breathe in deeply and hum to myself, moving rhythmically, close my eyes and sway gently from side to side. I lift my arms into the air, my t-shirt hemline rising up to expose my midriff to the warm woodland breeze, I wave my arms in time with nature's sounds, feeling the air lap either side of me, tightening my skin, the woodland sounds drumming a percussion beat, rustle flutter tweet-tweet, rustle flutter tweet-tweet. I sway and hum and my mood soars, the regular cracking of twigs add to the drum beat, rustle flutter tweet-tweet crackle crack, sway and hum, rustle flutter tweet-tweet crackle crack scrunch, clomp clomp crackle crack scrunch...

I'm quickly brought back to my senses. *Footsteps.* I'm not alone. I spin in the direction of the sound and my breath freezes in my chest.

Jasper.

'Eouuugh!' I cry out, and look around in panic. But there's nobody to hear.

He's standing six feet away, silent, watching. How long has he been there? An icy fear spreads through me and I take an involuntary step backwards.

'Well if it isn't the little freak girl,' he growls through his teeth. There is no pretence at politeness, his lip curls in disgust and his eyes are dark with something ugly.

'Having a little dance are we, Sweet Pea?' he says, his sneering voice jarring with the peacefulness of the woods.

'What do you want?' I spit, trying to sound brave. He's balanced on the raised roots of a tree with one foot forward as though ready to pounce. His arm is out of the splint now, and both hands are shoved in the pockets of his cargo pants, and he's jingling the coins in his pocket, rattling them around. Jangle, jangle, jangle. The sound is menacing.

'I want the next dance,' he says quietly, the smile on his mouth never reaching his eyes. 'We have unfinished business, you and me.'

I'm frozen to the spot, my legs won't move. 'What do you want?' I say again, playing for time.

'I was enjoying your little dance. I want you to dance for me.'

I edge backwards. I know it's pointless trying to run but I can't just stand there. My legs feel like lead and my heart's hammering in my chest.

I turn and start to stumble through the undergrowth. Perhaps I can hide. I hear him laugh behind me. I try to run faster but my legs won't move fast enough, it's like wading through treacle, my feet are too big, my muscles won't work. I hear his breaths, just behind my right ear, his feet clomping alongside me. He's laughing, enjoying this. He's not even out of breath. *I'm dead.*

His strong hand clamps down on my arm and I come to an abrupt halt, I try to slip out of his grip but he has tight hold of my hair. I open my mouth to scream but nothing happens. He's sweaty and hot, I can't think what to do. He towers over me, his black hair glistening with sweat. I cry with pain as he yanks my arms behind my back and pushes me against a tree. I can smell pungent stale sweat and old beer.

'So you got lucky last time, but you won't today.' He belches loudly and bile rises into my mouth. 'If you want to see your precious daddy again, you'll do as I say.'

I kick out at him and struggle, his mention of my dad has enraged me and I'm kicking his legs, kicking and kicking and kicking. How dare he mention my dad.

'Shut your fat mouth!' I shriek at him. 'Shut up, SHUT UP, you know nothing about my dad, you're not even good enough to say his NAME. You shut up you, you…' I scratch around in my head for the most offensive word I can think of but my head is empty. 'You, you…BLACK-WING!' I shriek.

What?

But it's as though I've slapped him. There's total silence and I hold my breath. He stands motionless, gaping, the colour drains from his face until it's grey. And then white. White with rage. Terror grips me.

'You BITCH,' he booms at me and my head jerks up on shock. *What did I say?* I turn my face away from him and close my eyes as though to shield myself from his anger. He looks like he really wants to kill me. *What have I said that's so bad?*

He's rigid with rage, as though he's rooted to the ground. *Do something.* His big dirty hand is clamped onto my shoulder and I quickly bite down on his arm, hard, it's the arm I twisted the other night. 'Ow!' he yells, loosening his grip just long enough for me to slip beneath his arm, he snatches at my wrist but I yank it out of reach, he grabs my hair and I cry out as she drags my head downwards. As I lose my balance I grab at his clothing. I hear a ripping sound as his shirt tears, he loosens his grip on my hair as my nails dig into the skin on his chest producing a river of red, I kick him again, hard, then leap to my feet and run like hell.

This time I really surprise myself, I'm leaping through the woods, my legs are strong and muscular and my back feels like a well-oiled motor, I can feel the adrenaline flowing through my veins, my tissues. Just like the other night, coming from my shoulders, where my wing marks are, my centre of strength. I'm leaping over the ground like a panther. I hear Jasper panting and lumbering behind me but I can tell that I am leaving him behind. I feel so light on my feet like I'm flying; my feet touch the ground and my whole body bounds upwards and onwards. I almost want to laugh. I've never run so fast, I had no idea I could do this. Something inside tells me this is not normal, this is something to do with that weird thing that happens, to do with the changes, the muscles, the wings. The rage. But I don't care, I feel strong, I feel in control, I am free. I laugh and I glance round to see where he is, he's way behind. He doesn't stand a chance. It's almost pathetic, he's running like hell but I'm so much faster. Stronger, better. I laugh out loud. I can see him way, way behind. He's so far back that...THUCK!

My world goes black.

I can feel a searing pain in my head. I open my eyes. Hurts.

I'm lying on the floor beneath a large tree. I must have run right into it, head first. *Oh God.*

I can't move my arms, my legs. I can't think how to move. I hear him lumbering towards me, and his six-foot body leaps on top of me. I move my hand limply. Ow. Ow.

He leans over me. I feel his whole weight on me, crushing me.

'Nobody calls me a *Black-Wing* and lives,' he says. 'What do *you* know about the Black-Wings? What do you know? Did your dad tell you? Did he?'

He's squeezing my arm tightly. Hurts.

'No,' I cry. 'I don't know anything. I made it up.'

His eyes narrow, his face is inches from mine, I can smell his sour breath. I try not to breathe.

'You really are a freak aren't you, that's not normal the way you run.' I feel his breath on my face. He looks puzzled, like he's trying to work something out. The feeling is starting to come back in my body, but my head hurts like hell. He studies my face as though it holds the solution to some kind of strategic puzzle. I lie very still and close my eyes. *Perhaps if I pretend I'm dead.*

'But you're not just a Fae are you, you're too fucking strong.

Of course you are!' He rolls his eyes to himself as though he has realised something he knew all along. 'Of course you're not just a Fae. You're a Sage. You must be, you're Tate's kid!'

My eyes snap open. I stay silent. What does he know about Tate? And what's a Sage? My head's whirling. It starts to feel fuzzy, sounds like he's talking through a glass of water. It's echoing and wobbling. And then he throws his head back and starts laughing, like I've said something really funny. I feel a cold fear creeping over me. My head is pounding and my vision is coming and going. I want to sleep. Perhaps if I sleep now, I'll wake up and this will all be a dream.

His knee is digging into my chest just below my rib cage and I can hardly breathe. He's squeezing hard and as he laughs his body is vibrating. My ribs hurt. My chest hurts. My head's numb.

It's gone quiet. Has he gone? Still hurts. Still can't breathe. His hands are around my neck, his knee still wedged under my rib cage.

'It's a hat trick!' he suddenly says with a menacing laugh. 'I've got the mother, and the father, and now the daughter.' He looks towards the sky and groans with pleasure. 'And she's a Sage. It just gets better and better.' He's laughing again. I feel cold, ice cold from head to toe. I try to breathe out. I just want to die quickly now. *Am I dead yet?*

I focus my mind on Dad. What happened, Dad? What does this beast know about you? And how does he know Tate? Did he kill you both? What's a Sage? I can't breathe at all now, my chest hurts and there's a roaring sound, I've never known pain like it...

'Yeh, I can't wait to tell your precious daddy and mummy how I've violated their baby daughter, their precious little girl, I can't wait to see the look in their eyes when I tell them.'

I stare at him. I don't understand. Dad's alive? Tate's alive? He knows where they are?

'Oh yes.' He's still talking, he's moved his knee now and the air is starting to squeeze back into my lungs, he reaches into his pocket and pulls out a small roll of black Duck tape. *Dad's alive?* I don't understand. I concentrate on breathing and staying conscious. He leaps up onto his feet, his hands clamped around my arms, and he starts to drag me along the ground by my arms, my shoulders are nearly wrenching out of their sockets. My muscles still feel weak and shaky, he pulls me to my feet and props me up against the tree, hard, I can't move, he's too strong. *Dad's alive somewhere?* My spine is crushed against the rough bark of the tree, it hurts. As I'm gaining consciousness, I'm also starting to feel frightened, terrified.

'Oh yes, little freaky FAIRY,' he says, pressing his whole weight against me to pin me even harder against the tree, his face coming towards me until his nose is just an inch from mine. 'This time you don't get away.'

He laughs nastily, congratulating himself, and pulls the tape out of the roll with a ripping sound. A bolt of pain shoots up my arm as he rams it back against the tree, binding me to the tree tightly so that my shoulders, arms and waist are held hard against the hard trunk of the tree.

I kick weakly at the tree; the tape is too strong for me. Jasper steps back to view his work with a nasty grin.

'Oh yes,' he says, his voice low and husky, he licks his lips slowly, winks and clicks his tongue, and then his grubby hand starts to unbutton his cargo pants. I shudder and look up to the sky. I can't move my shoulders, my arms, my body. All I can do is kick but I can't get any strength behind it because my body is strapped so hard to the tree.

I'm angry at myself, why did I let him catch me, I'm stronger than him, faster than him, I can beat him. I've done it before, I can do it again. I start to feel the hot rage filtering through my veins, just like the other night. I just have to wait. I can be stronger than him. *I can do this.* I just have to wait to recover, for the strength to filter from my spine into my shoulders and then into my muscles. I concentrate my thoughts into my back, where my wings are, it seems to be the centre of my strength. I can feel it getting warm, hot, can feel the build up of molten liquid behind my shoulder blades, in my spine, and I smile inwardly, I'll have the power to overcome him soon, just have to wait for it to build and then flood into my muscles. I'm sure that's how it works. And then I'll go and find Dad. *Dad's alive.*

It's getting hotter and hotter in my spine, I know that it will start to flood out into my body soon, through my muscles, they will come alive, they will start to bubble and develop. It's getting hotter and hotter. Actually it's really hurting. I try to shift my back on the tree stump but I'm held tight against the tree. I can't move, and the build up of power, the fuel, it's going nowhere. My back is strapped too tightly, restricting me. It's building and building but it can't energise my limbs, my body. It's like a hot molten fuel inside me, wanting to burst outwards. My body is going to implode. The heat is burning through my shoulders, my back, racking my body with pain. Stop, stop, I scream in pain, in frustration.

Jasper laughs even more. It's a callous, sinister sound.

'Kick all you like little fairy girl, as long as you're strapped to the tree, you're as weak as a kitten. Just like your sweet ginger cat when my dog caught it and snapped its neck.'

What?

The world is silent and still for a split second whilst I absorb what he said.

'You BASTARD! You BASTARD! You BASTARD!' I spit and kick. *He killed my cat.* His bloody ugly dog. He killed my cat. My Jelly Tot. I can't move my chest, my arms. My lower body's free and I kick out at him but my legs feel weak, pathetic. The rage is eating back into me, a flesh-splitting pain ripping through my spine. I'm so tightly bound that the energy has nowhere to go and it's turning in on me, starting to eat me, burn me from inside out. I scream out with the pain and I'm crying openly now. My poor little cat, poor Jelly Tot.

'I'm going to KILL YOU!' I scream. 'I'm going to KILL YOU AND YOUR UGLY DOG!'

Jasper steps away from me and laughs, enjoying my pain, the whole forest echoes with the sound of his laughter. I scream louder and louder. My screams bounce off the trees whilst the raging pain rips down my spine as I try to free myself.

'You're not so strong now, are you, freaky fairy.' He steps towards me. I can feel his acid breath on my face. I feel powerless. The burning rage in my spine is starting to fizzle, the pain is easing, and I know it's dying. I feel limp, lifeless. Why is he calling me a fairy? I don't understand. *How does he know?*

'Let me go you CREEP,' I spit at him. 'You're a bully, let me go. Why are you doing this? Why me?'

Jasper laughs again, but it sounds more like a snarl.

'You really don't know do you?' he sneers. 'Haven't you worked it out yet?'

What's he talking about?

He has sweat running down his face, glistening, horrible. He lifts his arm to wipe the sweat from his face. As he turns away the rip in his shirt comes apart to reveal his bare back. And I nearly vomit. I stare at his back. It's revolting. Revolting. He sees my reaction and laughs. He turns and removes his torn shirt, proudly revealing the thing in the middle of his back, between the shoulder blades. It looks like a black slug. Horrible. A cold, icy fear creeps over me. I think it's sort of shrivelled black slimy...BLACK WINGS.

I scream.

Chapter Nineteen

'Oh yes,' Jasper says. 'I'm a Black-Wing.'

He laughs and licks his lips.

'And now I'm going to take what every Black-Wing wants. A *fairy*.' He's laughing like he's unhinged. 'And it's just so EASY.'

Terror grabs me by the throat and I can't breathe. I don't quite know what he's talking about but I know I'm in grave danger. Ainsel said Black-Wings are dangerous to Fae. And somehow he knows I'm a Fae. He presses against me. I want to throw up.

'Nice,' he rasps, he's breathing heavily, almost panting. I try to scream but there's no air in my lung, I open my mouth and he presses a hot dirty hand over my lips, the smell makes me gag. I try to kick out but his legs are pinning my hips back to the tree, I have no strength, it's like I'm burnt out. He's still laughing, a dirty, guttural laugh. I bite his hand and scream again. He pulls his hand away.

'Ow, you bitch!' he slaps me hard across my face, my head spins round with the force of the blow, the world sways for a moment and then stills. It hurts like hell. I blink to force back the tears.

'Tying a girl to a tree is not a show of strength,' I say, trying to make my voice deep and brave, but it sounds squeaky in my ears. 'It just shows what a COWARD you are. Why not cut the tape, and we'll have a fair match.'

'Shut up, freak,' he says, 'or you'll never see your father again.' His laugh is coarse and raucous, his eyes black and wild.

'What do you know about my dad?' I spit at him. 'You're just low life. You don't know *anything* about my dad. You are clutching at straws. YOU'RE the freak, you're the one with the slimy thing on your back, *you're* the big ugly FREAK, and you'll NEVER be as strong as me.'

I wheeze and then cry out in pain as his body crushes hard

against me, his hips grinding into me, he laughs loudly as I try to kick, his hand fumbles towards my jeans. I feel utterly helpless. I close my eyes tight and retch as his hand grasps my flesh so hard it hurts. I open my mouth to scream again, but no scream comes, my throat's dry, there's no sound left. My ears start to roar and my vision blurs, I hear shouting, and then nothing. It feels like I'm free from that monster's vice-hold grasp, muffled voices from far away, shouts and crashing thumps. I keep my eyes tight shut. Don't understand. Can't see, cold, very cold, trembling, I know I'm lying on the floor now, it's quiet, he's gone. Gone.

I pass out.

Someone's saying my name, I'm thirsty, throat hurts, head hurts, ribs hurt, mouth hurts, eyes won't open. I tremble, shiver, shiver, and remember, and scream. This time it works. I scream again, louder.

'Shhhhhhh,' comes a soothing voice, I'm being held, gently, but my arms lash out, I scream again, trembling violently.

'It's okay,' comes a voice, a kind voice. 'It's okay, Scarlett, you're safe now.'

I cautiously open my eyes a fraction. I'm under the oak tree, I'm sure. I can tell. The smell. Comfortable. Home. I can't focus my eyes. Can hear somebody sobbing, then I realise it's me. I let the tears flow, I'm shivering, whole body shivering, the person holds me tighter. It feels good. Warm. I want this person to hold me tight and never let me go. I'm not sure what's happened, I can't remember, it's all very blurry, I try to remember.

I was sitting under the tree, nice, calm, warm. Then the fairies, pretty lights, tinkly sounds, lovely colours, friends, niceness, goodness, pretty, sweet, like a dream sleepy, warm but not scary. So why am I scared? Scared. Scared. I was in the woods, spoke to Sasha. Strange. Very strange. She ran off. I was dancing. Dancing and humming, lovely. Birds singing, sung through the trees, warm, happy, secure. Then Scared. Why? Scared. Somebody there, somebody there. JASPER.

I jolt and fling my arm out to steady myself. 'Jasper!' I splutter, struggling to sit up, looking around with wide scared eyes. 'Jasper, the monster, he tried to hurt me, he caught me, he hurt me, please, he laughed, sneered, he tried to...' I'm shaking like a leaf, eyes feel wild with terror.

'Shhhhh,' comes the voice again and holds me even tighter. Holds me tight and safe. I close my eyes tight shut again. 'Shhhhhh, he's gone, he'll never touch you again, I heard your screams, it's okay now. I heard you all the way from my cottage.'

I trust this voice. This voice is good. I gasp and shudder, and let another sob escape. The person with the voice wipes away my tears with his fingers. His fingers smell nice, of paint and leather. They feel soft and I hold the hand between my own fingers and hold it to my lips. Nice smell. Comforting, I kiss the soft part, I can taste my own tears.

I open my eyes again, slowly. I look around. I see the familiar branches of the old oak tree. I *am* sitting under the oak tree, and I'm wrapped up with a lovely soft boy. I look at the arm that's around me. A thin arm, a nice hand. A good hand. I knew that hand; I've seen it before somewhere. I've held that hand. Perhaps I should look at the face now.

'Luke,' I sigh.

Then I open my eyes wide again.

'Where is he? What happened? Did he, did he...'

'Shhhh, it's okay. No, he didn't touch you. I got to him first.'

I sigh in relief.

'So what happened?' I say sleepily. 'How did you get rid of him?'

'Well you see that large plank of wood over there?' Luke points in the direction of the bushes.

'The tree branch?' I say, eyeing a massive lump of wood about six inches in diameter.

'Yeah. Jasper didn't take kindly to being whacked over the head with it. He decided to leave.'

I can't help but smile. I gulp and my breath comes in a shudder. Luke's arms tighten protectively around me until my breathing calms once again.

'Was he hurt badly?' I look up into Luke's eyes.

'Well he's going to have a cracking headache for the rest of the weekend.'

I close my eyes again and snuggle my face deep into Luke's shoulder, inhaling the scent of turps and soap.

'Do you want me to take you to the police station?' Luke says softly.

I'm quiet for a moment whilst I process the facts. Jasper shouldn't get away with that, I know what would have happened if Luke hadn't turned up. But Luke did whack him over the head with a plank of wood; will he get into trouble for that? And there are other things I can't explain easily to the police. Like me beating Jasper up last week. And Maggie, poor Maggie will never let me out of her sight again never mind go on holiday, if she finds out what happened. And what will I say to the police, when they ask me where I've been all day and what I was doing? I can hardly say I've been talking to fairies in the woods. And the wings. What if they want to examine me? What if they see my wings? Would they show up on an x-ray? I shudder. Oh my God, am I going to have to hide away from doctors for the rest of my life?

'No,' I say firmly to Luke, and smile weakly. 'I just want to go home.'

Luke nods and snuggles me closer. He's squeezing my painful ribs but I don't complain. I just like being held. Luke may be thin and lanky, but he feels soft and warm, like a huge fleecy scarf wrapped around me.

Then a sickening memory materializes in my head. My little cat. My poor little cat. His brutal terrier dog killed Jelly Tot. A little sob escapes as I remember my lovely little ginger and white cat. She was so gentle, would never hurt a fly. She never even chased mice or birds, not ever. She was such a sweet little cat. She slept on my bed every night from the day Dad brought her home, and whenever I put my hand out in the night I'd feel her there all warm and curly and purry. I start to cry again.

'He killed my cat, Luke,' I wail. 'Jasper's dog killed my Jelly Tot.' The tears flow down my cheeks and I'm crying like a baby. Luke wipes my cheek and hugs me closer. 'And he said other stuff,' I gasp between sobs, 'about my dad, he said my dad was still alive. What did he mean, Luke?'

He bends down and kisses me lightly on the top of my head. We sit there for a long time, both silently processing everything that's happened.

'I don't know,' he says, after a while. I've almost forgotten what he's responding to. 'But if your dad's still alive, we'll find him.'

I struggle to sit up but everywhere hurts, and I still feel weak and shaky. Luke takes a bottle of water out of his bag, twists the top off and holds it to my lips. I take a greedy gulp and some of it dribbles down my chin.

'We need to get you back home before it goes too cool,' he says, and helps me to my feet. We begin to pick our way through the woods, towards home. Luke has his arm around my shoulder and is guiding me. It really hurts because that's where Jasper grasped me. But the pain is good compared with everything else that's happened this evening.

I wonder what he would've done with me. You know, afterwards. Perhaps he would have tried to kill me or something? And what about Sasha – did she lead me into his trap? Just like the night at the cinema, and the green drink. They're just evil, both of them.

'That creep Jasper and his vile sister should've never been born!' I mutter.

Luke is quiet and I suddenly remember about him and Sasha, I feel terrible, and after he's been so sweet to me.

'I'm *so* sorry, Luke. That was insensitive of me.' I could kick myself.

Luke screws up his face, looking puzzled. 'What do you mean, why should I care what you say about them?'

'I'm sorry, I shouldn't have mentioned Sasha's name.' I feel really bad, why did I mention Sasha. After all, I have no hold over Luke.

'What do you mean? It's *you* she was nasty to. I could have killed her that last day at school when she upset you. That's why I got away quick after the exam, I wanted to thump her. And I don't hit girls. At least I got the chance to belt her disgusting brother.'

'No I don't mean what Sasha said to me, I'm talking about you and Sasha. She told me that you went with her, you know, slept with her.'

I can't meet his eyes, and I have no idea how he's going to react. But it's out there now. It's been said. I bite my lip and glance up at him.

'What?'

Luke looks like he doesn't know whether to laugh or explode. He pushes me away from him, places a hand on each shoulder, forcing me to look at him.

'What are you talking about?' His eyes flash with anger.

Oh. *Ooops.*

'Well…Sasha *said*…' I splutter. 'She told me she had sex with you. She said you were obsessed with her.' Well, I might as well just say it now, even though I can tell he's really angry with me. Me and my big mouth.

Luke shakes me lightly on the shoulders and his eyes bore into me.

'First of all, Sasha is vain, conniving and twisted, and I wouldn't go near her if she was the last girl on the planet. Second of all, she's my *cousin*.'

'Oh? Oh.' *Oh.*

'Sasha and Jasper are my cousins. But to be honest it's not something I'm likely to broadcast, I can't stand them. Any of them. Jasper, Sasha and their vile father Ethan.'

Luke's almost breathless with rage. 'And no, just to be clear, I've never slept with Sasha.' He's still breathing hard, but his eyes soften.

'Scarlett, just for the record, I've never had sex with *anybody*.'

Chapter Twenty

It's barely dawn the following morning and I'm back in the woods. I duck straight into the Fae world without hesitation. It's so easy now I know how. As I pass through the membrane I can detect the split second when the everyday world dissolves into the Fae world, like swimming through a muddy ditch into a lake of sparkling mineral water.

Eldridge is close by, collecting wood. I can see him better today, my eyes must be getting used to the brightness.

He's wearing the same red shorts that he wore yesterday and I wonder about their laundry arrangements. Typical teenage boy I suppose. Typical except for his wings. They sit high on his back between his shoulder blades. They're quite short, hardly reach his shoulders. As he works they flicker and quiver, moving so quickly that they remind me of a shimmering halo.

'Hello,' I say shyly and he spins around. I'm struck by how strong and toned his body is for a boy of fifteen. He looks a lot like his sister except for the slightly darker skin. He smiles suddenly and his face lights up. His amber eyes twinkle beneath his thick black lashes. He has a sooty mark over his forehead and a smear down one cheek.

'Where's Ainsel?' I say.

Eldridge nods his head past my right shoulder and I turn to see Ainsel dancing towards me.

We both smile in greeting and she wraps her arms around my shoulders, lifting herself off the ground and I notice she's as light as a feather. We both sit down beneath the oak tree and I kick off my shoes, I'm surprised to see Eldridge come over and sit quite close to us.

Ainsel folds her wings skilfully, tucking them up behind her. They fold into almost nothing, they are so fine and delicate. I want to touch them, but I daren't.

She looks almost like a real person, except for her dress sense. Or lack of it. Both Ainsel and Eldridge look like they've forgotten to get dressed. Their clothes barely cover them, although I'm getting used to Ainsel's virtual nudity now. In fact I think it might be nice to take a few clothes off myself. *Don't be stupid.* What do they do if it's cold? Or is it warm and sunny all the time?

'Where are the clouds?' I say out loud, realising that the sky was cloudy earlier in my world, but when I came through to the Fae world is was immediately clear and pure deep blue. 'And rain and wind? Do you get weather?'

'We don't get clouds because our air is so pure. Most of your clouds are created by the smog rising into the air and collecting, then falling back to the ground as mucky rain.'

'It's *not* mucky.'

'Yes, it is,' she argues, her wings twitching with annoyance, she pulls at her ear and I laugh. She glares at me.

'The wind is caused by the air feeling so suffocated that it has to move around quickly.'

'You don't have wind?' My eyes open wide in astonishment.

'Well of course we have air movement, it has to move around or it would become stale. And there's moisture in the air, it falls as dew from the rivers and lakes. We get a kind of rainfall but you wouldn't recognise it as such, it's more like a mist, like a cool steam. But the air movement is like a gentle breeze, strong enough to move the leaves, air the grass and dry the dew.'

'Do you get night and day?' I say. 'Does it ever go dark?'

I hear Eldridge snort and without even looking at him I know he's rolling his eyes. Ainsel shoots him a warning look.

'We live on planet Earth just like you.' Ainsel explains slowly to me, like you would to a small child. 'So the Earth still goes round the Sun and we get night and day just like you.' Ainsel looks amused, but I hear Eldridge sigh loudly, for my benefit. I turn to look at him and he glares back obnoxiously. *He thinks I'm stupid.*

He suddenly jumps up and runs lightly over to a shrub just behind me, and plonks back down. I feel uncomfortable with him sitting so close. His face is mostly hidden by the foliage but I still turn away so he isn't in my line of vision. Who wants to look at a half-naked obnoxious Elf?

His bare feet are just a few inches from my hand. I steal a glance at them out of the corner of my eye. I find myself fascinated by his toes. Clean. Well, a bit dusty. But kind of, well, nice feet. Cute stubby toes. My fingers play with my hair whilst I watch his little toes wriggling. Mesmerised. Then his toes dig into the sand and flick upwards; a mist of fine sand sprays into my face and stings my eyes. I yell and shut my eyes tightly, they water and I reach in my pocket for my hanky. I can hear him chuckling. *Unbelievable.*

'Stupid Elf!' I shout.

'In fact,' Ainsel continues as though there's been no interruption, 'some colours in your world have disappeared because of the smog. For instance this colour here...' She stoops and plucks a flower from a shrub.

'The true colour of this flower is *primo*. I'll bet you've never seen *that* colour before.'

I let out a little laugh. 'Primo?' I peer at the little flower, and look away quickly as my eyes sting. I jump as Ainsel suddenly leaps into the air, light as a feather, her wings shimmering against the deep blue sky.

'Look, here it is again!' she says, pointing a dainty finger to a flower on a nearby tree.

'My eyes are still hurting from the sand in my eyes!' I glare at Eldridge.

'No, it's because the colour is too pure for your eyes,' Ainsel says. 'You have to get used to it. Use your peripheral vision until your eyes get used to it, or you'll harm your eyesight.'

I look at the flower cautiously. I can't understand what I'm looking at. The colour is nothing I've ever seen before, it isn't red or blue, there's no yellow. It's a completely different colour, amazing. Now I can see this particular colour all over the woods. Primo. I can see that there's some of the colour in the oak tree's leaves, and also in other trees and flowers. Different variations of the colour.

'That's awesome!' I breathe, thinking about Luke and suddenly wanting to show him this. Maybe this is what's missing from his life, his painting. No wonder he's been striving to create something else, another type of colour. Many centuries ago this colour was part of our life. And now we can't see it at all. I have a really strong need to show Luke the Fae world.

'This is totally different from anything I've ever seen before,' I say. I study everything all around me, occasionally having to shield my eyes from the blaze of colour.

'Yeah,' says Ainsel looking pleased that she's impressed me, 'you thought there were only three primary colours, but there are four – red, yellow, blue and primo. In fact primo was the original first prime colour, which is why prime colours are called prime colours, from primo. But as it hasn't been seen in the everyday world for hundreds of years, people have forgotten about it.'

I feel excited. 'So that's why the colours look so different here. There's a whole different range of colours, primo mixed with red, primo mixed with blue, primo mixed...'

Eldridge snorts again, and rolls over onto his front, facing away from us so I'm looking at the back of his head. He plucks a blade of grass and blows hard on it, making a haunting screeching wailing sound. I jump. Ainsel seems oblivious to his childish, attention-seeking behaviour, and continues talking. 'Are you in Transition yet?'

'What?' My mouth must have dropped open because she peers inside, seeming to count my teeth.

'Well stop me if you disagree,' she sings out, 'but I'm guessing that you must be about sixteen or seventeen, so you are probably going through Transition by now?'

I stare. 'What?' I say again. 'What's Transition?'

'Oh my God, you really know nothing do you?'

She pauses dramatically for effect, but when I don't respond she continues, 'We Fae have our wings and gifts from babies, but Fae *Hybrids* are just everyday people until they reach sixteen, and then they go through Transition, and develop into a full-Fae. Transition can last anything up to two years. That's when the Hybrid's wings develop and strengthen. You get your Fae strength and stuff.'

I cross my legs and shuffle nervously.

'Stuff?' I hardly dare ask.

'Well, y'know, gifts and stuff. We all have a gift, some Fae can heal, some can see into the future, and we all have this really impressive strength. Whatever.'

That strength. That must be why I was able to beat up Jasper. 'Oh!' It's starting to make sense now.

'Oh, and the sex stuff too.'

She has my full attention now. 'Sex stuff?'

'Yeah.' Her face breaks into a wide mischievous grin and she jumps up into the air, landing gracefully on her feet, does a twirl and announces, lifting her arms into the air, 'We, the Fae people are sex Gods and Goddesses!' She looks over at me with a knowing look. 'And it all starts for you at Transition. It's a *wild* time.'

Ainsel giggles and Eldridge snorts again. I feel the ground sway. I close my eyes until the feeling has passed. When I open them, Ainsel's nose is inches from my face and I jump.

'So are you sixteen yet?'

'Yes, I was sixteen last week.'

I feel myself blush bright red. I hear a boy laugh. I turn to glare at Eldridge but am astonished to see another boy lying in the grass quite close. Too close. Maybe ten feet away. He looks a little older, maybe eighteen or nineteen. And he's staring right at me.

It takes me a moment to get my breath. He's lying on his back with his hands clasped behind his head. Watching me. *How long has he been there?* His skin is dark brown and toned, and there are marks on his arms, patterns, like a tribal tattoo. He has a shadow of dark hair shaved very short. His eyes are deep and intense, almost black. His lips are thick, round and full, and his gaze blatantly lustful. *Oh God.* I feel naked, as though with a single look he has stripped me of all my clothes and I'm sitting naked in the grass. He makes me wish I was naked. I want to be naked. *Oh my God stop it.* I feel a heat beginning to smoulder deep within me. My skin tingles and my muscles tighten inside. I don't know why I'm reacting this way. I feel myself blush, my face, my neck, like a warm sweet caramel being poured over my skin, downwards, down into my breasts. *Stop it.* But I can't tear my eyes away from his; he's holding me in his gaze. What a strange boy. *But quite beautiful, in a boy sort of way.*

Finally he breaks eye contact, leaps to his feet and turns away from me. He has the most stunning wings, not large, shimmering and quivering with vibrant colour, strong, they suddenly unfold like a silver pulsating canopy. I feel a dart of excitement. A man with wings. I swallow hard. My heart is hammering in my chest. He looks back at me and smiles, lighting up his whole face and setting fire to my insides, my breath hitches. And then he speeds off into the woods like a graceful streak of liquid light, leaving a warm ache though my body from head to toe. I feel my breathing coming in gasps and I realise I've been holding my breath. *What was that?* Elf. Fairy. I watch him as he disappears, flitting between the trees.

'Orion,' Ainsel murmurs, smiling knowingly. 'You fancy him.'

'I do not!' I spit, and then sniff, astonished at how passionate that came out. 'Rubbish.'

'It's not your fault,' Ainsel says. 'We are all highly sexual around Transition, and he's just showing you how it can work. Orion's toying with you. He means no harm. But he could have you any time he likes, and he knows it.'

'No he could NOT!' I snap, not very convincingly.

Ainsel laughs and I glare at her. She doesn't even know me. How can she say things like that?

'NEVER!' I say. 'Never. We don't have such a casual attitude towards sex. It's disgusting.' In my head I can hear Sasha's 'Sandra Dee' skit of me. Maybe it's true, maybe I really am frigid like Sasha said. My cheeks smart just thinking about it.

'Don't worry,' Ainsel says, 'once you go into Transition, you won't feel so prudish. It's really not that big a deal, it's only sex.'

Chapter Twenty-One

'So what's *your* special gift?' I say to Ainsel, anxious to change the subject. I don't feel comfortable talking about sex in such a casual way. *Sandra Dee.*

'Both Eldridge and I are Travellers. We can space-hop,' says Ainsel.

'Space-hop?' I screw my face as an image of a large orange bouncy ball with a painted face pops into my head.

'That's what we do. Space-hop. We can literally disappear…' She laughs. I jump in shock as I'm suddenly staring at thin air, she's vanished and I didn't even see her go. I hear her voice behind me, I spin round and Ainsel's walking out of the woods towards me. '…and reappear wherever we like. So we can travel around wherever we like within the Fae world. It took me a while to perfect it, though. We just disappear and then think ourselves to reappear in another place. It's quite useful if you want to get somewhere fast and can't be bothered walking or flying.'

'Yeah, like you'd ever get tired of flying!' I laugh.

Ainsel glares at me and her wings twitch just like Jelly Tot's tail used to when she was cross. I don't know what to make of her. *Is she making fun of me?* It sounds like something from Enid Blyton's Magic Faraway Tree.

'So what's the point in that anyway? Being able to jump about the place?'

'We protect the Fae world!' she announces proudly. 'That's our job. If there's any danger, or somebody comes through the membrane who shouldn't, we can hop deeper into the woods really quickly, and warn the other Fae.'

I remember the last time Ainsel spoke of danger, she mentioned Black-Wings. When she went all scary and crouched down like a tiger. And also Jasper's reaction when I called him a Black-Wing. And the image of those black slimy things on his back. What does it mean? I don't want to mention Black-Wings to her, not after last time. I daren't ask her. I daren't. I mustn't. Not until I know her a bit better. I'll have to find out some other way. I really mustn't mention Black-Wings.

'Ainsel, what are Black-Wings?' I hear myself say, and brace myself, expecting her to react. But she just looks right through me, as if she hasn't heard.

'We can travel great distances in just a second, we can hop *anywhere* within the Fae membrane. And we can carry people with us, like a transport service. We can take other Fae right to the other side of the Fae world!'

'So not that far at all then,' I snort derisively. 'The Fae world's only a mile or two wide.' I laugh rather rudely. Ainsel glares at me and scratches her head, then tugs at her ear quite aggressively.

'Actually,' Eldridge pipes up loudly, 'I think you'll find that the Fae world is at least fifty lengths wide, and twice as deep.'

I spin round, when did he get back?

'Fifty lengths? What's a *length*?' I say, with my hands on my hip. 'I know how big Gossamer Woods is, I've seen it on the map, and it's two miles in diameter or thereabouts.'

'Well it's the *thereabouts* that makes the difference,' says Eldridge glaring at me. 'The Lakes and Mountains are only one length away and that doesn't even go half way into the centre. And it's *far* bigger on the inside than the outside, don't you know anything?' And he promptly disappears in a puff of fairy dust as though to demonstrate his great talent.

I sigh loudly but don't bother to argue. *Lakes and Mountains indeed*. They clearly live such a sheltered life they have no idea what a lake or a mountain is. Their 'Lake' is probably a garden pond, and the 'Mountain'…well it's probably an ant-hill.

'So how many Fae people live in these woods?' I ask Ainsel. There can't be that many Fae people squashed into this little woodland.

'One thousand, nine hundred and fifty-six,' says Ainsel.

I laugh, and Ainsel scowls and pulls at her ear. She turns her back on me.

'Oh, plenty of space for everybody then!' I say sarcastically.

'Oh yes,' she says, spinning back to face me, the sarcasm lost on her. 'We're fairly scattered about really, each Fae family has a large cabin. There are nearly a thousand cabins in total.'

She actually looks as if she believes it to be true. I'm honestly beginning to wonder if she can even count. Pur-lease, a thousand cabins in these woods? *I don't think so.*

'Do you go to school?' I say. Clearly they've never learnt about basic maths. After all, the woods are roughly circular, about two miles in diameter, so even if they were to walk all around the outer circumference of the woods they would only be walking about, what, I screw my nose up while I do the quick calculation in my head, about six miles. I smile at the image of a whole family squeezed into a tiny garden shed, and lots of sheds all lined up together like beach huts.

'No'—Ainsel shakes her head—'we don't *need* school.'

'Everybody needs to learn,' I say rudely.

'We learn,' a voice says, right behind my right ear and I spin round. Eldridge again.

'Oh *you're* back.'

'Never went away,' he snorts. I'm starting to feel giddy with all the coming and going.

'Of course we learn,' Ainsel says, as I turn my back on Eldridge. 'We learn everything we need to know from nature, from our surroundings. Nature is full of mathematical solutions, scientific experiments, geological masterpieces...they all intermingle, they're all part of the same theory, they're connected by nature. You can't learn one without understanding the other. We don't have to get on an aeroplane to know how to fly. We don't have to go to Florida to experience pure sunshine and we don't have to get in a car and drive for miles to find pure beauty.'

But you can't count.

Eldridge has moved round and is now sitting beside Ainsel, staring at me insolently. *Ignore him.* Ainsel is still patiently trying to explain.

'You sit in a classroom and study a diagram of a leaf in a book, when you could go outside and learn from the tree. The tree will teach you all you need to know. Nature knows about symmetry. Nature is balanced, plants and animals are balanced – you are exactly the same on the left as the right. More or less.'

She leans forward and peers rudely at a spot on my cheek. I cover it self-consciously with my hand. *I should put gel on that tonight.*

'Some animals learn to look like their surroundings, camouflage, take this butterfly...'

I frown. What butterfly?

Ainsel reaches out and plucks a flower from a nearby clump of flowers growing from the earth close to her. As she holds the flower out to me, it flaps its wings and flutters away into the sky.

'Oh my God!'

Ainsel smiles and then narrows her eyes.

'The butterfly didn't learn about camouflage from a book. You learn about the Sun, Moon and stars from a television programme. We look upwards, we know which star is going to be where, and we know why – you can't learn that from looking at a TV screen. We can read the sky, we can see, sense, any asteroids long before your scientific telescopes have even been switched on...'

'Ainsel, what are Black-Wings?' I interrupt her mid-flow; somehow I can't wait any longer. Her reluctance to tell me is just igniting my curiosity. She ignores me and continues talking, but I'm only half listening now. Patience isn't my thing.

'We watch and listen, and we also learn through our people, the knowledge is passed down through generations of Fae.' Ainsel lightly touches her lips, her ears, and then her heart. 'It's inside us, *this* is where learning begins. And it's inside *you* too – you just have to release it.'

'Yeah yeah, but what's a *Black-Wing*?'

'So whilst you are watching a nature programme on TV, we're watching it happen in real life.'

'I see your point,' I say a little too curtly, 'but what's *Black-Wing*, what does that mean?' I say more softly, moving closer to Ainsel. 'Please?'

Ainsel looks away and studies a leaf that is hanging low on a nearby tree. 'What?' she says. Like she's playing for time.

'Please? I don't understand. Everything's gone crazy since my dad went missing. And I've just found out my mother was Fae and I think she may still live here, and I keep having these strange dreams, and—'

'Your father's missing?' Ainsel says, looking alarmed. I have her full attention now.

'Please Ainsel, what does Black-Wing mean?'

Ainsel looks uncomfortable, she looks at Eldridge and he looks back at her. I hold my breath. Someone might finally tell me what is going on.

Ainsel studies my face, my expression. She looks haunted.

'What?' I look around cautiously. 'What?'

Why won't they answer my question? I quickly open my bag and scratch around inside it. My fingers fold around a sheet of paper and I drag it out, nearly ripping it on the zip of my bag. I hold it out to her and poke the page with my finger.

'Look!' I point to my father's handwriting at the top of the sheet of paper. 'Look, this is one of the last things my dad wrote before he disappeared. On the top of this sheet. *Shadow Fae.* That must be something to do with the Fae world?'

I hear a sharp intake of breath.

'Put that away, quickly,' pleads Ainsel, pushing the sheet of paper back towards me, 'please, don't show that to anybody. You have to get rid of it.'

I don't understand. They haven't answered my question at all. *What does it all mean?*

'Scarlett, you ask about the Black-Wings? You want to know what the Black-Wings are? And then you show us *this*?' She pokes her finger at the paper. I pull it away from her quickly. She looks so angry. I don't know what she means. What any of this means. She's glaring at me.

'What?' I say.

'The Black-Wings *are* the Shadow Fae,' blurts Eldridge, and his eyes narrow suspiciously, watching my reaction carefully. Oh my God. *Oh my God.*

'Ainsel, please, please I'm not messing around, this is important. I need to know. If the Black-Wings are dangerous I need to know why. They seem to be mixed up in all my problems at the moment. First of all Dad disappearing. And then this boy who has been trying to hurt me, he went ballistic when I accidentally called him a Black-Wing.'

Ainsel screws her face up in a question.

'Oh, it was after you went peculiar the other day, and mentioned Black-Wings. It was on my mind and I accidentally...well anyway he went crazy and then I saw that he had this black stuff on his back. Like black wings.'

Ainsel's face clouds over fearfully. 'What do you need to know?' she whispers.

'I really need to know about the Black-Wings.'

Ainsel puts her arm hesitantly around my shoulder. Her eyes are just inches from mine and she looks deadly serious.

'There are no Black-Wings left,' she whispers, 'so you must be mistaken about the boy with the black wings.'

'If there are no Black-Wings left, why are we whispering?'

Ainsel exhales noisily. I flop down into the grass, suddenly exhausted. I'm fighting back my frustration. Ainsel lies down next to me, so close we are touching, our legs stretched out in front of us and our bare toes wriggling. Her hands intertwine with mine, I can't be sure where Ainsel ends and I begin. I sigh in frustration.

Ainsel suddenly sits up and pulls her legs up close to her. I sit up too, and mirror her posture. Eldridge is watching Ainsel closely, he suddenly bottom-shuffles forward and peers at me.

'You say your mother is Fae and she lives here in Gossamer Woods?' he says.

'Yes, I think so. She'll be about thirty-two now. She has red hair like mine. Her name is Tate, or Tatham.'

Eldridge and Ainsel lock eyes for a long moment, and then they both stare back at me, two identical sets of big amber eyes. They both lean forward and peer at my face. Both with their faces very close to mine as though they're studying an insect. I feel uncomfortable. Has my spot grown huge or something?

Ainsel slowly shuffles round behind me and lifts up my t-shirt. I jump in surprise. Eldridge is there too, staring at my back. I hear them both gasp.

They pull my t-shirt back down and bottom-shuffle back round to the front. Clearly the examination is over, I'm not sure if I've passed the test or not. Their faces are pale and drawn, and very serious. Everything is deathly quiet all of a sudden, as though the whole of the Fae world has come to a standstill.

'Blimey,' says Ainsel.

'Blimey,' says Eldridge.

They're both staring at me with their mouths open.

'What?'

They look at each other, and prod each other as though compelling each other to speak. Finally Ainsel speaks.

'You're Tate's daughter.'

'Yeah, I *know*.'

'But you're *Tate's* daughter.'

'Yes. But how can you tell that from looking at my back?'

'Your tattoo.'

'I don't have a tattoo.'

'Yes you do – your wing mark. Tate put that on your back after you were born, so that she would know you again. For sure.'

'Oh!' I swallow hard. They know Tate. They actually know my mother. That's where my wing marks came from. It's a tattoo. *A tattoo?*

'My mother had a tattoo put on a newborn baby? With needles and stuff?'

'No, no,' says Ainsel quickly, 'It's just henna soaked in ethereal. It's harmless but it works like a permanent tattoo. Quite a few Fae have them.'

I nod, remembering Orion, the sexy boy. He had tattoos on his arms.

'What's she like?' I say, shyly.

'Who?' says Ainsel.

'Tate' —I swallow hard—'my mother.' Those words sound so strange on my lips.

'She's kind of sweet and funny. And beautiful.' Ainsel scowls. 'Like you.'

'Can I meet her?' I say meekly, feeling a blush come to my face.

'Who?'

'Tate. My mother.' A shiver goes down my spine again as I say it and my heart is pounding in my chest. I'm going to meet my mother. Ainsel and Eldridge look at each other again. *For goodness sake.*

Eldridge speaks, Ainsel just stares. 'Tate's gone.'

I want to scream. What are they talking about?

'What do you mean, *where's* she gone?'

They both look at each other and then stare at me again. 'Well that's what we were hoping *you'd* tell *us*.'

'I don't *know* where she is, I've only just found out she's my mother!' I say, almost shout.

'We're not sure where she is either,' Ainsel says quickly. 'She disappeared about three months ago. We've hunted everywhere. She's just not here anymore.'

Chapter Twenty-One

An icy fear creeps over me.

'Is it likely that she's been harmed by the Shadow Fae? The Black-Wings?' I ask urgently. 'For some reason?'

'Why, what do you know?' asks Ainsel suspiciously.

'I don't know ANYTHING,' I'm shouting now. 'I keep TELLING you!'

'OKAY, okay,' says Ainsel quickly, and Eldridge nods to her.

'Okay, we'll tell you what we know about the Black-Wings.' She shuffles back so that she's leaning against the great trunk of the oak tree.

'So Black-Wings are another name for Shadow Fae?' I say.

'We call Black-Wings the Shadow Fae because they're kind of our archenemies. But they aren't Fae at all. They're like the exact opposite to us. But they can exist pretty much in the Fae world or in the everyday world,' says Eldridge.

'But they *hate* us,' pipes up Ainsel. 'The one thing on the Black-Wing's mind is to destroy the Fae. They've tried it time and time again through the generations. But over the last hundred years or so, we've managed to contain them, even started to wipe them out. The very last Black-Wing in these woods was called Zoran. He was evil. He lived many years ago. He kidnapped a young Fae Hybrid girl and held her captive. She was only sixteen.'

'Oh God that's awful, poor girl. The same age as me.'

'But Zoran was no match for Layla,' Eldridge interjects proudly.

Both Ainsel and Eldridge turn to look at me with strange expressions on their faces.

'Layla? Was she the girl who was kidnapped?'

Ainsel sighs.

'Layla is our *queen*, she's the strongest, wisest and most powerful Fae in the whole of our world.' Ainsel says this so proudly it brings a tear to my eye, I've no idea why.

'Wow, you have a queen?' I say, and Ainsel looks at me oddly.

'Layla *killed* Zoran, and freed the Fae girl,' says Eldridge excitedly. The two sweet Fae teenagers beam at me happily, two sets of pearl teeth, two pairs of honey-coloured eyes.

'So if Zoran was the last Black-Wing, and Layla killed him, then there shouldn't be any more Black-Wings then?' I say, puzzled.

'Well that's just it. When Layla rescued the kidnapped Fae girl, she was pregnant with Zoran's baby.'

'Oh, no. Poor girl.'

'But the baby died soon after birth.'

'Oh no! That's terrible!'

'No not really. There's no place for a Black-Wing baby in the Fae world.'

'So where's the Fae girl now, the one who had the Black-Wing baby?'

'Pandora went back to live in the everyday world.'

I gulp. I'm suddenly breathing very quickly and I feel a little dizzy. Oh my God that's where Pandora comes into all this. So Pandora is the kidnapped Fae girl. And her Black-Wing baby didn't die. Of course it didn't. The Black-Wing baby grew up to have two children called Jasper and Sasha.

Ainsel and Eldridge are looking at me expectantly.

'Do you know for *sure* that the Black-Wing baby died?' I say.

Ainsel and Eldridge glance at one another, and then shake their heads.

'There's a grave, where the baby was supposed to be buried. Many years ago. We were told never to go near it. Never to touch it. But recently...well after Tate disappeared...some of the Fae had a bad feeling. Just a feeling. And one of the Fae decided to look. Just to make sure. And when they dug up the grave...it was empty. There was no baby there. So we don't know for absolute sure that the Black-Wing baby died.'

Oh God. I stare off into the distance. What do I say? I have to tell them.

'Well,' I say, with a loud sigh, 'I think the Black-Wing baby *didn't* die. I'm fairly sure his name is Ethan Curnow and he lives in the everyday world, in a large house on the edge of the woods. He's very wealthy and he has two children, a boy and a girl.'

Ainsel and Eldridge don't look at all surprised. They both nod.

I quickly try to work things out in my head. Luke's their cousin, he can't be a Black-Wing, he's no blood relation to Ethan. No wonder Luke hates them so much. He said that his Uncle Ethan was vile. So Sasha's a Black-Wing too? I wonder if she knows. She's only just turned sixteen so won't have started to get her wings yet. Oh my God, she'll hate it if she gets those horrible black slimy shrivelled wings.

'Is Layla still alive? Your queen?' I say.

'Yes, Layla's quite frail now, but she lives at the Palace, deep in the centre of the woods where we can protect her,' says Ainsel. 'She'll be anxious to meet you, Scarlett.'

'Me?' I say, my face creasing with puzzlement.

Why would the Fae Queen want to meet me?

Ainsel's looking at me with her head at an angle, with shining eyes and a mischievous look.

'What?' I say.

Eldridge giggles.

'What?' I say again, feeling a bit stupid.

'Layla's your grandmother,' Ainsel blurts.

My eyes open wide. Ainsel and Eldridge look like two nodding dogs in the back of a car. I'm silent for a long moment and they continue to stare at me. Like they're waiting for the penny to drop. Am I being dim or something? What have I missed?

And then it clicks. Oh my God. Oh my God.

'I'm related to the Fae Queen?'

Ainsel and Eldridge are laughing.

'Stop it!' I shout. 'What are you laughing at?'

'You still don't get it do you?' says Ainsel.

Ainsel springs lightly to her feet. Eldridge stands next to her. As though to attention. I tilt my head upwards so that I can see them. *What are they doing?* They are still giggling like a pair of little kids. I feel uncomfortable.

'What are you doing?' I say.

Ainsel carefully places one foot behind the other, Eldridge puts one arm across his chest and the other behind his back, and together in perfect timing, Ainsel curtseys and Eldridge bows.

'Welcome to the Fae world, *Princess Scarlett*!'

'What?'

Oh my God. Oh my God. *Oh my God.*

'Oh yes very funny!' I say. 'You can stop laughing now.'

It just gets better. I was just getting used to being a fairy. *Now I'm a bloody fairy princess?*

Chapter Twenty-Two

I need to speak to Pandora.

She said I could trust her so I'm going to take her at her word.

And I'm going to run there, to Luke's house. Just for the exercise. Because exercise is good, right? And I've been neglecting my body since the exams started, spending so much time studying I'm not as active as I'd normally be. Because normally I'd be out and about, running or doing some other activity, well, every few days really. Well at least once a week. When I could. And if I missed a week I'd do a bit more to make up...

Okay, okay I almost never do exercise out of school. Yes, I know I should, but I don't. But it's never too late to start is it? I've been thinking a lot about, you know, exercise and running and...

Okay, okay, I admit it. I really want to try out my new muscles. It's sort of like a new toy, I can't stop thinking about it, how it felt the other day when I was running from Jasper. I was able to run like the wind. My body has changed so much, I have really toned-looking muscles and the thighs of a seasoned athlete, my calves are pure muscle. But not in a bad way, it looks amazing.

I can say that can't I, just to myself?

And I'll tell you a secret...I'm super-strong! I was messing with this piece of tree branch I found lying in the garden, and it just snapped like a twig! So I found this big old metal hinge – the type you put on garden gates. And it just bent in my hands! Like it was a pipe cleaner or a bit of wire.

So I thought I'd have a go at running again, just jog over to Luke's house to see if his gran's there. I don't know how much Luke knows about all the Black-Wing stuff, or even the Fae stuff, so I need to be careful what I say in front of him.

I pull on my old Lycra shorts and they stretch really tight over my thighs. Hmm, they're going to split. I wriggle out of them and step into my denim shorts. They look rather filled out too, but quite sexy if I'm honest.

I squeeze into a sports top and drag it down over my bra, it's a bit short and skimpy and it keeps riding up. It makes me look, well, kind of curvy. But it's no worse than Sasha wears. I can't believe I'm comparing myself to *Sasha*. In fact I can't believe how different I look now. Usually my t-shirts just hang there, with no shape, but – well let's say it isn't hanging now. My bras are a little snug, so I borrowed a couple of old ones from Maggie's drawer, she probably won't miss them.

I pop my trainers on and I'm ready. I stand in front of the mirror, and turn this way and that. Blimey.

I pull my hair back and tie it up at the back, feeding it through my baseball cap like they do in America. *Wow.* I can't believe how conceited I'm becoming.

I open the front door and look down the path, suddenly feeling self-conscious. Our old postman is sorting out the mail on his bicycle at my gate. He glances up as I bang the front door closed. He double-takes as though he's seen something unexpected, then stares barefaced at my chest as I approach. *Pervert.* As he goes to open our gate, his eyes on my bottom, he catches his foot on the bike pedal, yanking the bike, which clatters down the wall, his post-bag vomits its contents across the pavement and Mr Postman falls splat on top of his bike.

I begin to jog along the pavement, slowly. My muscles feel so tight and strong. I go a little faster, until I'm bounding along at a normal pace, really enjoying the breeze whipping past my cheeks, my hair is bobbing from side to side, my breathing is even and I'm not really pushing myself. Not like at school when we were competing against the others on the track. It's nice to just be jogging along, normal pace.

In fact there's really quite a breeze getting up now, I can feel the cool air on my face. My eyeballs feel cold.

And then I notice. People are looking at me. But not in a good way. I glance down, are my shorts half way down my legs or something? Nope. I'm jogging alongside the town bus, it's driving really slowly today, perhaps there's a traffic accident ahead, I wonder what it is? A woman inside the bus is staring at me in a weird way, I smile at her and wave, and she looks panic-stricken. Strange, perhaps she's unwell. The scenery seems to be whizzing past me, I'm really getting the hang of this now, quite enjoying it. Perhaps I should speed up.

But hang on, actually the cars aren't going that slowly, I've left the bus behind now and passed a couple of cars in front.

Oh My God, it's me.

I'm overtaking the cars. *Oops.* I'm running faster than the cars. And I'm not even trying.

I slow right down and then stop, nearly trip over my feet. I lean over with my hands on my knees, pretending to anybody who's watching that I'm out of breathe. But the truth is, I've hardly broken into a sweat. And Luke's house is just around the corner. And I've run here in just under…it's only taken me four minutes. To run two miles. That's impossible, surely. That means I've been running at a speed of…well, fast anyway. And I wasn't even trying.

I'm thinking maybe I won't run in public any more. Better not to draw attention to myself like that again. I take off my baseball cap and shake my hair loose, try to walk sedately towards Luke's cottage, ignoring the stares. As I approach I pull my hair forward so that it covers my chest a little.

Luke's standing in his front garden, working on his painting, the foundations of his next masterpiece being baked onto his canvas by the early morning rays of the sun.

He looks up as I open the creaking front gate, and flashes me a smile.

'You look *great!*' he says, staring at my body. My stomach flips and I feel my cheeks slowly turning red.

'Are you okay? Ya know, after...Jasper,' he looks awkward.

'Yeah I'm fine.' I nod. 'I'm okay.'

'I heard he spent two days in hospital with concussion, he told them he ran into a door,' Luke says in a serious voice. I bite my lip, but I see the corner of his mouth twitch. And we both explode with laughter.

'Is your gran home?' I say, looking past him and through the open front door to his cottage.

'No, she got the bus into town, she'll be back after lunch, d'ya want her?'

'No, it's okay,' I say. 'It can wait.'

I have no idea whether he knows about the Fae world, or the Black-Wings. I don't want to say anything to him until I've spoken to his gran. And it can wait till later.

Luke plants his big painty paintbrush in a jar. He looks happy.

'What're you painting?' I say.

'You.'

'What?'

'Will you sit for me? In the woods. Please. That big painting I'm working on. There's something missing and I want to do some sketching and painting, try some things out. Experiment a bit, and I need a model. I want to capture the light coming through the trees; it was so awesome the other day when we were in the woods. Please?'

'Nude?' I say, anxiously. My heart is hammering.

There's silence and I glance up to see the look of amusement on his face. He has a cheeky twinkle in his eye. 'No, course not. Unless you're offering?'

I feel so stupid. What am I thinking? How embarrassing. Why did I say that? That's the bloody half-naked fairies putting stupid ideas like that in my head. I glance down at myself, old denim shorts and an old sports top that I'm bursting out of.

'Okay,' I say, 'of course I'll sit for you.'

'And the lighting's perfect today.' His attention's returned to his canvas.

I feel surprisingly comfortable with the thought of him painting me. In fact I'm looking forward to it. I've been so busy dashing about the place being beaten up and stuff in the last week I relish the thought of a day relaxing in the woods.

'Anyway we've plenty of time,' Luke says, his eyes twinkling in the sun. 'Let's have a drink.'

Luke brings some cans of Coke from the fridge and we sit out on the terrace chairs as we suck at our cans. As the ice-cold fizz quenches my thirst, Luke gulps down his drink as though he has been in the desert for weeks without water, I smile. I sigh loudly and relax back into my chair.

He's watching me through his floppy blond fringe. His hair's quite long – just short of his shoulders. His fringe is unruly, and partly obscures his eyes. I wonder if he spends hours trying to get that 'bed-head' messed up hairstyle. No, he definitely just falls out of bed and shakes his head, maybe runs his comb through his hair occasionally. I doubt he even owns a mirror; his clothes are a mishmash of different colours and textures, surf-style shorts, laced pumps, plain white shirt, denim jacket with the arms cut out.

But I like what I see. He has a lightly tanned complexion and dark lashes curling over those vivid blue eyes. His eyes look intense, sort of sulky, but they break into a twinkle when you least expect it. His teeth are perfect. His mouth, mmmm, soft pink lips.

Chapter Twenty-Three

An hour later, I'm wondering what kind of a bloody fool I am to be sitting in the damp grass with a swarm of flies worrying around my face, while Luke sketches me. He's brought a few different pads, a couple of blank canvas boards and a selection of paints and brushes.

I settle back into the soft mossy grass and try to ignore the insects. I watch Luke as he squeezes out some paint onto his palette; he comes alive when he's painting. There's a passion, eagerness, almost greed as he loads his brush with colour. He makes a few brush strokes at a time onto his canvas and then looks over at me. I wonder if he likes what he sees. His eyes are lapping my body, his fingers moulding my outline into the canvas, making love to his canvas, making love to my image.

He chats incessantly as he sketches; his shyness dissolves as his hands carve out the beginnings of the painting onto his board. His words clatter in and out of my thoughts, only compelling me to listen when I choose. His hair flops over his face as he works and he flicks his face up now and then to scrutinise me. He looks so intense as he works. I close my eyes and enjoy the feeling that his eyes are watching me, lapping over my body as I lie in the soft earth.

He told me to sit anywhere I liked, in a position I'd be comfortable to hold for half an hour at a time. So I flopped beneath the oak tree in a patch of grass. And decided to lie, rather than sit, so that I could relax and close my eyes, listening to the sounds of the forest, inhaling the scents and feeling the textures beneath my fingers and toes.

I feel warm and fuzzy inside. All sorts of thoughts are whirling through my head, I can feel the flicking on my ear again and I know that if I weaken even a little bit I could so very easily be drawn back, back into the mysterious Fae world. I sense a familiar fluttering in my spine as I settle deep into the soft blanket of moss. My fingers play with the hem of my t-shirt and it creeps upwards exposing my belly and midriff to the warm air, my skin tingles, the fluttering feeling deep in my spine strengthens.

'Scarlett,' I hear Luke's voice but he sounds fuzzy and faint. Although the sun is hurting my eyes, I can see him, poised with his canvas. 'Scarlett, I need to nip back to the cottage to get my hog brush, are you okay here for a bit or do you want to come with me? There's no way Jasper will be around today as he's still confined to the house with concussion.'

'Mmmm,' I say, feeling sexy and enjoying what my body's telling me, 'I'll just stay here and have a snooze.'

The sun's hot on my skin now, and my soft mossy mattress is warm. I can smell the forest, an earthy, herby aroma. I hear the faint rustling of movement, the familiar wafting of winged insects nearby and open my eyes. I know I'm in the Fae world, the colours are so intense they are painful.

My eyes are drawn to a figure moving between the trees a little way off. Orion. He's wearing thin white surf shorts. Nothing covering his deep brown torso. Again I'm struck by his dark beauty. He turns and looks at me, I glance around to see if Ainsel or Eldridge are here but I'm alone. Alone with this strange sexy elf boy. I'm confused, and strangely excited. My eyes are drawn back to him, partly hidden in the trees, flitting from tree to tree as though he's as light as a feather and yet strong. His muscles are well defined beneath his dark skin. I call out 'Hello' and he turns and smiles. I swallow hard. Although I can't see him clearly, I sense that he's expecting me.

I shuffle backwards until I'm leaning against a large root of the oak and close my eyes again. The sun beats against my eyelids and I watch a kaleidoscope of imagined colours dancing around my head. I feel movement and body heat very close and I sense that he's sitting on the ground beside me. My heart races a little, and my palms tingle. I can hear the trees rustling in the distance, and the birds are circling above. I smell a faint masculine, musky scent, I inhale deeply and a ripple of pleasure drips slowly through my body. The ground's warm and dry but a light cool whirl of air creeps beneath the fabric of my top. My spine tingles. I press my back against the ground and a bolt of pleasure shoots through my body. I feel him touch my hand and my back arches. I'm trembling, my whole body prickling with anticipation.

I open my eyes and turn to face him. *Wow.* He's even more striking close up, and a little older than I had thought, maybe nineteen or twenty. His skin is deep caramel and smooth with a dark shadow of stubble around his chin. His hair is shaved close to his head, perhaps three or four days' growth. His eyes are black and shamelessly lustful, framed by thick black lashes. He leans forward and I feel his breath on my cheek, his lips are full and fleshy. I almost convulse with excitement.

'Do you know my name?' he says, his voice deep and smooth.

'Yes,' I say, trying to control my breathing.

'Say it to me.'

'Orion.' I like the sound of his name on my lips. 'I'm Scarlett,' I add.

'I know.'

He leans close as he speaks, his face inches from mine. I feel his warm breath on my face. He drags his finger slowly up my arm causing a warm fuzzy ripple to run deep inside me, I press firmly against the hard tree root beneath me, a hot wave pulsates up and down my spine, increasing in intensity. I feel the fluttering start between my shoulder blades. Like my wings are going manic inside my body, crazy to be freed. I cannot peel my eyes away from his.

The world is silent for a brief moment as I drink in the image of his beautiful face and melt inside his jet black eyes, enjoying the sensations that are happening inside my body.

My face creases into a questioning frown and I open my mouth to speak, but then close it again. I think about Luke, and then immediately erase him from my mind. I frown.

Orion draws his finger across my forehead, removing the frown. I tremble with the softness of his touch, my skin tingles and I sink lower into the ground, my eyes never leaving his. I settle into the warm dry sand, feel like my clothes are too tight, like I'm bursting out of my top.

His eyes lap my body, exploring my tiny exposed waist, my rounded hips, which seem to be spreading and pulling at the stitches on my tiny shorts. I feel mixed up, dizzy, hot, my flesh sizzles with the warmth of my feelings. He leans over me, a perfect face, so smooth. His skin is warm and soft. His fingers brush my cheek. He lowers his face, his lips brush mine, surprisingly soft and cool, a bolt of electricity shoots through my body as he kisses me, gently at first and then less tenderly, urgently, pulling me in, his lips warm and wet, urgent, something inside me takes over and I snatch at him, pulling him down, losing myself.

He pulls away and looks at me, runs his thumb across my lips, I struggle to control my breathing. I don't know how but my top is up around my neck, the cool air on my skin, his firm muscles pressing gently against me. I can't quite read his expression. His hand lightly slips beneath the fabric of my bra, my skin tightens with anticipation, he murmurs gently as his fingers caress, I close my eyes and feel his lips gently follow his fingers. I'm tugging him down to me, the silky skin of his chest is pressed against me, warm and firm, and as his lips touch mine again, passionately, his lips open mine and I want to reach inside him, I can't get close enough. I can feel that he wants me, his kiss so sexy, a mixture of softness and urgency, my body aches in a way I can't understand, but he's starting to slip away…disappearing…just beyond my grasp…I feel confused. My eyes shoot wide open. Everything is groggy and dull. The sun has disappeared.

'Scarlett,' I hear my name, I smile softly and turn my head.

'Scarlett,' he says again a little more urgently.

'Scarlett!' he's shouting now. But not Orion, Luke, he's rushing over to me. I sit up quickly and look around, startled. But there's nobody else. Was I dreaming?

'Scarlett, are you all right?' Luke's eyes are boring into me.

'Er, yes, why?'

'I couldn't find you, you'd disappeared. You'd gone. I called you, walked back along the path a way looking for you. But when I got back here, there you were. Asleep. How did you *do* that?'

'I went for a walk.' I waft my arm vaguely in the opposite direction.

I'm confused. Luke is looking at me strangely, and I quickly pull my top down over my exposed skin, still damp from Orion's lips. *How embarrassing.*

I can't work out where reality ended and the dream began. Was it all just a fantasy?

I feel different, alive. I look around me, convinced I will see Orion moving through the trees. *I'm going mad.* I brush myself down, reach into my bag for my drink. I'm filled with a strange longing, an aching deep inside. As I bend over my bag, my top gapes, and I feel something brush my skin. I shudder and drop the bag. I vaguely feel something flutter past. It's very quick.

'Scarlett, you sure you're okay?' Luke's eyes are filled with concern. 'You're shivering.'

'I'm absolutely fine,' I say, but I can't stop trembling. I flop back beneath the tree, exhausted. 'I think I might have had too much sun or something. Did you get the brush you wanted from home?'

'No, I couldn't find it. I'll go into town tomorrow morning and get a new one. Come on I'll take you back now.' Luke glances around at his easel and paints spread across the floor of the forest. 'Do you still want to come back to mine and talk to Gran?'

'No, Luke, finish your painting, I'm fine now.' I take out my bottle of water and slug it down. I'll visit Pandora tomorrow morning when he's out buying his paints.

'Okay…if you're sure,' says Luke. 'I'll just finish this bit and then I'll walk you home.'

The sun is indistinct behind a bright white haze. Luke squeezes out some more paint and his brush teases out shapes in his thick oil paint, his fingers carving me into the painting, teasing his paint into my shape.

Suddenly a sharp pain ricochets across my brain and a white flash of light blinds me, As though I've been smacked over the head, my mind spins and my heart races with anxiety. Ow, ow, ow, that hurts, that's not a normal headache. It's more like one of those bloody migraines.

I close my eyes tight but the pain increases, my head is going to burst. I want to cry out but it's too intense. After a moment it begins to clear, I keep my eyes tight shut, the pain's diminishing, the bright white light's flickering, hazy, colours and shapes are forming. I try to open my eyes. The bright light shuts down and everything's dull. It's dark now, blackness, I can't see anything. I feel a waft of air, like a breeze from an open window, and my eyes are starting to adjust to the light.

Somehow I know I'm not in the woods any more, I'm back in that dream. At that place. The place where I saw Dad. I peer into the darkness, I know he's here. I can make things out now; it's a shed, or barn, same as before. And it's like I'm inside it again, I've been here before.

It's cold and dank. I can smell animals, hay, and something dirty like soot. I make my way carefully towards the back wall, where the desk was last time, where Dad was. I concentrate; I don't want to wake from this dream. Or whatever it is. I can see some horse paraphernalia. A man, and a woman, they're lying on the floor together, holding on to each other so tightly it's almost as though they think they might fall off the floor. But I can see clearly now, it really is Dad, *Dad! Dad!* I call out to him. Where is he, why can't he hear me? He looks asleep. I can see his wavy brown hair, it looks quite long, it's grown, and he needs a shave, he's dirty.

Just then Dad wakes and starts coughing, he's clutching his chest like his lungs hurt, coughing. The woman wakes and puts her hand on his arm as though to comfort him. *Dad!* But who's the woman? She's lying beside him. She has long hair, red hair. And, and green eyes.

Could it be, could it be... Oh my God, oh my God. It's the Angel Lady. It really is. It's the woman who used to visit me at night times. *It's the woman in my photo frame.* But she looks a little like me. Actually she looks a lot like me.

And she's looking straight at me. I gasp, I think she can see me. I stare back at her. Wow, that's my mother. But Oh my God, she really *can* see me, her mouth's moving. She's shaking her head, she's looking straight at me and seems to be mouthing something, I can't hear her voice, I strain to hear. But yes, I can hear, I can hear her; it's soft, so soft it's difficult to make out... 'Scarlett,' she's saying. It's very muffled, and I can't hear properly, there's a roaring sound in my ears, what's she saying now? I can see her mouth moving. I can hear her now, the Angel Lady. I can hear her voice, faint and weak.

'Scarlett, stay away from the Black-Wings.'

Oh my God where are they? *Where are you, Dad?* I try to see if there's a window, where is he? I see a huge door, at the end of the building, and windows. Dirty windows. The white flashes are making it difficult to make anything out. No, don't go. Dad where are you? The smell of chemicals is overbearing, like paint or creosote.

The floor feels gritty and cold, hard beneath my bare feet. The sun is streaming through a skylight in the roof; on the desk are glass tubes. Test tubes. And there's a case, like an aquarium, with black stuff in it. Like tar. Black sticky tar.

There's a noise from the doorway, and another man emerges at the door. He looks familiar. Oh my God it looks like Ethan. Sasha's dad. He's growling something at my dad, my dad is looking up at him, saying something, they're shouting at each other, I strain to hear but I can't make out the words, Dad's shaking his head, saying No. And...OH MY GOD, Ethan has just struck Dad over the head. No! I lunge forward at the man, NO! I try to swipe the man but it's like he's just air. Or is it me? Perhaps I'm air. Dad's holding his head. I'm crying now. 'Dad!' I'm shouting, perhaps if I shout loud enough, 'Dad!'

But it's all fading away, going, darkness, darkness and fuzziness, I'm crying, 'Dad!' And Luke's holding me. 'It's okay,' he's saying. He's crouched over me, his arm around me, rocking me like a baby.

'He was here,' I say to Luke. 'Dad was here, but the man, he hit him, Dad was hurt!'

'It's okay,' says Luke, 'it was just a bad dream, it's okay.'

My heart is hammering in my chest and my lungs feel they're going to burst.

'It was just a dream?'

'Yeah,' Luke says. 'You were calling out in your sleep. It's just a bad dream. A nightmare. I'm sorry I shouldn't have asked you to come back into the woods with me. Not so soon after Jasper attacked you. But it was just a dream. It wasn't real. It's okay now.'

'Okay,' I smile weakly and slurp on my bottle of water, concentrating to stop my hand from shaking. I squeeze Luke's hand reassuringly. He seems to have finished painting and has packed away his kit. I put on my trainers and stand up, holding onto the tree trunk to steady myself. I walk over to where Luke was sitting. 'Can I see?'

'No way,' he growls, he seems embarrassed. 'I never show my paintings until they're finished.'

'Please?'

He looks hesitant.

'Please?' I say again.

'Well, okay.' he says. 'But before you do I have to explain...'

I can't wait for him to finish what he's saying. I dash round to the front of the canvas and peer at the painting. I gasp. He has painted me totally naked. Well, as good as. The picture shows me as I had lay beneath the oak tree, but my breasts are round and full, and bursting out of a sexy floaty dress made from a lemony-cream translucent sheer fabric with hardly anything left covered, my bottom and thighs are rounded and voluptuous, and my long legs parted in a provocative pose, the buttons of my dress are coming apart to reveal my thighs and hips, and a little rounded belly. My hand goes down to my stomach self-consciously.

'It's...it's...' I gasp, clutching myself with shock. 'But...'

'Please don't be offended,' he pleads. 'Let me explain.'

'No it's okay,' I say quickly. 'It's okay, it's...well, it's beautiful!'

And it is. But Luke's face is still creased with concern, his eyes soften and turn to the floor. He looks red and flustered.

'Why did you paint me like that?' I say gently.

'I don't know,' he says. 'I got a bit carried away. Are you offended?'

'No,' I reply, 'no, I'm not offended.'

As we turn to walk home, I furtively trace the contours of my body with my fingers, it's as though I've grown from a child into an adult, literally in a week. I'm confused.

Chapter Twenty-Four

'There you are, dear.'

Pandora hands me a warm mug of hot chocolate. I'm sitting in Luke's gran's kitchen surrounded by her old-fashioned appliances and the wonderful savoury smell of some kind of casserole in the large oven.

'Luke's gone into town to get some new brushes,' Pandora says. 'You just missed him.'

'That's okay, I just popped in on the off-chance that he'd be here,' I lie.

Of course I knew Luke wouldn't be home, he'd told me he was going into town today to get art materials and I'd waited until I was sure he'd be out of the way before I'd knocked on the door. It isn't Luke I want to see today, it's his gran. But now I'm here, I don't know where to start.

Pandora looks younger today. She seems so at home in her old-fashioned cottage full of strange out-dated appliances. Her lined face is smiling and she hums to herself as she potters around her little kitchen. She looks like somebody out of a seventies sitcom with her pinny tied around her middle and her hair pulled back and tied up in a bun, a silver curl escaping at the front.

This is the first time I've seen Pandora since that day on the bus, and as I sit here in her kitchen I reflect that such a lot's happened in just two weeks – Jasper's attack and the strange feelings of rage that seemed to come with it, and the links to the tingling feelings in my back and the rather peculiar sexual stuff. *And the wings.* And the sudden change in my physical appearance, the muscles and the strength. And speed. Then there's the Fae world stuff – my mother being a fairy called Tate, being left in the woods as a baby, meeting Ainsel and Eldridge. *Am I going mad?* Then the letter from Dad, the photo frame with Fae on it, and the stuff in his folder with his handwriting mentioning the Fae. And now the revelation that Pandora is mixed up in all of this, she's the mother of a Black-Wing. And she was there in the woods when I was found as a baby, and then the hanky – its strange healing qualities.

But what am I going to say to her? It all sounds so crazy. But then she may just be able to tell me what's going on. Maybe she can help me. She did say I could trust her. But how on earth am I going to ask? *Hey, old lady, do you know anything about fairies?* I don't think so. I'd better just go. I slurp back the last of the hot chocolate and pick up my bag to leave.

'Thank you so much for the hot chocolate,' I say, 'but I don't want to take up any more of your time.'

As I stand to leave, Pandora sits down at the table opposite me, and sighs. I can almost hear the creaking of her joints as she eases herself into her chair.

'Don't ever get old, my dear,' she says, her face creasing into a smile. Her face lights up, warming me from inside. I'm not sure what to say. I sit back down and drop my bag onto the floor. I suddenly feel very shy.

'I think maybe you wanted to ask me something?' she says softly. She holds my gaze steadily and just for a moment I can't breathe. I break eye contact and stare down at the table, fiddling with the Claddagh ring that Sasha gave me at Christmas, a token of her friendship. *Huh.*

I can't think how to start. The kindness in her face makes me want to cry.

'It wasn't meant to be like this,' she suddenly says softly. 'I'm glad you came to talk to me today. Your father hid the truth about who you are because he wanted you to live like a normal girl in the everyday world until you reached Transition. He was going to tell you everything, when you reached sixteen. About yourself, your mother. And what's happening to you. He isn't here to talk to you now, but I know that he would have wanted me to help you all I can.'

She reaches out her hand and it closes over mine. I hold my breath but can't prevent a gulping noise coming from my throat. She leans forward and lightly squeezes my hand. 'You can trust me, Scarlett.' She says it so softly it's barely a whisper.

And to my utmost embarrassment, my face creases up and I start to cry. There are so many questions I want to ask, and all I can do is cry.

Pandora is silent; she just holds my hand. I feel soothed. I sniff loudly and realise she's placed a cotton hanky on the table in front of me. I pick it up. It has embroidered yellow Orchids on it, just like the other hanky. I wipe my eyes, snort noisily and then blow my nose. As I breathe into the cool hanky it has a calming effect. It smells faintly of lavender.

We sit in silence for a while and I stare at Pandora's hands. They're wrinkled with large brown patches, like huge freckles. I wonder if they're old scars where she has hurt herself, or just something to do with old age. Her nails are oval shaped and very pretty. She wears a pale pink semi-translucent varnish. Pandora remains silent, waiting. I take a very deep breath and decide to just plunge right in and ask a stupid question.

'What can you tell me about the Fae people?' I say, looking directly into her eyes expecting her to laugh at me or something, but she doesn't even blink, she just smiles kindly and nods.

'The Fae are very *special* people, they live in clusters all over the world, but there is a group who live here in the woods. They're genetically very close to humans, but they've chosen not to integrate with us so-called 'sophisticated' folk living in the everyday world. They're much closer to nature than us. They have found a way, over the years, to protect their world from the pollutants that we discard in our modern life, by separating their atmosphere from ours. They are very good, pure people, and they possess very special and powerful gifts.'

'Oh!' The relief must show on my face because she laughs, and I start to laugh too. But for me it's a kind of hysteria and I wonder whether I'll ever be able to stop.

'So it's a sort of colony?' I say, gulping and wiping my eyes again.

'Mmmm. Not really. They're more like another species of humankind. Fae people are basically human, but they have an extra component, a substance called ethereal, which makes them slightly different to everyday humans.

'Originally the Fae would have lived within our communities side by side with us. But as the years have gone by, particularly this last century, our air has become intolerable for them and now they have to remain within their own world, behind a membrane. Everyday humans can enter the Fae world, and can thrive there for a short length of time, but not indefinitely. But Fae people cannot survive in the everyday world, they would suffocate in our atmosphere.'

'Oh!' So I can't be a Fae because I would have suffocated by now. I should be feeling relieved.

'Oh,' I say again, and the disappointment must show on my face. 'Somebody told me that I was a Fae.' I laugh a little self-consciously.

'Oh yes, Scarlett, you *are* a Fae!' Pandora says, smiling kindly. 'Your father is human but your mother's a Fae. If a Fae person and an everyday person have a baby together, the baby is called a Fae Hybrid, but the baby has to live in the everyday world until he or she reaches Transition. That's why your mother left you in the woods for your father to find.

'But now you're sixteen, that's the age when Transition begins, now your lungs are fully developed, you can choose whether you want to live here in the everyday world, or in the Fae world.'

I stare down at the kitchen table, not sure what I'm feeling. So *that's* why my mother abandoned me, I would have died in the Fae world.

'There are certain Fae characteristics that you would associate with Fae people – like, for example, the shape of their ears.'

Pandora lifts her hair back and I see that her ears come to a point at the top. My fingers self-consciously go to my own ears and follow the shape around at the top. Pandora laughs, it sounds melodic.

'Maggie said you were in the woods that day, when I was found as a baby?'

'Yes, dear, I'm a Fae Hybrid too. Just like you. Tate's family and my family go back a long way. Tate asked me to bring you through to the everyday world for her and I've kept an eye on you ever since.' Pandora's eyes twinkle. 'You were a beautiful baby. And you've grown up to look just like your mother.'

I'm silent for a few moments whilst I take this in. It's nothing I didn't already know, but it's somehow more powerful to hear the story from Pandora. More real. My heart's hammering in my chest. *I really am a Fae.*

I'm a fairy.

My hand goes to my ear and feels the shape. I subconsciously pull my hair forward over my ears. *I need to buy a hat.*

'Have you visited the Fae world yet?' Pandora says.

'Yes, yes, I've met Ainsel and Eldridge.'

'Ah, yes, the twins. They're such a sweet pair.'

'They're twins?' I say, surprised. 'Ainsel said Eldridge was younger than her.'

Pandora laughs, and dabs at her eyes with a clean hanky. 'Well Ainsel is nine minutes older than Eldridge. I was there at their birth.'

'So you still visit the Fae world then? I thought...I thought...' My voice trails away. Me and my big mouth. How do I say *I know that your Black-Wing baby didn't die?*

'Yes, I still visit occasionally, maybe once a year or so.'

Pandora excuses herself and walks over to the oven to turn it down. She opens the oven door and the kitchen is bathed in a wonderful cheesey-mincey cooking smell.

I lean over slightly so that I can see the old lady's shoulders, and crane my neck to see her back. *Phew, no wings.* Pandora turns round and I look away quickly. Of course they can't have wings, they are just another tribe of humans, and the wing thing is just imaginary. An illusion. Whatever I do or say, I mustn't mention wings. *Don't mention wings.* Do *not* mention wings. *Do NOT mention wings.*

'Pandora, have you got wings?' I bite my lip hard.

'No, dear. Not anymore. I did grow wings when I reached Transition, as all Fae Hybrids do.' *Oh my God.* 'But your wings will only thrive if you spend enough time in the Fae world.'

Pandora comes to sit back down again. 'The air here in the everyday world is too polluted to sustain Fae wings, and so they will shrivel and be absorbed into your body over a number of years. They'll only develop and break through your skin if you spend time in the Fae world, breathing the pure Fae air. And even after they've broken through, they'll rarely appear in the everyday world, only in the Fae world. So you don't need to worry about wings suddenly appearing half way through your maths class.' Pandora laughs.

My heart is hammering in my chest and I'm feeling dizzy. I feel I want to cry again, but I swallow it back.

'So you know my mother? You know Tate?' My voice is husky.

'Yes, Tate's a very important person in the Fae world, she's a Sage Fae. The Sage Fae family are the monarchs of the Fae world. They're the strongest, purest and most gifted of all the Fae people.'

'Wow.'

I feel a burst of pride. So it's true what Ainsel and Eldridge said. My mother really is a fairy princess.

'So does that mean that when I become a Fae, I will be a Sage Fae too?'

'Yes, you already are, dear. You *are* a Sage, a Fae Princess. You are very special in the Fae world.' Pandora smiles eerily.

'Did Dad know all this? About the Fae stuff?'

Chapter Twenty-Four

'Yes, he knew.'

I sniff loudly and Pandora reaches over and places a cool bony hand over mine.

'After you were born, Tate asked me to bring you through to the everyday world and leave you with Sam. Tate was broken-hearted. She had lost the man she loves, and also her baby daughter.'

'So how they find each other again? Dad and Tate?'

'Well it was quite a while later. You were about two or three. Tate came to me. She asked me to talk to Sam, to show him the way through the Fae membrane. She couldn't be without him. So I started to take Sam through into the Fae world, he and Tate would meet up regularly.

'After a while Sam worked out how to get through the membrane all by himself. He was determined, he practised for hours and hours but finally managed it, which was no easy task for a non-Fae. He was going to talk to you about the Fae world when you reached Transition. I know that he was looking forward to introducing you to your mother.'

I smile weakly through my watery eyes, I'm glad Dad found his love again. And I feel even more sure that he's stuck in the Fae world somehow.

'So you haven't met Tate yet?' Pandora says. 'I know she was eager to meet you.'

'No,' I say sadly, 'Ainsel says that Tate seems to have disappeared around the same time as my dad. I like to think they're somewhere in the Fae world together. Do you think they've found some way of being together or something?'

Pandora's face creases in a frown, she looks uncomfortable.

'Disappeared?'

I don't know whether to say anything about the Black-Wings or not. I'm looking intently at Pandora and she's looking at me. *Just say it.* No, no I can't do it. I can't mention about Jasper. It just isn't right. I can't say it. You can't go around accusing people of kidnapping. On a hunch. Especially not to that person's grand-mother.

I break eye contact and look down at the table, focus on my hand, on my mug. Change the subject.

'Can I ask you, Pandora, what exactly happens at Transition?' I feel embarrassed, but Pandora seems quite relaxed.

'Transition is a bit like puberty in the Fae world. Fae Hybrid children don't develop much during their early teens, but soon after a Hybrid child turns sixteen they rapidly develop their physical appearance and their Fae gifts, their wings grow, and they develop sexually.' I pull my cardigan over me and fold my arms. *I know what she means.*

'Pandora, what's your gift? If you don't mind me asking?'

'I'm a Fae healer. I have the gift of healing.'

'Ahhhh,' I say, 'the hanky!'

'Well I did hope that the hanky would help ease your bumps and bruises. And also maybe mend your heartache a little.' Pandora chuckles. 'My gift is not as potent as it was, but I usually have a stock of hankies which are impregnated with the Gossamer Orchid balm. I collect it when I visit the Fae world. The Orchid flower has healing properties too.'

I nod. That's why the sap from the Orchid stem healed the cuts on my hand.

Just then the front door bangs shut and I hear Luke's voice booming through the hall. 'Hi, Gran I'm home!'

'In here, Luke, your friend's here,' Pandora calls back. I hear the door to Luke's studio being opened and a thud as something is thrown down. I suddenly gasp as realisation dawns, I struggle to control myself. I was so obsessed with who was a Black-Wing that I didn't, I hadn't...

'Luke's a Fae too?' I whisper.

Chapter Twenty-Five

'Luke's a Fae Hybrid like you,' says Pandora as she shuffles over to the huge white Belfast sink, rinses out her cup and places it on the shelf.

I can hear Luke sorting his shopping in the hall. 'Does he know?' I say in a hushed voice.

'Yes of course, he's always known, but he's never been very interested. He says that everything he needs in life is here in his studio, and in this village.'

'Oh!' Luke exclaims as he comes through the door, and nearly trips over his feet.

'Hi, Luke, I came over to see you but I forgot you were out this morning, so your gran made me a drink,' I blurt unnecessarily.

'Hey.' Luke's face splits into a grin and I look down at my hands. He chucks some paint brushes onto the table.

'I bought a new hog brush but couldn't get real sable, they were too expensive,' he says to his gran. 'Did you know sable brushes are made from real sable fur? It's taken from the tail. Tried to find out if they harm the animal to get the fur to make the brush, but the woman in the shop was a bit dim. She said they take the tail off the sable and it's perfectly fine which I think is unlikely. Anyway I can't afford fifty quid for one brush, so I got synthetic. Probably just as good.'

I start to laugh, imagining lots of sable creatures running around without tails. Luke gives me a look and I snort, trying to stifle my giggles. It reminds me of the time my dad told me they don't harm lambs for our 'leg of lamb' on a Sunday dinner – they just remove one leg and the lambs hop around in the fields on three legs until the fourth leg grows back. And I used to believe him.

I watch as Luke takes his new things out of his bag. He's standing opposite me, lost in his new paints and brushes. As he leans against the table, the fabric of his shorts stretches across the front, revealing the shape beneath. I go hot, I feel a flush rise to my cheeks and I concentrate hard on my empty mug, fiddle with the handle and shift awkwardly in my chair.

I've never actually seen a man's, you know, *thing*. Not properly. Even when Jasper…well I didn't really see anything. Not properly. And it's not like I was looking. And anyway that doesn't count. I mean obviously I've seen TV programmes, when I was staying at Sasha's and she would watch late night films. But usually you would just see the girl; you'd see loads of shots of boobs and bottoms and her bits and pieces. But the men you'd just get fleeting shots. We used to try to pause the TV but we could never get a proper full-frontal. You know, in full view. And I've never seen a proper one. In real life. Or even felt one, even through trousers.

Sasha used to boast about how many she'd seen and how they were all different so I sometimes kind of wonder, if I saw one, how you know if it was, you know, normal. Big. Or whatever. I glance back to Luke's shorts and then look away quickly.

Pandora stands up, her eyes twinkle. *Oh bloody God she saw me looking.*

'I'm just popping out to the shops,' she says. 'Scarlett, it's been really lovely talking to you, please pop by any time for a chat – it's always nice to have a visitor.'

She leaves the room and I hear the front door close behind her. My face is still hot with embarrassment.

'D'ya want another cup of hot chocolate?' Luke says innocently as he leans over and takes my empty mug out of my hands. I can breathe again now he's moved away.

'No, but a Coke would be nice,' I say, a little shakily.

'So, what would you like to do today?' he says as he hands me an ice-cold can. I snap it open and gulp it down.

'I think we should visit the Fae world,' I say, expecting a reaction.

'Aw no,' he says, 'boring.'

'What?'

'What?'

'So you knew I was a Fae too?' I say.

'Yes, of course.'

'How did you know?'

'Gran told me. About you being a Sage. But she said I shouldn't tell anybody. Because of you being special and stuff.'

'Well, that's where we're going today, the woods,' I say decisively.

'Okay.' He peers at me through his curtain of messy blond hair. 'I'll take my paints.'

'No, we're going to the Fae world,' I say firmly.

'That could be a problem,' he says, gulping down the last of his drink and crushing the can with his hand, 'because I have no idea how to get there. The Fae world. Never been there, never really been interested.'

'I'm surprised.'

'Surprised? Why?' He sits down in the chair next to mine; his knee is touching my leg. My leg jerks away like it's been touched by an electric current.

'Because of the colours, they're so amazing.'

'Colours in the woods *are* amazing. It's the woods. They always are. That's why I like to paint in the woods.'

'No, Luke, you don't understand. The colours in the Fae world are so pure, and fresh. The air is so clear – and the extra colour makes every single colour look different.'

'What do you mean *extra* colour?'

'You know – the fourth prime colour. Primo.'

'Primo?' He screws his nose up.

'Oh my God. You don't know, do you?' I tingle inside at the prospect of finally knowing something before somebody else.

'What?' Luke is looking at me like I've gone mad.

'Oh my God, Luke,' I say, 'you're in for such a treat. Come on.'

I grab his hand and drag him out of his cottage towards the woods.

'Just focus on my finger and then let your eyes relax.'

I shove my finger an inch from his nose and Luke stares cross-eyed at my finger whilst he concentrates. We're sitting under the old oak tree, and I'm trying to teach him how to pass through the Fae membrane into the Fae world.

'What now?' he says slowly, his eyes starting to glaze over. He looks like something from a zombie film.

'Can you see it?'

'See what?'

'What are you looking at, what can you see?'

'Your bloody finger.'

'You're trying too hard.'

'What?'

I sigh hard and feel like stamping my foot. 'Just let your eyes relax, like when you look at those magic eye pictures. Focus on my finger and then when you are focused, look through my finger at the—'

'I can't see a thing with your finger stuck there!' he says, pushing my hand away roughly. 'I don't know what you're on about, I can't see anything, and I don't know what you mean by magic eye. I'm sorry, Scarlett, I'm just not gonna be able to do it. What's wrong with the everyday world anyway?'

I glare at him.

'And it's no use you looking at me like that,' he glares back at me.

'Pah!' I say, jumping up and stomping away from him. I want to scream. We've been here in the woods for over an hour and it feels like he just isn't trying. He's such a child. I feel frustrated, I was so eager to show him the Fae world, to see his expression when he saw all the new colours and sights. I just know he'll love it, and want to paint it. I want to see his excitement when he sees the beautiful colours. I want to be the first one to show him, to take him there, to my special place.

He flops back against the tree, lazily. 'Why don't we just sit and enjoy the moment here in the woods?' he suggests.

'And do what?' I snap, wanting to slap him.

'Well we could just sit here and enjoy each other's company?'

'Pah!'

'You could tell me about the colours, describe that new colour to me. What's it called, Primark?'

He starts to laugh and I glare at him.

'Very funny.'

'Come on, Scarlett, I'm sorry. Maybe if I take a look at one of those magical eyebrow pictures.'

He wiggles his eyebrows up and down fast, grinning from ear to ear.

'Not funny.'

I sigh. I know I'm being childish, it's not his fault. I sigh again, louder.

'Well, how about you tell me all about all your fairy friends,' he says.

'Oh never mind,' I snap. 'If you are going to patronise me then we might as well go home.'

'I'm not patronising you, I'm just saying I can't seem to get into that Fae place, but does it really matter?'

He leans towards me and touches my arm. I push him away roughly. He leans towards me again and lands a quick kiss on my cheek, I turn away. I feel a burning behind my eyes as I fight back tears of frustration.

'I just like being here with you,' he says. 'I'll get the hang of it one day if it's really that important to you. I'll practice. I'll ask my gran. Don't get upset, please. It's just that Fae stuff – it's just not important to me. I guess I'm just not a fairy sort of person. I have everything I want right here in this world. My painting. My life.'

I feel hot and unreasonable. 'Well you just stay here in the everyday world with your paintings and your perfect life – I'm off to the Fae world.'

I spin round to face the oak tree and quickly focus on the Fae world. *My world.* And as I slip through the membrane, I hear Luke calling out, 'Scarlett, I'm sorry. I'll try again. Please, Scarlett, come back.'

I close my ears to him. I feel angry and crushed, but I'm not sure why. I kick the tree hard and yelp in pain. I kick it again and then fall to the ground clutching my foot. *Ow.* I can still make out Luke's outline on the other side of the membrane. Inches away from me, still shouting to me. I reach out my hand towards him and prod the membrane. I can't feel the membrane, but it feels all tingly as it reshapes around my hand, and I'm able to touch Luke's face without actually feeling anything.

'Oy!' I hear Luke's muffled voice through the membrane. I can just make out his outline, brushing away an imaginary insect.

Luke's fuzzy figure starts to move away. I sit down hard on the floor and watch him disappear. I feel empty and alone.

A swarm of butterflies flits past my face, leaving a kaleido-scope of patterns in the air. I'm captivated. I wonder whether our world was like this hundreds of years ago. I sigh. I wish Luke could see this.

I lie back in the warm grass and close my eyes. My fingers play in the warm clean sand beside me. My back is tingling, I can feel my wings, strengthening, getting ready to burst into life. I wonder how long it will be before they are ready. I lift my legs up and push back against the ground, setting off more vibrating just beneath the skin. I smile to myself. As the feeling radiates through me, it feels like my whole body is boiling with some emotion, something I can't describe. Don't understand. I enjoy the feeling and take deep breaths. I force air into my lungs, breathe, breathe.

'Hello again.'

My eyes snap open and I sit up quickly. *Orion.* The sun's behind him and he looks like a tall dark angel with a halo encompassing his whole body. He's wearing white surf shorts, nothing else. *Seriously, don't they ever wear clothes?* His chest is darkly tanned and well-toned. I'm struck by how tall he seems. And strong. Solid. Mature. *Sexy.*

'Are you all right?' he says, a frown appearing above his dark chocolate brown liquid eyes.

I swallow hard.

'I've just had an argument with a friend. It seems to be happening a lot lately. I'm not sure I belong in the everyday world anymore.' I feel surprised by my own words. I hadn't realised I felt like that.

'Would you like me to sit with you for a while?' he says. His eyes are smiling at me, melting my reserve. I feel a quivering excitement inside.

'Yes please,' I'm shocked to hear myself say.

He sits on the ground next to me and places a strong arm lightly around my shoulder.

'It's a confusing time for you,' he says. It's more a statement than a question.

'Yes,' I say.

He gently pulls me towards him, his large hand covering my shoulder. A warm cocoon, a warm sexy cocoon. A stranger, and yet I feel safe. I can feel how firm his muscles are, one arm is holding me close to his chest, and the other hand is gently rubbing my arm. I press my face against his skin, hot and dry from the sun, he smells musky and masculine. I snuggle my face into his chest and close my eyes, drinking in the scent of his body.

His warm dry hand is running up and down my arm, soothing, he takes hold of my hand and kisses gently inside my palm. I nearly explode; his lips feel soft and warm. A damp tingling is left where his lips were. I open my eyes and watch as his lips travel up my arm, gently kissing and nuzzling my shoulder.

'I can make you feel better,' he says as his eyes look deep into my soul. *I know you can.*

I close my eyes as I feel his lips touch my neck, gently, and a small groan escapes my lips. His kisses are moving upwards sending me into spirals of sleepy pleasure. His lips casually brush my ear, and his tongue teases, I moan gently as I feel his sharp teeth gently nibbling. He buries his face in my neck beneath my ear and burrows his face in my hair. My nerve ends are on fire; ripples of delight running through me.

'Let yourself go,' he whispers. I slide back into the sand and he lowers himself beside me, his arms encircling me. I close my eyes as his hand circles my back, round and round, the circles getting smaller and lower until I'm almost panting, drunk with pleasure. I can feel throbbing, deep, deep in my back, I know it's my wings, sending little electric shivers to the nerve endings in my skin like little arrows shooting through my body.

'Scarlett,' he murmurs. I shiver at the sound of my name. I like it. I can't believe this is me, I feel so different here. *I belong.* His hand slides down beneath my bottom and he pulls me towards him, wrapping my leg around his hips, tucking me in tight and I nearly implode as I feel a hard knot push against me. Ripples of pleasure start to pulsate deep in my belly and ripple out towards my spine; it feels as though my wings are controlling my whole body, my feelings, my senses.

His silky wings stand out like erect proud ensigns, vibrating from deep inside his body, reverberating through his body and echoing into mine. As I clutch him hard against me I start to move gently, wishing there was no fabric between us, I can't get close enough.

He quickly slides on top of me, his lips find my mouth and he kisses me hard, forcing my mouth open with his tongue, circling and sending my senses into a whirl of desire, I clutch at the smooth hot skin on his back, his neck.

'Scarlett,' he whispers, his fingers caress my breast through the thin fabric of my bra. I push into his hand, want him to touch me. *It's the wrong face.* I cry out with pleasure and guilt, battling with myself as I run my fingers across his velvety head and pull his mouth to my breast, watch his lips close around my nipple, sucking through the wet fabric of my bra. He groans as I push the fabric away, his hot breath and cool wet tongue on my skin, sucking, flicking and nibbling and sending my pleasure soaring to a deeper intensity. I can't get close enough, my fingers tug at him as he devours me, my skin prickling with arousal. *It's the wrong man.*

He roughly unwraps my legs and rolls away from me, looking at me, searching, his eyes haunted, dark with desire.

'Are you sure?' his voice is serious. I smile back and run my hands over his firm dark body. Then I slowly slide my hand behind the waistband of his flimsy shorts, not knowing exactly what to expect.

'Oh God,' he moans gently, he's naked beneath and I gasp, shocked, my head spins, my senses whirl as I feel the full size of him.

'Scarlett, are you sure?' he says again, more urgently. 'Oh God,' and he shuts his eyes and pushes himself into my hand, I close my fingers around him and feel him moving gently, my stomach jolts with anticipation. *It's not the right man.*

His fingers reach urgently beneath the waistband of my jeans, I like it, my jeans are tight, Orion thrusts his hand low and I cry out. Delighted. Horrified. Thrilled. The vibrations in my spine, my back, my wings, are intensifying and I suddenly feel a searing pain, as though the muscles are ripping away from my rib cage, biting stabbing pain and yet a strange ecstasy as my head whirls, dizzy with desire. *It's wrong, the wrong man. The wrong man.*

'I don't know, I'm not sure!' I cry out.

He stares at me, panting heavily, his eyes are black as night.

'I'm sorry,' I say, in a voice that doesn't sound like mine. He stops immediately. 'I'm so sorry, no. It's wrong.' I'm breathing hard. He nods once.

'I'm sorry, Orion, this isn't right for me. I can't do this. Not yet. I'm so sorry this really isn't like me. I don't do this.'

'That's okay,' he says after a brief moment, and he runs his finger slowly down my exposed breast. I quickly cover myself with my top.

'It's okay,' he says again. He releases me and lets out a shuddering sigh, jumps lightly to his feet and holds out his hand to pull me up.

He tries to rearrange his silky shorts naturally over his awkward shape. He shrugs and pulls a face, and I start to giggle. He kisses me lightly on the forehead.

'You know where to find me,' he whispers. And then he turns and quickly walks away.

I want to laugh, cry, scream. I feel burning frustration mixed with dizzying relief.

Chapter Twenty-Six

After Orion's gone I groan and slump back down to the floor. I'm still hot all over, drained. My jeans are uncomfortable, I'm all swollen and out of shape, everywhere. I don't recognise my own body. I straighten my clothes and fasten my jeans. *What's happening to me, what am I turning into?*

My heart is still thumping hard in my chest, my body still tingling. My legs are wobbling like a jelly. I not only feel uncomfortable physically, but I feel ashamed.

I close my eyes. The sun is on my face and it starts to relax me. The dry heat makes me warm and muzzy. I sense the flutter of insect wings, and can hear the buzz buzz of a nearby bee looking for nectar to harvest. The hot sun is bright on my eyelids, different lights dancing around and getting brighter and brighter until it hurts. I shield my eyes with my arm, but the light is still getting more intense, bright white light. My head is almost cracking with pain, I can't open my eyes and I can't see, but then the light starts to dim and I know without opening my eyes that I'm in that strange barn again. I'm back in my recurring dream. I can smell it, the unmistakable sooty chemical smell.

I peer through half-closed eyes. My dad is there. He's sitting at the desk this time. It's more like an old bench. I can see clearly this time. The bench is cluttered with documents and bottles, and the papers have markings on them. Like chemistry or formulas or something. Dad is studying some kind of black oily substance in a glass tube. Like a test tube. It looks like Dad's lab at the university, except he's in a barn. No, it's a stable; I can see horse tackle, and a saddle. It's old tackle, as though it hasn't been used for years. Old and dusty.

There's that smell, like soot. An inky, chemically smell. It makes me want to retch.

'Dad!' I say softly, but he doesn't react. He's breathing heavily, as though he's been running and is out of breath. He doesn't look well, there's a grey pallor to his skin, and his hand is shaking. 'Dad!' I say louder. 'Dad!' What's going on? Why is he sitting in a stable doing chemistry experiments? Is he unwell?

'He can't hear you.' It's a woman's voice. It's Tate. 'He can't hear you.'

I turn to face her. She smiles. She has piercing green eyes, and long wavy red hair, not as curly as mine. And there's no doubt about it, she's the person in the photo frame.

Tate's sitting cross-legged on the floor, but she gets to her feet and walks towards me. She's tall. I take a hesitant half step backwards, unsure how to react.

'Don't be afraid,' she says.

'Is he…is this real?' I say.

'Yes,' she says. 'Sam…your dad…can't see you but I can, Scarlett. I'm Tate. I'm your mother.'

I nod.

'You used to visit me, when I was little,' I say, and smile. 'I thought you were an Angel.'

'Yes,' she says, her eyes glistening. 'I was never sure whether you knew I was there. You looked so sweet and cosy tucked up in bed with your little ginger cat.'

Wow, Jelly Tot. My eyes prickle as I remember lying in bed as a child, Jelly Tot curled up at the foot of my bed, and Angel Lady telling me a story about a world of fairies and a magical land full of winged creatures and dragons and unicorns.

'There's so much I want to say to you,' she says.

Dad starts coughing, he sounds as though he's going to cough his own lungs up. His face goes red, and he's wheezing. He holds a handkerchief to his mouth and coughs blood red sputum into the white cloth. Tate's eyes cloud over.

'What's Dad doing? Why doesn't he come home? Is he sick?'

'It's not his fault, Scarlett. He's heart-broken about leaving you. But some people are keeping us both captive. I don't know if you've heard of the Black-Wings. They're making him do things, scientific experiments.'

I turn back to look at Dad. He's screwing his eyes up trying to get a teeny bit of the black sludge onto a slide, gasping for breath, his hands are shaking. His eyes look bloodshot and tired. I hold my hand out towards him, he looks up and for a moment I think he can see me.

'Dad!' I cry. But he looks right through me, and then continues his work on the slide containing the grey sticky yuck.

'What's he doing?' I say. 'What's that black stuff?' It reminds me of Jasper's black slimy wings and it's starting to make me feel ill.

'It's called Ethereal Black, it's the main constituent of the Black-Wings' genetic makeup, it's been extracted from Jasper's wings.'

'What's Dad doing with it?' I say, my voice high and shrill. 'Where are you?'

'Our captors are making Sam cultivate a synthetic version of Ethereal Black so it can be made in large quantities.'

'Why?' I say, my face screwing up, why would anybody want to cultivate that revolting stuff?

'I don't know. All I know is Ethereal Black is very destructive to the Fae world. We don't know what they want these chemicals for. But to the Fae world, a large supply of Ethereal Black is the equivalent to a country stock-piling chemical weapons. The only possible use for this stuff is for destruction.'

'Oh my God! Dad's being forced to make a chemical that could destroy the Fae world?'

Tate's emotionally-charged silence answers my question.

'Is that why Dad looks sick? Is the chemical affecting him?'

'No, the chemical can't do him any harm. It's only harmful to Fae people. He's ill because he's trapped in the Fae world, and he can't tolerate the Fae atmosphere. It's too pure for him. That's why he's sick.'

'Why don't you both try and escape?' I say, horrified.

'We can't, the stuff your dad's working with, it would be really poisonous to me, to any Fae. And there is so much of it around this place that it would be too dangerous. It's all around the entrance to this building, and if I walked through it, well...' Her voice trails off. I clamp my hand over my mouth.

'And they've told Sam that if he tries to escape, they'll harm me.'

'Is that why they captured you first? As leverage over Dad?'

'Gosh you know a lot already. Yes, they trapped me into coming here, then they sent a message to Sam to come, said I was in trouble.'

'Where are you?' I say quickly. 'I have to get you both out of there.'

'Please don't try and find us, Scarlett, it would be too dangerous for you.'

It's fading. The vision is fading, slipping away. 'Tate!' I shout. 'Tate, where are you, where are you?'

But it's too late, she's gone. I spin round, look around me. I'm still in the woods. I must have fallen asleep. That strange dream again. My head aches.

I need to get home, Maggie's coming home tonight.

Chapter Twenty-Seven

'It's seven thirty in the morning!' I object, as I open my front door the following morning to see Luke standing there, beaming. I find it hard to meet his gaze.

I can hear Maggie stirring upstairs. She arrived home late last night all blustery and excited from her holiday. She looked fabulous, more like the old Maggie. She has a gorgeous deep brown tan and she'd discarded that frown she's been wearing for the last two months. We didn't get to bed 'til gone midnight, but I had a disturbed night's sleep with strange dreams, sort of mixing up Orion and Luke. Okay, so it was a kind of action replay of what happened with Orion, but it was Luke instead. Yes I know, sad. But, wow!

'Hey!' Luke announces brightly as he bounces through the doorway, past me and straight through to the kitchen.

He digs into his backpack and pulls out sheets of paper with what look like coloured dots all over them. He spreads them out on the kitchen table.

'I've got the magic eye!' he says, beaming all over his face. 'I've got it, I can do it.'

'What're you on about?'

'I downloaded loads of those magic eye pictures, and printed them out. And I was up all night learning how to do them. And I can do it now, easily. See…'

He picks up one of the pictures and puts his finger on his nose, then moves it slowly towards the picture. I struggle to keep a straight face.

'See! This is a picture of a dinosaur. I can see it clearly.' His eyes are all glazed and he's concentrating hard. 'See, I can look all around the picture now, see everything. Once you learn how it's easy. So I'll be able to go with you to the Fae world now.'

He looks so pleased with himself. I feel a pang of guilt as I remember what I was doing with Orion whilst he was learning this magic eye stuff.

'You were up all night learning how to do this?' I say, incredulous. 'What possessed you to do that?'

'Well if that's what I need to do to make you like me and hang out with me, then it's a small price to pay,' he says, leaning forward and pecking me on the cheek.

I stare at the floor, feeling unsettled. 'You don't have to do all this to make me like you,' I mumble.

I sit down hard on the kitchen chair and take a deep breath, feel my face flush. I can hear Maggie coming downstairs; her voice rings out through the hallway. 'Who was at the door, Scarlett?'

'Maggie, this is Luke from school,' I say quickly as she appears in the doorway. 'We're working together on a project about, erm...'

I cast Luke a warning look, I didn't tell Maggie about the Fae stuff last night. She was on such a high from her holiday and I was so pleased to see her. And something told me that I need to choose my time carefully before I introduce her to the concept that I'm a fairy.

'The environment,' Luke chimes in, still breathing hard from his two mile power-walk. His face is begging me to rescue him but my lips turn up at the corners as he flounders on. 'We have to do some research for next year at school. About the world around us and how it affects the atmosphere.'

He's flushed and is babbling. I glance warily at Maggie, she must wonder what kind of weird boy he is, not only does he look eccentric, he also talks a load of rubbish.

'So we need to go into the woods today and do some...observation...' Luke finishes, his voice trailing off. He looks at me as if to say, 'Thanks a million'.

Maggie rubs her eyes and rummages through her handbag for her car keys, yawning widely. She suddenly stares at me as though she's seeing me for the first time.

'What on earth have you been doing whilst I've been away?' she says, looking at my top, and then my jeans.

I immediately feel guilty and embarrassed. Can she tell what I've been doing, thinking? *Those* kind of thoughts? Can she tell just by looking at me? Is it written all across my face? I feel my face blush deeply.

'Just hanging out and stuff, why?'

'Look at the state of your jeans.' Maggie points. 'The stitching is all splitting down the side. I think maybe we need to get you some new clothes, and that top's way too small for you. What have you been eating whilst I've been away?'

Virtually nothing actually, when I think about the number of meals I forgot to eat.

I stare down at myself. *This top fitted me fine last week.* But now I'm bursting out of it. And my jeans look as though they're straining to keep me inside.

'I've got to go,' Maggie says, glancing at her watch.

She grabs her bag and gives me another quick hug, then rushes out of the kitchen. I listen as the front door closes and her heels clip down the pathway to her car.

'Come on then,' says Luke, as he gathers up his magic eye papers. 'Let's go and explore your Fae world. And you can show me this Primark colour.'

'Primo.'

'Whatever.'

I grab some drinks and snacks from the fridge, stuff them into Luke's backpack and follow him outside.

We walk in silence for a while, I'm thinking about Sasha. She must be a Black-Wing too. But does she know? Does she know I'm a Fae? Actually I don't think she does. Does she even know that Luke's her cousin, and that Pandora's her gran?

I know she has her nasty side, but she always seemed glad to get Jasper and Ethan out of the way. But those bruises. Did Jasper make those marks? Or her dad? Are they treating her badly? Or was it just a trap? I screw my eyes up whilst I try to work it out. Argh it's just too complicated.

We've arrived at the old oak tree; Luke drops his backpack down on the floor and unzips the top, drags the magic eye pictures out.

'You do realise that you are not actually stepping inside the magic eye picture with the dinosaurs…it isn't Jurassic Park,' I say.

'Ha bloody ha,' Luke says, and reaches out to slap me.

'Ow!'

He leans back against the oak tree and I sit cross-legged, facing him. There's so much I need to think about, Sasha and Jasper, Ethan. What if that recurring dream is somehow a warning. What if it's right? If Jasper and Ethan are holding Dad and Tate captive somewhere? I shake my head lightly as though to rid my head of its current train of thought.

'Go on then,' I say, shoving one of the magic eye pictures in front of Luke's face.

'Shut up, I need to concentrate.'

Luke puts his finger in front of his face and starts to move it backwards and forwards, he goes cross-eyed. I see him try everything, blinking, squinting, opening and closing his eyes. He tries so hard and I feel really sorry for him. He stares at his dinosaur magic eye picture in dismay. 'I can see the dinosaur clearly,' he says, 'so why can't I see the fairy stuff?'

After an hour of this, he has a headache and I pull the drinks out of his bag. We eat snack bars and break open our not-quite-as-cold-as-they-should-be cans of Coke. I start to giggle. Luke tries to slap me. I giggle even more and Luke pulls cross-eyed faces to make me laugh even more. Luke starts to laugh. I roll back on my back and cross my legs helpless with laughter trying not to wet myself. Luke tickles me, leaning over me. I try to push him away. He pins me down, and I stop laughing and bite my lip. *He's going to kiss me.* Luke smiles down at me. I smile too. *He's going to kiss me.*

He runs his tongue over his lips and I wait. *He's going to kiss me.* I'm breathing quickly. I can see that his chest is rising and falling rapidly too. *He's nervous.* My lips tingle in anticipation. He leans towards me slowly and I feel his breath on my cheek, his hair flops over my face, tickling my cheek. I close my eyes in anticipation, his lips gently brush mine, my lips part and our lips touch again, still gentle, soft. The kiss lasts for just a moment, and then he pulls away. When I open my eyes his face is inches from mine, his eyes still closed. He opens his eyes slowly, and smiles. I'd like him to kiss me again, but he pushes himself up on his elbow and brushes my cheek with his thumb. We don't say anything for a long moment. The kiss was lovely. So…soft, gentle…loving. So…not sexual.

'Luke…' I say hesitantly, 'how old are you?'

'Fifteen.'

I can hear a humming sound in the distance, a sound I should recognise, and I'm trying to place it. I've heard it before, I can see from the corner of my eye that the sun has come out and it's quite bright now, and then I realise. It's the sound a hundred butter-flies fluttering together in the sky, it's getting closer. We're in the Fae world. Somehow during our kiss, we've slipped through into the Fae world. I must have brought Luke through with me while I was holding him.

I beam at Luke.

'Welcome to the Fae world!' I announce loudly, and his mouth drops open.

'Bloody hell!' he says, and gets to his feet shakily. 'Bloody hell!'

'Look!' I point at the cloud of butterflies that are now overhead, the colours changing as their position varies, like a massive multicoloured carpet.

I beam at him proudly. 'I knew you'd like it.'

'Like it?' he gasps, still staring all around him. 'Like it?

Bloody hell!'

He spins round to me. 'Well how the fu— er, I mean, how did we get here? How did that happen?'

'I'm not sure,' I chuckle. 'Maybe, er, because I wasn't paying attention...because I was distracted...I managed to slip through the membrane and because you were in my arms, you came too. After all, it would seem that you can bring inanimate objects through, maybe you can bring people through as well.'

'Bloody hell!' Luke says, and keeps repeating himself for quite a while whilst he explores his new surroundings. I search around but there's no sign of Ainsel or Eldridge. Or Orion, thank God.

Quite a while later Luke is still in a state of shock. I glance at my wrist but I've left my watch at home.

I sit on the floor and inhale deeply. Okay, despite the fact that Luke is ignoring me now, I'm feeling blissfully happy. *Luke kissed me*. Okay maybe not blissfully happy, but it's good, isn't it? Luke kissed me, he kissed *me*. Luke kissed me.

And yet I feel strangely unsettled. Not disappointed, of course not. But something. Well a first kiss is never going to be perfect is it? Or sexy? *Orion's kiss was*. Well Luke's only fifteen, I argue with myself, it'll be different when he's in Transition. And I can wait. It's only...it's only a year.

I suddenly realise Ainsel is sitting just a few feet away from me, on a fallen tree trunk. She's humming softly to herself and somehow the woodland creatures are joining in, it feels like a symphony of the most enchanting sounds. I glance over at Luke; he doesn't seem to have noticed her.

I can't help but be slightly worried how he'll react when he sees her. Her being naked and everything. Okay, so she's not naked but she might just as well be. And he's never seen me naked or anything. Of course. Obviously. And she's so pretty. And young.

Ainsel is looking at me questioningly. I suppose I'll have to introduce her. Just then Eldridge appears from nowhere. He's wearing the same red shorts.

'Luke,' I call over to him. He wafts his arm vaguely in my direction as though he's far too busy to stop and listen. 'Luke!' I say again, a bit louder, and he turns. And stares.

'This is Ainsel and Eldridge,' I say to him. 'They're twins.' Ainsel scowls at me.

I turn to Ainsel. 'Luke's Pandora's grandson.'

Well I suppose I could have predicted their reaction. If I'd really thought about it. After all, the last time we talked about Pandora, I told them Pandora's grandson was a Black-Wing.

'Aaarrrrrgh!' yells Luke as the twins pounce on him, pinning him to the ground. They're making hissing and growling sounds like wild creatures and their eyes have turned a kind of green-black.

'Gerroff!' moans Luke. Eldridge has his foot on Luke's thigh and is holding his shoulders to the ground, whilst Ainsel is hovering over him brandishing a sort of stick thing that looks like it's been sharpened to a spear.

I want to laugh but I suppose it's not really funny. I wouldn't be laughing if Luke really *was* an evil Black-Wing. But still, it's kind of funny to see Luke pinned down by these two half-naked fairies.

'It's okay, it's okay,' I shout to the twins. 'Luke's not a Black-Wing, he's not Ethan's son.'

But the twins don't move an inch.

'Eldridge, let Luke go. What's he going to do with you for goodness sake? You're the one with the spear!' I gesture at the stick thing that Ainsel is holding.

'Prove it!' hisses Eldridge through his teeth, and snarls.

Oh God.

'Scarlett! Go and get Gran!' shrieks Luke. 'Get your grubby hands off me you slimy little elf!'

Chapter Twenty-Eight

When Pandora and I arrive back at the oak tree, Luke and the twins are sitting in a circle chatting. Clearly they've resolved their differences. As soon as the twins see Pandora they spring to their feet and come dashing over.

'Pandy!' shrieks Ainsel, and jumps up into Pandora's arms like she's a bag of feathers.

'Hello Ainsel,' laughs Pandora, placing her back on the ground with a wince, and Eldridge rushes over to give Pandora a huge bear hug. He might only be fifteen but he towers over Pandora.

'What's this I hear about you terrorising my grandson?' Pandora says with a mock-scolding voice.

'Oh no!' says Ainsel. 'That's all sorted out now. Luke is *Grace's* son, not Ethan's!'

'I *told* you that!' I interject, but nobody's listening.

I sit a little way away, feeling sulky. Pandora digs into her handbag and hands out chocolate bars to the twins. They rip off the wrappers and start chomping away. *Chocolate?* Hello, I thought the Fae were supposed to be all 'living off the land' and 'natural' and stuff. Okay I know I'm being childish, but, I mean, *chocolate*?

Ainsel gathers an armful of soft vegetation and moss and places it on a tree stump, Pandora lowers herself onto it. She beckons me to come a little closer and it crosses my mind to be stubborn and say no, but I know I'm being stupid. So I move in closer and sit on the ground next to Pandora. She beams round at us, as though we are all her grandchildren.

Pandora chats with the twins for a while, asking after different people who are clearly Fae people I've never heard of – Elidir, Dagmar, Pepin, Cosmo. I move my feet around in the sand, making shapes and marvelling at how lovely and warm the soft dry sand gets when it's in full sunlight. Like beach sand, and just as clean. As I hear the twins chatting and giggling and Pandora's soft voice interacting with them, my eyes are drawn towards the trees deeper in the woods.

A figure is standing, watching me. *Orion.* He's drawing me in, like he's a magnet and I'm made of iron filings, the pull towards him is so great I put my hand out and grasp a chunk of long grass and keep a tight hold. He's quite a distance away but my eyes are locked onto his. There's a tugging deep inside, my hands are starting to sweat and slip on the chunk of grass. My heart is bounding with excitement. I want to go to him. But then he turns and walks away. I watch until I can't see him anymore, and then I keep on watching for a long time. I feel a chill and hug my cardigan around me despite the hot sun beating down on my back.

I glance towards Luke to see if he noticed, but he's staring at Eldridge, his eyes seem to be fixed on Eldridge's sweet little wings. He's probably thinking about the time when he gets his boy wings, when he reaches Transition. I can't quite read Luke's expression as he watches the Fae boy, but I smile to myself. I can see Luke is going through some of the emotions I experienced when I first discovered the Fae world.

'Scarlett tells me Tate's missing?' I hear Pandora say gravely.

Ainsel and Eldridge both nod wildly. 'Nobody's seen her for at least a couple of moons now,' Ainsel says.

'That's months,' Pandora says for the benefit of Luke and me. I nod politely. Why didn't they *say* months then?

'That's around the time Dad disappeared too,' I say. 'He disappeared on the first of April.'

'I think Tate was gone at least a couple of weeks before that,' says Eldridge, 'because I picked some of the Orchids to take to her and she'd already gone.'

'The Orchids first bloom at the end of March,' says Pandora, 'so she probably disappeared a week or two before Sam.'

I drag Dad's piece of paper out of my bag excitedly.

'Look, I found this with Dad's stuff.' I lay the sheet of creased paper on the floor and straighten it out. 'It was dated first of April, the day Dad went missing. But does anybody know where Gossamer Paddock is? And he mentions the Shadow Fae.'

Everybody looks at Pandora as the colour drains from her face.

'Yes,' she says quietly, 'Gossamer Paddock is on Ethan's estate.'

'I thought that the Black-Wing baby who died was called Ethan?' says Eldridge loudly and Ainsel punches him hard on the arm.

'What?' says Luke.

Pandora sighs, and looks round at us all, one at a time. Eldridge stares at Luke insolently and carefully folds his wings behind him, lies down. He plucks a strand of grass and holding it across his mouth, blows against it making the most ridiculous horrible screeching noise. Luke glares at Eldridge with something wild in his eyes.

Pandora straightens her skirt over her knees. She delves into her handbag again and pulls out a couple of bags of cheese and onion crisps, hands them to the twins. They pull them open and start munching away at them. What? I mean, Crisps? *Crisps?*

'I think I'd better tell the story, the whole story, from the beginning,' says Pandora, crossing her legs over at the ankles and touching Luke's hand affectionately.

'Many years ago, when I was a girl, there was one Black-Wing Fae left. Zoran. He was as evil as they come and he desperately wanted a child to carry on the Black-Wing heritage. Obviously no Fae girl in her right mind would partner with him, and a Black-Wing needs to partner with Fae blood in order to continue the Black-Wing line.'

Luke glances sideways at me and I know he's thinking the same as me, *that's why Jasper tried to rape me.* We share the thought for a moment and then both turn our attention back to Pandora's story.

'I'm a Fae Hybrid, and I had just turned sixteen. Like you, Scarlett, I had recently discovered my Fae heritage, and it was all very new and exciting. I thought all the Fae people were wonderful and kind and sweet when I met this handsome boy called Zoran. He was very charming. He was older than me and seemed to be very sophisticated and wise, strong and fit. He had tiny black wings, which fascinated me, but he would never let me touch them. That should have alerted me to the fact that something was wrong, but it didn't. I fell in love with him, or rather the person I thought he was. And I started meeting him in secret. One day I agreed to go back with him to his cabin.'

Pandora smiles sadly as though recalling the last happy moment of her life.

'And afterwards, when I tried to leave...'

There are tears running freely down Pandora's cheek but she makes no attempt to dry them.

'He wouldn't allow me to go home. He said I had something of his. He was referring, of course, to the baby I was carrying inside me. He kept me captive for nearly nine months.'

'God that's terrible!' blusters Luke. 'He kept you prisoner?'

'Of course the Fae village were incensed when they found out, they tried to rescue me. But there was bloodshed. The thing is, you see, the Black-Wings, they are very strong. Their Black-Wing blood not only makes them evil, it also makes them very tough, much tougher than the average Fae.'

Pandora smiles at me weakly.

'The only Fae who stood a chance of overcoming the Black-Wing boy was the Sage Fae, Layla. The Sage Fae is the strongest and oldest family strain in the Fae world, and the only Fae to compare to the Black-Wings.'

'Layla was my grandmother,' I say, and Pandora nods. 'So Layla came to your rescue?'

'Well no, not at first. Layla was pregnant at the time – she was carrying her first baby. She didn't want to risk harming her unborn child.'

'Was the baby my mother, Tate?' I say, puzzled and confused about timing.

'No, it was long before your mother was born. This was a baby boy. He was due about the same time as my baby.'

Pandora puts her hand protectively over her abdomen as though protecting her baby son all over again. Her other hand covers her mouth, as though remembering is just too painful for her.

'Zoran wanted his Black-Wing baby so much, he couldn't wait until I gave birth naturally in case Layla tried to rescue me and he lost control over me and the baby. So he decided to cut the baby out of me. I was almost full term.'

'That would have harmed you wouldn't it?' Luke asks, his eyes flashing.

'Yes it would have killed me. But he had no use for me any longer. He just wanted his Black-Wing baby.'

Pandora's hands are shaking.

'Zoran came to me that day, to take the baby. I can see the blade now. He came towards me, his face pure evil. I cowered like a cornered animal, defenceless against him.

'But Layla burst into the cabin and killed him. Right there and then. Layla took the knife that he was going to use on me and cut off his Black-Wings. He died horribly. He bled out revolting black slimy blood, the smell was repulsive. But he put up quite a fight.'

Pandora looks down at her hands; her words are coming in jerks now. I suppress a vision of Jasper's horrible slimy Black-Wings. Oh my God, my grandmother killed Jasper's grandfather. Pandora puts her arm around me and pulls me close.

'But Layla lost her own baby that day. Zoran kicked her hard and she knew her baby couldn't have survived it.'

'No!'

'And later that evening I gave birth to a baby boy. It was so unfair. *So* unfair. My baby boy was healthy and pink and beautiful, and Layla's baby boy was born grey and lifeless.'

Luke cradles his grandmother in his arms until her sobbing subsides.

Pandora gets out her white cotton healing hanky and gently mops her face. She blows her nose and clears her throat. She takes Luke's hand, and my hand, to continue the story.

'Layla saved my life, killed Zoran, lost her baby, and helped deliver my Black-Wing child all in the same day. We both knew what had to be done. The Black-Wing baby could not be allowed to live. Too many people had died at the hands of the Black-Wings. Too much blood had been shed and this was our one chance to rid the Fae world of all Black-Wings. My baby was the last living Black-Wing. I knew that he would have to be destroyed.'

Pandora pauses; we are all holding our breath.

'But I couldn't do it. I tried. Layla wanted to take the baby right away. So that I didn't see him. Didn't hold him. But I insisted. I was responsible for this baby being born, I was responsible for the Fae prince's death, and I was not going to allow anybody else to suffer.' Pandora sighs.

'But I couldn't do it. I sat and cradled my baby in my arms. I fed him. I dug a hole in the earth. I filled it in again, and then I took him and ran away. Ran away to the everyday world. I thought maybe, just maybe, if my baby grew up in the everyday world, he would grow up normal. No baby is born evil. Or so I thought. But I was wrong.

'He was my first-born child, Ethan. Nobody in the Fae world knew he had lived. I kept it a secret. But Ethan grew up to ruin people's lives, to cause heartache and destruction, and he produced two more offspring who were no better than himself.'

'Do you regret not killing Ethan when he was a baby?' Ainsel says, her eyes wide with innocence.

'No,' says Pandora after a short moment's thought. 'No. Although I suspected Ethan would be a handful, it's wrong to assume that any baby is evil. There's a place for every child, every creature born on this planet. We all start off with the same choices. We choose our own path in life. I still believe that Ethan had a choice, as a Black-Wing he clearly had a genetic disposition towards evil, but I brought him up knowing right from wrong and I still prefer to believe that he *could* have chosen a different path.

'Hindsight is a wonderful thing, Ainsel, and looking back it's clear that the world would be a better place if Ethan had not existed at all. He's responsible for misery and death of innocent creatures and good people. But he *does* exist, and I don't believe anybody has the right to say who should live and who should die.'

There's a sad silence as everybody processes this information. Something catches my eye and I look round. A little way away, almost hidden by a gathering of bushes, is a girl my age. She's crouched on the floor, her long dark hair covering most of her face. But I can see she's silently crying. She's almost directly behind the twins and Pandora, but she's listening to every word spoken. She looks up and my heart lurches, her eyes lock onto mine for just a moment, appealing. Tears spill down her cheek and she's shaking. I incline my head fractionally in a nod. She smiles weakly in response. My heart warms, even after everything that has happened, Sasha and I still understand each other. Then 'pop' she disappears.

Nobody in my group seems to have noticed. They are still processing what Pandora has told us. I wonder how long Sasha was sitting there. Did she hear everything that was said?

'So Layla was wrong to ask for the baby to be killed?' I say.

'No, Layla saw it from a different perspective. There are always different views of the same thing. The Black-Wings have been responsible for the death of many, many innocent Fae people over the years, over the generations. Layla made that decision to protect her people, on behalf of the Fae world. It's like a leader making the decision to go to war. There is bloodshed, there is pain and suffering. But sometimes few have to suffer for the good of the majority, and the future of the people. And she was right.'

'How could you be right, and she be right too?' says Eldridge, his nose crinkling.

'There are always different shades of the same argument, Eldridge. For example, two people with different religious beliefs. They can't both be right. Can they?'

'No,' pipes up Luke, 'that's why there are so many wars over religion – we did a whole term about it in school.'

Eldridge snorts. 'Well they teach you rubbish in school then!' he says. Luke glares at him.

'Well, think about this,' says Pandora. 'If you all to think about how you are *feeling* right now. At this precise moment. Think of *one word* to describe it, and hold that word in your head.'

We all stare at Pandora, concentrating.

'Now, tell me, one at a time, what word you are thinking.' Pandora looks at each of us in turn.

'Baffled,' says Luke, his brow creasing.

'Happy,' says Ainsel, beaming at Pandora.

'Irritated,' says Eldridge, glancing sideways at Luke.

'Worried,' I say.

'So which one of you is right?' says Pandora.

Chapter Twenty-Nine

'How did Ethan get to be so wealthy?' I ask Luke in a hushed tone, thinking about that massive house and all the expensive stuff inside it. And Sasha's ponies. And her designer gear.

It's the following morning and Luke and I are sitting in Pandora's kitchen, eating crisp hot crumpets dripping with real butter and smeared with sweet local honey. I couldn't sleep last night and judging by the number of texts Luke sent me all through the night, neither could he. So I walked over to Luke's house early. I can hear Pandora moving around in the bathroom above.

'I'm not exactly sure,' says Luke, 'but he started with nothing. Gran and Granddad kicked him out when he was about sixteen. They wouldn't let him near the house.'

'That's a bit harsh,' I breathe. 'Why did they kick him out?'

Luke goes over to the sink and washes the grease off his buttery hands.

'It was something to do with my mum, Grace. He did something to her.' He comes back to sit at the table, his eyes flashing with emotion.

The floor creaks and we both spring round. Pandora is standing behind us. She silently goes over to the sink and fills her teapot with water from the kettle. *Please don't let her have heard what I said.*

She sits at the table, facing Luke and me. Her hands are shaking a little and she looks severe. *Oh no.* I want to kick myself. I've upset her. I've made her angry. Oh God why can't I 'undo' the last two minutes. My face is hot with shame and I can't meet her eye.

I feel a warm bony hand over mine, and I look up to see she has taken both Luke's and my hands in hers.

'I need to tell you about Ethan, my dears,' she says, and she smiles sadly at us both.

Her eyes are strained and watery and her hand still shakes slightly as she pours milk into her china teacup. She places a knitted tea cosy over her teapot.

'Gossamer House, the house where Ethan lives with Sasha and Jasper, used to be owned by a lovely couple, Hilda and Horace. They lived there with their son Joe. They were very kind to me when I came back to the everyday world. I was young and single and had a very young baby. In those days, there was a name for girls who had babies at sixteen out of wedlock. But Hilda and Horace didn't judge me, they never asked questions, they offered me a job and a room. I was taken on to do some cleaning work in the house, and I was able to look after my baby at the same time. They were very kind.'

'Hilda and Horace?' says Luke, clearing his throat. 'Weren't my great-grandparents called Hilda and Horace?'

'Yes, dear,' says Pandora, smiling. 'Their son Joe was a little older than me, and very handsome.' Pandora's eyes twinkle. 'He was away at college but he came home for holidays and sometimes weekends. We became very close.'

Pandora pours herself a cup of tea from the pot, and takes a sip.

'Ethan was six or seven when Joe and I got married. We bought this little cottage at the edge of the woods, close to Hilda and Horace. And Grace was born two years later. We were very happy.'

Pandora pauses whilst she butters a slice of toast. Luke and I wait in silence for her to continue.

'We struggled with Ethan. We thought at first it could be jealousy. But his behaviour got worse as he grew older. And we couldn't have him hurt his little sister in that way.'

'What exactly did he do?' says Luke, his lip starting to quiver.

'Ethan was nine years older than Grace. He had always been a handful – we used to get reports from school about bullying, and inappropriate behaviour. And he would hurt animals. We found dead animals around the garden and fields, they had been tortured and, well I think he actually enjoyed hurting them. He got pleasure from their pain. I believe these days they call people like him sociopaths. No understanding of right or wrong.'

I stare down at the table top as I remember the day Jelly Tot went missing. Sasha and I hunted in all the gardens all morning, calling her name. Eventually it was Sasha who found her in the field behind Gossamer House, her little ginger fluffy body limp and lifeless, a huge red gash in her middle where Jasper's dog had ripped the life out of her. I blink hard, determined not to get upset again. Pandora pauses whilst she tops up her tea from the teapot.

'But the final straw was when Grace was six or seven. We had noticed she was becoming withdrawn, and she was reluctant to go to bed at night. Ethan was fifteen or sixteen, and it came to light...' Pandora sighs heavily. 'It came to light that Ethan was interfering with our daughter, my precious little girl. He was...well we never really found out the full extent of what he had done, but we found him in her room at night, more than once. Grace was a very unhappy little girl. That was why we sent Ethan away.'

I take a sip out of the can of Coke in front of me, and wipe my mouth with the back of my hand. Luke's face crumples and Pandora walks round to him and holds him.

I feel uncomfortable, like I'm intruding on a family matter. I get up from the table and walk out into the garden. I sit on a wooden bench just outside the door and look up towards the sky. I can hear Pandora and Luke talking but can't hear what they are saying. I close my eyes, the air is crisp and there's a light breeze, but the sun is hot on my eyelids. I can see a swirl of colours inside my eyes. The occasional word drifts from the kitchen, Grace...bedroom...darkness...not sure...

I try to picture what it is they are talking about. What Ethan was doing to the poor little girl? Horrible. I can imagine Grace in her bedroom, a place which should be her safe haven. How frightened she must have felt, when she saw her bedroom door opening. I can imagine it; see it in my mind's eye, a little girl, probably blonde like Luke, with big wide vivid-blue eyes just like Luke and Pandora's. In bed, her safe haven. The light from the hallway lights up her face. She is holding her breath. Poor little thing. The boy at the doorway smiles at her. 'Hello, angel,' he says. His voice is boyish, he approaches the bed and there is a strangled cry of fear from the little girl.

I jolt myself. Why am I thinking about this. *I am sick.* I try to snap myself out of my thoughts, but I can't. I try to open my eyes but all I can see is the room, the dark room. I can smell petals, innocence. I can't stop myself from thinking this, it's as though there's a television screen in front of me and I'm watching a replay in my head. The boy is pulling back the bedclothes. She's wearing pink pyjamas. The little girl curls into a ball, she is whimpering. The boy laughs. His hand reaches out. I want to shout out but I can't seem to control it. It's like I'm stuck in a video replay.

I try to tear my eyes away from what's happening, I feel nauseous. The little girl has her eyes tight shut, her face fills my replay screen, her eyes are closed, I see fear, revulsion, dread. Her face turns away from the boy. I won't look. I won't look at what he is doing to her. I won't. I tear myself away...I try to scream. For the little girl. For me.

But then it's as though the television channel has changed. I can't control it. But I breathe in relief. It's in the countryside. There's a lake. Grass. There is an elderly couple. They look so sweet, they are holding hands. They are dressed quite old-fashioned; she wears a blue flowery dress and a straw hat. The dress is tied with a belt at the waist and a white cardigan with the top button fastened. They're walking alongside the lake. Smiling. Looking into each other's eyes. They must be around the same age as Pandora. My heart lifts, I don't know what's happening but this is better than that scene in the bedroom.

A boy approaches the couple and they turn and smile at him.

'Hello, Ethan,' the old lady calls to him. And I freeze. Ethan? My TV image zooms into his face. He's older. Older than the scene in the bedroom. But the same boy. The old lady looks at him fondly, and the man pats him on the back. Ethan must be in his early twenties. He looks fit and tanned. He smiles at the elderly couple, he's talking to them, telling them about the flowers he's going to plant in their garden. Does he work for them? They must be his employers.

I feel as though I'm privy to a private conversation, eavesdropping. I feel uncomfortable. I want to leave but can't seem to. I try to open my eyes but it's like they are already open. It's like an action replay, of something that has already happened.

Ethan is walking beside the couple, talking animatedly. They are listening intently. The old man has a walking stick and limps slightly. The elderly lady is laughing. The sweet old lady stoops to pluck a pretty blue flower from the edge of the lake, and she feeds it into the man's buttonhole. There's a camera slung over Ethan's shoulder, and he takes it out of its case, points the lens towards the elderly couple. The man straightens his tie, and places his hand around the lady's shoulders. They smile for the camera. They look happy. As my vision seems to pan around the field, I realise what I am looking at. Where. It's the Gossamer Estate. Ethan's estate. I don't understand. He's a gardener at the estate? How did he get from being a gardener to owning the estate?

The vision goes back to him. Ethan. He's laughing with the old couple and the man is slapping him on the back jovially.

And then it happens. They are quite close to the edge of the lake. Ethan is walking between the elderly couple, has his arm resting over their shoulders. The man stumbles, the old lady lurches. Ethan's hands are on their back, pushing, pushing them towards the edge. The water. I shriek out but no noise comes out, I want to grab them, but all I can do is watch. They both tumble into the water. The lady cries out as she rolls into the lake. The water's deep, a huge splash, the couple come to the surface clutching each other, gurgles, gasping, shouting. The look on the lady's face. Terror. The man reaches out for the bank, grabs some grass. Ethan kicks his hand away from the bank. Just for a second the look on the old man's face, it seems to freeze-frame, he looks horrified, betrayed...and he slips down into the dark water alongside his wife. I'm crying out in my head but no sound, I want to help, I have to help.

But there's nothing I can do. I can't interact. I can't change history. It has happened. Ethan is watching. He has killed them. Murder. I want to be sick. The lake surface is broken with the ripples, which are still moving outwards, a couple of air bubbles rise to the surface. And then stillness. Ethan smiles.

As he turns the image of his face fills my view, for a fleeting second, just a moment, I swear he looks straight into my eyes. My mind fills with something black and horrible, I shudder. And then he turns away and saunters casually towards the large house. Gossamer House.

And then I'm back. I'm back in Pandora's garden. I blink. I've come out of my horrible video. Thank God. I gasp for air. I'm shaking, filled with disgust. I can't get the image of Ethan's vile face out of my head, and that lovely couple as they tumble into the water, and the little girl, Grace, Luke's mother, as she tries to block out what is happening to her.

I struggle to stand; my legs have turned to jelly. All my muscles feel like blobby things, they won't work properly. I sit back down and breathe. In, out. In, out. I try again, holding on to the arm of the bench. I can't wipe it out of my head. The faces of that lovely old couple. The little girl. That horrible wicked immoral boy.

I shakily walk into Pandora's kitchen. Luke and Pandora are

still sitting at the table talking. There's a book of photos in front of Luke and he's pointing to a photograph. I can't hear what they are saying; the words are merging into one big 'blah'. Just noise. It's like I'm hearing the conversation through a wall of water. I lower myself into the chair, reach for my drink. But I can't grasp it, my hand is shaking and my teeth are chattering. Pandora and Luke are looking at me. Kind words, I can hear kind words and a roaring sound in my ears, my face feels cold, my arms are sweating, a cold sweat, I want to throw up. The world goes black.

When I come round, I'm lying on Pandora's kitchen floor with my legs raised on a cushion. Luke passes me a glass of water.

'Okay?' he says.

I glance around, Pandora is placing a cool cotton hanky on my forehead and I feel the blood return to my face. I must have fainted. I deliberately shake all thoughts from my head. It was just my mind playing tricks on me. The scene in my head about Ethan. And Grace, Luke's mum when she was a girl. And the elderly couple. It was all my imagination. What's the matter with me? *Am I going mad?*

'I'm okay,' I say, struggling to sit up. 'Sorry about that.'

I pull myself to my feet. I feel okay. Maybe a bit wobbly. Pandora brings me a cup of tea. I take a sip and swallow, grimace. It's sickly sweet.

As the colour starts to return to my face I feel a little foolish. Fancy reacting like that, I must have dropped off to sleep. Strange dream. Kind of daydream.

I pull the Pandora's book of photos towards me. They are colour photos but they look like they have been sitting in this album for decades.

'That's my mum when she was a baby,' Luke laughs, as he sees me looking at a photo of a tiny pink baby being cradled by a young woman.

I peer at the photo. It has 'Grace at one week' written beneath it in almost copperplate handwriting. I look at the woman holding the baby.

'Wow,' I say. 'Is that you, Pandora?

Pandora laughs. 'Yes, dear, I was a lot younger then.'

I peer at the photo. A lovely young woman with a radiant smile looks back at me.

'You look so happy,' I say.

'I was, dear,' she says.

I turn the page in the book, more photos and faces, all looking happy. More photos of Pandora and a man who I assume must be her husband Joe. A spaniel dog features in most of the photos too. My eye stops at a pretty photograph, of a little girl sitting in a field of daffodils. She looks about seven or eight years old. She has fair hair, vivid blue eyes and a haunted expression. My heart leaps into my throat. *Oh my God.*

'Is that Grace?' I say hesitantly, a creeping feeling at the back of my neck. But I know it is. I know because she looks exactly the same as she did in my daydream. In the little video that my sick brain forced me to witness. The little girl in her bedroom. I turn the page quickly trying to banish the image from my mind.

But it gets worse.

On the next page is a photograph of an elderly couple. I gasp. A sweet elderly couple. They are laughing and the man has his arm around his wife. They look so happy. A lovely photograph. The woman wears a blue floral dress and a straw hat. The man has a stick, and he has a blue flower in his lapel. They stand at the edge of a lake; they are beaming at the photographer. The person behind the camera.

But all I can see in my mind's eye is the shocked look on the same old lady's face as Ethan's hand firmly pushes her into the lake. Just moments after the photograph was taken. Oh my God, how could I have known? How could I have known what they looked like?

'That's Hilda and Horace,' says Pandora, as I struggle to

control my breathing. I cannot faint again, I mustn't.

'They employed Ethan as caretaker after he left home. He worked in the gardens at Gossamer House. But they both died. It was very sad, they both drowned in the lake. Together. It was a terrible accident. Nobody knows what happened.'

I freeze. *I know.*

But I don't know. How can I? It was just in my head. It was just a freaky dream or something.

'So why didn't you and Joe go back to live in Gossamer House?' Luke says. 'After Hilda and Horace died. How come Ethan is living there and we're living in this cottage?'

Pandora sighs. 'Joe was Hilda and Horace's only son, but they left everything to Ethan, not to Joe. The Will had been changed just a week before their accident. They must have been very fond of Ethan, and they left him everything. The whole estate and all their money. He became a very rich young man overnight.'

Luke gasps, and there's a shocked silence as he takes this in. I feel sick.

'Couldn't Joe could have contested the Will?' I protest angrily.

'He could have done, yes' —Pandora clasps my hand— 'but we were happy in our little cottage, and frankly we didn't want to get into a legal battle with our son. We were glad he was at last happy, he had got what he wanted, and we hoped he might turn a corner. He was a young man now, and had inherited consid-erable wealth. We hoped this would satisfy his greed.'

We are silent for a long while. There's an air of sadness, everybody lost in their own thoughts.

I clear my throat. I need to move the conversation away from anything related to those horrible daydreams I had. Whatever they were. I shake my head, as though to sort out all the facts, I seem to be confusing reality with fantasy. These visions are just not normal. *I'm* not normal. Unless...unless...

'Pandora...what's Tate's special Fae gift?' I say, almost afraid of the response.

'Tate's a Visionary, she can see things,' Pandora says. 'She gets visions of something that is happening somewhere else, to other people, or flashbacks of something that's happened in the past. You'll probably have the same gift – it's passed on through the family.'

I'm breathing really fast and my hands are shaking.

Oh my God. Oh my God. Oh my God.

I spend the next half hour disclosing my visions of Dad and Tate in the stable, and my suspicions that they are somehow being held captive on Ethan's estate. After I've finished I look from Pandora to Luke, waiting for them to tell me I'm crazy. But they don't. They sit in silence. Eventually Pandora speaks.

'Mmm, that doesn't make sense,'

'Why?'

Pandora looks serious.

'Tate couldn't survive in the everyday world, the air would choke her. So if they are together, they're in the Fae world.'

'But if your dad's been stuck in the Fae world since April he'll be suffering from Fae sickness by now,' blurts Luke. Pandora shoots him a warning glance.

'Fae sickness?' I say, a cold fear creeping through my veins as I remember how grey and sickly Dad appeared in my visions. 'What's Fae sickness?'

'It's a little like altitude sickness,' says Pandora softly. 'Everyday people find the Fae atmosphere too rich, after a while they can have symptoms, breathlessness, dizziness, nausea, nosebleeds.'

'That's how Dad looked in my dream, he was coughing and he looked grey and sickly.'

'But if Sam and Tate are at Gossamer Paddock, it can't be in the Fae world. It's just not possible,' says Pandora kindly. 'The Fae membrane surrounds the woods, but it can't possibly stretch as far as the buildings on the Gossamer Estate.'

I feel crushed. It seemed like I had all the answers. Luke sees my crestfallen expression and touches my arm.

Pandora gathers her bags. 'I've an appointment in town, but I don't want either of you to go anywhere near the Gossamer Estate.' I smile weakly. You'd think we were twelve-year-olds. Pandora looks pointedly at Luke.

'It's okay, Gran, don't worry, we're not going anywhere near there. Not on the basis of a dream Scarlett had.' He laughs and I glare at him.

I feel deflated, I was kind of hoping Luke might be the one person who would help, would understand. Now I know my visions could be real, that Dad and Tate could be alive somewhere, held captive, trapped, I'm all fired up and want to do something.

Luke leans over and gives his gran a kiss on her cheek, and I force myself to smile. I feel let down.

'See you later, Gran,' Luke says, and takes her teacup and saucer over to the sink to wash.

We sit silently in our chairs, listening to his gran walking down the hallway. We hear the door softly close behind her. Luke waits a beat and then leaps up.

'C'mon, let's go and find your dad.'

Chapter Thirty

'You saw her too, didn't you?' Luke says as we make our way towards Gossamer House.

'Who?'

Luke just looks at me.

'Yes, I saw her,' I murmur. I have been haunted by the memory of how forlorn Sasha looked the other day, huddled behind the bushes, gently weeping as Pandora told her story.

I peer between the chestnut trees and view the huge house rising before us. Gossamer House. The last time I came here was three months ago. Just before Dad disappeared.

'Do you think she heard anything?'

'Yes,' I say, remembering about how distraught Sasha looked as she huddled behind the bush. 'I think she heard everything.'

As we approach the house we veer off to the right. The edge of Gossamer Woods borders the estate to the left and rear. The outbuildings lie to the right of the house. I can see now what Pandora meant when she said that the Fae membrane couldn't possibly stretch as far as the outbuildings.

I glance nervously towards the house as we scurry past, crouching low beneath the window. Two cars sit proudly in the driveway, Jasper's red MG sports car and Ethan's black Range Rover.

As we slip round the side of the house we're less visible from the house. We make our way out towards the outbuildings, past the new stable block, the field where Sasha keeps her ponies and the paddock where Sasha's favourite horse is grazing.

I glance back. Despite its grandeur, the large house looks bleak and lifeless.

One of Sasha's horses lumbers over in the hope of an apple, nudges my arm.

'Not today, Spangle,' I whisper to the lovely chestnut pony.

He nuzzles his face into my hand and I stroke his coarse mane and kiss him on his velvety nose.

'Here!' hisses Luke and I rush to join him. The small cluster of outbuildings stand before us like a row of rotten teeth, different types, shapes and sizes, in varying degrees of dilapidation. I cast my eye over them. None look familiar. I thought I would recognise one as being the barn from my vision, but I really can't tell. It could be any one of them.

'Be careful,' I hiss. 'If Dad and Tate are inside, then one of the Black-Wings will be close. Luke nods and glances around cautiously. A mist is creeping in over the field from the direction of the woods. I shiver and look up towards the sky. It feels as though the sun has never shone on this piece of land.

We slide around the back of the first building; it's made of brick with a broken corrugated roof. Luke tries the door handle but the door doesn't shift, it's either locked or jammed shut.

I peer in through the broken window. A huge mature sycamore tree dominates the interior space, growing up through the ground, bent double as it tries to find its way through the roof and towards the sky. Branches poke out through broken windows. I feel sorry for it. I'd like to tear down the building from around the tree, brick by brick, give it room to breathe, grow and develop.

I suddenly feel tearful as I crane my neck to see the higher branches hunched over, their puny anaemic leaves craving sunshine and rain. There's a peaty mouldy smell, I peer in through a broken pane. A branch with large hand-like leaves wafts close to the window. I reach out and touch it. The leaves feel soft but crinkled.

I'm about to pull my head back when something catches my eye. Something out of place. In the corner.

I can't breathe. I just stare.

'What?' Luke says. 'Your dad?'

I shake my head, and pull back for Luke to peer through the

window.

'Is that your dad's bike?' he says eventually. I nod my head, the words frozen in my throat. We both heave, the door crashes open noisily and we are propelled into the hut. We both stop and listen. No sound.

I make my way over the bike, pushing back branches of the poor gnarled sycamore tree.

I touch the handlebars with a trembling hand. *Dad*. There's no mistaking it. It's painted half red and half white. Dad was using up some old paint; he had two half-pots of paint left over wanted to mix the two together. 'You can't do that,' I had told him. 'You can't ride a pink bike!' He had laughed, told me life was too short to worry about such things. But I had insisted. So he painted half the bike red, and half white.

Luke folds his arms around me and we stand together in silence.

'He must be here,' I whisper to Luke, unnecessarily. 'We must be right.'

Luke screws his nose up. 'You think?' he says. I slap him.

We scurry over to the next cluster of buildings, leaping over clumps of grass, boulders and bits of fencing scattered around.

The next three buildings stand close together. All three look well-used and in reasonable order, they're built of brick and have slate tiled roofs. Their windows are cracked but intact.

I peer through a window of the first building. It's empty. Just some bales of hay stacked in the corner and sacks of feed in the middle of the floor.

We move on to the second outbuilding. It's the smallest of the three buildings and doesn't seem to have a window. Luke moves towards the door and puts his hand on it.

'Wait!' I hiss at him. 'Careful! I'm sure this is the building Sasha used to shove Jasper's dog in, when he was away.'

Luke pushes the door open and I stand behind him. It looks empty. As the daylight washes into the room, all I can see is dust and containers of black paint in the corner. And plastic storage boxes piled along the back wall. Broken toys spilling out, old camera equipment, car manuals. One of the boxes is cracked and something indescribable is oozing out onto the floor. The stench takes my breath away. Like ammonia and rotting flesh.

We back out of the building quickly and close the door. I look around nervously for the dog. If it's not in this shed, it could be in the grounds somewhere.

Luke makes his way cautiously towards the final outbuilding. It's brick like the others, with a window on each length, a brick wall facing us. It's larger and taller than the other outbuildings, more like a barn or disused stable. It's difficult to gauge its exact size as the end of the barn disappears into the grey mist that seems to emerge from the woods beyond. The doorway is just beyond our field of vision, cloaked by the mist.

And there's that same nasty smell. It's the same unmistakable stink that was present in my recurring dream. My vision. That sooty, chemically smell. My stomach wants to heave.

I tiptoe to the wall and lean with my back against it, Luke does the same, both pressed up against the wall. I suddenly want to laugh.

We slide along the wall until we're at the edge of the window frame. *This is it.* I'm breathing heavily. What will I see when I peer inside? *I'm going to see Dad.* My stomach gives an excited flip.

I turn and put my face to the window. It's filthy dirty and I can hardly see inside, there's a rusty metal grille fixed inside the window frame. But I recognise it straight away. It's the same barn. It's the right barn. It's the barn in my vision. I can see the dark walls, the desk in the corner, the bales of hay, some empty sacks piled in the corner, the horse tackle hanging on the hooks on the walls. The mattress and blankets on the floor where Dad and Tate were lying.

I rub at the murky window with my hand. I can make out vague shapes. I rub again. There could be a figure; an outline of somebody is sitting at the desk. It could be Dad. I can't see properly. Can't be sure.

'I think they're in there!' I whisper to Luke. 'But I can't see properly. It's all murky, *you* look.'

Luke moves past me and peers in at the window, his hands above his eyes and his face pressed up against the glass. After a few moments he moves away and shrugs.

'I can't see anything. You sure it's the right barn?'

'Yeah, I'm absolutely certain.'

'You *sure* though? A lot of barns must look alike.'

'Of *course* I'm sure,' I hiss at him loudly. 'There's the desk where Dad was sitting. And the blankets on the floor where Tate was lying. And I thought I saw a shape of a person.'

'Well let's go inside and look properly.' Luke takes a step towards the doorway.

'But it could be Ethan!' I say. 'It looked like a person, but I couldn't make it out properly. The window was too dirty. I can't be sure.'

Luke ducks beneath the window, edging towards the farthest end of the barn. The mist is still lingering round the doorway and I glance behind to see where it ends. There's no mist over the fields, it just seems to be around the outbuilding and into the woods. Funny, I've never seen mist like this before. In fact it's more like smog. A sooty black fog.

'LUKE!' I hiss, grabbing his arm.'

'What...' I clamp my hand over his mouth and push him back against the wall.

We're not alone. To my horror a man has appeared as if from nowhere, he's standing just a few feet away from us.

It's Ethan, there's no mistaking him. The same man I saw in my flashback killing the elderly couple. The same man who crept into his sister's bedroom in the middle of the night. And the same man I saw in my vision hitting my dad over the head. He's the spit of Jasper, but older. And shabbier. He's lighting a cigarette.

He has something slung over his shoulder. A shotgun. I stop breathing. And any second now he's going to look up and see us. We both freeze-frame, bracing ourselves.

But then there's a loud scream, it comes from the direction of the paddock. Ethan spins towards the sound. Sasha's standing in the middle of the paddock, screaming and waving her arms around.

'Dad, DAD!'

Luke and I both slam our backs flat against the wall. Because just at that minute Jasper appears too, emerging from the black fog. I hold my breath.

Sasha screams again and flings her arms in the air.

'Quickly, COME QUICKLY!' she yells.

'What's the stupid bitch up to now?' splutters Jasper, and they both move away, towards Sasha.

'That was close,' hisses Luke, his face is grey.

'Come on,' I whisper, and we both slip behind the outbuilding and race across the field towards the woods. My heart is pounding in my chest. We dive behind a tree.

'What a stroke of luck she screamed at that moment,' whispers Luke, gasping to get his breath. 'I wonder what's wrong with her? Probably broke a nail.' He sniggers but I glare at him. He really is slow sometimes.

'There was no *luck* in it,' I hiss back. 'Sasha must have seen us, she was distracting them. She did it for us!'

Luke's still breathing heavily, his eyes bulging. 'Why would she help us?'

'I don't think things are quite as straightforward as they appear. There's something going on with that family. Something not right.'

'It's not just the family that's weird,' Luke says. 'That fog stuff, that's not normal. I don't know what it is, but it stinks. And did you hear the 'sloop' noise as Jasper appeared through it? It's not right that, it was as if they came through a doorway or something. And it closed behind them. Sloop sloop.'

I glance nervously at the fog, it stinks. Thick, suffocating. Just like the smell in my vision. It must be right, this is definitely the place. Dad's here somewhere. But Tate is right; we can't get into the barn. That smell must be something to do with the poisonous Ethereal Black. It's pure poison. Just like the Black-Wings.

'Come on,' says Luke, jabbing me in the arm. 'We're not going back there, not today anyway.'

I glance towards the paddock. Sasha's dad and brother have joined her and I can hear a heated discussion.

'It was Spangle, I thought he was lame!' she's protesting. 'I was worried!'

'You brought me out here for *THAT!*' Ethan growls, and I'm horrified to see him bring his hand backwards and swipe Sasha hard across the head, knocking her to the ground.

'No!' says Luke and starts to scramble. I pull him back.

'Stay here!' I say. 'There's nothing you can do, look, it's over now, look...'

Jasper and Sasha are marching back towards the fog, they disappear into the smoggy murkiness and it closes behind them like a screen door.

'Shit,' says Luke. 'That's just wrong. There's something sinister going on here.'

Sasha pulls herself up to her feet and darts across the field towards us, glancing back furtively towards the fog where her brother and father disappeared. As she approaches I want to rush up to her, to hold her. But I don't. I can't. I just stand there.

'Go!' she hisses. 'Go, they'll be back out soon and if they find you here they'll kill you both!'

I reach out and touch Sasha's arm gently. She recoils at my touch as though she's been electrocuted, hugging herself. Her arms are bruised badly, worse than before.

'Sasha,' I say quickly, 'where's my dad and Tate?'

Sasha shakes her head, 'I honestly don't know, Scarlett,' she says. There are tears in her eyes. 'They don't tell me anything.'

There's a growling noise and Jasper's vicious dog suddenly emerges as if from nowhere.

'GO!' Sasha gasps and she turns and runs towards the house, her legs stumbling and sliding across the mud and gravel.

I freeze. This is the dog that killed my cat, my lovely gentle cat. I hate this dog.

The ugly canine hurtles towards us, the hackles on its back standing on end, low throaty growls escaping from behind its yellow teeth. It comes to within six feet of me; its eyes fixed on mine, and stops abruptly.

'Stay absolutely still!' hisses Luke, his voice sheer panic.

I feel such hatred for this dog, I want to kill it. I don't feel fear. I lock eyes with it, the dog glowers back giving out low rumbling growls, those teeth, my poor cat. But it doesn't move any closer. And then strangest thing happens. The dog begins to back off, to cower. I want to kill it, it killed my cat, I want to...I take a step towards it and the dog yelps, shrinks back, and lowers its gaze. It won't look at me.

Luke grabs my arm and yanks me back against the tree just as Jasper emerges from the fog again.

'Gnasher! Go get the silly bitch, Gnasher, ATTACK!'

Jasper points towards Sasha, laughing like a madman. The dog turns and hurtles after Sasha.

'He's turned the bloody dog on his sister!' Luke gasps.

We both watch in horror as the ugly little dog tears across the field, catching up with Sasha, snapping at her ankles with blood-curdling snarls. We hear a thump as she reaches the back door and slams it shut in the dog's face.

'Let's get out of here,' says Luke.

Chapter Thirty-One

It's four days since Luke and I found that barn at Gossamer Paddock. I know Dad and Tate are there, on the other side of the fog. But I don't know how to get to them. Tate said that Ethereal Black stuff was lethal to Fae people, and the only non-Fae person I know, who is going to believe a story about fairies, is Maggie.

And she's sitting on the settee right now, staring at me. Her eyes are wide open, her cheek is twitching and her wine glass is slipping from her fingers.

'You want me to WHAT?' she finally says, her voice loud but squeaky. 'You say you come from a land of *fairies*, and you have had a *vision* about Sam being held by people with black wings. And you want me to walk into a dangerous black fog to save them and bring them home?'

I stare down at my hands and focus on my nails. They need cutting; they're all torn and split from spending so much time in the woods. Why did I ever mention this to Maggie? I really thought she would understand. I thought she believed. I thought—

'It's that LUKE boy isn't it!' Maggie is saying. 'He's odd that boy. Just like his grandmother, she was always hanging around when you were a young. She's a bit strange but her kids are definitely not right.'

'No, Maggie, I've got to know Pandora quite well, she's lovely, she gave me the hanky with the Gossamer Orchid balm on it, that's what healed my hand, you said yourself that the Gossamer Orchids had healing qualities.'

The minute it's out of my mouth I know it's a mistake. Maggie's eyes are like thunder.

'Those Orchids are EXTINCT, Scarlett.' Her voice is getting louder and louder, she fishes around in her handbag for her cigarettes and lights up as though her life depends on it.

'That barmy family have been planting weird ideas in your head. They're taking advantage of your grief, that's what they're doing. I knew I shouldn't have gone away and left you alone.'

Maggie looks like she doesn't know whether to cry or explode.

'I remember stories about Pandora's son, Ethan,' she says, pausing to suck the life out of her cigarette. 'He was always getting into trouble when he was young, mixed up with the police, there was a rape charge, and there was talk about...' Her voice trails off as she's trying to remember what it was she heard.

'Maggie, please listen to me. Luke's not Ethan's son, Ethan's his *uncle* not his father. Ethan is the Black-Wing!'

Maggie is looking at me as though she thinks I'm having some sort of breakdown. But I can't stop now, I need to explain. I need her to understand. To believe me.

'Just listen, Maggie, Luke's a Fae too, and so is Pandora – *that's* why she took an interest in me as a baby. She was the one who left me in the woods as a baby, Tate asked her to bring me to Dad to keep me safe.'

'Tate?' says Maggie, the sound of Tate's name seeming to soften her a little. 'What's Tate got to do with all this?'

'Dad's *with* Tate, they're stuck in the Fae world. That's the world that you both used to visit when you were little. In the woods. When you used to play with Tate. That's why you thought she was a fairy, she really *is* a fairy. A Fae. And that's why Dad couldn't find her...'

My voice trails off as I realise how bonkers this all sounds. To be honest if three weeks ago somebody told me this story, I'd think they'd lost it too.

I start to cry. Maggie puts her arm over my shoulders and holds me close. It's nice to be held.

'I'm sorry, Maggie,' I say after a while, 'I think I'll get to bed now. I've not been feeling so well these last few days. I think with Dad's disappearance and everything, and the story you told me about Tate, and Dad finding me in the woods. I think maybe I'm getting a bit confused.'

I peer at Maggie through watery eyes. She looks concerned but relieved that I'm finally talking sense.

'I'm sorry if I freaked you out, Mags,' I say. 'It's just that I've had some funny dreams lately and I started to wonder if they were real.' I laugh a little. And to be honest, I'm beginning to wonder if maybe I *am* going a little crazy.

'I want you to stay away from those woods,' says Maggie gravely, 'and stay away from that Luke boy too. What about Sasha, do you still see her? She's a *nice* girl.' Maggie is smiling kindly at me. I want to laugh at the irony of it, but can hardly tell her that Sasha is one of those Black-Wing people who are trying to hurt my dad.

'Okay, Maggie,' I say, resigned. 'I'll ring Sasha tomorrow.'

Maggie smiles broadly. In Maggie world, shopping is the cure-all for any ill. Even madness.

I climb the stairs to bed slowly, I'm feeling tired. Exhausted. My muscles ache. My head aches. I climb into bed and text Luke. DONT COME TO HOUSE. CONFIDING IN MAGS BAD IDEA, SHE THINKS I'M MAD.

Luke can't stay away from the Fae world now, he's brought all his paints and canvasses, and the twins let him stash them in their cabin. I watch as he sets up his easel and canvas in the sunlight. Eldridge is sitting nearby. Luke and Eldridge got off to a bad start but they seem to have made up their differences now. They're the same age, and they really seem to have hit it off.

I smile as Eldridge swipes his brush and holds it between his teeth like a rose, ducks and dives as Luke grabs out at it, swearing at him. All I can hear is loud boyish belly laughs as they race around. Luke retrieves his brush and sits back at his easel, stretches his long skinny tanned arms.

He's stopped drawing pictures on his arms. He's a different person now. Back at school he was a loner, kept himself to himself. Here he seems as though he's found his place. He always said he was searching for something in his pictures, but I suspect he was also searching for something in his life. And I think he's found it here in the Fae world. He looks at peace.

I haven't told Luke about my flashbacks about Ethan and Jasper. It was all a long time ago. And how can I be sure that it *was* Ethan who murdered Hilda and Horace. Or that a ten-year-old Jasper killed Luke's parents. There's no evidence, and it would hardly stand up in court.

But the main reason is that I don't want to hurt Luke. A voice inside keeps telling me that he has a right to know. But he's so happy at the moment and this would just dredge up pain for both him and Pandora. I'm beginning to realise that this gift of mine carries a huge responsibility.

Maggie and I haven't mentioned our 'conversation' since last evening. She was quiet at breakfast, but when I told her I was meeting Sasha in town and she brightened up. I feel bad deceiving her like this, but hey, look what happened when I tried to tell her the truth.

'So has Maggie banned you from coming to the Fae world?' mumbles Luke, stuffing all his brushes between his teeth to stop Eldridge from stealing them.

'Well,' I say, thoughtfully, 'if the Fae world is just a figment of my imagination, Maggie can hardly ban me from coming here can she?'

Luke grins and several paint brushes slide from between his teeth and clatter to the ground like a game of Pick-up Sticks.

'So asking Maggie to walk into the magic-eye fog to rescue your dad and Tate is out of the question?' He wiggles his eyebrows and I can't help but laugh.

Eldridge sits next to me and smiles. He seems different these days too. Luke has tamed him. He follows Luke around like a big brother, his eyes filled with something like admiration, almost awe.

'I can't work out if Sasha's trying to help us, or it's some kind of honey-trap,' says Luke, concentrating hard as he screws a cap onto a tube of oil paint.

Ainsel suddenly leaps to her feet and dances over to the fallen tree bough, holding out her arm. Three or four large butterflies land on her hand. She turns and holds her arms in the air and turns her face upwards, feeling the fresh breeze given off by their wings as they flutter into the air.

She's so childlike. I can't be affronted by her refusal to be sucked into my problems. It's a kind of innocence, like a child who doesn't quite understand the scale of a problem and is easily distracted. She's like a breath of fresh air.

'So tell me again,' I say, '*why* can't Dad and Tate be inside that barn and also within the Fae world? You said that the Fae membrane moves when you move inside it, so why is it so unbelievable that they have somehow managed to push the membrane outwards to include part of their land?'

Ainsel sighs, as though she's dealing with a naughty child who refuses to understand a simple instruction. Her lower lip plops out in a silly fairy pout, making both Luke and I grin at her. She dances over and flops gracefully onto the grass just below a beam of sunlight. Like a dancer taking centre stage. She lays her hands out either side of her, spreading her long graceful fingers in the short lush green grass. The beam of sunlight is like a spotlight, bouncing off her short dark hair giving it sheen; her little pointed ears look delicate with the hair cropped short around them. She's wearing a pretty, turquoise dress, which is transparent in part; semi-transparent where silver and gold strands knit together in a kind of skirt around her middle, which only just covers her modesty. She's the most beautiful creature I've ever seen and I can never get enough of her. I'm both amused and amazed that Luke seems to be so untouched by the beauty of this girl. If I were a boy, I would fancy her so much. Blimey, I'm a *girl* and I very nearly fancy her!

'It's just not possible,' Ainsel explains slowly. 'The only place where the membrane is thin enough for people to pass through is *here*, at this clearing by the oak tree. That's why Eldridge and I stay here most of the day. We are space-hoppers and—'

'Yes, I *get* that bit,' I interrupt rudely. 'But why is it not possible that the membrane has somehow thinned out and stretched somewhere else?'

'In any case,' says Ainsel, ignoring my question, 'the Fae membrane cannot pass through buildings.'

She smiles triumphantly.

'But it passes through trees and stuff,' I argue. 'You said yourself, trees and fixed things are there on both sides of the membrane, it's only the creatures and people who live on one side or the other.'

'Duh!' exclaims Eldridge. 'There's no way they could fill the barn with Fae atmosphere. It's impossible!'

He glances at Luke as though looking for approval, but Luke is just looks blank.

'Okay, so think of the Fae membrane as a huge rubber balloon containing the Fae atmosphere,' Eldridge says slowly, as though he's explaining it to a classroom full of young children, and I want to kick him.

'If you press the balloon to a building with holes for windows and doors, the building might shape itself around the building. But the air inside the balloon won't mingle with the air in the building, will it? The only way you could get Fae air into that building would be literally to pierce a gaping big hole in the balloon at the entrance to the building. And that's *impossible!*'

I lean back and close my eyes. Okay, okay, so it's not possible. The Fae membrane cannot have wrapped itself around the barn, at least if it did, nobody could get in and out unless they pass through the membrane. And the membrane is too thick to pass through.

'There is literally only one compound that could dissolve the

Fae membrane,' Eldridge is saying, 'and that's Ethereal Black. It turns the membrane into a black fog, making it thinner.'

I feel a prickle on my forearms. What did Eldridge just say? I blink open my eyes, Luke has a strange look on his face too. Sort of as though we've just invented cold fusion or something.

'Black fog?' breathes Luke.

I can't talk, so I nod my head violently at Luke.

'What?' says Eldridge. 'What?'

'The building, where Tate and Sam are being kept,' says Luke, 'it's covered in black fog. And there's Ethereal Black, everywhere. It's all over the place. That must be what they are using to dissolve the membrane.'

I pause for breath, my heart pounding. The twins are staring at me with huge frightened amber eyes.

'Ethereal Black?' repeats Ainsel, she has gone deathly white. 'But—'

Eldridge is shaking his head.

'It *couldn't* be,' he says.

'Oh my God, Luke, that chemical has dissolved the membrane and changed it into a black fog. The Ethereal Black. Somehow they have managed to pierce a hole in the membrane and that's how they are getting in and out of the Fae world.'

'But LISTEN,' says Eldridge, raising his voice. 'There isn't enough Ethereal Black in the whole *world* to create a fog that size,' interjects Eldridge. 'Even if you cut off the wings of a Black-Wing, there wouldn't be enough Ethereal Black inside them to make even a pinprick in the membrane. You would need buckets full of the stuff, and apart from in Black-Wings, it has never known to exist anywhere else, like ever. So where are they getting enough Ethereal Black to make a black fog?'

Luke and I look at each other. I make a gulping noise. Somehow I can't meet their huge innocent amber eyes.

'They're forcing my dad to produce the stuff synthetically, so they probably *have* bucketfuls of the stuff by now,' I say, staring at Luke.

Luke nods his head wildly, his eyes like saucers.

'Which means that Dad and Tate *are* in that barn,' I whisper.

We all sit in silence in a circle. There really is nothing more to be said. The sun's beating down on my back, but it just feels hot and uncomfortable.

'We're in big trouble,' says Eldridge eventually.

'Why is your dad helping them?' asks Ainsel, crinkling her nose. I want to cry. I feel as though I've let them down somehow.

'If he doesn't make the stuff they'll hurt Tate.'

'But why *him*?' Ainsel says. I stare down at my feet, focusing on an amazing pure white butterfly that's just landed on my toes, its white wings fluttering so fast that it looks like a white silvery dust is emanating from the wings.

'But why *him*?' Ainsel says again, poking me in the arm with her thin finger to get my attention. I sigh and look at her.

'He's probably one of the few scientists in the country who would know how to reproduce that stuff synthetically. That's what he does at the university. Whenever somebody finds a natural cure for something, like a herb or a flower or something, he tries to break it down and then reproduce it synthetically. Like recently somebody discovered that some remote tribe in the Amazon rainforest never ever get cancer. Ever. So they researched it and got it down to some flower that was found very high up in the trees, and it was very, very rare. But the tribe in that part of the forest used to harvest the flower every summer and mix it into some kind of drink or something. It had something inside it that had anti-cancer properties. So Dad had to find out what it was made of, and try and reproduce that synthetically.'

'So did he do it, did they find a cure for cancer?' asks Luke, his eyes shining.

I stare back down at my feet, really wishing I could tell him what he wanted to hear.

'No,' I say. 'He managed to reproduce it synthetically but it turned out to be useless. It wasn't the flower that had the anti-cancer agent inside it after all. So they went back to the Amazon to try and find out what it was.'

'Did they find it?'

'No,' I say sadly. 'The project ran out of money and they had to pack up and come home before they found the cure. It happens a lot apparently.'

'So the Black-Wings are forcing your dad to make poison, when he should be out there finding a cure for cancer!' announces Ainsel crossly. I smile. That is just *so* not the point.

I shiver, feeling cold despite the hot sun on my back. I feel trapped. But that's nothing to how Dad and Tate must be feeling. Being forced to make some stuff that could harm the person you love. And now he's made a load, what are they going to do with him?

'So Tate and your dad are stuck in that barn, and they can't get in or out without passing through the black fog?' says Ainsel, seeming suddenly to catch on. I nod. 'And it's not harmful to everyday people like your dad, or Black-Wings obviously, but it's harmful to any Fae person?'

Again I nod. There just doesn't seem to be a solution. Unless. Unless…

'I need to speak to Tate again,' I say suddenly. 'I think I might have an idea. But I really need to speak to Tate. I need to somehow bring on another of those vision things.'

'How're you going to do that?' says Luke. 'Can you just bring one on any time you like?'

'No. I don't know,' I say, sucking the air in through my teeth. 'But I need to find out, fast.'

I turn to Ainsel.

'Is there any way you can bring on your gifts, you know, control them, so you can have them whenever you want?'

'You learn to control it over time,' says Ainsel. 'But we've been practising for years. We had our gifts from birth. You only went into Transition a few weeks ago. There's absolutely no way you can control it, not yet.'

'Actually it's only three weeks,' I say, thinking back to my birthday, 'since I went into Transition.'

Is it really only three weeks since all this began?

'Have you noticed when you get the visions, what you're doing just beforehand?' asks Luke. 'What brings it on? Gran used to say that when she first went into Transition, her gift would be strongest when she was like really emotional, upset, or angry.'

'Sex,' says Ainsel, and we all stare at her. 'Sex might be able to bring on your gifts. You can't get more emotional than sex can you!' Her wings twitch so rapidly they lift her off the ground.

Luke starts to laugh.

'There you go then, you'll just have to have sex!' he says, wiggling his eyebrows at me.

My heart starts to pound and I feel my face blush deeply. Because the last few times I had a vision of Dad and Tate in the barn, it was after an encounter with Orion.

Chapter Thirty-Two

Okay, don't laugh, but I'm lying flat on my back, on my bed, in the dark. Stark naked.

I think Ainsel has a point. My visions do seem to be brought on by a sort of sexual thing, and it seems to be all mixed up with the feelings in my back, my wings. Like every time I get worked up, or aroused. That's when it happens. That's when my wings start to flutter, as though they're growing, developing. And that's when things change. My muscles. And that must be when I get my powers. My visions. When I can see Dad and speak to Tate. Ainsel said it was a highly sexual time. Transition. So perhaps sex brings it on. Makes it happen faster.

So what now? Maggie's out at her friend's wedding party tonight. So I can do what I like.

But I can't seem to get in the mood, I'm too distracted. Probably want it too much. It's bloody useless. I've tried everything. Pushing myself against the floor, like before. Pushing my hands into my back, like before. See if the wings will start fluttering, that usually starts things off. I've even tried other stuff. You know, sort of touching myself, you know – there. And it just felt silly. And was a bit sore and got hot and uncomfortable.

But perhaps if I relax a bit, I can get into the mood. And if I get into the mood, if I can get myself worked up enough…it should bring on a vision. I need to speak to Tate. And whenever I had the vision, it was when I was relaxed and exhausted. Afterwards. But I need to relax, I can't do it just because I want to.

I know, I'll try that relaxation stuff we used to do in the gym, after aerobics.

I lie back and breathe slowly and deeply. In. Out. In. Out. Concentrate on my toes, wriggle them around, and then relax them. Stretch out my legs and let them relax, go heavy. Breathe.

In. Out. In. Out. Arms, heavy, shoulders heavy, Heavy. In. Out. In. Out. Relaxed and sleepy. Sleepy. Sleeeeepy. Sleeeeeeeeepy.

Actually not that sleepy. Or relaxed.

Okay concentrate, try again, let all the tension of the day flow outwards, I can do this. I can even hear that woman in the gym talking us through the relaxation technique. My head, feeling heavy on the bed, my whole body heavy and floating, floating and relaxed and…oh hang on, is that my mobile? Perhaps it's a text. Maybe it's important. I grab my phone.

It's just an alarm I set to remind me to take the chicken out of the oven for Maggie. Yesterday. No wonder the chicken was burnt last night, I set the alarm for the wrong day.

Okay, concentrate. This is no good. Why can't I relax? Why can't I do it? I think back to the when I got my first vision. In the bedroom, when I first felt my wings flutter. I was exhausted after all that squirming around and stuff. And a bit worked up. Feel embarrassed now. What about the other two times? When did I have the vision the other night?

Oh yes. Oh yes, I remember. *Orion.*

I get up slowly, walk over to the wardrobe, pull out a long thick pullover. *Nothing else.* It comes down almost to my knees. *Nothing underneath.* I quiver, but not with cold.

I grab a torch.

This is for Dad. I slip out of the front door and close it quietly behind me. *This is for Dad.* A little cynical voice is laughing inside my head. *Yeah, sure it is.*

It's dark outside and I pick my way along the pathway through the woods. The sky's clear, black, filled with stars and a sliver of moon. The air is still warm – as though the trees have formed a giant green blanket to keep the crisp night air out for as long as possible. It smells dry and earthy. I feel myself unwind as I pass deeper into the woodland's comforting arms.

It looks different at night. My torch lights up the way but I feel sure I could find my way in complete darkness.

I begin to doubt myself. What if all the Fae are in bed? Perhaps they don't even stay out after dark. Perhaps it's bad for their wings or something.

When I reach the old oak tree I sigh and flop down, wondering how easy it will be to enter the Fae world in the darkness – how can I re-focus my eyes if I can't see anything? And how will I know whether I'm in the Fae world, with nothing to look at?

But I needn't have worried. I close my eyes and open them. And feel giddy. I put my arm out to steady myself. For it's no longer dark. The sky is still midnight blue but the whole place is lit up by tiny lights, filling every inch of the sky, glowing, like somebody has thrown fairy dust into the air and it's just hanging in space, sparking, a kaleidoscope of colourful wings – moths and butterflies, dragonflies, and other winged creatures. Like being inside a snow globe full of fluorescent fluttering petals. I quiver with delight. It's awesome.

'I'd close your mouth if I were you, you might catch a night-wing.'

I spin round. Eldridge.

'Oh, hello,' I say.

Oh God, he wears even less clothing at night-time. If that's at all possible. A pair of skimpy stretch boxer shorts and they don't hide much. Like a skimpy satin band loosely draped across his hips, half way down his bum in fact. And only just cover his, well his *thing* I suppose. But they are so…clingy. It looks pretty damn sexy and… He coughs and glares at me.

Oh God no I think he saw me looking. I feel the blood rush to my face. There's an awkward moment. But then he chuckles and turns away, I see that his tiny baby wings are also shimmering and luminescent.

'I'll get Ainsel shall I?' he peers past me as though he's looking for somebody else.

'Erm, no,' I pause, still hot with embarrassment. 'Actually it's not Ainsel I wanted to speak to. I glance around nervously. It's Orion.'

'Okay,' he says, 'I'll get him.' And he disappears. *Thank God.*

I sit on the ground, hug my knees, and enjoy the floor show. I'm fascinated by the sight, the colours, lights, contrasting with the ultra-black midnight sky. Eldridge called them night-wings, that seems a fitting name for these fantastic creatures. And right now I wouldn't want to be anywhere else. I feel happy. Peaceful. I feel...

'Hello.' I jump. And then gasp. *Orion.* Eldridge smirks and then disappears.

I'm astounded, all over again, by Orion's sexiness. I let my eyes openly wander his body, feel everything inside tighten with anticipation.

He's also wearing his nighttime attire. Like Eldridge, this comprises simply a pair of skimpy shorts. White, barely there, almost transparent. As though he's just stepped out of a pool and the wet fabric's clinging to his shape. They're thin and silky, and just hang off his body bits, revealing the shape of him beneath. I swear I can virtually see everything. I swallow hard and feel my chest rising and falling with emotion. I feel like I'm going to hyperventilate.

He's standing maybe ten feet from me. He doesn't come closer and I don't invite him to. He watches me as my eyes explore his body. My heart begins to pound as I notice changes beneath the flimsy silk of his shorts. His eyes are intense and black with something hungry, searching my shape beneath my sweater. I feel my nipples react to his greedy gaze, and become sensitive to the soft woolly fabric resting against them.

He licks his lips, deep and full. I remember his lips on my skin. I feel the skin on my breasts tighten, as though they might burst out of my jumper. My muscles clench with anticipation.

His shoulders are broad; his chest is rising and falling. He knows why I'm here. I know why I'm here. My hand touches my throat lightly. I can't find the words.

'Come with me,' he says, his voice deep and gravelly.

'Just a minute,' I gasp breathlessly. 'I don't want…everything.'

He nods. He understands. I trust him.

'Come, I'll take you to my place.'

I nod, step towards him and he takes my hand.

We walk for about an hour. My breaths are coming in bursts. His breathing is heavy too. I watch the shape of his shorts as he walks. His long legs. The way the waistband of his flimsy shorts dips at the back to reveal a hint of what is below. And the way the shape at the front changes as he walks. I'm shivering, there is a musky aromatic smell, the ground is covered in a velvety moss, which is soft and springy beneath my bare toes.

We pass people. Many people. Beautiful people. Winged people. Wild people. Gentle people. Fae people. But we are moving quickly, they come towards us to look, to stare. And then they dissolve back into the landscape, foliage, trees, into the darkness and mystery of the Fae world.

The sky is illuminated by a radiant glow of wings. Like a million tiny glow-worms floating through the air. It's so pretty, romantic. They light up the pathway, Orion's darkly tanned skin shimmers in the soft glittery light. He frowns deeply as he walks, breathing heavily but holding my hand gently. As the path narrows Orion leads me through a dark unlit passageway in the undergrowth, dipping his head and holding his hand out behind him while I follow.

His wings fascinate me, they're luminous and shimmering, vibrating, they emerge just between his shoulder blades rising from his back for about seven or eight inches, arch outwards and then dip downwards about a foot below their base. They are magnificent, strong and somehow masculine in a weird kind of way. Every now and then they close up, folding into themselves. I want to touch them. I reach out my hand tentatively and brush my fingers over a wing; it feels silky and almost fluid. 'Oh!' I exclaim as a wild dart of erotic electric current ripples through my body like a thousand vibrating strands of fibre-optic silk.

Orion turns and his frown unfolds into a deeply seductive smile. As though he carries the wisdom of a thousand thoughts. As though he can read my mind. No, it's more like he can read my body, my feelings. This is nothing to do with thoughts, it's as though we are bypassing thoughts and communicating directly from one body to another.

'Soon,' he says, and I almost convulse with anticipation.

We begin to descend, passing down into some kind of under-ground tunnel. The air is peaty and earthy; the roof just skims Orion's head. The tunnel is filled with glowing winged creatures, millions of flea-sized floating specks, which look like a glitter of ice crystals. It reminds me of Santa's grotto. I'm aware of constant change around me, the walls of the cave, the ceiling, the air, alive with movement.

Despite the constant drifting of these night-wing creatures inside the tunnel, everything feels muted, a dulling of sound. The quiet you get after a heavy fall of snow.

There are creatures, bat-like birds, almost invisible but shimmering with a muted green glow, they glide close to the walls of the cave, slipping past each other stealthily like stingrays in a large aquarium, hugging the sides of their tank. I tingle with a mixture of fear and wonder.

'Baterflies,' says Orion, seeing me eyeing them. I laugh, thinking he's joking. But he looks deadly serious. 'They could snap through your neck in one bite.' It's his turn to look amused at my reaction. 'But they won't,' he says quickly, squeezing my hand lightly. 'They only kill to defend the Fae.'

Oh, that's all right then.

As we begin our ascent towards the outside world, I hear the sound of running water and it makes me wonder if I need to pee, or whether it's just the strange feelings going on below. I stop and gulp in the fresh night air, enjoying the freshness and frankly glad to get away from those skulking bat things. I hold my hand in front of me and the night-wings melt around my arms like a slipstream.

I look for the water, perhaps it's the same stream that eventually emerges into Luke's cottage garden. The path opens up and I see a large double-fronted wooden chalet-type building with a painted veranda. The veranda spans the whole length of the chalet, and there is a swing-type seat at the front like you see in the American films. A black Labrador dog sits by the green front door, he stands and wags his tail as we approach, but then lies down again when he sees Orion. As though he was expecting someone else. In the large sloping roof is a dormer style window, with green moss-covered slates.

'Wow, I wonder who lives there?' I say.

'I do,' Orion says. 'It's my cabin.' I glance round at him to see if he's joking. You'd hardly call it a *cabin*.

Orion laughs at me, I'm not sure why. But I'm quickly distracted. As I approach the house the sound of water is amplified, and the woods open up to a huge lake. The slice of moon is reflected in swirling squiggles as a waterfall tips copious amounts of water ungraciously over a clifftop high above, the water crashes into the large lake beneath.

A huge fountain of water explodes up from the centre of the lake, rising perhaps thirty feet into the air and then splatting ungraciously back into the massive expanse of water. Okay maybe it's not the size of Windermere, but it's no garden pond either.

I'm disquieted by what I see. Because far beyond the lakeside, way past the cliff face where the water is being dumped into the lake, past the treetops and the middle landscape, way up high, almost reaching the black night sky...are the most enormous snow-capped mountains. Yes, mountains. In the middle of Gossamer Woods. I'm disorientated. Where am I? How can I be surrounded by a mountain range, taller than any mountains I've ever seen in this part of the world? *Bloody odd.*

But all questions are quickly wiped from my mind as I gaze across the amazing expanse of water. The lake is alive with movement from the waterfall and fountain, but there's swirling in its depths as though a thousand food mixers are churning and swirling the crystal clear water, causing ripples and waves to break across the surface.

The lake reflects millions of twinkling winged insects – dragonflies with colourful luminous wings hovering over the surface of the water creating a constant buzzing and fluttering sound only just perceptible above the crashing of the water. Butterflies, although sense tells me they must be moths, flit by inches from my face. The woodland trees surround the lake and I can't even see the pathway through the woods.

The air feels fresh and crisp on my face. It smells musty. Rich, dark and earthy. There's a whiff of something herby, perhaps minty. Orion leads me towards his cabin. I can't take my eyes off the clear swirling water.

He lightly strokes my neck with his finger and I turn to face him, brought back to the moment. I stop breathing, his hips brush mine, it's difficult to control myself, I feel like I might have wet myself or something. He inclines his head, gesturing towards the lake, his eyebrows raised in a question. I follow his gaze.

'Let's swim,' he says.

He steps away from me, turning away, and slides his barely-there shorts down his legs, steps out of them. My heart nearly stops. I can't tear my eyes away. Naked. So toned, tanned. No white lines, his back deeper brown, lower down paler but no ugly tan lines. Such a lovely bottom, small, rounded, so…I can't get rid of the feeling I want to…I want to get down on my hands and knees and just touch him, kiss him. Bite him. I want to—

OH MY GOD.

He's turned to face me. I cannot believe what I'm seeing. OH MY GOD. How on earth is that supposed to, well, you know…

Chapter Thirty-Three

Orion smiles at my reaction. I want to be naked too. My hand touches my woolly jumper. I feel overdressed.

My fingers grasp the hem of my jumper and I quickly peel it up over my head. I hear him gasp, I like it. I feel my skin tightening as the air laps over my body. I run my hand down, his eyes chase my fingers. They glint with anticipation, dark and feral.

I enjoy teasing him, I see him change shape before my eyes. I want to touch but I daren't. He's standing just a few feet away, his eyes following my hand. As he reacts, I do too, I can feel things happening, I allow my fingers to circle my belly, trying to keep control of myself. I hear him murmur. He moves towards me and takes my hand roughly, slips my fingers between his lips and bites gently. I nearly explode, his lips soft and full, his teeth sharp, his mouth cool and moist. His eyes are blacker than black, gleaming. I touch his chest, smooth and dark, broad with well defined muscles. My fingers brush his tight little nipples. I have an uncontrollable need to… I bend and gently kiss his nipple, my tongue swirls and he groans loudly, I bite, I feel I'm going to explode. My hand pulls at his firm flesh. He pushes me away gently, he's panting. As though he's struggling to keep in control.

I glance downwards, can't believe he could be still changing. I want to touch but don't know how to. My flesh is aching, wanting, my muscles deep inside tightening. I want something that I don't completely understand.

'Not yet,' Orion gasps, reading my body.

He holds me at arms' length, just for a second his eyes bore into me. It's a look of raw lust. The second lasts forever.

And then he turns and dives into the lake. I gasp as the icy-cold spray shocks my skin like a scald. I crouch at the side of the lake, and then sit, letting my legs dangle in the water. I struggle to control my breathing.

Then I lower myself into the deliciously cold water.

The lake is deep, I can't feel the bottom, beneath me it feels as though a dozen mermaids are whirling and reeling in the lake's dark depths. Orion swims over to me and turns me in the water so he's holding me from behind, I melt against him. He runs his hands over my stomach, my breasts, my head leans back against his shoulder. My mind whirls, the water swirls gently around us, icy, caressing every inch of skin and heightening sensation.

He moves us towards the centre of the lake where the natural spring is bursting through the surface of the water. He is holding me tightly. His body feels firm. Hard. I turn my face upwards and close my eyes. The noise of the fountain is almost deafening. We tread water beneath the spray, ice cold and yet my body feels on fire.

Orion pushes me over the fountain and I'm surprised to feel the spray of water as it rises from beneath, supporting my weight. The spray of water that was rushing into the air ceases as I cut off the flow. I can feel the force of the water beneath my legs raising me up, so I'm supported by the spray, just beneath the surface. Orion is behind me, his arm around my waist. I can feel him pressing into me from behind; the cold water has not cooled his ardour. I want to raise myself on top of him, want to feel him beneath me, against me. Inside me.

'No,' he says brusquely as he feels me push against him. 'No, let me...'

He grabs my thighs and parts them roughly, so I'm straddling the water spray rising from the earth. I feel the powerful icy cold water spring forcing up against me, around me, inside me, vibrating against me, millions of bubbles bursting against me, I widen my legs further, it's almost unbearable, something feels like it comes alive inside like a thousand red-hot bees are shimmying up and down my spinal cord. I cry out loudly but the sound is immediately deadened by the sound of the water. I feel his hands grasping hard at my thighs, hot breath on my neck, he moans gently.

I feel on the brink, struggling to keep control. I turn my head towards the sky, black with millions of exploding stars, night-wings and a splinter of bright white moon. I'm flooded with an ecstasy so intense that it's almost agony. *Oh my God.* Bubbles rise all around and dance to the surface, so cold it feels hot. I close my eyes. Feel the icy water caress my skin. I come alive inside, my wings vibrating beneath my skin, my muscles tighten and relax, pulsating, my body and mind opening up to the dancing water, wider and wider as I embrace the feeling, my breathing coming in bursts.

'Let go.' Orion's fiery breath on my neck sends thrilling ripples up and down my spine. He bites my ear, my neck, a wonderful burning scorching pain. The water bubbles rush around me, his hands are around my breasts, the water around my body, I can't breathe, my wings are beating in time with my heartbeat, deep inside my chest so hard, my breaths coming in shudders, can't get the air inside, the pain building, pleasure building, intensity building. I hold my breath. And everything begins to explode inside, like a hundred fireworks in my belly, in my spine. I feel as though my back is splitting. I imagine I can see glorious wide wings either side of me. I want to fly away, to lift into the air from this water hurricane. I look to the side and there's nothing there.

I cry out as a spasm of pulsating hotness rips through my body, every muscle clenching tight, so tight. His hand is beneath me as I feel my body surrender, supporting me in the water, clutching me, biting into me, I hear him groan in response to my pleasure. He gently moves me away from the spring and it suddenly feels very warm away from the icy cold fountain.

I'm exhausted yet sensitised; every nerve in my body is on fire. He turns me around and his lips are on my mouth, he is pulling hard against me, I tug at him, wrap my legs around him, feel the hard ridge of his body, the warm water swirls as he moves gently against me, and I begin to swell and grow once again, I kiss him hard, bite, salty, can feel his passion growing, parting my lips, his tongue swirling with mine, his body searching mine.

'Please,' I murmur, moving against him. 'Please, I'm ready.'

'No,' he says, he sighs and shakes his head reluctantly, pulling himself away from me. 'I'm sorry, no.' His face is flushed, his eyes angry with regret.

Moments later I'm sitting on dry land, in a shallow cave behind the waterfall, covered in a large towel, which Orion has brought for me, sipping ice cold spring water from a glass, still breathing hard. Orion has gone again. I said I didn't want everything, and he's as good as his word. So for now I'm guessing he's staying away from temptation.

I sigh and open my eyes. The vision before me is almost too much, too beautiful to take in. Dawn is breaking and the sky has turned deep orange-red, I'm watching the sun rise through a wall of moving water. I'm still sizzling but I feel exhausted. Satiated.

I close my eyes and lean back against the cool rear wall of the cave. A shiny crystal rock with a woven carpet of dry tree roots and damp mossy foliage. It smells damp, limey, peaty. I allow the smells and colours to envelope me, I have no idea how I'm going to get home and I don't care. I'm not even sure what or where home is any more.

Daylight is increasing and filtering through the wall of water, playing with the kaleidoscope of colours already embedded in the cave rock, like a wall of bright silvery light, dancing and flashing. The sound of the crashing water is loud but strangely comforting.

Amazing silvery stalactites and stalagmites cling to the cave entrance, for every spike coming downwards there is a matching one coming up from beneath, like a perfect set of lion's teeth. They seem to be exactly symmetrical either side, and the distance between each pillar is, to my eye, exactly identical. I am marvelling at this, it reminds me of the rows of desks lined up in the exam hall just a few of weeks ago, and yet a million lifetimes ago now. I briefly reflect on everything that has happened in such a short time. How much I have learned. How I have changed.

I sense movement beyond the waterfall. *Orion.* He's moving around, just at the edge of the lake. His wonderful dark tanned body. Naked. I'm about to call out to him when I realise it's not him. The fall of water lessens, and there's a gap, like a window out onto the lake. He's moving around, this person. He's facing away from me and doesn't seem to know I'm here.

He's very like Orion. Same skin colouring, same toned body. *Same lack of clothing.* Same black hair but longer. His hair is shoulder length, dark, dark shiny black. Same sexy translucent wings, held erect away from his body as he concentrates on what he's doing. The tip of the wings are quivering erotically and it's doing something to me. *God are all Fae men this sexy? And naked?*

He's holding something, like an animal or something. It's furry, cradled in his arms. It's a white dog, or a fox or something. No, it's a cat, a very large cat. A large white striped cat. With amber eyes, large paws. OH MY GOD, it's a white tiger! A snow tiger. It's only a bloody snow tiger cub.

I hardly dare breathe. Who is he, and what's he doing with a lion? And anyway, what's a snow tiger doing here? In the UK? Is it a zoo or something? Yet he seems to know exactly what he's doing. It's like he's talking to it, without saying anything. I'm mesmerised. The young cub is looking at him, eye contact. The cub is so sweet, is it tame? He's examining the cub's paw; the boy's wings are quivering, held erect outwards and the tips moving so fast, flicking and shimmying. *I wish they'd stop doing that.* Something's happening to my wings, I can feel them inside, begin to flutter, like they are answering the call of this boy's erotic wing movements.

I feel a little panicky and look past the boy to see if I can see Orion, but there's no sign of him. My body's shuddering involuntarily, my wings beating hard against the inside of my back, as though they're trying to get out, my body jolts forward and I try to control my breathing, try not to make a sound. Luckily the water is still crashing down noisily so the sound of my panting is not audible above the waterfall. I feel a ripping pain in my back, the muscles in my shoulders go into spasm and I can't stop myself from crying out, my eyes still transfixed on the boy. On the wings. On the wild animal. Ow, ow, that really, really—

'Oooeeeuuuuuw!' I suddenly scream loudly.

The boy spins round. Two pairs of eyes on me, two wild amber tiger eyes glaring at me with animosity, and two dark sultry eyes, equally fierce, equally hostile, equally dangerous. His face is quite perfect. Like Orion but younger. Softer. Wilder. With a light soft covering of dark facial hair around his chin, trimmed very close. And dark feral eyes.

I hold his stare for a moment before I remember I'm wearing no clothes. I pull my blanket towards me and lightly cover myself. I glare back at him impudently, still panting with the pain from my spine. He doesn't attempt to cover his nakedness. Frankly I'm happy about that. There is something utterly amazing about the image before me. Man and wild creature. And yet also repellent. I want to look away but I can't. How long has he been there? Did he see us in the water? Was he there all the time?

As his wild eyes burn into me, the movement of his wings intensify, they flicker and vibrate as though they have lost control. The boy looks uneasy. His eyes flash. He clutches the cub closer as though hiding behind it.

'Argh!' the pain from my back suddenly increases, ripping through my body violently and I scream out. The boy drops the animal and rushes towards me, I'm blinded by a white flash, searing pain and whiteness, my head is going to burst open. 'Argh!' I scream out again, and then it starts to clear. I look for

Orion, for the other boy. The tiger.

And then Tate looks up and smiles. Oh God I must be back there, in the stable. I'm in my vision. Was the boy real? *I hope so.* I feel a bit ashamed, I'd almost forgotten that this was the objective in coming here this evening – to bring on a vision. *Of course it was.*

'Hello,' I say, still breathless from my ordeal. I glance down at myself to check I'm not naked, but I'm back in my day clothes. Tate whispers hello and then nods anxiously towards the wall behind me. I turn around and see a man sitting on a chair in the corner with a shotgun leaning up against the wall. Ethan.

He's looking straight at me. I recoil in horror, stumble backwards and yet he doesn't seem to see me at all, he's looking right through me. Like I'm a ghost that only Tate can see and hear. Tate looks anxiously at me. How can I have a conversation with her when she can't talk to me?

'Tate,' I say to her, and she deliberately doesn't look directly at me. I hear Ethan shuffling his feet around behind me. 'Please, I know you can hear me, but that you can't talk to me. Please can you visit me instead? Tomorrow morning, around ten o'clock, after my aunt has left for work? Like you used to when I was little, when you came to my bedroom. I have to do something to help. Please, you come to me. I know that you can do this too, this vision thing. You come to me then we can talk properly to each other.'

Tate nods her head a couple of times.

'What's up with you?' A voice comes from the other side of the barn, he sounds slurred, I notice a bottle of beer on the floor beside Ethan's chair. He's glaring at Tate.

'I've a stiff neck,' she snaps back to him. Dad stirs on hearing Tate's voice. He coughs, a raspy, hard cough.

I move towards Dad, I know he can't see me. I hold out my hand to him but can't feel him. My hand just passes through his. *Weird.* I look around. I don't know what I'm looking for. There's a smell of thick oily smog, which makes me want to cough.

The desk that Dad was working at is pushed into the corner, stacked high with boxes and tubes and containers. As though his work is nearing its conclusion. I shiver. I hate to think what they will do with Dad and Tate once their work is over. I move towards the desk, there's a notebook with Dad's writing. Like a formula. Chemical symbols and marks. A large glass tube sits in an open box with black tar-like stuff inside.

Dad is lying on a dirty mattress on the floor. Tate is sitting beside him. I move back to Ethan. He has no idea I'm standing just inches away from him. I feel such hatred for this man, considering I've never met him. He takes a swig from his beer can and places it on the floor beside him, belches loudly, shuffles to get comfortable. He's wearing a red check lumberjack shirt, and jeans. Doc Marten boots. He really shouldn't wear those jeans. They're Levi's, quite a trendy style, but they look gross on him. I peer at his shotgun. I wonder if it's loaded.

The light is streaming in through the grubby side window, the one Luke and I peered through the other day. Without thinking I reach out to wipe the dirt, my finger pokes right through the glass. Because, of course, I'm not really here. *Duh.*

Over at the far end of the barn is a large stable door, wide open. Almost daring its prisoners to try and make a run for it. But surrounding the door is a black thick sooty fog, hovering ominously around the frame of the doorway. Like the oily fumes from the exhaust of an old motor. I shiver. Anybody walking through that doorway would get coated by that black stuff. And if it's as poisonous as Tate says, then there is no way in or out of the barn for a Fae person. Not through the doorway anyway.

So that's decided then. We will just have to get Dad and Tate out through the walls. *Somehow.*

I smile at Tate with a confidence that doesn't reach my heart, and she smiles back fondly. *I wonder if my eyes are beautiful like that.*

She inclines her head fractionally and I feel my eyes fill with emotion. As I blink back the tears, I wake from my vision.

I'm back at the oak tree. Eldridge is there, he smiles knowingly and I can't meet his gaze. Does he know? Do they all know? I glance down and am wearing my large thick pullover once again. Orion must have re-dressed me. *I hope.*

'How did I get back?' I ask sheepishly.

'I brought you,' Eldridge says, matter-of-factly. I look around, no sign of Orion.

'Oh,' I say. Of course it makes sense; Eldridge can take people places with his space-hopping or whatever they call it.

'I saw somebody else there,' I say hesitantly, 'by the lake, a boy. He looked a bit like Orion.'

'Sebastian,' says Eldridge. 'Orion's brother.'

I shiver.

'He had a wild animal,' I say. 'A tiger or something?'

'Yeah, they're Whisperers. Orion and Sebastian. Sebastian's a bit of a recluse. He's only really interested in animals. But Orion uses his gift for people, to read body language, what you want, how you want it. And he can make people like him. It's quite a gift.'

I'm surprised to see that Eldridge looks mildly jealous, and I wonder who *he* would like to use his charms on, if he had Orion's gift.

'Do you have someone special?' I say gently.

'No,' he says sulkily, digging his toes into the sand. But his face has turned pink. I smile and he turns away shyly. There's a sadness in his eyes that I can't quite read.

Chapter Thirty-Four

As I sneak into my bedroom I hear Maggie stirring in her room, just getting up for work. Surprisingly I don't feel tired any more. Must be adrenalin or something. Plenty of time to sleep afterwards. I slip into my pyjamas and wander downstairs, feigning a yawn.

'Morning, sweetheart.' Maggie yawns back.

'Morning, Mags.' I slump in a chair and help myself to some cereal. 'Did you enjoy the wedding?'

Maggie tells me all about her friend's wedding day whilst I eat my cereal in silence, tuning in and out of her conversation.

'When do you need to enrol for sixth form?' she suddenly says, and I nearly drop my spoon.

I shovel a large spoonful of cereal into my mouth and mutter something indecipherable like 'blurb smurf flombin mooh'. The fact is, I don't want to go back to school. And it's not just because of Sasha or the problems I had on my last day. I just feel I've moved on. But how can I explain this to Maggie? She has no idea what's going on. How can I say 'I'm not going back to school because I'm a fairy princess and I'm needed to save the fairy world' for goodness sake. Maybe Dad will be able to explain it to her better; hopefully he'll be home this time tomorrow. My stomach does a little warm flip of excitement. This time tomorrow, everything is going to be fine. *Either that or I'll be dead.*

Tate comes early. It's nine thirty and I have only just got back into my bedroom after eating my breakfast. I'm sitting on my bed thinking about when she used to visit me when I was little. She would sit on my bedroom chair, her beautiful wings spread beside her, her long red hair falling down her front like waves. She used to—

'Scarlett, can you hear me?'

I look up, and then shrink back. It's as though she's actually in the room with me, and yet not there at all. Like the ghost you see on movies, part there and part not there. She's fuzzy too, out of focus, with a kind of shiny haze around her. Like somebody has sprayed around her with glittery dust. She's sitting on my bedroom chair, the same chair she used to sit on to talk to me when I was a little girl. I can see now why I thought she was an angel.

'Tate,' I say eagerly, 'are you okay?'

'Yes,' she says, and smiles weakly, 'but it's dangerous for you at the barn, the black fog is poisonous.'

'We need to get Dad out of there, he looks sick.'

'Yes, he's suffering quite badly with Fae sickness.'

'Why are they forcing him to make all that Ethereal Black stuff? What do they want with so much of it? Surely it's not *just* to create a fog to keep you in the barn?'

'We don't know for sure, all we know is that it's very dangerous for the Fae world. It would be like giving a machine gun to a toddler.'

'Oh my God. I have to get you both out of there.'

'That's just it. I'm inside unable to get out, and you can't get in without harming yourself. You can't come, it's too dangerous. And both Jasper and Ethan are staking out the stable, taking shifts, we're never alone. And they have a shotgun. You'd be walking straight into their trap.'

'But Dad could die! *You* could die!'

'The Fae world needs a Sage Princess to carry on the Sage heritage. You need to stay safe. You and I can't both die in this barn.'

I'm quiet whilst I think this through. Tate sits silently in the corner, perched on a chair and it strikes me how ridiculous this would look to anybody else.

'I don't care,' I say to Tate loudly. 'I think I can find a way without touching that fog stuff. I'll find a way. How weakened are you by being cooped up there for months?'

Tate smiles. 'I rather hoped you'd say that.' I suddenly want to hug this woman. A woman I didn't even know existed a few weeks ago. My mother. *Wow.*

'I'm in pretty good shape. But Sam is sick, he can't fight. He's vulnerable.'

'Which of them is the stronger? Jasper or Ethan?'

'Oh, Jasper definitely. Ethan's fond of his beer and he drinks through most of his shift. But they have a shotgun.'

'Tate, I have a plan,' I say. Although to be honest my plan is only half-cocked currently. Well okay, I don't have a plan. But I will have a plan by tonight. I know I will.

'I'm going to try and get you both out tonight, without them even knowing.' I smile at her with a confidence that I don't feel.

'I'm not sure,' says Tate and my skin creeps with disappointment.

'What?'

'Well, I'm not sure I want it to be like that.' She looks straight at me with an expression I can't read. As I look into her piercing green eyes I feel a surge of excitement. Like looking directly into a green flame.

'You and I, Scarlett, are the Sage Princesses of the Fae world. We're not going to just sneak away from these Black-Wings when their backs are turned, like cowards. The Sage don't run away. If you *have* found a safe way to come here tonight,' she pauses and I feel my face smart. Oh my God she knows I don't have a plan. *She knows.*

'If you find a way to come here tonight without passing through that lethal fog, then we fight.'

'Fight?' My voice sounds like it is travelling through water.

'Oh yes,' Tate says. 'Definitely. In fact that's something I might even enjoy.'

What a strange mother I have. I feel a sudden thrill of excitement.

Chapter Thirty-Four

'I'll see you this evening then,' I say with certainty.

Tate beams. But then she frowns and bites her lip.

'Scarlett,' she says hesitantly, 'this feud between the Sage and Black-Wings has gone on for long enough, generations of Fae have battled with generations of Black-Wings. If we are going to fight, we fight fair, and it ends today. We are going to show those Black-Wings who is the most powerful Fae clan in the forest. So come prepared for a battle tonight. Two on two. Two Sage Princesses against two Black-Wings. We can do it. I know you're not at full strength yet but I can tell you have been working on your gifts...'

She frowns.

'Incidentally, how on earth did you manage to control your gift so early in Transition? How did you bring on the vision last night all by yourself? Normally the vision is very sporadic for the first few months, even years.'

I feel myself blush.

'Don't ask,' I say, carefully folding my bedclothes. I brush my duvet straight with my hand and tuck it around my pillow.

'Scarlett,' she says.

'Yes?' I look up and meet her eyes.

'I'm proud of you.'

And in a blink of an eye she's disappeared.

Okay, so now I just have to work out a plan.

Three hours later I perch on the edge of my bed and take a deep breath. I pick up my mobile and dial a familiar number. My heart is pounding in my throat, a lot depends on this phone call and I could have got it so very wrong. I stand and walk over to the window. I look out into the distance, to a point in the distance that I can't see because of the thick trees lining Gossamer Woods.

I count the rings, one...two...three...I gulp. Perhaps a made a mistake. Four...five... I'm just about to end the call.

'Hello.'

There's a pause while I catch my breath.

'Hi, it's me.'

There's silence for along anxious moment, and I swear my heart has leapt into my throat.

'What do you want?'

Harsh words, a voice loaded with emotion.

'I need your help.'

Silence again. A lot hangs on the next few words spoken. I hear nervous heavy breathing at the other end of the phone.

'What do you need me to do?'

'Can we talk?' I say. 'Please?'

'I'll come to yours, give me half an hour.'

'Thanks,' I say, my eyes filling with relief and affection.

Twenty minutes later there's a timid knock on the door, I swing the door open.

'Thanks for coming, Sasha.'

Chapter Thirty-Five

The warmth from the day is starting to diminish. Luke, Ainsel and Eldridge are looking at me gravely, awaiting my instructions. I take a deep breath.

'Listen, Ainsel,' I say. 'Can you and Eldridge space-hop through a brick wall, carrying somebody else?'

Ainsel's large ochre eyes look back at me.

'I don't know,' Ainsel shrugs. 'I've never tried it.'

'I have,' pipes up Eldridge and all heads are turned to him. 'It wasn't a brick building, but it was that tunnel up near the Lakes and Mountains.'

He turns to me with a mischievous twinkle in his eye, 'You must have seen the tunnel, it's up near Orion's place where you were last night.'

Eldridge stares at me with innocent saucer eyes. My eyes narrow as I look back at him. He holds my stare for a moment and I drop my eyes to the floor.

'You visited Orion last night?' Luke says, looking puzzled. 'Why?'

'I needed his advice on the plan for tonight,' I lie, glaring at Eldridge.

'I remember!' shouts Ainsel gleefully, jiggling on the spot, totally oblivious to the direction the conversation has taken. 'The tunnel collapsed at one end, and one of the Fae children was trapped inside. Eldridge space-hopped into the tunnel and brought the boy out.'

Luke jumps to his feet. 'Let's try it!' he says. Eldridge leaps up eagerly.

'No!' I say. 'We don't have time for messing around.'

We form a circle. There's a deathly hush as I outline my plan to my three friends. When I have finished nobody says anything. Three faces look at me apprehensively. I take a deep breath.

'There's just one more thing,' I say, 'there's one more person joining our team. Please don't over-react.'

Sasha timidly appears from behind a tree. Both Ainsel and Eldridge sniff the air, Eldridge hisses loudly and then they both spring to their feet, landing on all fours and crouch down like wild cats, crawling forward with their chins close to the ground. The hairs on the back of my neck stand on end to see the change in them, their lips curl menacingly as they creep forward like wild animals stalking their prey.

Luke starts to laugh and Ainsel turns and hisses at him. He shuts up and looks alarmed.

'Hey, it's okay,' I say. 'Sasha's a Black-Wing but she's my friend, I trust her and she's going to help us.'

Ainsel hisses as I say the word 'Black-Wing'. Luke is laughing behind his hand, I glare at him and mouth 'HELP', but he just grins insanely.

Sasha's eyes have filled with tears and she starts to turn away. I grab hold of her hand and pull her towards me, my arm around her. She smiles weakly. She looks so different today. No makeup, and just leggings and a t-shirt. Granted it's a fifty quid Hollister t-shirt, but nevertheless it's not in-your-face expensive. She looks nice actually, I always thought she looks great without makeup, and the plain clothes show off her figure just as well as the low cut clingy fancy stuff. She looks younger, and quite lovely.

'Listen you two, I'm putting my trust in Sasha, and you need to too. If I'm your Sage Princess, and if you really *do* believe in your monarchy, you need to believe me and trust me.'

I'm shocked to hear the words from my own lips. Have I really just pulled rank with my friends? Like I'm a real bloody Princess? I'm just about to apologise and take the words back when Ainsel and Eldridge both get up from their crouched position and bow low to me like I'm royalty. Why did I say that? Luke is nearly falling off his log laughing.

'Get up, you twits!' I say to the pair of them.

Sasha's eyes are like saucers.

'Listen, we can trust Sasha. Okay so she's a Black-Wing, and she's done some dumb things recently,' I lock eyes with Sasha and she gives me a watery smile. 'But she wants to make amends. She's going to be working with us today, to make sure things happen how we want them to happen.'

Luke glances at Sasha as though he has a bad taste in his mouth. But says nothing. Eldridge eyes Sasha suspiciously. Ainsel cautiously approaches her, peering in her face and sniffing at her. Sasha looks towards me anxiously. Ainsel prods her shoulder rudely and Sasha looks freaked out but says nothing.

'Okay then,' I say, hoping the awkward moment has passed. 'Do we all know what we have to do?'

My four best friends in the world nod back at me.

'Okay, let's do it.'

Sasha nods and disappears back into the everyday world.

I sit back and wait to hear from Tate. Sasha's first job is to take a cup of hot chocolate to Ethan; it contains a mild sleeping powder and should buy us some time to get Dad out of the barn before Jasper arrives.

All of a sudden a voice breaks into my thoughts.

'Scarlett.'

I jump. 'Did you hear that?' I say, everybody just stares at me. They all look dumb and shrug their shoulders. Okay so it was just me. *That's reassuring. Voices in my head.*

'Scarlett, it's me, Tate.' I spin round thinking I will see her.

'I'm just talking to you directly. We can do this.'

'Oh, okay,' I say out loud.

'What?' says Ainsel.

'No,' says Tate. 'Don't speak to me out loud, just listen and reply with your mind.'

'Can you hear me now?' I say inside my head.

'Yes,' says Tate. I check again to see if anybody is watching me. No. I lie back in the grass and close my eyes. Ah that's better.

'What is it, Tate?' I say. 'What's wrong?'

'I need to talk to you about when we're alone with the Black-Wings. Strategy.'

'Okay.'

Oh yeah, strategy.

'Rule number one, we don't use weapons. We use our strength and our guile, our power and our wisdom. But we don't cheat and we don't use weapons. But they might, so we have to be better than them.'

'How do we do that?'

'We *are* better than them. We just have to show them. We concentrate and watch. We use our minds. We use our gifts to anticipate their moves.'

Oh, is that all then.

'Just read their moves and use it against them. If we do that, together with our superior power, it should be a walk in the park.'

'Wow, Tate, really?'

'No!' she says. And then she laughs. She has a very strange sense of humour. 'Seriously it will be fine. Just remember to attack first, take them by surprise, don't wait 'til they make a move. We're at a slight disadvantage in that I'm not fit and you're not full strength. But even at half strength we should be okay, don't worry, I won't let anything happen to you.'

'Okay,' I say. There is silence for a moment and I wonder if she's gone. Then her voice comes again.

'Scarlett?'

'Yes?'

'A girl has just come into the barn, tall with dark hair, she's given Ethan a hot drink. Is that part of the plan?'

'Yes, it's Sasha, Ethan's daughter. She's helping us.'

'WHAT?' Her voice comes quick and harsh like a knife cutting through ice.

Chapter Thirty-Five

'It's okay, I know what I'm doing,' I say, sounding more confident than I feel.

'She's just gone,' Tate says, her mind-voice almost a whisper. 'He's drinking the drink. God he's a revolting indulgent slob. And he wasn't very nice to his daughter.'

'Where's the shotgun?' I say.

'It's by the side of him.'

There is radio silence for a few moments and I'm not sure if she's still there. Just then I hear an urgent voice in my head again.

'He's asleep,' she says.

I turn to my friends and take a deep breath. I want to cry now.

'Okay,' I say, steadying my voice. 'Game on. Ethan's asleep. We go now!'

I look around; all three are beaming at me. You don't get better friends than this. I feel a bit choked.

'It's okay, Scarlett,' says Luke gently. 'We all know what we have to do. It'll be fine.' I catch his eye and he holds my gaze for a few moments before he looks away.

Eldridge quickly wraps his arms around my waist and Ainsel walks around, checking he has a good hold. Then she quickly wraps her arms around both of us.

And before I realise what is happening, we're all inside the barn. There was no jolt landing, or noise, or even feeling. We're suddenly *here*. Three of us standing in the middle of the barn. There's a stink of male sweat, rotted horse manure, sooty chemicals and stale beer. Ainsel and Eldridge quickly release their arms from around me and I glance anxiously towards Ethan. He's snoring loudly with his mouth open.

Ainsel tiptoes over to where my father lies. He's asleep on his side, but his breathing is laboured and his hands are loosely tied together in front of him with rope. Ainsel deftly unties his hands and Dad opens his eyes and gasps.

Ainsel places her hand over Dad's mouth so he can't make a sound, and gestures not to speak. Dad nods. He understands immediately, he looks over to me and his eyes open wide.

Dad. Just for a moment I feel overcome with emotion. *Dad's here.* I swallow back a choking feeling in my throat. *Dad.* This is real, not a dream or a vision. *Dad.* My legs feel wobbly and my heart feels as though it's going to jump out of my body. Everything sounds muffled. I glance around for something to hold on to, as if maybe I'm going to fall. The world goes blurry as my eyes fill with tears of relief.

But there's no time. I can't go all soppy now, this is dangerous. I snap myself back to the moment, blink back my tears.

Dad's breathing seems to improve as he comprehends what's happening and adrenalin starts to recharge his body. He sits up, shakes his wrists and arms, his eyes still darting back to me. Ainsel presses her finger to her lips to remind him to keep very quiet.

Eldridge is edging over towards Ethan. The sleeping man's fingers are tightly curled around the barrel of his shotgun. Eldridge turns and gestures to Ainsel to space-hop Dad out of the barn, out of danger. Ainsel immediately wraps her arms around Dad and the next second they're both gone.

Dad's safe. Easy as that. I fight to control my breathing. *Dad's safe.* Again I feel a stinging behind my eyes. I blink hard. Time for that later.

Eldridge tiptoes back over to me and whispers, 'If I'm going to take the gun, I'm going to have to disappear with it the minute I touch it. It's risky and it could wake him, but it's the only way.'

I shrug and look anxiously over at Ethan as he stirs and grunts.

'Okay,' I nod at Eldridge. Tate and I lie down on the mattress in the same position she and Dad were lying a moment earlier. I drag Dad's hessian blanket over myself.

And we watch.

Eldridge edges back towards Ethan carefully, until his hand is inches from the shotgun barrel. Ethan stirs again, and opens his eyes. He sees Eldridge, but by the time his brain has registered what's happening, Eldridge has grabbed the shotgun and disappeared into thin air, along with the shotgun.

Ethan blinks twice, looks down at his empty hand, then sits up and looks all around him with a puzzled expression. He glances over towards me and Tate – sees that Tate is still there, apparently asleep. He looks towards me and sees a dark lump under the blanket in the corner. He shrugs, sits back in his chair, takes a swig out of his beer bottle, and closes his eyes. Within thirty seconds he's snoring again.

Wow, that couldn't have been easier. Now we just have to wait for Jasper to join us. Sasha should be waiting outside the stable door, hiding in the black fog, ready to jam the door behind Jasper once he's entered the stable. And then it's up to us. Me and Tate. *Me and my mum.* Showtime. *Or bloodbath.*

I don't know how long we wait. It could be ten minutes, twenty, or even longer. I hear the thud, thud of Jasper's footsteps on the pathway outside. I watch the stable door open. I pull the blanket over my face, but I sense him entering the stable, hear a shuffle of feet as he turns and closes the door.

'Dad?' he says gruffly, I hear him kick at Ethan's foot. 'Wake up, you prat.'

I peep from behind my blanket. He looks very different from the night at the cinema. Sure, he's still wearing trendy jeans, he's still groomed to within inch of his miserable life, and his leather jacket must have cost more than my dad earns in a month. But as I see him today, he just looks like a pathetic, miserable spoilt boy.

I wait for the sound of Sasha closing the stable door, as planned. I peer anxiously towards the doorway but Sasha is standing in the middle of the opening, as though she's rooted to the spot.

I feel an icy chill – surely Sasha's not going to let me down now? Was I wrong to trust her?

Jasper senses Sasha's presence and spins around.

'Get out of here you nosey little bitch!' he shouts, wafting his arm in her direction as though swatting away an irritating bluebottle.

She continues to stand, just staring at her brother, and then her father. I swallow nervously. *Close the door, Sasha.*

'Get out of here, this is nothing to do with you,' Ethan slurs in her direction. 'Go and play with your ponies.'

Sasha speaks clearly and slowly.

'This is for all those times you hurt me Dad, all the times you came into my room when I was little and told me I was your special girl, and then showed me things to me that no six-year-old should ever see. This is for all the times you both hit me, and hurt me, and left me bruised and in pain. This is for all the times you heard me crying and laughed at me. And this is for those times you forced me to have sex with you, Jasper. Scarlett's my *real* friend. She's the only family I have. You're both disgusting and I hope you get what you deserve.'

Jasper's face is a picture, a mixture of disbelief and rage. Sasha looks determined and strangely at peace. Jasper lurches towards the doorway but Sasha is faster, she dodges back and slams the stable door shut in his face. There's a satisfying metal thuck as she firmly shoots the large bolt in place, and a thud as a tree branch is wedged against it.

Thank God for that.

'Eh?' mutters Ethan.

After a split second of dawning, both men spin round to face us. I whip my blanket away and jump to my feet. Tate flips onto her feet gracefully; her huge wings unfolding dramatically like a huge translucent silver parachute. As her wings unfurl, her lip curls back and she hisses menacingly at the Black-Wings.

I'm shocked to find myself mirroring Tate's facial expression, my lip twisting back over my teeth, my muscles pulling me towards the ground, my breath escaping my lips in short sharp hisses. It's as though I have no control over my body, my muscles pulling me into a crouch-like squat, Tate is beside me in the exact same stance. We both hiss and spit like wild cats.

'Fuck,' Jasper utters in a strangled voice, he tries the handle of the stable door but it doesn't budge.

Chapter Thirty-Six

'Where's the fucking shotgun, you prat?' Jasper snarls at his father in panic. Ethan's arms are desperately flailing around, as though he hopes the gun will suddenly manifest itself.

My muscles have loosened up and I find myself able to stand normally, and Tate is unwinding too, her wings relaxing into a more natural semi-folded position.

'Now that's no way to speak to your father,' Tate says mockingly as she flexes and stretches her muscles, her eyes shining with anticipation.

Ethan stumbles to his feet and lurches towards her, as quick as a flash Tate pirouettes on the spot like a ballerina caught in the spotlight on stage, her wings tightly bound to her back, spinning once, twice, on the third spin her foot connects neatly with Ethan's kneecap. His leg bends sideways awkwardly, he shrieks as he crumples to the floor.

'Oh, sorry,' she says, 'me and my big feet.'

I stand straight and proud. *That's my mum.*

I feel movement from Jasper. I've been here before, and I know his moves. He steps towards me and pauses, weight on his front foot, forms a fist with his right hand, another step forward, right arm pulls back, starts to transfer weight to his front foot, preparing for a punch – probably aimed at my face. I watch his movements as though in slow motion, I wait, wait, wait until his arm has reached the end of its backward momentum, his weight on his back foot, the split second before his fist moves forward along with the weight of his whole body to the front foot again and out with his punch…at that precise moment I lunge forward, grasp his forearm and dance on the spot – turning full circle and again hear that wonderfully satisfying sickening crunch as the bones and tendons in his arm splinter and twist.

'Arrrrghghgh! Shit! You BITCH!' Jasper screams out. He drops to the floor, nursing his damaged arm. I'm tempted to kick him hard in his sensitive bits, just like I did a few weeks ago, but decide to allow him a chance to recover before I plant my next move on him.

As the two men writhe on the floor, Tate and I smile at each other. Tate raises her eyebrows. 'This is going to be easier than I thought,' she says, feigning a yawn. 'Shall we play *I-Spy* whilst the boys catch up?'

But as she smiles over at me, I see Ethan's arm grab outwards and something glints before my eyes. A knife. I scream a warning towards Tate as he swings the knife within inches of her leg. She hops out of the way but he catches her calf on the next swipe and a red ribbon of blood flows down her leg.

'Mum!' I scream, and for a split second our eyes lock in wonder. *Oh my God I called her Mum.*

'Come 'ere you slag,' Ethan slurs towards Tate, and her head snaps back towards the job in hand. He's still dragging himself across the floor, towing his damaged leg behind. His arms are waving around, swiping madly at us both with the blade. We dance out of the way, Tate's leg now worryingly red with blood but it doesn't seem to be slowing her down.

Tate whizzes round on the spot and delivers a neat punch to Ethan's ribs, Jasper grabs out to the knife and I quickly leap in the air and knock him off balance, he staggers backwards and Tate kicks his legs from beneath him. Ethan tries to pull himself up on a chair and I knock the chair from under him, watching him crash back to the ground still nursing the knife in his hand.

I can't believe how easy it is, Tate and I are delivering our moves like an expertly choreographed dance.

'Give it here you useless piece of shit,' Jasper growls at Ethan, lunging across the room and snatching the knife from him.

Jasper turns and rushes at me with the knife held high. Tate screams. Jasper's using his undamaged left hand and he's wielding the knife clumsily and dangerously. I step backwards and feel the wall of the barn behind me. The daylight is dimming and the knife glints as it catches the light from the window. I can't see where it is, he's coming at me and I have nowhere to go. I'm aware of Tate on the other side of the desk, rooted to the spot, weighing up the situation. Everything stops for a second; the world goes silent whilst I pause for breath.

'Not so clever now are we, little freak girl,' he sneers. 'I'm going to cut that smile off your face, and then I'm going to cut your little cutie pie wings out of your back. And then before I kill you and your fairy queen mother, the very last thing you feel before you die will be me, enjoying your pretty little fairy body. How does that sound?'

Ethan's laughing raucously from the other side of the room.

'Go for it, lad,' he rasps, his voice coarse and disgusting. 'But save one for me, I've always had a thing for a woman with wings.'

'Shut up, you idiot!' Jasper snarls at his father.

I catch my breath; he's closing in on me, slowly, menacingly. My back is against the stable wall. I'm cornered. I can't see, feel, think. I'm dodging around but the blade is missing me by inches each time. He lunges. I move my arm but not quick enough. I feel a sudden dull coldness in my arm followed closely by a red-hot smarting and a warm trickle. A stream of dark red blood is pouring down my arm. I'm blinded by sheer panic.

Concentrate, concentrate, the words come into my head and a calmness soaks through me, my invisible wings start to pulsate in my back like a catalyst setting off a reaction, flooding through my body like a tranquilising drug, steadying me, concentrating my thoughts, my movements.

Watch his arm, watch the blade – concentrate Scarlett. The voice is soothing. I focus on his hand wafting to and fro. As the blade passes inches from my face I wait as his arm travels to the end of its journey, and I muster all my strength and my foot comes up to strike him hard in the gut. The air poofs out of him and he wobbles on the spot.

Without missing a beat my arm rises towards the knife, my fist punches his arm hard in the muscle, taking him by surprise, his hand opens and the knife flies up into the air. His eyes are wide with shock and pain. But my eyes are following the track of the knife through the air as it returns towards the ground, and I'm underneath it, catching it deftly in my hand.

He stares in disbelief, still bent double clutching his stomach. A small shove to his chest from the flat of my hand and he topples over like a skittle. He lands in a dazed crumpled heap onto the floor. 'No, please, no,' he wheezes as he sees the knife in my hand. 'Please, please.'

I chuck the knife into the corner of the barn, well out of reach.

'Get up, you snivelling idiot,' I say.

I want to laugh, he looks so pathetic. He stumbles to his knees, cradling both arms together in front of him. I glance at Tate, questioningly. She's leaning back against the stable wall with her arms folded in front of her.

'Go for it,' she says.

'Okay,' I shrug. And I spin round and my foot connects neatly with Jasper's rib cage. His whole body jolts to the side and he crashes to the floor, his eyes closing as his head hits the ground.

I quickly check on Ethan. He's quivering in the corner, his leg lying at a strange angle.

'It was all him,' Ethan blusters like a baby. 'It was Jasper, it was all his idea, it was nothing to do with me.'

Tate's lip has curled in disgust and her wings are wide and erect once more. She hisses loudly towards Ethan and he yelps in shock.

'May I?' she says to me, her eyes flashing with amusement.

'Oh yes,' I say, 'be my guest.'

She steps towards Ethan, her wings shimmer like a million stars as she is lifted lightly off the ground, hovering gracefully, looming over Ethan with her auburn hair flowing down her body like a river of liquid copper, her wings spread out like a huge silvery parachute. Her lips draw back and she hisses at him, the sound menacing, low and drawn out.

Ethan cowers, covering his head with his hands, watching through his fingers. But my eyes are transfixed on Tate's wings, like shimmering sheets of liquid crystal. She returns gracefully to the ground, her wings folding inwards towards her spine, she shakes her thick wavy hair and pulls her it forward over her right shoulder, smoothing it with her hand.

'Is that what you really think, Ethan? Is that what you think all Fae women are for? For your entertainment?'

Tate runs her hand across her body seductively, Ethan's eyes widen with astonishment and delight. He licks his lips.

And then Tate bends forward and punches him hard in the face. His head flips and he spins back against the wall of the stable, groaning loudly, clutching his face. The skin over his nose has split, blood runs down his face from the cut and oozes out of his nostrils. His nose looks crushed and bent. He's lying awkwardly, limp and useless, he closes his eyes and groans. She pokes him. He opens his eyes.

'Ethan Curnow, you are a depraved corrupt perverted psychopath who should have been killed at birth. If you ever come near me, my daughter, or my friends again I will kill you. Do you understand?'

'Go to Hell,' he mutters as he slips into unconsciousness.

Tate dances over to me and we hug. I cling on to her, she feels wonderful.

'Wow, that was great!' she says. 'We should do this more often!'

I start to laugh and I'm not sure I'm ever going to stop. Tate is laughing too and I realise that she and I not only have the same sense of humour, but we have the same laugh.

She touches my face with her finger, as though testing whether I'm real or not and it strikes me that she's probably as amazed by me as I am by her.

There's a creaking sound from behind me, from the doorway, like a rusty gate hinge. Probably Sasha, we told her to stay outside until the end. Tate glances over my shoulder and I feel her stiffen in my arms, the colour drains from her face. I turn.

Sasha is standing in the open doorway holding her father's shotgun. It is raised to her shoulder, her cheek pressed against it, her right eye looking along the barrel. Her finger is on the trigger. And it is aimed at us. Tate freezes, I freeze. I go cold from head to toe.

'Sasha! Sasha, don't!' My voice sounds squeaky. My legs are frozen to the spot. 'Please, don't, please!'

Tate steps from behind me and pushes me gently to one side. The gun is aimed at Tate's chest.

Sasha momentarily takes her eye off her target and stares at me. It's as though she's somewhere else, her eyes are glazed, wild, driven. She just stares. Then her head turns towards Tate.

'Is he dead?' she says.

'No, no, of course not!' Tate answers. 'He'll be okay in a few days!'

'Sasha, please!' I plead.

Sasha's head turns back to me for just a second, and then she lines up her shot again. The gun is held steady; the only part of her that moves is her lower lip as she speaks out of the side of her mouth.

'Scarlett, please would you ask your mother to move aside whilst I shoot that evil perverted bastard who calls himself my father.'

There is a split second pause whilst we adjust our understanding. I can't breathe. Tate also seems rooted to the spot. She is directly between Ethan and Sasha, in the line of fire.

'No, Sasha, it's not the right way,' says Tate gently, her face filled with horror.

Sasha is starting to cry silently and the gun is shaking in her hands, her finger still on the trigger. The feeling comes back to my legs and I move towards Sasha. Her eyes leave the target and look at me pleadingly, like a person lost and empty. I hold out my hand and she lets me take the shotgun off her, and place it on the floor. Sasha is as white as a sheet, I take her in my arms and hold her very tight, I'm aware of Tate picking up the shotgun and placing it in the corner, away from Ethan and Jasper. After a moment I lead Sasha to the corner of the barn and sit her on the chair beside Dad's make-shift work desk. She is shaking like a leaf, I place Dad's hessian blanket around her shoulders and she smiles weakly up at me and nods. I kiss her lightly on her forehead.

'I'm sorry,' I say, 'I didn't realise. I should have known, I should have known. I'm supposed to be your friend, I'm sorry.'

Tate knocks lightly on the barn window to signal to Luke that Ainsel and Eldridge can come and get us.

'What the…' says Eldridge when he arrives inside the barn, staring at the two crumpled men in the corner and Sasha sitting at the desk, pale and shivering. He gapes at Tate and me with a mixture of awe and fear.

'Whoop!' exclaims Ainsel when she sees the carnage, her eyes like saucers. 'Are they dead?'

'No, of course not,' I say, amused by her reaction.

Ethan stirs and groans. Ainsel sniffs at the air and shudders. I'm getting used to the horrible sooty cloggy oily smell of the Ethereal Black. Ainsel clutches my hand and I squeeze it. Then she shrieks as she notices my bleeding arm and Tate's cut leg.

'It's okay,' I say quickly, 'they're just flesh wounds. We're fine.'

As I hug Ainsel, I detect slight movement from the crumpled bodies in the corner and everything changes in a split second.

Jasper's hand is reaching up on a shelf above him, his fingers curled around a glass jar filled with Ethereal Black slime. I watch in horror as his hand drives the glass jar from the shelf, propelling it with all his force, through the air towards me.

I scream out and shove Ainsel away. In that same moment Sasha leaps up from her chair, discarding her blanket, and dives in front of me just as the jar of slime crashes into her and bursts open, emptying its contents across her back.

In one movement I'm across the room and pummelling Jasper, hard, I'm screaming and hitting him in the stomach, in the head, in the chest. He has slumped back down, his eyes rolling in his head, his breathing laboured, and I feel somebody's hands around me, dragging me off him. It's Eldridge.

'Stop, stop, it's enough, you'll kill him,' he pleads. But I push Eldridge away, I want to kill Jasper, I really want to kill him, he tried to rape me, he hurt Sasha, he captured my dad and Tate, he killed my cat. And he threw lethal chemicals at me, just as I got my family, my friend, my life back. I feel all the hurt and frustration of the last few months rising in me like a hot bolt of rage, energising me, strengthening me, I want to hurt him, I want to kill him, I want to...

What's the matter with me?

I stand back, clutching onto the wall, gasping for breath. Jasper is unconscious.

I hear Tate's voice.

'Come, Scarlett, it's okay, it's okay. It's over.'

I turn. Sasha has discarded her t-shirt, which is coated in slime, I know it's not harmful to Sasha but I suddenly feel tearful. I have that feeling, it all hurts so much, so much I turn and hit the wall of the barn with my fist. And then hit it again.

'OW!' I cry and drop to the floor. 'Ow, ow, ow.'

I'm fighting to breathe, Sasha is next to me, her turn to hold me tight. We clutch on to each other like sisters. Both sobbing.

'You saved my life,' I gasp and shudder. 'You saved my life.'

She hugs me tighter.

'I've missed you,' she whispers, and I smile into her stupid, silly, wonderful pouting face.

'Oh, Sasha, your t-shirt!' I say with a sudden giggle, knowing how fussy she is about her clothes.

'It was only an old Hollister t-shirt,' she says, and then whispers, 'I'm not sure I'd have risked my new Chanel blouse.' We both start to giggle and snort uncontrollably. We cling on to each other.

Ainsel is dabbing at Tate with Pandora's hanky. A tiny splash of the Ethereal Black slime has caught her wing.

'It's okay,' she assures me. 'It was just a tiny amount. The hanky will act as an antidote until we can treat it.'

Once Ainsel has finished, Tate hugs me and beckons to Sasha to join us. Sasha looks odd with just her bra and leggings but frankly who cares. The twins are half-naked anyway. Actually, if I'm honest, Tate is half-naked too. But I can't deal with that thought right now.

Eldridge and Ainsel choose that moment to wrap their arms around us and space-hop all three of us out of the barn together like a huge group hug.

Luke is waiting at the oak tree. He glances at Sasha and nods in respect. Then he immediately attends to Tate, coating her black smudge with a yellow oily gunge, which I can only presume is Gossamer Orchid sap. There's a bubbling as it starts to work its way into the silvery fibres of her wings, the black slime starts to rise to the surface.

'Dad?' I say as Luke meets my eye.

'He's fine,' he says. 'He's trying to explain it all to Maggie.'

'Oh my God, poor Dad.' I can't help giggling. I'd love to be a fly on the wall when he tells Maggie that my crazy story about fairies and black fog and black-winged people really was true.

Tate hugs me again. It feels so wonderful to be held by my mother and I'm starting to feel wobbly. Delayed reaction. Tate clings on to me and buries her face in my hair. She smells like flowers and freshness. I start to cry. And laugh. And cry.

'So what happened with the Black-Wings?' says Luke, and then looks apologetically towards Sasha.

'They're out for the count,' I say. 'We'll let them suffer for a few hours and then send Ainsel and Eldridge in to fetch them. Pandora can do some healing on them before we send them over to the hospital. I think we've taught them both a lesson they won't forget for quite a few years.'

I smile wickedly.

'Nobody messes with the Sage Princesses.'

Chapter Thirty-Seven

We're sitting in the grass, in the Fae world, lapping up the weak early autumn sunshine. Ainsel and Eldridge, Luke and Pandora, Sasha, me and Maggie, Tate and Dad. We've discovered that it's really easy to take people into the Fae world like I did with Luke that day, and we regularly take Maggie over with us for brief visits.

Maggie now understands everything that's happened, and she was really apologetic that she didn't believe me when I tried to tell her the truth. She gets on really well with Tate; she's even introduced Tate to the joys of drinking wine. *Hmm.*

The grass is damp. Pandora has laid out a massive waterproof tartan picnic rug and is delving into her large basket hamper, pulling out plates, plastic boxes of food and thermos flasks full of piping hot coffee. She smiles over at me and hands me an ice cold can of Coke. How on earth she kept it this cold I have no idea, and I appreciate her thoughtfulness.

Luke helps Pandora put out the food. He cuts every sandwich into quarters and takes out a large plate. He arranges the sandwiches neatly around the plate, facing the centre, starting the next layer half a sandwich in like a pyramid. I watch in fascination. He has one sandwich left at the end, he pauses, shrugs and I'm appalled to watch him shove it unceremoniously on top of his creation, spoiling the design.

I lean forward and move the offending sandwich, placing it on another plate.

Luke frowns thoughtfully, and then deliberately knocks the whole pyramid of sandwiches so they are all jumbled on the plate. He grins cheekily. *Why would he do that?*

I glare at him.

I pull the plate of sandwiches towards me, and start to re-build the pyramid. When it is finished I put the plate down and look at it, look at Luke. He holds my gaze. Oh my God he knows me better than I know myself.

I pull a sandwich out from the bottom of the pyramid and slap it on the top, deliberately spoiling my own masterpiece. There. I feel liberated.

Okay, I know it's only a plate of sandwiches. *Obviously*. But perhaps it doesn't matter if some things in life are a little wonky. Luke grins and nods.

Dad, oblivious to our strange sandwich battle, leans forward and takes a sandwich, shoves it all in his mouth at once, wiping his buttery hands on his shirt. He pushes his glasses up his nose and then takes another sandwich.

Dad's fully fit again, keeps saying he can't believe how much I've changed. It wasn't easy for him, trying to explain to the police where he'd been for those few months, but we managed to drum up a barely plausible story. We just told them what they wanted to hear – that he had walked out on his life but decided to return. Simple as that. It is perhaps a little worrying that they so easily accepted his explanation. The policemen smiled knowingly as if to say 'I told you so' as he signed off the paperwork.

Like me, Luke has decided not to go back to school. As he's not yet sixteen he's too young to leave school, but the art college were so impressed with his painting they have agreed for him to take a year out to research 'Colour, Form and the Chemistry of Colour'. Whatever that means.

Sasha is living deep in the Fae world. She can't return home for obvious reasons. I don't know how it's going to work out; it's the first time the Fae people have had a Black-Wing living in their midst since Zoran's days. Tate has granted her Sage immunity, which means she has the freedom to live in the Fae world alongside the Fae people as long as she doesn't cause any trouble. Only Tate (or me I suppose) can lift the immunity so she's safe here in the Fae world. She's found an abandoned cabin in the Lakes and Mountains close to where Orion lives, as far away as she could get from her vile Black-Wing family.

Luke and I kind of broke into Gossamer House whilst Ethan and Jasper were recovering from their injuries in hospital. We got all Sasha's clothes, makeup and girlie stuff, which cheered her up.

I haven't seen Orion since that night. I feel very confused. But I feel it's the beginning, not the end.

Pandora is still treating the black spot on Tate's wings where the Ethereal Black touched her. The mark has diminished to almost nothing, like a mole or beauty spot on her wing tip. But until it disappears completely I won't be happy.

Tate wants to take me to meet my grandmother, Layla, soon. Layla lives in some kind of palace (yeah, I know) very deep in the woods, which is apparently a very long way away. I still haven't got my head around how big everything seems from the inside of Gossamer Woods considering the map shows it as a small cluster of trees. And on the map there is *no mention* of lakes and mountains and definitely no hint of a palace where a fairy queen might live. My stomach flips just thinking about it.

I've spent a lot of time with Tate these last couple of months, getting to know her. I can't believe how alike we are, same sense of humour. Sometimes we laugh so much we can't breathe. So my life is complete. For now.

I lean back and sigh in utter contentment, here with my family, my closest and most wonderful friends, in the most amazing place in the whole world. I lazily snap open my can of Coke and grab an egg sandwich with the other hand. Perfect.

Luke springs up from where he's sitting with Pandora, his face brimming with happiness.

'I have something to show you all,' he announces proudly. 'I've finally finished my painting, the one of the woods, and I want to show to you all whilst we are here together.'

I'm aware that Luke has been spending quite a bit of his time in the Fae world with his precious painting. He has been researching the colours and pigments, and has created a paint in the primo colour that is compatible with his other oil paints.

He rushes to get the large canvas; he's been storing it nearby in a little hut that Ainsel and Eldridge use. He comes back out of the hut, puffing and dragging the painting behind him; it's covered with a cloth.

'I have finally found the thing I was looking for, the missing ingredient. I think I have finally painted the perfect picture!'

Fuckety fuck.

Has he painted me in it? Used the sketches he did of me that day in the woods? Almost naked. *Oh no. Nooooo!*

I swallow nervously. If I'm in the picture I hope he's put some clothes on me. And not painted me too sexy. In fact I hope he has missed me out completely.

I glance quickly at Dad. He's smiling encouragingly at Luke.

Oh bloody God crap, please PLEASE don't show Dad a picture of me sexy and naked.

'Is this the best time, Luke?' I say, trying to say a million things with my eyes. But Luke's on a roll. I've never seen him so determined. Or so happy. He steps back and turns the painting around for us all to see, grinning from ear to ear.

There is complete stunned silence.

He has captured the colours perfectly – I have definitely never seen a painting quite like it – the colours, the vibrancy, the realism. The trees and the woods, it's so lifelike you feel you need to touch it. The winged insects, the grass – it almost smells right.

'Oh my God, Luke,' I gulp. 'It's…it's truly fantastic.'

And I really mean it. It *is* fantastic. Of course, it all makes sense now, it fits. And I am so happy for him. For them both. I glance around the group to see people's expressions. Pandora looks surprised but there are tears of joy and pride brimming in her eyes; Dad's mouth has dropped open and I catch Tate's eye, she's grinning broadly. Tate winks at me and I want to giggle. Ainsel is beaming.

For Luke has not only captured the woods, the sunlight and the magic within the painting. He has also conveyed his unadulterated, pure and complete love for the person in the painting.

For there, the focus in the centre of the painting, wearing very little clothing at all except a lustful gaze, looking absolutely amazing with the most lovely translucent wings spread out behind...is Eldridge.

Details of Cally Pepper's books can be found at the author's website: http://www.callypepper.com

LODESTONE BOOKS

Lodestone Books is a new imprint, which offers a broad spectrum of subjects in YA/NA literature. Compelling reading, the Teen/Young/New Adult reader is sure to find something edgy, enticing and innovative. From dystopian societies, through a whole range of fantasy, horror, science fiction and paranormal fiction, all the way to the other end of the sphere, historical drama, steam-punk adventure, and everything in between. You'll find stories of crime, coming of age and contemporary romance. Whatever your preference you will discover it here.